Robert Ludlum's™

The
Moscow
Vector

Also by Patrick Larkin
in Large Print:

The Tribune

Also by Robert Ludlum
in Large Print:

The Janson Directive
The Sigma Protocol
The Tristan Betrayal
The Prometheus Deception
The Matarese Countdown
The Icarus Agenda
The Gemini Contenders
The Bourne Supremacy

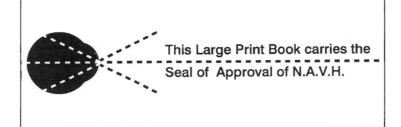

This Large Print Book carries the
Seal of Approval of N.A.V.H.

Robert Ludlum's™

The
Moscow
Vector

A COVERT-ONE NOVEL

SERIES CREATED BY

Robert Ludlum

WRITTEN BY

Patrick Larkin

WHEELER
PUBLISHING

Published in 2005 by arrangement with
St. Martin's Press, LLC.

Wheeler Large Print Hardcover.

The text of this Large Print edition is unabridged.
Other aspects of the book may vary from the original edition.

Set in 16 pt. Plantin by Elena Picard.

Printed in the United States on permanent paper.

Library of Congress Cataloging-in-Publication Data

Larkin, Patrick.
    Robert Ludlum's The Moscow vector : a covert-one
novel / [series created] by Robert Ludlum and [written by]
Patrick Larkin.
        p. cm. — (Covert-One novel)
    ISBN 1-59722-009-4 (lg. print : hc : alk. paper)
    1. Bioterrorism — Prevention — Fiction.
    2. Intelligence officers — Fiction.   3. Americans —
Russia — Fiction.   4. Moscow (Russia) — Fiction.
    5. Large type books.   I. Title: Moscow vector.
    II. Ludlum, Robert, 1927–   III. Title.
    PS3612.A65R63 2005b
        813'.6—dc22   2005015530

Robert Ludlum's™

The
Moscow
Vector

As the Founder/CEO of NAVH, the only national health agency solely devoted to those who, although not totally blind, have an eye disease which could lead to serious visual impairment, I am pleased to recognize Thorndike Press* as one of the leading publishers in the large print field.

Founded in 1954 in San Francisco to prepare large print textbooks for partially seeing children, NAVH became the pioneer and standard setting agency in the preparation of large type.

Today, those publishers who meet our standards carry the prestigious "Seal of Approval" indicating high quality large print. We are delighted that Thorndike Press is one of the publishers whose titles meet these standards. We are also pleased to recognize the significant contribution Thorndike Press is making in this important and growing field.

Lorraine H. Marchi, L.H.D.
Founder/CEO
NAVH

* Thorndike Press encompasses the following imprints: Thorndike, Wheeler, Walker and Large Print Press.

PROLOGUE

February 14
Moscow

Snow, blackened by auto exhaust and industrial pollution, lay heaped along the sidewalks of Tverskaya Street, a wide boulevard running right through one of the Russian capital's busiest commercial districts. Beneath glowing street lamps, pedestrians who were bundled up against the frigid night air jostled one another along the icy pavement. Streams of cars, trucks, and buses rumbled past in both directions. Their thick snow tires crunched over the salt and sand strewn to provide traction on the huge, multi-lane thoroughfare.

Dr. Nikolai Kiryanov hurried north along the right-hand side of the street, doing his best to mingle unobtrusively with the bustling crowds. But whenever anyone, young or old, man or woman, brushed past him, he twitched, fighting down the urge to shrink back or break into a sudden, panicked run. Despite the bitter cold, sweat trickled down his forehead from under his fur hat.

The tall, rail-thin pathologist clutched the wrapped gift box under his arm tighter, resisting the temptation to shove it out of sight inside his coat. Although Valentine's Day was a relatively recent addition to the Russian calendar, it was increasingly popular, and plenty of the other men around him carried their own boxes of chocolate and candy as presents for their wives or girlfriends.

Stay calm, he told himself urgently. He was safe. No one knew what they had taken. Their plans were still secret.

Then why are you jumping at every little shadow? the little voice inside his head asked drily. Have you forgotten all the odd looks and frightened glances from your co-workers? And what about those faint clicking noises you kept hearing on the telephone?

Kiryanov glanced over his shoulder, half-expecting to see a squad of uniformed police, the *militsia,* closing in on him. He saw only other Muscovites wrapped up in their own cares and concerns and eager to get out of the below-freezing winter weather. Momentarily relieved, he turned back and almost collided head-on with a short, squat older woman with her arms full of parcels of food.

She glared at him, muttering a curse under her breath.

"*Prastite, Babushka,*" he stammered, edging past her. "Pardon me, little grandmother." She spat angrily at his feet and scowled after him. He hurried onward, his pulse hammering in his ears.

Not far ahead, neon signs glowed brightly in the gathering darkness, standing out in stark contrast to the massive gray Stalinist-era apartment buildings and hotels lining the street. Kiryanov breathed out. He was close to the coffee bar where he had agreed to meet his contact, a sympathetic Western journalist named Fiona Devin. Once there, he could answer her questions, hand over his information, and rush home to his small flat with nobody in higher authority the wiser. He walked even faster, eager to get this dangerous clandestine rendezvous over and done with.

Someone crashed into Kiryanov from behind, shoving him forward onto a thick slab of slick black ice. His feet skidded out from under him. Arms flailing wildly, he lost his balance and fell backward. His head slammed hard onto the frozen pavement, and a white-hot wave of agony sleeted through him, drowning all conscious thought. Dazed and groaning, he lay still for a long moment, unable to move.

Somewhere in the swirling cloud of pain,

he felt a hand on his shoulder. Wincing, he opened his eyes and looked up.

A blond-haired man in an expensive-looking wool overcoat knelt beside him, offering profuse apologies. "My dear sir, I am so sorry. Are you all right? That was clumsy of me. Terribly clumsy." He gripped Kiryanov's arm tightly with both of his gloved hands. "Here, let me help you back up."

The Russian pathologist felt something needle-sharp stab deep into his flesh. He opened his mouth to cry out and then realized in mounting horror that he could not breathe. His lungs were paralyzed. Vainly he tried to draw in the air he desperately needed. His arms and legs twitched and quivered as more of his muscles locked up. Terrified, he stared up at the man leaning over him.

A faint smile ghosted across the other man's thin lips and then vanished. "*Da svidaniya*, Dr. Kiryanov," he murmured. "You should have obeyed orders and kept your mouth shut."

Trapped in a body that would no longer obey the commands of his mind, Nikolai Kiryanov lay rigid, soundlessly screaming, as the world around him faded into utter and unending darkness. His heart fluttered futilely for a few moments, and then stopped.

The blond-haired man stared down at the open-mouthed corpse for a second longer. Then he looked up at the ring of curious bystanders drawn by the commotion, donning a mask of astonished concern. "Something's wrong with him!" he told them. "I think he's had some sort of fit."

"Maybe he cracked his head too hard when he fell? Someone should call a doctor," a stylishly dressed young woman suggested. "Or the *militsia*."

The blond man nodded quickly. "Yes, you're right." Carefully, he stripped off one of his thick gloves and pulled a cell phone out of the pocket of his overcoat. "I'll punch in the emergency number."

Within two minutes, a red-and-white ambulance pulled up to the curb and stopped. The blue flashing light on its roof strobed across the small knot of onlookers, sending jagged, distorted shadows dancing across the pavement and nearby buildings. Two burly paramedics jumped out of the back, carrying a portable stretcher, followed by a weary-looking young man in a wrinkled white coat and a thin red tie. He carried a heavy black medical bag.

The ambulance crew doctor bent over Kiryanov for a moment. He checked the fallen man's fixed and staring eyes with a small penlight and felt for a pulse. Then he sighed and shook his head. "This poor fellow is dead. There's nothing I can do for him now." He looked around the circle of faces. "Right. Who can tell me what happened here?"

The blond-haired man shrugged his shoulders expressively. "It was an accident. We bumped into each other and he slipped and went down on the ice over there. I tried to help him up . . . but then he just, well, stopped breathing. That's really all I know."

The doctor frowned. "I see, sir. Well, I'm afraid you're going to have to ride along with us to the hospital. There are forms to fill out. And the militia will want to take an official statement from you." He turned to the rest of the bystanders. "What about the rest of you? Did anyone else see anything useful?"

There was silence from the crowd of bystanders. They were edging back with carefully blank faces, already drifting away down the street in ones and twos. Now that their initial burst of morbid curiosity was sated, no one wanted to risk wasting an evening answering inconvenient questions in one of Moscow's dreary, dingy emergency rooms or police stations.

The young doctor snorted cynically. He motioned to the two paramedics with the stretcher. "Load him up. Let's go. There's no point in wasting any more of our time out here in the cold."

Moving fast, they bundled Kiryanov's body onto the stretcher and slid it into the back of the ambulance. One of the paramedics, the white-coated doctor, and the blond-haired man climbed in beside the corpse. The second paramedic slammed the door shut and got in beside the driver. With its light still flashing, the ambulance pulled out into Tverskaya Street's heavy traffic and headed north.

Safe now from prying eyes, the doctor deftly rifled through the dead man's pockets and then under his clothing, checking and then discarding the pathologist's wallet and hospital ID card. He scowled at the others. "Nothing. There's nothing. The bastard is clean."

"Take a look inside this," the blond-haired man suggested drily, tossing him the package Kiryanov had been carrying.

The doctor caught it, tore off the wrapping paper, and ripped open the candy box. Manila folders full of documents tumbled out across the corpse. He scanned through them quickly and nodded in satisfaction. "These are the photocopied case records from the hospital," he confirmed. "Every last one of them." He smiled. "We can report a success."

The blond-haired man frowned. "No. I do not think we can."

"What do you mean?"

"Where are the blood and tissue samples he stole?" the blond-haired man asked pointedly, narrowing his cold gray eyes.

The doctor stared down at the empty box in his hand. "Shit." He looked up in dismay. "Kiryanov must have had help. Someone else has the samples."

"So it seems," the other man agreed. He pulled the phone out of his overcoat again and punched in a pre-coded number. "This is Moscow One. I need an immediate secure relay to Prague One. We have a problem. . . ."

PART ONE

CHAPTER ONE

February 15
Prague, the Czech Republic
Lieutenant Colonel Jonathan "Jon" Smith, M.D., paused in the shadowed arch of the ancient Gothic tower at the eastern end of the Charles Bridge. The bridge, nearly a third of a mile long, had been built more than six centuries before. It crossed the Vltava River, linking Prague's Staré Mésto, the Old Town, with its Malá Strana, the Little Quarter. Smith stood quietly for a long moment, carefully scanning the stone span before him.

He frowned. He would have preferred a different location for this meeting, one that was busier and had more natural cover. Wider and newer bridges carried the Czech capital's motorized traffic and its electric trams, but the Charles Bridge was reserved for those crossing the Vltava on foot. In the dreary half-light of late afternoon, it was largely deserted.

For most of the year, the historic bridge was the centerpiece of the city, a structure whose elegance and beauty drew sightseers and street vendors in droves. But Prague now lay shrouded in winter fog, a thick cloud of cold, damp vapor and foul-smelling smog trapped along the winding trace of the river valley. The gray mist blurred the graceful outlines of the city's Renaissance and Baroque-era palaces, churches, and houses.

Shivering slightly in the frosty, dank air, Smith zipped up his leather bomber jacket and moved out onto the bridge itself. He was a tall, trim man in his early forties with smooth, dark hair, piercing blue eyes, and high cheekbones.

At first his footsteps echoed faintly off the waist-high parapet, but then the sounds faded, swallowed by the fog rising from the river. It flowed slowly across the bridge, gradually hiding both ends from view. Other people, mostly government workers and shop clerks hurrying home, emerged from the concealing mists, passed him without a glance, and then vanished back into the haze as quickly as they had come.

Smith walked on. Thirty statues of saints lined the Charles Bridge, silent, unmoving figures looming up out of the steadily thickening fog on either side. Set in op-posing pairs on the massive sandstone piers supporting the long crossing, those statues were his guides to the rendezvous point. The American reached the middle of the span and stopped, looking up at the calm face of St. John Nepomuk, a Catholic priest tortured to death in 1393, his broken body hurled into the river from this same bridge. Part of the age-blackened bronze relief depicting the saint's martyrdom gleamed bright, polished clean by countless passersby touching it for good luck.

Moved by a sudden impulse, Smith leaned forward and rubbed his own fingers across the raised figure's.

"I did not know that you were a superstitious man, Jonathan," a quiet, tired-sounding voice said from behind him.

Smith turned around with an abashed grin. "Nothing ventured, nothing gained, Valentin."

Dr. Valentin Petrenko came forward to join him, holding a black briefcase gripped tightly in one gloved hand. The Russian medical specialist was several inches shorter than Smith and more solidly built. Sad brown eyes blinked nervously behind the pair of thick glasses perched on his nose. "Thank you for agreeing to meet me here. Away from the conference, I mean. I realize this is not convenient for you."

"Don't worry about it," Smith said. He smiled wryly. "Believe me, this beats spending another several hours rehashing

Kozlik's latest paper on typhoid and hepatitis A epidemics in Lower Iamsodamnedlostistan."

For a moment, a look of amusement flickered in Petrenko's wary eyes. "Dr. Kozlik is not the most scintillating speaker," he agreed. "But his theories are basically sound."

Smith nodded, waiting patiently for the other man to explain why he'd been so insistent on this surreptitious rendezvous. He and Petrenko were in Prague for a major international conference on emerging infectious diseases in Eastern Europe and Russia. Deadly illnesses long thought under control in the developed world were spreading like wildfire through parts of what had once been the Soviet empire, breeding in public health and sanitation systems ruined by decades of neglect and the collapse of the old communist order.

Both men were deeply involved in confronting this growing health crisis. Among other things, Jon Smith was a skilled molecular biologist assigned to the U.S. Army Medical Research Institute of Infectious Diseases (USAMRIID) at Fort Detrick, Maryland. And Petrenko was a highly regarded expert in rare illnesses attached to the staff of Moscow's Central Clinical Hospital. For several years, the two men had known each other professionally and had developed a respect for each other's abilities and discretion. So when a plainly troubled Petrenko pulled him aside earlier in the day to request a private conversation outside the confines of the conference, Smith had agreed without hesitation.

"I need your help, Jon," the Russian said at last. He swallowed hard. "I have urgent information that must reach competent medical authorities in the West."

Smith looked closely at him. "Information about what, Valentin?"

"The outbreak of a disease in Moscow. A new disease . . . something I've never seen before," Petrekno said quietly. "Something I fear."

Smith felt a small chill run down his spine. "Go on."

"I saw the first case two months ago," Petrenko told him. "A small child, a little boy who was just seven years old. He came in suffering aches and pains and a persistent high fever. In the beginning, his doctors thought it was only a common flu. But then, and quite suddenly, his condition worsened. His hair began falling out. Terrible, bleeding sores and painful rashes spread across most of his body. He became severely anemic. In the end, whole systems — his liver, kidneys, and ultimately, his heart — simply shut down."

"Jesus!" Smith murmured, imagining the

21

horrible pain the sick boy must have endured. He frowned. "Those symptoms sound an awful lot like high-level radiation poisoning, Valentin."

Petrenko nodded. "Yes, that is what we first thought." He shrugged. "But we could not find any evidence that the boy had ever been exposed to any radioactive material. Not in his home. Not at his school. Not anywhere else."

"Was the kid infectious?" Smith asked.

"No," the Russian said, shaking his head emphatically. "No one else around him became ill. Not his parents or his friends or any of those who treated him." He grimaced. "None of our tests turned up signs of a dangerous viral or bacterial infection and every toxicology exam came back negative. We could not detect any traces of poisons or harmful chemicals that might have done so much damage."

Smith whistled softly. "Very nasty."

"It was terrible," Petrenko agreed. Still clutching his briefcase, the Russian scientist took off his glasses, polished them nervously, and then pushed them on again. "But then others began showing up at the hospital, suffering the same horrible symptoms. First, an old man, a former Communist Party apparatchik. Then a middle-aged woman. And finally a young man — a sturdy day laborer who had always been as

22

healthy as a horse. All died in agony in a matter of days."

"Just those four?"

Petrenko smiled humorlessly. "Those four that I know of," he said softly. "But there may well have been others. Officials from the Ministry of Health made it clear that my colleagues and I were not supposed to ask too many questions, lest we risk 'provoking an unnecessary panic' among the general population. Or stir up sensationalist reports in the news media.

"Naturally, we fought the decision to the highest levels. But in the end, all of our requests for an expanded inquiry were denied. We were forbidden even to discuss these cases with anyone beyond a very small circle of other scientists." The sadness in his eyes intensified. "A Kremlin official actually told me that four unexplained deaths were trivial, 'mere statistical background noise.' He suggested that we instead focus our efforts on AIDS and the other illnesses that are killing so many in Mother Russia. In the meantime, the facts surrounding these mysterious deaths have been classified as state secrets and buried in the bureaucracy."

"Idiots," Smith growled, feeling his jaw tighten. Silence and secrecy were the bane of good science. Trying to conceal the emergence of a new disease for political reasons was only more likely to lead to a catastrophic epidemic.

"Perhaps," Petrenko said. He shrugged. "But I will not take part in a cover-up. That is why I have brought you this." The Russian gently tapped the side of his black briefcase. "It contains all the medical information relevant to the four known victims, as well as samples of their blood and selected tissues. I only hope that you and others in the West can learn more about the mechanisms of this new illness before it is too late."

"Just how much hot water are you going to be in if your government finds out that you've smuggled this data out?" Smith asked.

"I do not know," the Russian admitted. "That is why I wanted to give you this information in secret." He sighed. "Conditions in my country are deteriorating rapidly, Jon. I'm very much afraid that our leaders have decided that it is safer and easier to rule by force and fear than by persuasion and reason."

Smith nodded his understanding. He had been following the news out of Russia with increasing concern. The nation's president, Viktor Dudarev, had been a member of the old KGB, the Soviet Committee for State Security, stationed in East Germany. When the USSR crumbled, Dudarev had been quick to align himself with the forces of reform. He had risen fast in the new Russia, first taking charge of the FSB, the new Federal Security Service, then becoming prime minister, and finally winning election as president. All along the way many had wanted desperately to believe he was a man sincerely committed to democratic norms.

Dudarev had fooled them all. Since taking office, the ex–KGB officer had dropped the mask, revealing himself as a man more interested in satisfying his own ambitions than in establishing a genuine democracy. He was busy drawing more and more of the reins of power into his own hands and those of his toadies. Newly independent media companies were muzzled and then brought back under government control. Corporations whose owners opposed the Kremlin were broken up by official decree or had their assets confiscated in trumped-up tax cases. Rival politicians were coerced into silence or smeared into oblivion by the state-run press.

Satirists had dubbed Dudarev "Czar Viktor." But the joke had long ago worn thin and now seemed well on the way to becoming a harsh reality.

"I'll do what I can to keep your name out of it," Smith promised. "But somebody in your government is bound to trace this information back to you once the news

25

leaks. And it *will* leak at some point." He glanced down at the other man. "Maybe you should come out with the data. It might be safer."

Petrenko raised an eyebrow. "Seek political asylum, you mean?"

Smith nodded.

The scientist shook his head. "No, I do not think so." He shrugged. "For all my faults, I am a Russian first and forever. I will not abandon the motherland out of fear." He smiled sadly. "Besides, what is it the philosophers say? For evil to triumph, all that is necessary is for good men to do nothing? I believe that to be true. So I will stay in Moscow, doing what I can to fend off the darkness in my own small way."

"Prosím, můžete mi pomoci?" The words came floating toward them out of the mist.

Startled, Smith and Petrenko turned around.

A somewhat younger man, hard-faced and unsmiling, stood just a few feet away with his left palm held out as though begging for money. Beneath a tangled mane of long, greasy brown hair, a tiny silver skull dangled from his right earlobe. His right hand was hidden inside a long black overcoat. Two other men, similarly dressed and equally grimy, stood close behind him. They too wore small skull-shaped earrings.

Reacting on instinct, Smith stepped in

26

front of the smaller Russian scientist. "*Prominte.* Sorry," he said. "*Nerozumím.* I don't understand. *Mluvíte anglicky?* Do you speak English?"

The long-haired man slowly lowered his left hand. "You are American, yes?"

Something about the way he said it raised Smith's hackles. "That's right."

"Good," the man said flatly. "All Americans are rich. And I am poor." His dark eyes flickered toward Petrenko and then came back to Smith. He bared his teeth in a quick, predatory grin. "So you will give me your friend's briefcase. As a gift, yes?"

"Jon," the Russian muttered urgently from behind him. "These men are *not* Czech."

The long-haired man heard him. He shrugged blithely. "Dr. Petrenko is correct. I congratulate him on his acuity." The folding knife he'd been concealing inside his coat came out in one, smooth motion. He flicked it open. Its blade looked razor-sharp. "But I still want that briefcase. *Now.*"

Damn, Smith thought, coldly watching the three men starting to fan out around them. He backed up slightly — and found himself penned against the waist-high parapet overlooking the Vltava River. This is not good, he told himself grimly. Caught unarmed and outnumbered on a bridge in the fog. *Really* not good.

Any hopes he might have had about being able to just hand over the briefcase and walk away unharmed had vanished when he heard the other man use Petrenko's name so casually and confidently. This was not a run-of-the-mill mugging. Unless he missed his guess, these guys were professionals and professionals were trained not to leave witnesses behind.

He forced himself to smile weakly. "Well, sure . . . I mean, if you put it like that. There's no need for anyone to get hurt here, is there?"

"No need at all, friend," the knife-wielder assured him, still grinning cruelly. "Now, tell the good doctor to hand over that case."

Smith drew in a single, deep breath, feeling his pulse accelerate. The world around him seemed to slow down as adrenaline flooded into his system, speeding his reflexes. He crouched. Now! "*Policii!* Police!" he roared. And then again, shattering the fog-laden silence. "*Policii!*"

"Fool!" the long-haired man snarled. He lunged at the American, stabbing upward with his knife.

Reacting instantly, Smith leaned aside. The blade flickered past his face. Too close! He chopped frantically at the inside of the other man's exposed wrist, hacking at the nerve endings there.

28

His attacker grunted in pain. The knife flew out of his suddenly paralyzed fingers and skittered away across the paving. Still moving fast, Smith spun back around, slamming his elbow into the long-haired man's narrow face with tremendous force. Bones crunched and blood spattered through the air. Groaning, the man reeled back and fell to one knee, fumbling at the red ruin of his shattered nose.

Grim-faced, the second man pushed past his fallen leader, thrusting with his own blade. Smith ducked under the attack and punched him hard, angling up to come in right under his ribs. The man doubled up in sudden agony, stumbling forward. Before he could recover, Smith grabbed him by the back of his coat and hurled him headlong into the stone parapet of the bridge. Stunned or badly injured, he went down on his face without a sound and lay still.

"Jon! Watch out!"

Smith turned fast, hearing Petrenko's shout. He was just in time to see the shorter Russian scientist drive the third man backward with desperate, uncontrolled swipes of his briefcase. But then the wild glee in Petrenko's eyes faded, replaced by horror as he looked down and saw the knife buried up to the hilt in his own stomach.

Suddenly, a single shot rang out, echoing across the bridge.

And a small, red-rimmed hole opened in the middle of Petrenko's forehead. Pieces of shattered bone and brain matter flew out the back of his skull, driven by a 9x18mm round fired at point-blank range. His eyes rolled up. Then, still clutching his briefcase, the dying Russian staggered and fell backward over the parapet, toppling into the river below.

Out of the corner of his eye, Smith saw the first attacker scrambling back to his feet. Blood ran red across the man's face, dripping off his unshaven chin. His dark eyes were full of hatred and he held a pistol, an old Soviet-model Makarov. One spent cartridge rolled slowly across the uneven pavement.

The American tensed, knowing already that it was too late. The other man was too far away — well out of his reach. Smith whirled around and threw himself off the bridge, diving headfirst into the fog. Behind him, more shots crashed out. A bullet tore right past his head and another ripped through his jacket, sending a wave of white-hot pain searing across his shoulder.

He struck the surface of the Vltava in a white burst of spray and foam, plunging deep into its icy, ink-black waters. Down and down he slid into a freezing void of absolute silence and utter darkness. And then the river's swift current caught him in its grip, tugging at his torn jacket and his arms and legs, sending him tumbling and rolling as it dragged him north, away from the bridge's massive stone piers.

His lungs were on fire, screaming for air. Grimly, Smith kicked out, clawing his way up through the frigid, turbulent water. At last, his head rose above the rippling surface and he hung there for a long moment, gasping and panting, straining to draw in the oxygen his body craved.

Still caught in the current, he swung around. The Charles Bridge was invisible in the swirling fog, but he could hear shouts and panicked voices reverberating across the river. The sounds of gunfire seemed to have roused Prague's citizens from their late afternoon torpor. Smith spat out a mouthful of water and turned away.

He struck out toward the eastern bank, angling across the current sweeping him downstream. He had to get out of the river soon — before the bitter cold sapped his strength completely. His teeth began chattering as the chill penetrated his waterlogged clothes and bit deeply into his body.

For a long, despairing moment, the mist-shrouded shore seemed to hang just beyond his rapidly tiring reach. Aware that his time was running out fast, Smith made one last desperate effort. He kicked out again and this time felt his flailing hands touch a bank of mud and small pebbles at the water's edge. Straining, he hauled himself out of the Vltava and onto a narrow strip of withered grass and neatly trimmed trees, apparently part of a small riverside park.

Shivering and wracked by pain in every muscle, he rolled over onto his back and lay staring up at the featureless gray sky. Minutes slid past. He drifted with them, too exhausted to go any further.

Smith heard a startled gasp. Wincing, he turned his head to the side and saw a small, elderly woman bundled up in a fur coat staring down at him in mingled fear and amazement. A tiny dog peered out from behind her legs, sniffing curiously. The air around them seemed to be growing darker with every passing second.

"*Policii,*" he said, forcing the words out past his chattering teeth.

Her eyes opened wide.

Summoning up the last of his broken Czech, Smith whispered, "*Zavolejte policii.* Call the police."

Before he could say anything more, the fast-gathering darkness closed in around him and swallowed him whole.

CHAPTER TWO

Northern Operational Command Headquarters, Chernihiv, Ukraine

For hundreds of years Chernihiv had been called "the princely city," serving as a fortified capital for one of the princedoms at the heart of the Kievan Rus, the loose confederation of Vikings who had made themselves the masters of what would later become Russia and the Ukraine. Several of its beautiful cathedrals, churches, and monasteries dated back to the eleventh and twelfth centuries, and their golden domes and spires lent a quiet elegance to the little city's skyline. Every year, busloads of tourists made the short journey from Kiev itself, one hundred and forty kilometers to the south, to gawk at Chernihiv's ancient sites and artwork.

Few of those tourists ever noticed an isolated complex of Soviet-era concrete and steel buildings on the city's outskirts. There, behind a barbed-wire perimeter fence guarded by heavily armed soldiers, lay the administrative center for one of the three major combat organizations of the Ukrainian military — the Northern Operational Command. The sun had long since set, but lights were still on throughout the complex. Staff cars bearing flags from every major unit in the command filled the parking areas surrounding a floodlit three-story central headquarters building.

Inside the building, Major Dmitry Polyakov stood off to one side of a crowded briefing room. He had carefully chosen a position that gave him a good view of his boss, Lieutenant General Aleksandr Marchuk, the man in charge of the army's Northern Operational Command. The tall young major checked the folder under his arm yet again, making sure that it contained every report and draft order the general might need for this emergency military conference. Polyakov was well aware that Marchuk was a hard-charging, thoroughly professional soldier, one who expected his senior military aide to be ready to respond instantly to any need or order.

Marchuk, his senior staff officers, and Northern Command's division and brigade commanders sat around three sides of a large rectangular conference table. A detailed map of their operational zone stood on an easel set up at the head of this table. Each high-ranking officer had his own briefing folder, an ashtray, and a glass of hot tea set out before him. Cigarettes smoldered in most of the ashtrays.

"There's no doubt that both the Russians and Belarussians have dramatically tightened security along our joint border," the briefer, a full colonel, continued. His pointer tapped the map at several places. "They've closed every minor crossing point from Dobrjanka here in the north all the way to Kharkiv in the east. Traffic is only being allowed across at checkpoints set up on the major highways — and then only after intensive searches. Moreover, my counterparts at both Western and Southern Command report similar measures being taken in their areas."

"That's not all the Russians are doing," one of the officers sitting at the far side of the table said grimly. He commanded a Covering Force brigade, a new combined-arms formation made up of armored reconnaissance troops, scout and attack helicopters, and infantry units heavily armed with anti-tank missiles. "My forward outposts have observed company-strength and battalion-strength reconnaissance forces operating at several points along the frontier. They appear to be attempting to precisely locate the duty stations of our border security detachments."

"We should also keep in mind those

troop movement rumors passed to us by the Americans," another colonel added. The crossed hunting horns on his shoulder tabs identified him as a member of the Signals Branch, but that was only a cover. In reality, he served as the head of Northern Command's military intelligence section.

Heads nodded around the table. The American military attaché in Kiev had been distributing intelligence reports suggesting that some of Russia's elite airborne, tank, and mechanized infantry units had vanished from their bases around Moscow. None of the reports could be confirmed but they were disturbing nonetheless.

"So what is Moscow's official excuse for all of this unusual activity?" a heavyset tank division commander sitting next to the intelligence chief asked. He was leaning forward, and the overhead lights gleamed off his bare scalp.

"The Kremlin claims these are merely precautionary antiterrorist measures," Lieutenant General Marchuk answered slowly, stubbing out his own cigarette. His voice was hoarse and sweat stained his high uniform collar.

Major Polyakov hid a worried frown. Even at fifty, the general was ordinarily a strong, healthy man, but now he was ill — quite ill. He had not been able to keep any food down all day. Despite that, he had in-

36

sisted on calling this evening conference. "It's only the damned flu, Dmitry," Marchuk had rasped. "I'll get over it. Right now, the military situation demands my full attention. You know my rule: Duty first and last."

Like any good soldier given an order, Polyakov had nodded and obeyed. What else could he do? But now, looking at his leader, he was beginning to think he should have pushed harder to try to get the older man to seek medical attention.

"And do we believe our good Russian friends and neighbors, Aleksandr?" the tank division commander asked wryly. "About these so-called antiterrorist measures?"

Marchuk shrugged. Even that small movement seemed to take an effort. "Terrorism is a serious threat. The Chechens and others will strike at Moscow and its interests whenever and wherever they can. We all know that." He coughed hoarsely, paused for a moment to catch his breath, and then forced himself to carry on. "But I have not seen any information — either from our own government or from the Russians themselves — that would justify so much military activity on so large a scale."

"Then what should we do?" one of the other officers murmured.

"We will take precautions of our own,"

Marchuk said grimly. "To keep 'Czar Viktor' and his cronies in Moscow honest, if nothing else. A little show of force on our part should go a long way toward deterring any idiocy by the Kremlin." He pushed himself to his feet and stood facing the map. Beads of sweat rolled down his forehead. His face was gray. He swayed once.

Polyakov started forward, but the general waved him back. "I'm fine, Dmitry," he muttered. "Just a little light-headed, that's all."

His subordinates exchanged worried glances.

Marchuk forced a ragged smile. "What's the matter, gentlemen? Never seen anyone with the flu before?" He coughed again, this time a prolonged, hacking cough that left him head down and panting for air. He looked up with another faint smile. "Don't worry. I promise not to breathe on any of you."

That drew a nervous laugh.

Recovering slightly, the general leaned forward, supporting himself with his hands. "Now, listen carefully," he told them, plainly fighting for every word. "Starting later tonight, I want all Ready Force divisions and brigades brought to a higher alert status. All personnel leaves must be canceled. All officers away from their units for any reason should be recalled — at once. And by dawn tomorrow morning, I want every operational tank, infantry fighting vehicle, and self-propelled gun in this command fitted out with a full load of ammunition and fuel. The same goes for every transport and combat helicopter fit to fly. Once that is done, your units will begin moving to their wartime deployment areas to conduct special winter maneuvers."

"Bringing so many troops to full combat readiness will be expensive," his chief of staff pointed out quietly. "Extremely expensive. Parliament will ask serious questions. The defense budget this year is very tight."

"Screw the budget!" Marchuk snapped, straightening up in irritation. "And screw the politicians in Kiev! Our job is to defend the homeland; not worry about budgets." Abruptly, his face grew grayer still and he swayed again. He shuddered visibly, plainly wracked by a wave of terrible pain, and then folded slowly forward, collapsing facedown across the conference table. An ashtray crashed to the floor, spilling soot and cigarette butts across the frayed carpet.

Stunned officers jumped to their feet, crowding around their fallen commander.

Polyakov pushed through them, heedless of rank. The major touched Marchuk's shoulder gently and then felt his forehead. He yanked his hand away. His eyes opened wide in shock. "Mother of God," he whispered. "The general is burning up."

"Turn him over onto his back," someone suggested. "And loosen his tie and collar. Give him room to breathe."

Working quickly, Polyakov and another junior aide obeyed, tearing open shirt and jacket buttons in their haste. There were gasps from around the crowded room when parts of Marchuk's neck and chest came into view. Almost every inch of his skin seemed covered in raw, bleeding sores.

Polyakov swallowed convulsively, fighting against the urge to throw up. He swung away. "Fetch a doctor!" he yelled, horror-stricken by what he had seen. "For God's sake, someone fetch a doctor now!"

Hours later, Major Dmitry Polyakov sat slumped forward on a bench in the hallway just outside the intensive care unit of the Oblast Clinic Hospital. Bleary-eyed and depressed, he stared down at the cracked tile floor, ignoring the muffled, incomprehensible squawks of the PA system periodically summoning various doctors and nurses to different sections of the building.

A single pair of gleaming, highly polished boots intruded on Polyakov's view. Sighing, the major looked up and saw a dour, thin-faced officer staring down at him with evident disapproval. For an instant he bristled, but then he caught sight of the twin gold stars of a lieutenant general on the other man's white- and red-embroidered shoulder boards and jumped to his feet. He threw his shoulders back, and lifted his chin high, standing braced at attention.

"You must be Polyakov, Marchuk's senior aide," the other man snapped. It was not a question.

The major nodded stiffly, still at attention. "Yes, sir."

"My name is Tymoshenko," the much shorter, thin-faced officer told him coldly. "Lieutenant General Eduard Tymoshenko. I've been sent from Kiev to assume command here, by order of both the defense minister and the president himself."

Polyakov struggled to hide his dismay. Tymoshenko was known throughout the army's officer corps as a political hack, one of hundreds left over from the days before the Ukraine regained its independence from the disintegrating Soviet Union. His reputation as a field commander was dismal. Those who had endured his leadership spoke bitterly of a man more concerned with mindless spit-and-polish than with real combat readiness. These days he spent most of his time in various posts inside the Defense Ministry, energetically shuffling papers from one side of his desk to the other while making sure that influential politicians regarded him as indispensable.

"What is General Marchuk's present condition?" Tymoshenko demanded.

"The general is still unconscious, sir," Polyakov reported reluctantly. "And according to the doctors, his vital signs are deteriorating rapidly. So far, he is not responding to any treatment."

"I see." Tymoshenko sniffed, turning his head to stare contemptuously at the dreary surroundings. After a moment, he looked back at the younger man. "And the cause of this unfortunate illness? I heard some nonsense about radiation poisoning just before leaving Kiev."

"No one knows yet," Polyakov admitted. "The hospital is running a complete battery of tests, but the results may not come back for hours, perhaps even days."

Tymoshenko arched a single gray eyebrow. "In that case, Major, may I suggest there is no longer any purpose to be served by haunting these corridors like some little lost lapdog? General Marchuk will live — or he will die. And I am quite confident that he will do so with or without your presence." He smiled thinly. "In the meantime, it seems that I need an aide myself, at least until I can locate a more efficient and deserving young officer."

Polyakov did his best to ignore the insult. Instead, he simply nodded expressionlessly. "Yes, sir. I will do my best."

"Good." Tymoshenko nodded toward the exit. "My staff car is waiting outside. You can ride back to headquarters with me. And once we're there, I want you to arrange temporary quarters for me. Something comfortable, I trust. You can clear out Marchuk's billet bright and early tomorrow morning."

"But —" Polyakov began.

The dour little general stared up at him. "Yes?" he snapped. "What is it, Major?"

"What about the Russians? And the border situation?" Polyakov asked, not bothering to conceal his surprise. "General Marchuk intended to deploy the Command's fighting formations to their maneuver areas at first light tomorrow."

Tymoshenko frowned. "So I understand." He shrugged his narrow shoulders. "Naturally, I canceled those orders as soon as I arrived." He shook his head derisively. "Full-scale maneuvers in the dead of winter? With all the wear and tear on expensive equipment that entails? And all because of a few paranoid whispers about the Russians? Utter madness. I really cannot imagine what Marchuk thought he was doing. The fever must have addled his brain. Why, the fuel bills alone would be entirely prohibitive."

With that, the new leader of the Ukrainian army's Northern Operational Command spun crisply on his heel and strutted off, leaving Major Dmitry Polyakov staring after him in growing dismay.

The Pentagon

Corporal Matthew Dempsey of the Pentagon's police force whistled softly under his breath as he walked his night beat along the massive building's quiet, labyrinthine corridors. This was his favorite shift. The Pentagon never really shut down and lights still glowed under some office doors, but much of the grinding daytime hustle and bustle faded in the hours right around midnight.

The small radio receiver fitted in his ear squawked suddenly. "Dempsey, this is Milliken."

Dempsey spoke into his handheld radio. "Go ahead, Sarge."

"Dispatch reports an emergency call from an office inside the DIA's JCS Support Directorate. Somebody in there just punched in 911, and then left the phone off the hook. The operator thinks she can hear someone breathing, but she can't get anyone to respond. I want you to go check it out."

Dempsey frowned. The Defense Intelligence Agency's several Pentagon office suites were incredibly sensitive areas — ordinarily completely off-limits to anyone without at least a Top Secret clearance. He was authorized to override those restrictions if necessary, but doing so was going to raise one hell of a hornet's nest. Even if this was just a false alarm, he'd be spending the next several hours filling out non-disclosure forms and being interrogated.

He sighed and trotted off down the corridor. "On my way."

Dempsey paused outside the locked outer doors of the DIA section's office complex. A light on the electronic security station there shone bright red. Anyone trying to force their way through would automatically trigger alarms throughout the massive building. With another frown, he dug the shift-issued special police ID card out of his uniform pocket and ran it through the machine. The light shifted to yellow, indicating that he had been granted emergency permission to enter.

He pushed through the security doors and found himself in another hallway, this one leading deeper into the building. Several soundproofed glass doors opened onto this corridor. Silently now, the policeman moved faster toward the office his sergeant had identified as the source of the abortive 911 call, trying very hard not to look too closely at anything in the rooms he passed.

A painted sign on the door he was looking for read DIRECTORATE FOR CURRENT INTELLIGENCE — RUSSIA DIVISION. Dempsey knew enough about the different intelligence outfits to realize that the men and women who worked here were directly responsible for briefing the Secretary of Defense and the Joint Chiefs on all significant military and political developments. They were the top analysts charged with pulling together the bits and pieces of information gathered by human agents, from satellite photographs, and from intercepted radio, phone, and computer transmissions.

"Police!" he called out as he went inside. "Is anyone here? Hello?"

The corporal looked around carefully. The room was a tangle of desks, chairs, filing cabinets, and computers. The faint voice of the 911 operator still trying to get a response guided him toward a desk in the far corner.

Dozens of file folders and prints of satellite photographs lay strewn across the desk and the carpeted floor around it. Despite his best efforts, the corporal could not help reading the tags on some of them: 4TH

GUARDS TANK DIVISION — NARO-FOMINSK CANTONMENT, SIGNAL INTERCEPTS — 45TH SPETSNAZ BRIGADE, RAIL TRAFFIC ANALYSIS — MOSCOW MILITARY DISTRICT. Red warning stamps marked them all as being classified TOP SECRET or beyond.

Dempsey winced. Now he was in for it.

The computer on the desk hummed quietly to itself. A screen saver hid the contents of whatever document its owner had been working on and the police corporal was very careful not to touch anything around the machine. He looked down.

There, curled up next to an overturned chair, lay an older man. The skin on his face and neck was strangely mottled. He groaned once. His eyes flickered partly open and then closed as he drifted in and out of consciousness. He was still clutching the phone receiver in one hand. Clumps of his thick gray hair were falling out, revealing grotesque bald spots covered in a bright red rash.

Dempsey dropped to one knee, taking a closer look at the sick man. He felt for a pulse. It fluttered rapidly and irregularly under his fingertips. He swore once and grabbed his radio. "Sergeant, this is Dempsey! I need a medical team up here, pronto!"

47

February 16
Moscow

The ornate pinnacles and towers of the Kotelnicheskaya apartment block soared high above the city, offering an unsurpassed view west across the Moscow River toward the red brick walls and golden domes and spires of the Kremlin. Dozens of satellite dishes and radio and microwave antennae sprouted from every relatively open space on its elaborate facade. Kotelnicheskaya was one of Stalin's massive "Seven Sisters" — seven enormous high-rises built around Moscow during the 1950s to close what the increasingly power-mad dictator believed was a humiliating "skyscraper gap" with the United States.

Once home to Communist Party officials and heavy-industry bosses, the enormous high-rise now mostly housed wealthy foreigners and members of the new Russian governing and business elite — those able to afford the rents on luxury flats that ran several thousand American dollars a month. The very highest floors, those immediately below a towering central needle topped by a giant gleaming gold star, commanded prices beyond the reach of all but the richest and most powerful men. To bring in even more money, several apartments at the very top had been converted into high-prestige corporate offices.

A tall, powerfully built man stood at a window in one of those renovated penthouse office suites. There were strands of gray in his pale blond hair, a color matched by his ice-gray eyes. He frowned, staring out across the darkened city. The long winter night still held Moscow in its freezing grip, but the sky overhead was turning faintly paler.

A secure phone chirped suddenly on the desk next to him. A digital readout attached to the phone blinked to life, identifying the caller. He swung round and picked it up. "This is Moscow One. Go ahead."

"This is Prague One," a muffled, nasal-sounding voice said. "Petrenko is dead."

The blond-haired man smiled. "Good. And the materials he stole from the hospital? The case files and biological samples?"

"Gone," Prague One reported grimly. "They were in a briefcase that went into the river along with Petrenko."

"Then the matter is closed."

"Not quite," the caller said slowly. "Before we caught up with him, Petrenko had arranged a rendezvous with another doctor, an American attending the same conference. They were talking together when we jumped them."

"And?"

"The American broke free of our ambush," Prague One admitted reluctantly. "The Czech police have him in protective custody."

The blond-haired man's eyes narrowed. "How much does he know?"

The man known as Prague One swallowed hard. "I'm not sure. We think Petrenko managed to tell him something about the deaths before we arrived. We're also fairly sure that the Russian was planning to hand over the medical files and samples to him."

Moscow One tightened his grip on the phone. "And just who is this interfering American?" he snapped.

"His name is Jonathan Smith," the other man said. "According to the conference records, he's a military doctor — a lieutenant colonel — assigned to one of their medical research institutes as a disease specialist."

Smith? The blond-haired man frowned. He had the fleeting impression that he had heard that name before, but where? Somehow it seemed to ring a faint warning bell far back in his mind. He shook his head impatiently. He had more immediate concerns. "What are the Czech police doing now?"

"Dragging the river."

"For the briefcase?"

"No," Prague One replied. "We have an

informant inside the police headquarters. They're only looking for Petrenko's corpse right now. For some reason the American is keeping his mouth shut about what he was told."

The blond-haired man stared back out the window. "Will they find either one?"

"The body will turn up sooner or later," the other man admitted. "But I am confident that the briefcase is gone forever. The Vltava is wide and its current is swift."

"For your sake, I sincerely hope you are right," the blond man said quietly.

"What about this man Smith?" Prague One asked after a moment's uncomfortable silence. "He could become a serious problem."

The blond-haired man frowned again. That was true enough. The American doctor might not yet have told the Czech authorities what he had learned, but eventually he would report Petrenko's claims and the news of his murder to his nation's intelligence services. If so, the CIA and others were likely to begin paying entirely too much attention to new reports of other mysterious illnesses. And that was something he and his employers could not risk. Not yet anyway.

The man code-named Moscow One nodded to himself. So be it. Acting openly against this man Smith would be dangerous. If he disappeared or died, the Prague police would certainly begin asking even more awkward questions about the Petrenko murder, and passing those questions on to Washington. But letting him live was potentially more dangerous. "Eliminate the American if at all possible," he ordered coldly. "But do it carefully — and leave no one alive this time."

CHAPTER THREE

Prague

The tiny interrogation room near the back of the main Prague police station at Konviktská 14 was sparsely furnished. There were just two battered plastic chairs and an old wood table covered with dents, gouges, and the scorch marks left by countless cigarettes carelessly ground out on its surface. Jon Smith sat stiffly in one of the chairs wearing borrowed slacks and a sweatshirt. Even the slightest movement made him uncomfortably aware of his own aching cuts and bruises.

He frowned. How much longer were the Czech authorities going to hold him here? There was no clock in this little room, and his wristwatch had been ruined by its immersion in the icy waters of the Vltava. He glanced up. The faint light leaking in through a tiny window high on one wall showed that it was already past dawn.

Smith fought down a yawn. After they rescued him from the riverbank, the Czech police had taken down his account of the vicious attack that had killed Valentin Petrenko and brought in a medic to patch up the bullet crease across his shoulder. In the process, his belongings, including his wallet, passport, and hotel room key, had been hustled away for "safekeeping." By that time, it had been very nearly midnight and, after bringing him a late supper of soup, they had "suggested" that he use a cot in one of their empty holding cells. He smiled wryly, remembering the long, cold, and mostly sleepless night. At least they had left the door unlocked, making it clear that he was not exactly under arrest, only "helping the authorities with necessary inquiries."

Bells tolled somewhere close by, probably those of the Church of St. Ursula, calling the devout to early morning mass and young children to classes at the adjoining convent school. As if on cue, the door opened and a lean, pale-eyed police officer, immaculate in a neatly pressed uniform, came in. His light gray slacks, blue shirt, carefully knotted black tie, and darker gray jacket marked him as a member of the Prague Municipal Police — the more powerful of the two rival law enforcement agencies operating in the Czech capital. The ID badge clipped to his jacket identified him as Inspector Tomas Karasek. He dropped easily into the chair directly across from Smith.

"Good morning, Colonel," the police officer said casually in clear, comprehensible English. He slid a pair of police artist sketches across the table. "Please tell me what you think of these drawings. They are based on the statement you gave my colleagues last night. Do they match what you remember of the man who you claim killed Dr. Petrenko?"

Smith took the drawings and examined them closely. The first showed the face of a man with long, tangled hair, dark, brooding eyes, and a small skull earring. The second was identical, except that the artist had added a bandage over what appeared to be a badly broken nose and sketched in bruising all around it. He nodded. "That's him. No question about it."

"Then he is one of the Romany," Karasek said coolly. He tapped the pictures with one forefinger. "I believe you would call him a Gypsy in your country."

Smith looked up in surprise. "You've already identified this guy?"

"By name, no," the Czech police officer admitted. "No one matching his precise description appears in our files. But the earring, the hair, the clothing . . . these are all signs which tell me that he is one of their people." He grimaced. "By their very nature, the Romany are criminals. Even their youngest children are raised to be petty thieves, pickpockets, and beggars. They are nothing but troublemakers, scum, and vermin."

With an effort, Smith concealed his distaste for this expression of unthinking bigotry. For all their very real faults, the Romany, a poverty-stricken and rootless people, were commonly used as scapegoats by the richer, more settled societies in which they roamed. It was an old game and all too often a deadly one.

"Dr. Petrenko's death was not exactly an act of petty theft," he said carefully, reining in his temper. "More like cold-blooded murder. These guys knew his name, remember? That's pretty goddamned personal for a simple bunch of muggers."

Karasek shrugged. "They may have followed him to the Charles Bridge from his hotel. These Romany street gangs often prey on tourists, especially if they scent rich pickings."

Something in the way he said it sounded false to Smith. He shook his head. "You don't really believe any of that crap, do you?"

"I don't? Then what should I believe?" the other man asked quietly. The pale-eyed Czech policeman looked narrowly across

56

the table. "Do you have some theory of your own, Colonel? One that you would like to share with me, perhaps?"

Smith stayed quiet. This was dangerous ground. There were limits to what he could safely tell this man. He was sure that Petrenko had been killed to stop him from handing over the medical files and samples he had smuggled out of Moscow, but there was no real evidence left to back that up. Both the briefcase and the Russian had vanished in the Vltava. In the meantime, pushing the idea that this was a political murder was too likely to entangle him in an investigation that could drag on for weeks, and risk revealing skills and connections he had sworn to keep secret forever.

"I've read your statement over quite carefully," Karasek went on. "Frankly, it seems curiously incomplete in several important respects."

"In what way?"

"This rendezvous of yours with Dr. Petrenko on the bridge, for example," the Czech police inspector said. "It seems rather an odd place and time for an American military officer and a Russian scientist to be meeting. You see my point, I hope?"

"My work for the U.S. Army is purely medical and scientific in nature," Smith reminded him stiffly. "I'm a doctor, not a combat soldier."

"Naturally." Karasek's thin-lipped smile stopped well short of his pale blue eyes. "But I envy you your American medical training, Colonel. It must have been exceptionally thorough. I've met very few doctors who could survive hand-to-hand combat with three armed men."

"I was lucky."

"Lucky?" The Czech police officer left the word hanging uncomfortably in the air for a few moments before continuing. "Nevertheless, I would still like a more reasonable explanation of what you and Dr. Petrenko were doing together on the Charles Bridge."

"There's no great mystery," Smith told him, regretting the need to lie. "After two days of lectures and symposia, I needed a short break from the conference. So did Petrenko. And we both wanted to see a bit more of Prague. The bridge just seemed a reasonable starting point."

Karasek raised a skeptical eyebrow. "You were sightseeing? In the fog?"

The American said nothing.

The Czech policeman stared hard at him for a while longer and then sighed. "Very well. I see no reason to detain you here any longer." He stood up smoothly, moved to the door, and pulled it open. Then, abruptly, he turned back. "One thing more, Colonel. I should tell you that we

58

have taken the liberty of collecting your luggage from the conference hotel. It's downstairs waiting for you at the main desk. I imagine that you will wish to shave and change your clothes before making your way to the airport. The next connecting flight to London and New York leaves in a few hours."

Smith eyed him narrowly. "Oh?"

"In these unfortunate circumstances, I am sure that you will wish to cut short your stay in my country," Karasek explained. "This is regrettable, of course, but entirely understandable."

"Is that an order?" Smith asked quietly.

"At an official level? Not at all," the other man said. "Our two governments are close allies, are they not?" He shrugged. "Consider it instead a strong unofficial suggestion. Prague is a peaceful city, one whose prosperity depends largely on tourism. We try not to encourage Wild West–style shoot-outs on our scenic streets and historic bridges."

"So you're the sheriff and I'm the gunslinger you're running out of town before there's more trouble?" Jon said with a rueful grin.

For the first time, a hint of genuine amusement flashed across the inspector's face. "Something like that, Colonel."

"I'll need to contact my superiors,"

Smith said pointedly.

"Certainly." Karasek turned toward the hallway and raised his voice slightly. "Antonin! Please give our American friend here his phone."

A taciturn sergeant brought in the cell phone they had found securely fastened inside the waterproof inner lining of his leather jacket.

With a brisk nod of thanks, Smith took the compact phone, flipped it open, and hit the power button. A small color display blinked on. Small icons flashed across the miniature screen as the machine ran a quick self-diagnostics check, making sure that it was undamaged and that no one had tampered with its special subroutines and codes.

"A very intriguing piece of equipment," Karasek said coolly from the door. "Our electronics experts were quite puzzled by several of its more advanced features."

Smith made sure his face stayed blank. "Really? That's a shame. They're the hottest thing in the States right now. Next time, I'll be sure to bring the user's guide with me."

With a slight smile, the Czech shrugged his shoulders, conceding defeat. "I earnestly hope there will not *be* a next time, Colonel Smith. For now, I wish you a safe journey."

The American waited until the door clicked shut and then punched in a preset code. He lifted the phone to his ear. There was a short delay before it began ringing on the other end.

"Hold one moment, please," a woman's soft voice said politely. Then, after a musical tone chimed twice, confirming that both ends of this call were being encrypted, she said, "We're clear. Go ahead."

"This is Lieutenant Colonel Jonathan Smith calling from Prague," Jon said carefully. "Look, I realize that it's very late there, but I need to speak to General Ferguson. This is important. Fully urgent, in fact."

Anyone listening in would be able to confirm that Brigadier General Daniel Ryder Ferguson was the director of the U.S. Army Medical Research Institute of Infectious Diseases. However, the number he had auto-dialed was not associated with any office at USAMRIID. Instead, his call was passed through an automated relay — one equipped to detect attempts to intercept the signal — before arriving at the Washington, D.C., headquarters of Covert-One.

Jon Smith led a double life. Most of his work was done out in the open, as a scientist and doctor assigned to USAMRIID. But there were also times when he took on

61

special missions for Covert-One, a top-secret intelligence outfit, one that reported directly to the President of the United States. No one in Congress even knew it existed. Nor did anyone in the broader military and intelligence bureaucracy. Loosely organized around a small head-quarters group, Covert-One relied on a clandestine network of operatives, professionals in a number of different fields with a wide range of skills and expertise. Like Smith, they were largely free of family ties and other personal obligations that might hamper their secret work.

"General Ferguson has already gone home for the day, sir," Maggie Templeton, the woman who ran communications for Covert-One, said without missing a beat, playing along with the fiction Smith was weaving. The phrase he had used — "Fully urgent" — was a piece of voice code, a shorthand way for a field agent to report that he was in serious trouble. "But I can patch you through to the duty officer."

"The duty officer?" he repeated aloud. He nodded. "Yes, that would be fine."

"Very good. Wait one moment."

The phone went dead for a brief moment and then a familiar voice spoke in his ear. "Good morning, Jon."

Smith sat up straighter. "Good evening, sir."

The chief of Covert-One, Nathaniel Frederick Klein, chuckled drily. "You're not usually so formal, Colonel. I assume that the walls around you have ears. Maggie told me you were in hot water of one sort or another."

Smith hid a smile. He was fairly sure that at least one hidden microphone was busy recording his end of this conversation. Inspector Karasek was clearly suspicious of him. "I'm calling from a police station in Prague," he said simply. "Three men tried to kill me yesterday afternoon. They did kill a colleague of mine, a Russian research scientist named Valentin Petrenko."

There was a short silence on the other end.

"I see," Klein said at length. "You were quite right to report in. This is serious. Extremely so. You had better brief me, Jon."

Smith obeyed, recounting the attack on the bridge. For the moment, he was careful to stay within the framework of the story he had already told the police. If they *were* listening in, it made sense not to give them any more reasons to interrogate him further. And Fred Klein was smart enough to fill in the obvious gaps for himself.

"The men who attacked you were professionals," Klein said flatly after Smith had finished. "A hit team, with training in close-quarters combat and small arms."

"No question about it," Smith agreed.
"Were they Russians?"

Smith thought back, mentally replaying what he could remember of the long-haired man's voice. Once the lead attacker had dropped the beggar act and started speaking English, there had been some kind of faint, underlying accent, but Jon was not sure now that he could pin it down. He shrugged. "Maybe. But I wouldn't swear to it."

Klein was silent for another few moments. "And where did Dr. Petrenko work in Moscow?" he asked.

"He was a disease specialist attached to the Central Clinical Hospital," Smith told him. "A top-notch guy. One of the best in his field."

"The Central Clinical Hospital? That is interesting," Klein mused. "Very interesting, indeed."

Smith raised an eyebrow. From his position in the shadows, Klein had unhindered access to an incredible range of information and analysis. Were other U.S. or Western intelligence organizations already probing the disease outbreak in Moscow?

"All in all, I would have to say that you have been extremely fortunate," the older man continued. "By rights, you should be lying dead on that bridge."

"Yes, sir," Smith agreed. "By the way,

the police here share your assessment of the situation."

Klein snorted. "So I imagine that the Czech authorities have been asking awkward and inconvenient questions about just how you managed to survive this melee?"

"You could say that," Smith said wryly. "Add the words *non grata* to my *persona* and you'll get a pretty clear picture of my current status. They're shipping me out on the next available flight to London."

"Which is embarrassing, but not fatal. Either to your career or your cover," Klein commented. "More to the point: Are you still at risk from these men?"

Smith considered the question carefully. It was one he had been chewing on for most of the past night. Just how far would the agents who had murdered Petrenko go? Had eliminating the Russian scientist himself satisfied their orders or were they expected to silence anyone Petrenko had contacted? "It's possible," he admitted. "Not likely, maybe, but possible."

"Understood," Klein said quietly. The line went dead again. He was back in less than a minute. "I'm going to arrange some backup for you. It won't be much, not given the tight time frame, but I don't want you hanging out there all on your own. Can you sit tight for an hour or so?"

Smith nodded. "No problem."

"Good. Call me back before you leave that police station." Klein hesitated briefly. "And do try your best not to get killed, Jon. Filling out all the paperwork involved is pure hell on my end."

Smith grinned. "I'll keep that in mind," he promised.

A middle-aged man wearing a thick brown overcoat, gloves, a fur hat, and mirrored sunglasses hurried out the front entrance of the Konviktská police station. Without looking back, he walked briskly away, heading southwest toward the river.

Not far off, a black Mercedes sedan with tinted windows sat waiting for him in a narrow side street. Although the Mercedes was parked illegally, the diplomatic tag displayed prominently on its windshield had so far kept Prague's notoriously over-zealous traffic wardens at bay. Despite the overcast day, sunshades were drawn down across the sedan's rear windows.

Still moving quickly, the man pulled open the driver's-side door and slid inside behind the wheel. He took off his hat and sunglasses and tossed them onto the leather seat beside him. With one gloved hand he nervously smoothed down spiky tufts of newly cropped brown hair.

"Well?" asked a grim voice from the rear seat. "What did you find out?"

"The municipal police are still holding the American," the driver, a Romanian whose name was Dragomir Ilionescu, replied, looking up into the rearview mirror. He could just barely make out the shape of the man sitting behind him. "But not for much longer. As you anticipated, they have arranged a flight out for him later today. First to London and then on to New York."

"With what official security?"

"None, apparently. The Czechs expect him to make his own way to the airport."

"How far can we trust our informant?" the voice asked.

Ilionescu shrugged. "He has always been reliable in the past. I have no reason to doubt him now."

"Excellent." Teeth gleamed in the shadowed interior as the man in the rear seat smiled coldly. "Then we will be able to provide Colonel Smith with a most exciting journey. Signal the rest of the unit. I want everyone ready to move immediately. They know their parts."

Obediently, Ilionescu reached for the car phone. He flicked the switch that activated its scrambler. But then he hesitated. "Is taking this risk necessary?" he asked. "I mean, Petrenko is dead and the material he stole is gone forever, washed away in the river. We have accomplished our primary mission. Given that, what real difference does the life of one American doctor matter one way or the other?"

The man in the rear seat leaned forward out of the shadows. Pale light streaming in through the tinted windshield danced off his shaven skull. Gently, very gently, he touched the thick bandages covering his shattered nose. They were stained with patches of brown, dried blood. "Do you think the man who did this to me was *only* a doctor?" he said softly. "*Just* a simple physician?"

Ilionescu swallowed suddenly.

"Well, do you?"

Sweating now, the Romanian shook his head.

"You show some sense, then. Good. So, whatever this man Smith really is, let us make an end of him," the other man went on. His voice was now dangerously low. "Besides, our recent orders from Moscow were quite specific, were they not? No witnesses. None. You do remember the penalties for failure, I trust?"

A muscle around Ilionescu's left eye twitched at the memory of the gruesome photographs he had been shown. He nodded urgently. "Yes. I remember."

"Then carry out my instructions." With that, Georg Liss, the man who bore the code-name Prague One, sat back again, hiding his ruined face in the darkness.

CHAPTER FOUR

Near Bryansk, Russia

Four twin-tailed Su-34 fighter-bombers roared low over the rolling, wooded hills west of Bryansk. Advanced onboard radar systems allowed the attack aircraft to fly just high enough to clear the tallest trees and power pylons in the area. Streams of incandescent flares designed to decoy heat-seeking surface-to-air missiles blazed in their wake, wafting slowly downward toward the snow-covered ground.

Suddenly the Su-34s popped up, briefly gaining altitude while their onboard systems acquired multiple targets, transferred the data to their weapons, and calculated release points. Seconds later a cloud of precision-guided bombs and missiles fell away from beneath their wings and plunged onward toward the distant forest below. Instantly the four jets broke hard right, again diving for the deck to shake off any hostile radars as they exited the strike area and vanished to the north.

Behind them the woods began exploding,

erupting in huge pillars of blinding orange and red flame. Shattered trees were thrown high into the air, tumbling end over end for hundreds of meters before crashing back to earth. Billowing clouds of smoke and lighter debris drifted downwind.

Nearly a dozen high-ranking Russian army and air force officers stood on the roof of an old concrete bunker dug into the forward slope of a nearby ridge, watching intently through binoculars. More than one hundred heavily armed airborne assault troops wearing snow smocks and body armor were deployed along the ridge, guarding the generals. Command and electronics vans were set up behind the bunker, well hidden among the trees beneath infrared-resistant camouflage netting. Newly laid fiber-optic cables snaked away through the forest, feeding back to a secure communications network. To help preserve complete operational and strategic secrecy for this special set of maneuvers, dubbed WINTER CROWN, all radio, cellular, or standard landline transmissions were being severely restricted.

An army colonel, listening intently through a headset, turned to the short, slender man standing beside him. Alone among all the observers crowded onto the bunker roof, this man wore civilian clothes. He was snug in a plain black overcoat and scarf. The wind ruffled his sparse brown hair. "The exercise computers report all simulated enemy artillery batteries and mobile fire control radars destroyed, sir," the colonel told him quietly.

Russian president Viktor Dudarev nodded calmly, still watching through his binoculars. "Very good," he murmured.

A new wave of sleek ground-attack aircraft — ultramodern Su-39s — raced low over the nearest hills with their powerful turbojet engines howling. They flashed past the bunker at high speed, flying down the wide valley below the ridge. Hundreds of unguided rockets rippled out from the pods slung beneath their wings, streaking onward on trails of smoke and fire. The whole eastern edge of the forest vanished in a rolling series of thunderous explosions.

"All enemy SAM teams have been either suppressed or eliminated entirely," the colonel reported.

The Russian leader nodded again. He swung his binoculars to the left, peering east down the valley. There, in a growing clatter of rotor blades, came a stream of mottled gray-black-and-white helicopters, Mi-17 troop transports, each carrying a team of Spetsnaz commandos. Moving at more than two hundred kilometers an hour, the fleet of winter-camouflaged helicopters swept by the bunker and vanished into the thick smoke clouds now rising above the bomb and rocket-shattered forest.

Dudarev glanced at the colonel, "Well?" he demanded.

"Our special-action forces have penetrated the enemy front lines and are en route toward their primary targets — headquarters units, fuel depots, long-range missile complexes, and the like," his military aide, Colonel Piotr Kirichenko, confirmed, after listening closely to the reports streaming through his headset. He looked up. "The first echelons of our main ground attack force are deploying now."

"Excellent." The Russian president focused his binoculars on the distant opening to the valley. Small specks appeared there, moving fast and spreading out across the rolling, open ground as they drew nearer. They were tracked scout cars, BRM-1s, mounting 73mm cannons, missiles, and machine guns. Behind the scurrying reconnaissance units came masses of heavier armor — T-90 tanks armed with 125mm main guns. The T-90, clad in explosive reactive armor and equipped with IR jammers and anti-laser aerosol defenses to defeat enemy anti-tank missiles, was a significant upgrade of the older T-72. Designed to reflect combat lessons learned during the seemingly endless war in Chechnya, it was the Russian army's most modern battle tank. New computerized fire control systems and thermal sights gave the T-90's main gun range, accuracy, and firepower that was almost equal to that of the American M1A1 Abrams.

Dudarev smiled to himself, watching the formations of tanks maneuvering at high speed down the valley. Western intelligence believed most of Russia's T-90s were deployed in the Far East, facing the People's Republic of China. But the West's vaunted spy agencies were wrong.

Since gaining control over the Kremlin, the ex–KGB officer had worked hard to rebuild and reform his nation's dilapidated armed forces. Thousands of corrupt or lazy or politically unreliable officers had been sacked. Dozens of poorly equipped or poorly performing tank and motor-rifle divisions had been ruthlessly disbanded. Only the best formations were kept in the army's order of battle. And more and more money from Russia's growing oil revenues had been spent on making sure this smaller force of elite divisions was far better-paid, better-equipped, and better-trained than the massed conscript armies of the old Soviet Union.

Dudarev glanced at his watch. He tapped the colonel lightly on the arm. "Time to go, Piotr," he murmured.

Kirichenko nodded. "Sir!"

As they turned to go, the generals nearest to them snapped to attention and saluted.

Dudarev wagged a teasing finger at them. "At ease, gentlemen," he said. "Remember, no formality is necessary. After all, I am not really here. Nor have I ever been here. According to the Kremlin press office, I am off on a short holiday, spending a day or so at my dacha outside Moscow." A humorless smile creased his thin lips. He turned and motioned toward the dozens of tanks and tracked BMP-3 infantry fighting vehicles now rumbling through the valley below them. "Nor is any of this really happening. Everything you see is no more than a dream. WINTER CROWN is only a paper drill, a mere headquarters map exercise. Correct?"

The assembled senior officers chuckled dutifully.

Under the terms of various conventional arms treaties Russia had signed, all of its large-scale military maneuvers were supposed to be announced weeks and even months in advance. WINTER CROWN was a flagrant violation of those agreements. None of the foreign military attachés stationed in Moscow had been notified. And every element of the exercise itself had been very carefully timed to ensure that U.S. spy satellites were not overhead whenever the thousands of troops and hundreds of vehicles involved were actively maneuvering across the snow-covered fields and forests.

The same exquisite timing and elaborate security measures would soon be employed in other major exercises scheduled around the periphery of the Russian Federation, near the borders of Georgia, Azerbaijan, and the breakaway Central Asian republics. Anyone asking inconvenient questions about these intensive battlefield rehearsals would be informed that Russia was simply conducting "special antiterrorist training" for its rapid deployment forces. By the time the deception became obvious, it would be too late. Far too late.

With Colonel Kirichenko close at his heels, he trotted down the steps cut into the hillside at the back of the bunker. A stocky, gray-haired man stood at the bottom waiting patiently for him. Like Dudarev, he wore a drab dark overcoat and stood bareheaded in the bitter cold.

The president turned to his aide. "Go ahead and make sure everything is ready for our departure, Piotr. I'll be along shortly."

The colonel nodded. He walked away without looking back. Part of his duties included knowing exactly when to vanish — and exactly what not to see or hear.

Dudarev turned back to the gray-haired man. "Well, Alexei?" he asked softly. "Make your report."

Alexei Ivanov, an old and trusted comrade from the KGB, was now the head of a little-known section in the KGB's successor, the Federal Security Service, or FSB. On formal organization charts circulated by the Russian government, Ivanov's department carried the rather boring title of the Special Projects Liaison Office. But insiders called his shadowy domain "The Thirteenth Directorate" and tried very hard to stay out of its way.

"Our friends have signaled that HYDRA is in motion — and on schedule," he told the Russian president. "The first operational variants are taking effect."

Dudarev nodded. "Good." He looked up at the bigger man. "And what of those information leaks you found so troubling?"

Ivanov scowled. "They have been . . . sealed. Or so it is claimed."

"You are not sure?" Dudarev asked, raising an eyebrow.

The head of the Thirteenth Directorate shrugged his massive shoulders. "I have no real reason to doubt these reports. But I admit that I do not like this game of working by remote control. It is an imperfect process." He frowned. "Perhaps even a dangerous one."

Dudarev clapped him briskly on the shoulder. "Cheer up, Alexei," he said. "The old ways are dead, and we must move with the times. Decentralization and power-sharing are all the rage these days, are they not?" His eyes turned cold. "Besides, HYDRA is a weapon best employed at a safe distance and with total deniability. True?"

Ivanov nodded heavily. "That is true."

"Then you will continue as planned," Dudarev told him. "You know the timetable. Keep a wary eye on our friends, if need be. But do not interfere directly unless you have no other choice. Clear?"

"Yes, your orders are clear," the bigger man agreed reluctantly. "I only hope your faith is justified."

Amused, the Russian president raised an eyebrow. "Faith?" His lips twitched upward in a brief, icy half-smile. "My dear Alexei, you should know me better than that. I am no true believer — in anything or anyone. Faith is for fools and simpletons. The wise man knows that facts and force are what truly govern the world."

Tbilisi, Georgia

Georgia's capital lay in a natural amphitheater, surrounded on all sides by high hills topped by ancient fortresses, crumbling monasteries, and dense forests. On a clear day like this one, the far-off snow-capped peaks of the Caucasus Mountains appeared on the northern horizon, standing sharply etched against a pale blue sky.

Sarah Rousset, a correspondent for *The New York Times*, leaned on the railing of the balcony of her top-floor room in the five-star rated Tbilisi Marriott. She was only in her mid-thirties, but she had allowed her originally chestnut-colored hair to go mostly gray. Looking older than she really was somehow reassured both senior editors and potential news sources. With one eye shut, she focused through the viewfinder of her digital camera and began snapping pictures of the enormous crowd filling the wide, tree-lined avenue below.

She zoomed in on a diminutive white-haired woman holding a rose-colored banner aloft. Black mourning ribbons fluttered from the staff. Tears trickled unheeded down the woman's wrinkled face. With one light tap of her finger, Rousset froze the powerful image and stored it in her camera's memory. That one should make the front page, she thought. Right beside the lead article with her byline plastered on it.

"Marvelous," she murmured, still taking pictures.

"I beg your pardon?" the tall, square-jawed man standing at her shoulder said coldly. He was the chief of mission for the U.S. embassy here.

"All those people," Rousset explained, nodding at the Georgians packed below them. Beneath a sea of rose-colored flags and placards, the silent crowd was slowly flowing east toward the Parliament building. "There must be tens of thousands of people down there in the freezing cold. Maybe more. And all of them united in sorrow and grief. Just for one sick man." She shook her head. "It's going to make a marvelous story."

"More like a terrible tragedy," her companion said tightly. "For Georgia certainly, and perhaps for the whole Caucasus region."

She lowered the camera and glanced sidelong at him from under her long lashes. "Really? Would you like to explain why . . . in a way my readers can understand, I mean?"

"Not for attribution?" he asked quietly.

Rousset nodded. "No problem." She smiled delicately. "Let's say that you'll appear in print as 'an expert Western observer of Georgian politics.' "

"Fair enough," the diplomat agreed. He sighed. "Look, Ms. Rousset, you need to understand that President Yashvili is more than just an ordinary politician to those people. He's become a symbol of their democratic Rose Revolution, a symbol of Georgia's peace, prosperity, and maybe even its continued existence."

He waved a hand at the distant hills and mountains. "For centuries, this region was torn back and forth between rival empires, Persia, the Byzantines, the Arabs, the Turks, the Mongols, and finally the Russians. Even after the Soviet Union imploded, Georgia was still a wreck, ravaged by ethnic infighting, corruption, and political chaos. When the Rose Revolution swept him into office, Mikhail Yashvili began changing all that. He's given these people their first real taste of competent, democratic government in eight hundred years."

"And now he's dying," Rousset prompted. "Of cancer?"

"Maybe." The tall American diplomat shrugged gloomily. "But no one really knows. My sources inside the government say that his doctors haven't been able to identify the illness killing him. All they know is that his vital organs are failing rapidly, shutting down one by one."

"So what happens next?" the female *New York Times* reporter wondered aloud. "After Yashvili dies."

"Nothing good."

Rousset pressed harder. "Could other regions break away — just like South Ossetia and Abkhazia?" Fighting in those two self-declared "autonomous republics" had killed thousands and lasted for years.

"Or maybe even escalate into another all-out civil war?" she went on. Filing reports from a war zone was a risky business, but it was also the path to journalistic stardom. And Sarah Rousset had always been ambitious.

"Possibly," the tall man admitted. "Yashvili doesn't really have a clearly defined successor, at least not anyone trusted by all the different political factions, nationalities, and ethnic groups in Georgia."

"What about the Russians?" she asked. "There are still lots of native Russians living here in Tbilisi, right? If serious fighting broke out in and around the city, would the Kremlin send in troops to stop it?"

The diplomat shrugged again. "As to that, Ms. Rousset, your guess is as good as mine."

CHAPTER FIVE

The White House, Washington, D.C.
President Samuel Adams Castilla led his guest into the darkened Oval Office and flipped on the lights. With one hand, he loosened his carefully knotted bow tie and then unbuttoned his formal dinner jacket. "Take a pew, Bill," he said quietly, motioning toward one of the two armchairs set in front of the room's marble fireplace. "Can I get you a drink?"

His Director of National Intelligence, William Wexler, shook his head quickly. "Thank you, but no, Mr. President." The trim, telegenic former U.S. senator smiled fulsomely, evidently hoping to take the sting out of his refusal. "Your wine stewards were very generous at dinner tonight. I rather think that one more glass of anything might tip me right over the edge."

Castilla nodded coolly. Some members of the White House social staff seemed to harbor the unexpressed conviction that guests at state dinners should always be offered enough rope to hang themselves —

or, in this case, enough alcohol to put a whole regiment of U.S. Marines under the table. Guests who were wise resisted temptation and pushed away their wineglasses before it was too late. Guests who were not wise were rarely invited back, no matter how influential or popular or powerful they might be.

He glanced at the ornate eighteenth-century clock ticking softly on one curved wall. It was well past midnight. Again he waved Wexler into a chair and then sat down across from him. "First, I appreciate your willingness to stay on so late tonight."

"It's really no trouble, Mr. President," Wexler said in a rich, professional politician's baritone. He smiled again, this time revealing a set of perfect teeth. Although he was in his early sixties, his deeply tanned face showed very few lines or wrinkles. "After all, sir, I serve at your pleasure."

Castilla wondered about that. Stung by a series of damaging and very public failures, Congress had recently enacted the first major reorganization of America's intelligence-gathering apparatus in more than fifty years. The legislation had created a new cabinet-level post — the director of national intelligence. In theory, the DNI was supposed to be able to coordinate the U.S. government's complex array of competing intelligence agencies, departments, and bureaus. In practice, the CIA, FBI, DIA, NSA, and others were still waging a fierce bureaucratic war behind the scenes to severely limit his powers.

Overcoming so much powerful institutional resistance would take a very shrewd and strong-willed man, and Castilla was beginning to have serious doubts that Wexler had either the will or the mental dexterity. It was no real secret that the former senator would never have been his first choice for the position, but Congress had dug in its collective heels and refused to approve anyone but one of its own. With even nominal control over a total intelligence budget of more than forty billion dollars, the Senate and House of Representatives were very interested in making sure the DNI post went to someone they knew and trusted.

Wexler had served as a senator from one of the smaller New England states for more than twenty years, compiling an earnest, if relatively undistinguished, legislative record, and earning a reputation as a decent, hardworking member of the various Congressional committees overseeing the armed forces and intelligence agencies. Over his years of service, he had accumulated a great many friends and very few serious enemies.

A solid majority of the Senate had believed he was the perfect choice to head the U.S. intelligence community. Privately, Castilla was convinced that Bill Wexler was a painfully polite, well-intentioned pushover. Which meant that the reforms intended to streamline and strengthen the management of U.S. intelligence operations had only added yet another layer of red tape to the whole system.

"What exactly can I do for you, Mr. President?" the national intelligence director said at last, breaking the small silence. If he was at all puzzled by Castilla's decision to pull him aside at the state dinner to arrange this unusual and highly irregular late-night conference, he hid it well.

"I want you to redirect our intelligence-gathering and analysis efforts," the president told him flatly. Like it or not, he realized, he had to try working through this man — at least for now.

Wexler raised a single quizzical eyebrow. "In what way?"

"I want more focus on political and military developments inside Russia, and on events in the smaller countries around its borders," Castilla said. "And that's going to require extensive shifts in the allocation of satellite time, SIGINT translation priorities, and analyst assignments."

"Russia?" Wexler was astonished.

"That's right."

"But the Cold War is over," the intelligence director protested.

"So they tell me," Castilla said drily. He leaned forward in his chair. "Look, Bill, for any number of overriding geopolitical reasons we've cut our good *friend* Viktor Dudarev a lot of slack over the past couple of years, right? Even though that's meant turning a blind eye to some of the nasty moves he's made against his own people?"

Wexler nodded reluctantly.

"Well, the trouble is that while we've been tied down in Afghanistan, Iraq, and a dozen other hellholes around the globe, Dudarev has been busy building a new autocracy in Russia, with him sitting on top of the heap as the supreme ruler of all that he surveys. And I don't like that. I don't like it one little goddamned bit."

"The Russians have been extremely useful allies against al-Qaeda and other terrorist groups," the intelligence director pointed out. "Both the CIA and the Pentagon report that we've obtained a substantial amount of actionable intelligence from their prisoner interrogations in Chechnya."

Castilla shrugged his big shoulders. "Sure." He gave the other man a lopsided grin. "But, hell, even a two-bit thug will help you kill a rattlesnake — so long as you're both stuck at the bottom of the same canyon, that is. That sure doesn't mean you should turn your back on him."

"Are you suggesting that Russia is again becoming an active enemy of the United States?" Wexler asked carefully.

Castilla made an effort to hold his temper in check. "What I'm suggesting is that I don't like flying blind around a guy like Viktor Dudarev. And right now the intelligence analysis I'm getting from the CIA and the other agencies pretty much reads as though they're just clipping newspaper articles."

The DNI smiled weakly. "I've made the same comments to my staff," he admitted. "I've even passed those complaints along through the various appropriate interagency coordinating committees."

Castilla scowled. The "appropriate interagency coordinating committees"? Leadership by memo and committee? And this was the guy who was supposed to be cracking the whip over the CIA and the other intelligence organizations? Wonderful. Just wonderful. He gritted his teeth. "And?"

"Apparently, there are . . . well . . . problems in some of the analysis sections," Wexler said hesitantly. "I don't have all the details myself yet, but I've been told that several of our best Russia specialists have fallen seriously ill over the past couple of weeks."

Castilla stared hard at him for several seconds. "Maybe you had better fill me in, Bill," he said grimly. "From the top, and starting right now."

Moscow

It was full daylight now. Pallid rays cast by the weak winter sun winked off the ice-choked Moscow River and sent back dazzling reflections from the windshields of the cars and trucks grinding slowly in both directions across the bridges visible from the windows of the Kotelnicheskaya high-rise. Even twenty-four floors up, their blaring horns could be heard faintly. The Russian capital's morning rush hour was in full swing.

The blond-haired man sat at his desk, again rapidly skimming through the set of highly encrypted e-mails sent to his computer over the past several hours. Most were short, usually containing only a name and title, a location, and a single-line status report:

Marchuk, A., CINC, Northern Command, Ukraine — infected. Condition: terminal.
Brightman, H., SIGINT Specialist,

GCHQ, Cheltenham, United Kingdom — infected. Condition: dead.

Yashvili, M., President, Republic of Georgia — infected. Condition: terminal.

Sundquist, P., Senior Political Analyst, CIA, Langley, U.S.A. — infected. Condition: dead.

Hamilton, J., Manager, A2 (Russia Group), NSA, Fort Meade, U.S.A. — infected. Condition: terminal.

The list of those now ill and dying or already dead ran on and on, more than thirty men and women in all. He read to the end with growing satisfaction. It had taken years of painstaking research to perfect the biological weapon called HYDRA — the ultimate, precision-guided silent killer. Months of preparation had gone into selecting targets for the first HYDRA variants and then finding ways to deliver them undetected to the chosen victims. Months more had been spent in secretly acquiring the necessary materials to build each specialized variant of the weapon. At last, all of that intricate planning and dangerous work was coming to fruition.

In retrospect, he thought dispassionately, those preliminary tests in Moscow had been largely unnecessary, a waste of resources and a breach of operational security, but HYDRA's creator had insisted on running them. Controlled experiments in the sterile confines of a laboratory were no substitute for field tests on real people, he had said. Only by setting HYDRA loose on random targets could they be sure that other doctors and hospitals, those outside the secret, would not be able to detect his creation, or to cure those infected by it.

The man code-named Moscow One shook his head. Wulf Renke was brilliant, ruthless, and, as always, utterly determined to have his own way. In the end, those sponsoring the HYDRA Project had yielded to his will, eager to see for themselves that the weapon's performance matched his extravagant claims. Well, it had, but only at the cost of alerting Doctors Kiryanov and Petrenko and sending them haring off to warn the West.

Then he shrugged. What did it really matter? Kiryanov and Petrenko were both dead. And soon the only Westerner with whom they had shared their fears would join them.

He reached out for his phone and dialed a local number.

A cold, clear voice answered on the first ring. "Well?"

"The first phase is largely complete," the blond-haired man said quietly.

"Have you informed Ivanov?"

"I gave him a preliminary report late last night," he confirmed. "Before he left to join Dudarev for the WINTER CROWN maneuvers. I'll brief him more fully once he returns to Moscow."

"I assume our friend from the Thirteenth Directorate was pleased?" the voice said.

"I suspect Alexei Ivanov would be far more pleased if he filled my shoes — or yours," the man known as Moscow One said sardonically.

"No doubt," the voice said. "Fortunately, his master is more sensible and more accommodating. Now, how soon can we begin the next phase? Our friends need to know when they can ramp up their military preparations."

The blond-haired man checked the last status report on his computer screen, one sent by Wulf Renke himself. It would be best to confer personally with the scientist before deploying the next variants by courier. "I'll need a plane out of Sheremetevo-2 later tonight."

"I will arrange it."

"Then I should be at the HYDRA lab early tomorrow morning."

CHAPTER SIX

Prague

With his overnight bag and laptop slung over one shoulder, Smith pushed through a crowd of patrolmen and traffic wardens coming back to work from their mid-morning coffee break. Cold air rushed in through the open front doors of the Konviktská station, bringing with it the cloying reek of gasoline and diesel fumes trapped in the Old Town's maze of narrow streets.

Jon stepped outside onto the pavement and immediately felt the frigid Prague winter climate wrap itself around him. He stopped and blew on his hands, already regretting the loss of his leather jacket, torn and soaked beyond repair. Before signing out of the police station, he had changed into a pair of jeans and a black turtleneck sweater, but the thin gray windbreaker he wore over the sweater offered little real protection against the piercing cold. Over his cupped hands, his eyes were busy scanning the surrounding environment.

There, he thought.

Just across the street from the police headquarters, a big, beefy, bearded man leaned casually against the side of a parked taxi, a Czech-made Skoda sedan. Beneath the caked-on grime and mud, the cab had so many dents and scrapes from minor accidents that it was hard to tell where its original paint job left off and the primer began. The driver looked Smith up and down, hawked once, spat to the side, and then slowly straightened up to his full height. "Hey, mister!" he called out in heavily accented English. "You need a taxi?"

"Maybe," Smith said cautiously, crossing the street. Was this huge bear of a man his promised contact? "How much would you charge me for a ride to the airport?"

It was a natural question. Prague's independent cabdrivers were notorious for doubling and even tripling their regulated fares for unwary or naïve tourists. Even on the short run to Ruzyně, the city's only international airport, that could add up to serious money.

The big man grinned broadly, revealing a mouthful of tobacco-stained teeth. "For a rich businessman? I would charge a thousand crowns." He lowered his voice. "But for a scholar like you? A poor professor? Nothing. You will pay me nothing."

Smith allowed himself to relax slightly. *Scholar* was the recognition word Klein had selected for this rendezvous. Against all appearances, that meant this rough, boisterous taxi driver was the Covert-One asset activated to help him get out of the Czech Republic in one piece. He nodded quickly. "Okay. You've got yourself a deal. Let's go."

With one final look around, he slid into the back seat and waited while the driver squeezed himself in behind the wheel. The Skoda rocked under the big man's weight.

Before putting the taxi in gear, the driver swung round to look the American in the eye. "I have been told that you wish to arrive at the airport safely and discreetly," he rumbled.

"That's right."

"And that there may be others who do not wish to see this occur. Correct?"

Again, Smith nodded, tight-lipped this time.

The big man smiled widely again. "Do not worry, Scholar. All will be well. You can rely on Václav Masek." He unzipped his bright red ski parka just far enough for Jon to see the butt of a pistol in a shoulder holster, and winked theatrically. "And on my little friend here if there is any trouble."

Smith tamped down a worried frown.

The head of Covert-One had warned him not to expect too much. "I can only get one man to you in time, Jon," Klein had said. "He's a contract courier, not a field operative, but he is mostly reliable."

Smith made a mental note to have Klein update his file on Masek. The bearded giant seemed too boastful and far too eager to flourish his concealed weapon. That was potential trouble. It meant that the Czech cabdriver was either badly frightened and talking big to hide his case of nerves — or that he was too aggressive, spoiling for a chance to prove himself ready for more exacting and rewarding assignments.

He stayed quiet while the taxi driver took them through the labyrinthine streets of the Old Town, across the Vltava, and up the winding road east of the Castle, a massive complex of churches, convents, towers, and government buildings dating back centuries. Through it all, the other man kept up a running commentary, pointing out tourist sights, swearing profanely at other drivers, and offering repeated assurances that they were making good time.

Definitely nerves, Smith decided. For all his bulk and bravado, Masek was a small, scared man on the inside. The Czech driver might be a competent clandestine courier, but Klein should never have asked him to step so far out of the safety of the shadows. Be fair, Jon, his mind coldly reminded him. This guy probably knows that a hit team has already tried to kill you once and that it may try again.

He sighed. Hell, he was feeling pretty twitchy himself. He stared out the window, seeking calm in the neatly manicured gardens visible on either side. The roof of the Belvedere, a lovely royal summerhouse built during the Renaissance, rose above the surrounding trees, sheathed in blue-green copper.

Minutes after heading downhill again just north of the Castle, the Skoda curved three-quarters of the way around a busy traffic circle and came out heading west on a wide boulevard. Smith sat up straighter. They were on Evropská, a modern thoroughfare that ran straight to the airport. Off to their left, he could make out a sprawling patchwork of suburban houses, schools, and small industrial parks. On the right, a chain of three hills crowned with evergreens, oaks, and beeches climbed steeply above more rows of detached houses and shops. These forested heights stretched away to the north and east, reaching toward the river behind them.

Masek accelerated, pushing the taxi up to and then beyond the posted speed limit. Signs sliding past overhead indicated that the airport was only a few kilometers away.

Soon Jon caught fleeting glimpses of a narrow artificial lake through the bare branches of the trees lining the north side of the boulevard. Beyond the lake, the ground fell away into a rugged, broken landscape of dark woods and gray limestone cliffs.

"That is the Divoká a Ticha Sárka, the valley of the Wild and Still Sarka, a place of legend and violence," the taxi driver explained grandly, nodding his massive head toward the shadowed gorge visible on the other side of the stretch of gray-green water. "Some say men and women fought a cruel and bloody war there long ago, before the dawn of history. It was a war waged for absolute power and dominion. According to the stories, a beautiful young maiden named Sarka lured the chief warrior of the men into that forest. There, she made love to him, plied him with strong drink, and then murdered him in his sleep."

Smith grinned. "Not exactly a cheerful place, I guess."

Masek shrugged his broad shoulders. "Well, actually, it is a nature preserve now. Many people from Prague swim and camp there in the summer, when it is hot. We Czechs may be romantic, but we are also very practical."

Suddenly, brake lights glowed red as the

cars in front of them began slowing down. A line of orange cones angled across the boulevard, closing off the fast lanes heading west. By the side of the road, a portable electronic sign blinked on and off, repeatedly flashing a warning message in Czech.

"Shit," Masek muttered. He took his foot off the accelerator and stomped down hard on the Skoda's brakes. The taxi decelerated sharply. Frowning and grumbling under his breath, he swung into the suddenly crowded right lane, forcing his way into the narrowing gap between an old Volvo and a brand-new Audi. Horns blared behind them in protest.

Smith leaned forward. "Road construction?" he asked quietly. "Or an accident?"

"Neither," the big man replied, nervously chewing at his lower lip. "That sign says the police have set up a special traffic checkpoint and that we must be prepared to stop."

"What are they looking for?" Jon heard himself ask.

Masek shook his head irritably. "I do not know. Drunk drivers? Drugs? Stolen goods? Or maybe only bald tires and broken taillights." His knuckles whitened as he tightened his grip on the steering wheel. "It could be any of those things. The authorities greatly enjoy handing out tickets and collecting special fees."

Smith peered through the windshield as the taxi inched slowly ahead. They were roughly one hundred meters from the exit marked *Divoká Sárka*. It fed onto a much narrower side road that veered off into the woods. A lone patrolman wearing the peaked cap, black winter jacket, and blue snow pants of the Czech national police stood there, rhythmically waving a bright orange baton to keep the traffic moving. Every so often, he would step out with an upraised hand and signal one or more of the oncoming cars or trucks off onto the exit beside him, emphasizing his orders with short, sharp jabs of the baton.

The American watched closely, looking for a pattern in the way vehicles were selected. He frowned, unable to detect one. The bored-looking patrolman seemed to be allowing most cars and trucks to roll right on past him, only occasionally pulling others off the boulevard in ones or twos. That meant this was probably just a random spot check.

Probably.

"Shit," Masek muttered again as the policeman jabbed his baton at them. They had been plucked out of the passing parade. Glumly, the cabdriver spun the steering wheel sharply to the right. They turned onto the exit, trailing the short line of other cars and trucks already diverted off Evropská.

Smith glanced back through the Skoda's rear window. A late-model black Mercedes with tinted windows swung onto the park access road close behind them. Frowning now, he turned around.

They were in among the trees now. Light filtered down through a maze of bare branches overhead. The police checkpoint was just ahead. He could see a pair of unmarked cars, also Czech-manufactured Skodas, parked on the shoulder, near another row of orange traffic cones. Two more uniformed patrolmen were posted there, apparently asking the drivers of each vehicle a few quick questions before waving them on.

One of them approached the taxi. He looked old for his rank, with a gaunt, sallow face. Under his peaked cap, his eyes were expressionless. He bent down and rapped sharply on the driver's side window.

Masek quickly rolled it down.

The policeman held out his hand. "Show me your driver's license. And your taxi permit," he snapped in rapid-fire Czech.

Hurriedly, the big man obeyed, handing over the required papers. Visibly fretting, he waited uneasily while the patrolman skimmed through them. Apparently satis-

100

fied, the sallow-faced officer contemptuously tossed both the license and the permit back into Masek's lap. Next, he peered into the backseat. One dark eyebrow went up. "Who is this fellow? A foreigner?"

Smith kept his own mouth shut.

"Nobody important. An American businessman, I think. He's just a fare I'm taking to the airport," Masek mumbled in answer. The big man was openly perspiring now. Tiny droplets of sweat slid down his forehead. Smith could sense the fear growing inside the cabdriver, gnawing away at his confidence and self-control. "He says he has a flight out this morning."

"Don't panic," the patrolman said with a disinterested shrug. "The American should still make his trip on time."

"Then we can go now?" the cabdriver asked hopefully.

The policeman shook his head. "Not quite yet, friend. I'm afraid this is not your lucky day. The government has another flap on about vehicle safety, especially for taxis. That means a complete inspection." He turned away, calling toward his colleague. "Hey, Edvard! We'll take this one."

Smith's eyes narrowed. Something about this man's profile tugged at his subconscious, sounding a faint but insistent alarm. Looking more closely, he noticed a tiny perforation, some kind of piercing, in the man's earlobe. That was odd, he thought. How many middle-aged Czech cops wore jewelry off-duty?

The policeman looked back at Masek. "Park over there," he said, pointing toward the side of the road, indicating a space between the two unmarked cars. "Then just sit tight. We'll have you out of here as soon as possible."

"Yes. Yes. Of course." With a shaky smile, the taxi driver nodded obsequiously, bobbing his massive head up and down. He steered the Skoda over onto the grassy shoulder, backed in carefully between the parked cars, and then slowly reached down to switch off the ignition. His hands were trembling.

"No, don't," Smith said abruptly, still looking out the window. "Leave the engine running for now." Both of the Czech policemen were bending down to talk to the driver of the black Mercedes. There were no other cars waiting to go through the checkpoint. The tree-lined access road behind them was completely empty.

He shook his head, irritated at himself. What was he missing? Those little alarm bells inside his head were growing louder. It was time to play it safe, he decided. "Give me your pistol, Václav," he said quietly. "Now."

"My pistol?" The big man's eyes widened in surprise. Warily, he glanced over his shoulder. "Why?"

"Let's just say that I'd like to avoid any unfortunate accidents," Jon told him, careful to speak calmly. There was no point in spooking the other man — not yet, anyway. Not until he could figure out why his fight-or-flee instincts were hammering so hard on the gates of his conscious mind. He thought fast. "Do you have a permit for that weapon?"

Reluctantly, Masek shook his head.

"Swell. Just swell." Smith frowned. "Look, these cops are already looking for trouble. Getting a ticket for something like a burned-out brake light is bad enough, a real pain in the ass. But do you really want to get nailed for carrying an illegal firearm?"

The cabdriver turned even paler beneath his full, tangled beard. He swallowed hard. "No, I do not," he admitted. "The penalties for such offenses are very . . . severe."

"Then give it to me," Smith said forcefully again. "Let me handle this."

Eagerly, Masek unzipped his parka and tugged the pistol out of his shoulder holster. His big hands were shaking even harder now.

Jon reached across the seat and took the weapon away before the other man could drop it. The pistol was a CZ-52, a Czech-manufactured autoloader using the same 7.62mm round as the Second World War–era Soviet Tokarev. Once a standard Warsaw Pact military sidearm, thousands had been sold as "surplus" to private citizens — both legally and illegally. He made sure the manual safety was still set in the middle "safe" position and then hit the magazine release. There were eight rounds inside the small clip, the standard load for a pistol of this make. He slid the magazine back in and again glanced out the window.

Outside, the two Czech policemen slowly straightened up from the black Mercedes. After exchanging a few muttered words, they turned in unison and stalked back toward the parked taxi.

Smith stiffened.

Each man's face had become a rigid, unreadable mask, utterly without any discernible emotion. It was as though some terrible force had erased all traces of humanity from them, leaving the surface features, but wiping away any real sign of life and personality. One of them, the older patrolman who had checked Masek's papers reached down almost casually and drew the sidearm holstered at his side.

And suddenly Jon knew where he had seen this man before.

On the Charles Bridge, he realized

grimly. Fading back before Valentin Petrenko's wild, desperate swings right after burying a knife deep in the Russian scientist's stomach. Like his two comrades, the gaunt-faced man had been wearing a small silver skull, a death's head, in that tiny piercing in his right ear.

This "police checkpoint" was a trap, a carefully arranged killing ground.

For one long, terrible moment, time itself seemed to stop, but then Smith's trained reflexes kicked in. A sense of movement and the ability to act came flooding back into the once-frozen world around him. "Get us out of here!" he shouted to Masek. "It's a setup! Go! Go!"

Horrified, the big man slammed the Skoda into gear, stamped down on the accelerator, and reversed, frantically trying to get enough maneuvering room to pull forward out onto the narrow road. Smith thumbed off the safety on the pistol he had taken from Masek, pulled back on the slide and let it go, moving a 7.62mm round from the magazine into the firing chamber.

And then he was thrown forward as the taxi crashed into the empty car parked close behind and rocked to a stop. Glass and torn metal crunched. Jarred by the collision, the Skoda's engine stalled out and died.

Desperately, Masek fumbled with the

gearshift and ignition, trying to restart his battered cab.

It was too late, Smith realized abruptly, watching the gaunt-faced man bring his Russian-made Makarov up on target in what seemed like slow motion. The second phony cop had his pistol out, too. Hell.

Jon was already diving sideways toward the right-side passenger door when the windows on the left side shattered. Cubed shards of safety glass flew inward, shattered by the impact of several shots fired rapidly at close range.

One round hit Masek just above the left ear. The big man's head exploded, blown apart by a copper-jacketed bullet moving at more than a thousand feet per second. Blood and bone fragments sleeted across the Skoda's front seat and dashboard.

Another round punched into the cloth-covered seat close by Smith and ripped through a tangle of coils and springs. It ricocheted off the cab's steel frame, tumbling upward in a shower of sparks, smoldering pieces of torn fabric, and white-hot metal splinters. Christ! He grabbed the handle, shoved the rear door open, and threw himself out onto the ground.

Moving fast, he rolled to the right and came back up crouched behind the taxi's right rear tire. He risked one quick glance over his shoulder. Not far behind him the ground fell away sharply, descending ever deeper into the surrounding woods. Most of the trees here were ancient oaks and beeches, standing tall and leafless against the gloomy, overcast sky. There was almost no undergrowth, just a few small saplings and withered weeds.

Not really enough cover, Jon thought coolly. Just the tree trunks themselves. Anyone in pursuit would not have to work too hard to get a clear shot at him. If he wanted to run, he would somehow have to buy himself a decent head start.

More shots rang out and the Skoda rocked sharply, hit several times in rapid succession. More glass shattered. More metal tore. Ricochets spanged off the engine block and frame and whirred off into the trees, splintering branches and twigs.

Smith breathed in. One. Two. Three. Now.

With his pistol held ready in both hands, he reared up over the back of the taxi. His narrowed eyes flickered rapidly from side to side, hunting for the men who were trying to kill him. There! One of the fake cops, the older man, was standing just meters away, steadily squeezing off aimed rounds from his sidearm, methodically shooting up the taxi from front to back.

Smith whirled toward him, moving fast. Both the front and rear sights of his Czech-made pistol settled on the other man's chest. He squeezed the trigger and the pistol barked once, bucking upward as the slide slammed back, feeding in another round. Quickly, he brought the weapon back down on target and fired again.

Blood splashed high in the air. Hit twice, the gaunt-faced gunman spun toward the American who had shot him. His mouth fell open in stunned disbelief. Then, slowly, he fell to his knees and pitched forward onto the road. More blood pooled red on the black asphalt.

His colleague, a younger, heavier man, dropped prone. Grim-faced, he immediately fired back at Smith without bothering to aim carefully. He was clearly shooting wildly in an effort to drive the American back into cover.

One bullet from the Makarov whip-cracked through the air close to Smith's ear. Another ripped across the top of the taxi's trunk, tearing a fiery crease through the rusting metal and cracked and peeling paint.

He ignored them. Instead, he swung his own pistol through a short arc, zeroing in on the prone gunman. He squeezed off two more rounds. The first missed narrowly, sending broken chunks of asphalt and bits of gravel spinning away. But the second 7.62mm bullet tore off the top of the younger gunman's skull.

An eerie silence fell across the little clearing.

Smith breathed out slowly, scarcely able to believe he was still alive. He could feel his heart beating at an incredible tempo, only gradually falling off as his pulse settled. Now what? he wondered.

Suddenly he heard car doors slamming open. The people inside that black Mercedes were coming out, he realized. Still kneeling behind the bullet-riddled taxi, he swiveled. He caught a quick glimpse of two men, both of them wearing thick brown overcoats and fur hats, dropping into cover on the other side of the big luxury sedan. They were heavily armed. Each carried a compact Heckler & Koch MP5K submachine gun cradled in his gloved hands.

Smith grimaced. One of those men had bandages plastered across his narrow face — no doubt covering the mangled remains of the nose Smith had crushed yesterday on the Charles Bridge. So he was facing two more enemies, and there was no chance whatsoever of surprising them.

He glanced down at the pistol he held in both hands. Four rounds. He had just four rounds left in the magazine. He shook his head. That was not enough. Not against two high-powered automatic weapons that could easily shred the taxi he was crouching behind into a smashed heap of mangled metal.

Staying here meant dying. It was time to go.

He dropped back behind the ruined Skoda. Then, staying low, he loped away, sliding right over the edge of the steep slope leading down into Divoká Sárka, the shadow-filled valley of the Wild Sarka.

CHAPTER SEVEN

Georg Liss rose slowly from behind the Mercedes, sighting carefully along the short barrel of his MP5K submachine gun. His finger tightened on the trigger.

Nothing moved anywhere on the narrow stretch of road or behind the bullet-torn taxi slewed awkwardly across the shoulder. His face darkened. Two of his best field agents lay sprawled on the ground. They were both dead, gunned down by this damned American. The corners of his mouth turned down in frustration. First the near-catastrophe on the Charles Bridge, and now this disaster. The ambush he had planned should have been perfect, a mere matter of killing an unarmed man, like a sheep led to the slaughter. Instead, it had come apart in sheer bloody ruin. Where had that devil Smith gotten his hands on a weapon?

Still peering intently at the wrecked cab, Liss stood motionless, waiting for something, for anything, to shoot at. Suddenly, he heard the distant sound of dead leaves crackling somewhere in the woods beyond the road. The American was already running, heading straight down into the rugged Sarka valley. What would the men in Moscow say to him if Smith escaped now? More to the point, he thought grimly, what would they *do* to him?

"Dragomir!" he snapped to his driver. "Signal Eugen and get him up here from the main road." He nodded toward the two dead men wearing Czech police uniforms. "Shove those bodies into the trunk and take the American's luggage. Then both of you clear out. Head for the airport. If you see Smith arrive, kill him if you can. Otherwise, make for the safe house. I will contact you there later."

"What about our other vehicles?" the Romanian asked.

"Leave them," Liss growled through gritted teeth. "They are clean. Nothing inside can link them to us."

"Understood." Ilionescu nodded. He hesitated. "But what will you do?"

The man code-named Prague One glared back at him. "Me?" He nodded down at the compact submachine gun gripped in his hands. "I am going hunting. I have unfinished business with the inconvenient Dr. Smith."

Jon Smith bounded down the steep,

wooded slope, skidding and slipping across patches of loose soil and damp rock. He was running all-out now, letting gravity work in his favor, narrowly dodging tree trunks and low-hanging branches as they loomed up suddenly in front of him. He knew he was going too fast, much too fast, but the danger he sensed somewhere behind kept him moving at top speed.

And then his feet slipped out from under him as he raced through a pile of dead leaves. He came down hard and started sliding, completely out of control now. Swearing silently, Smith rolled and tumbled downhill, clawing frantically with his hands, stabbing his fingers into the dirt in an effort to slow his descent. Instead, he slammed shoulder-first into the trunk of an old gnarled oak. Pain flared across the whole left side of his body. The impact knocked the air out of his lungs.

For several endless seconds, he lay right where he had fallen, groggily trying to reclaim his scattered wits. Get up, his mind demanded at last. Get up if you want to live.

Still winded, Smith sat up slowly. He winced as muscles driven well beyond their natural limits protested wildly, sending sharp flashes of agony spiking all along his nerves and into his brain. Ignoring the pain with an effort of will, he pushed himself back to his feet. He flexed his dirty, cut, scraped, and aching fingers, and then stopped.

His pistol! Where was it?

Smith spun around, staring back up the steep slope he had just come tearing down. Heart pounding, he started climbing, closely examining the swathe of torn and gouged earth and the scattered drifts of fallen leaves.

There! He spotted the pistol beside the base of another tree, a towering beech still dappled with a few red, orange, and brown leaves. He leaned down, scooped it up, and checked the weapon over, quickly brushing away clumps of dirt caked around the muzzle and the hammer.

Then a submachine gun chattered, firing a short, three-round burst from somewhere up the hillside. Nine-millimeter rounds snapped past him and smacked into the tree trunk at waist-level, spraying jagged chunks of bark across the forest floor. Reacting instantly, Smith threw himself flat and rolled behind the trunk.

Another burst tore the ground just to his right.

With the pistol extended out in front of him, Jon rolled back out to the left, squeezed off a single shot, firing blindly uphill, and kept rolling across the slope. He ended up crouched behind another tree. The submachine stuttered again. More bullets hissed past, tearing at the forest around him. Smaller tree boughs and branches shattered. Other rounds whirred away, bouncing off boulders farther down the gorge in showers of rock splinters and fragments.

Smith risked a quick glance around the bole of the tree. He caught a glimpse of a man in a brown overcoat and fur hat moving cautiously downhill toward his position. There were bandages plastered across the man's narrow face.

He ducked back into cover. Hell. The range was about a hundred meters. Too far for a pistol — especially one with only three rounds left in its magazine. He would have to keep running, trying to stay out of the gunman's sights long enough to break clear or find a better fighting position. Frowning, he looked back over his shoulder, rapidly considering his options. None were especially good.

Below, the ground fell away even more suddenly, plunging down a steep, forty-degree incline all the way toward the distant floor of the Sarka gorge. Smith shook his head. Trying to move fast in that direction meant risking another wild, rolling tumble. And he couldn't afford that, not with an enemy close behind him and in hot pursuit.

That left only one real alternative.

Smith took a deep breath and then exploded out from behind the tree he had been using for cover, sprinting fast across the slope to the left. Caught off-guard by this sudden move, the gunman who had been advancing downhill stopped in his tracks and swore aloud. Then he opened up again with his MP5K, firing a series of rapid, aimed, three-round bursts at the American crossing his front.

Smith saw the ground ahead of him kicking up, ripped apart by 9mm bullets. He angled left again, dodged another tree, hurtled over a small boulder half-buried in the ground, and kept going.

The man hunting him stopped shooting.

Jon ran on through the woods, zigzagging wildly between trees and around little clumps of saplings to avoid giving the gunman a steady target. The downhill slope on his left grew ever steeper. Soon it fell almost vertically to the valley floor, well over forty meters below. There were fewer trees and the ground near the edge of this cliff was rockier, dotted here and there by cracked and weathered slabs of limestone spearing up through the soil.

He raced on, straining to draw enough air into his lungs. He stumbled once, forced himself upright again, and kept moving. The spot right between his shoulder blades tingled as he anticipated the sudden agonizing impact of a 9mm round fired at close range.

Suddenly Smith came out into a large clearing, a wide, open meadow carpeted in winter-browned grass and tufts of taller weeds. Another copse of sheltering trees beckoned on the far side, but those woods were at least three hundred meters away. To his right, the meadow stretched all the way to the distant upper rim of the valley. On the left, the clearing ended abruptly in the craggy limestone cliff he had been following, which plummeted toward the bottom of the gorge.

He grimaced. Trying to cross that open space would be a fatal error. Long before he could possibly make it back into cover, the gunman pursuing him would have a clear shot. He had run right into another damned kill zone. Good move, Jon, he thought wryly. He'd managed the difficult trick of leaping out of a frying pan straight into a nuclear furnace.

Smith spun around, looking back the way he had come. The forest there, a mix of widely scattered evergreens and small, leafless saplings, was too thin to offer real concealment. Nor were any of the rock slabs poking through the earth big enough to provide decent cover.

That left the cliff.

Heart pounding, Smith turned again and moved out into the clearing. With his pistol in hand, he loped along the edge of the precipice, trying to spot a path — or even just a series of handholds and ledges — that he could use to make his way down to the forested valley floor. He craned his head over the side, peering intently down the jagged, jumbled rock face. Up close, he could see that there were clumps of brush and even a few small trees growing out of the cliff, clinging somehow to narrow fissures and outcroppings in the angled layers of gray limestone. In other places, rivulets of water seeped from cracks, trickling slowly down the rock wall.

He stopped, again considering his chances. They narrowed down awfully fast, ranging from pretty damned slim on that cliff face to none at all up here out in the open. Sighing, Jon made sure the pistol's safety was on and then shoved it into the waistband of his jeans. He leaned farther out over the precipice, breathing deeply now, mentally preparing to lower himself over the edge. The trees and moss-covered broken boulders at the base looked tiny, as though they were miles away. His mouth went dry. Go on, Smith told himself angrily. There isn't much time left.

And then, quite suddenly, there wasn't any time at all.

Another sharp, staccato burst of gunfire rang out, shredding the earth and air all around him in a sudden hailstorm of lead.

From fifty meters away, Georg Liss heard the American cry out, and saw him spin round and topple over the edge of the cliff. He bared his teeth in a vicious, satisfied grin. So much for Dr. Smith, he thought coldly.

Slowly, very slowly, the dark-eyed man lowered the smoking muzzle of his MP5K and rose from behind the shallow slab of limestone he had used for cover. He moved forward cautiously, stripped the nearly empty clip out of his submachine gun, and slapped in a full magazine. Then he brought the weapon back up, slowly swiveling from left to right, scanning the open ground before him over the MP5K's front and rear sights. He kept his finger poised on the trigger.

There was only silence — and then, still far off in the distance, the sound of sirens drawing nearer.

Liss scowled. He would have to break away soon, before the Czech police arrived and began searching the woods. The American must be dead, he thought. No one could survive a fall from that height. Nevertheless, it would be best to make sure. If nothing else, Moscow One would insist on a confirmation of the kill.

Still grinning in cruel satisfaction, the man code-named Prague One prowled closer to the precipice. He leaned out over the rim, peering straight down that jagged wall of rock, eager to see Smith's corpse lying broken at the foot of the cliff.

Jon Smith lay sprawled on a shallow ledge only a few meters down the cliff face, with his back wedged against the trunk of the small evergreen that had helped brake his rapid, nearly uncontrolled descent. Through narrowed eyes, he stared up through the sights of his own weapon, holding it extended in a two-handed marksman's grip — waiting, just waiting.

Then he saw the dark-eyed man's head and shoulders appear over the edge. This close, he could even see the faint dried bloodstains on the bandages covering the man's broken nose.

Say good-bye, Smith thought grimly. He pulled the trigger twice, holding the pistol down firmly as it kicked back after each shot.

The first 7.62mm round hit the bandaged man in the throat, shattered his spine, and tore out through the back of his neck. The second blew a neat hole right between his eyes.

Already dead, the dark-eyed man

dropped to his knees and then tumbled headlong off the rim of the cliff. His limp body thudded onto a rock outcropping, bounced off, and plunged downward, cartwheeling and spinning in eerie silence all the way down the jagged wall.

Smith lay quietly for several seconds, staring up at the cloud-covered sky. Every bone and muscle in his body ached, but he was alive. When that last submachine gun burst had ripped through the air around him, he had taken the biggest chance of his life so far, allowing himself to fall backward toward the tiny shelf of rock he had just marked as the start of a relatively safe path down. By some miracle, his wild-eyed gamble had paid off, using up every ounce of luck he could reasonably expect in any one lifetime.

Slowly, he lowered the pistol, flipped the safety on, and tucked it inside the pocket of his windbreaker. His hands shook slightly as the adrenaline coursing through his bloodstream ebbed away.

Still feeling weak and with his nerves twitching, Jon turned over, sat up, and then looked carefully over the side of the narrow shelf of rock. There, forty meters below, the body of the man he had killed lay twisted and broken atop a large boulder. Blood smears around the corpse marked the final point of impact.

In the distance, he heard sirens, still faint, but growing steadily louder. It was way past time to get out of Dodge, Smith thought wearily. NATO allies or not, there was no way the Czech government was going to look kindly on an American military officer involved in a murderous, gangland-style shootout on the outskirts of its national capital. Again he glanced down at the dead man heaped at the base of the cliff.

Smith frowned. Before he ducked back into the shadows, he needed a closer look at that guy and at whatever he was carrying. Right now Jon had no idea what the hell was going on. One thing was only too clear, though. Somebody was very interested in making sure that he wound up dead.

Slowly at first, and then with growing speed and confidence, Smith climbed down the rugged limestone bluff, making his way from outcropping to outcropping and handhold to handhold. He dropped the last meter or so onto the floor of the Sarka gorge and then moved determinedly toward the shattered corpse splayed across a nearby boulder.

PART TWO

CHAPTER EIGHT

Baghdad, Iraq

Darkness had fallen across Baghdad. In the eastern half of the city, bright lights shone along the wide, modern avenues, gleamed from the windows of barricaded government ministries, and illuminated the still-crowded bazaars. West of the Tigris River, the cramped alleys of the Sunni-dominated Adhamiya district were lit only by the dim lamplight spilling from tiny shops and shanty teahouses, and out through the latticed windows and gates of older homes. The night air was cool and crisp with just a hint of the clean smell of rain lingering from a brief storm earlier that evening. Men in traditional Arab *kaffiyehs,* checked pieces of cloth worn over the head, lounged in small groups outside the teashops, smoking cigarettes and exchanging the day's news and gossip in low voices.

Abdel Khalifa al Dulaimi, a former colonel in Iraq's once-feared Intelligence Service, the Mukhabarat, walked unsteadily down one of the narrow alleys. He was much thinner now than in his days in power, and his hair and mustache were streaked with gray. His hands trembled. "This is madness," he hissed in Arabic to the woman following modestly in his footsteps with a full shopping basket in her arms. "This place is still a stronghold of the mujahideen. If we are caught here, death would be a kindness — and one we would not be granted either quickly or easily."

The slender woman, cloaked from head-to-toe in a shapeless black *abaya,* drew a step closer, narrowing the gap between them. "Then the trick is not to get caught, isn't it, Abdel?" she said coolly in his ear in the same language. "Now shut up and focus on your job. Let me worry about the rest."

"I don't know why I'm doing this," Khalifa grunted sourly.

"Oh, I think you do," the woman reminded him. Her voice was ice-cold. "Or would you really rather face a war crimes tribunal? With your choice of the gallows, firing squad, or a lethal injection? The ordinary people you and your thugs terrorized for so many years haven't exactly been forgiving, have they?"

The former Mukhabarat officer swallowed hard and fell silent.

The woman looked ahead over his

shoulder. They were drawing nearer to a large, two-story mud-brick house, one built around an inner courtyard in the traditional Iraqi style. Two hard-faced young Iraqi men stood in the open courtyard gate, carefully eyeing passersby. Each guard held a Kalashnikov AKM assault rifle casually at the ready.

"All mission teams, this is Raid One," the woman murmured in Arabic, speaking into the throat microphone concealed beneath her *abaya*. "Source One and I are moving into position now. Are you set?"

In turn, other voices ghosted through the small radio receiver fitted in her right ear. "Sniper teams ready. Targets zeroed in. Assault teams ready. Extraction team ready."

"Understood," she said softly. She and Khalifa were only meters away from the gate now. "Stand by."

One of the AKM-armed guards stepped out into the alley, blocking their way. His eyes were narrowed in suspicion. "Who is this woman, Colonel?" he growled. "The general summoned you to this meeting. Only you. No others."

Khalifa grimaced. "She is my wife's cousin," he stammered uneasily. "She was afraid to walk home from the market alone. She has heard the Americans and their pet Iraqi dogs, the Shia collaborators, are

127

raping women caught on their own, without a man to protect them. But I only agreed to bring her this far."

The woman lowered her dark eyes modestly.

The guard moved closer, still frowning. "You have compromised our security," he muttered. "The general will need to know this. Bring the woman inside."

"Raid One, this is Sniper Lead," she heard over her radio. "Just say the word."

The slender woman looked up again with a faint smile on her lips. "You may fire when ready, Sniper Lead," she said quietly. "All teams move now. Now!"

The guard's eyes widened in sudden alarm at the expression he saw on her face. He began raising his Kalashnikov, thumbing the firing selector off safe.

There were two soft *thuds*. Both guards crumpled in a mist of blood, shot through the head by high-powered rifle rounds fired from a rooftop more than a hundred meters away. Before they even finished falling, a group of six men who had been lounging outside one of the nearby tea stalls rose briskly and moved toward the open gate, bringing silenced Heckler and Koch MP5SD6 submachine guns out from under their loose-fitting jackets. Two of the gunmen dragged the bodies into the courtyard and dumped them in the deep shadows near one wall. Then they turned and sauntered back to stand at the gate in place of the dead sentries. No one looking out from the house would see anything amiss.

The woman pulled her own weapon, a 9mm Beretta pistol fitted with a silencer, out from under the food piled in her shopping basket. Together with Khalifa and the four other men, she drifted silently into the courtyard, carefully staying in the concealing shadows. She checked her watch quickly. Less than thirty seconds had passed. Faint sounds of music, the eerie keening of a popular Arab male singer broadcast on Syrian State Radio, filtered out through the shuttered windows of the house.

Satisfied, she signaled the assault team toward the front door of the house.

Moving in pairs, the four men sprinted up the steps. Covered by the others, the point man gently tested the solid wood door, making sure it was unlocked. He nodded once to his teammates and held up three fingers to signal the beginning of a three-second countdown.

They tensed. One. Two. Three.

Suddenly the point man kicked the door open and burst inside, followed closely by his comrades. There were a few muffled shouts, but they were immediately cut short by the harsh stutter of silenced sub-machine guns.

The woman crouched near the open door, holding her pistol ready. Trembling openly now, Khalifa waited with her. The former Mukhabarat colonel was praying frantically under his breath. Ignoring him, she listened closely to the staccato reports pouring through her radio earphone.

"Hallway secure and front rooms secure. Two hostiles down."

"Back rooms secure."

Another submachine gun chattered briefly.

"Staircase secure. One enemy down."

There were more shouts somewhere inside the house, followed by yet another quick burst of silenced gunfire.

"Top floor secure," a calm, confident voice said over the circuit. "Two more hostiles down. We have one prisoner. Raid One, this is Assault One. The house is clear. No friendly casualties."

The woman rose to her feet. "Understood," she said again quietly into the throat mike hidden by her *abaya*. "Source One and I are coming in." She motioned Khalifa ahead of her with the Beretta.

Inside the house, bodies littered the tiled floors, along with spent shell casings. Most had been shot while reaching for their weapons — a mix of Soviet-made assault rifles and pistols. The faintly metallic smell of blood blended with other odors, harsh, unfiltered tobacco, cheap aftershave, and boiled chicken. A radio somewhere still played music.

With Khalifa in tow, she took the stairs up to the second floor two at a time and made her way to an expensively furnished room at the back of the house. Thick carpets covered the floor. There were imported teak tables, chairs, and a desk topped with a softly humming portable computer. The machine appeared undamaged. She smiled.

One man wearing a robe and slippers lay facedown on one of the carpets with his hands bound behind him with strong plastic twist ties. Two of the attackers stood close by, covering their lone prisoner with their submachine guns.

At her signal, they rolled him over.

The woman stared down intently, mentally comparing the hawk-nosed, bearded visage before her with the file photographs she had studied. Angry, red-rimmed eyes stared back at her. She nodded in satisfaction. They had captured Major General Hussain Azziz al-Douri, one-time commander of the Mukhabarat's Eighth Directorate, the unit directly responsible for developing, testing, and producing Iraq's biological weapons.

"Good evening, General," she said politely, with a faint smile on her lips.

He glared back at her. "Who the devil are you?"

The woman flipped back the hood of the *abaya*, revealing her short blond hair, straight nose, and firm chin. "Someone who has been hunting you for a very long time," CIA officer Randi Russell told him coolly.

Dresden, Germany

Large flakes of wet snow drifted down from a dark, overcast sky. Spinning lazily in the calm, cold air, they settled softly across the plaza surrounding Dresden's floodlit Semper Opera House. A thin white blanket softened the stark outlines of the equestrian statue of King Johann of Saxony rearing high above the open square.

People bundled up in overcoats hurried across the plaza with their umbrellas hoisted high to ward off the falling snow, joining the excited crowds gathering outside the brightly lit entrance to the Opera House. Placards and banners posted around the city announced this evening's premiere of a new, ultra avant-garde version of Carl Maria von Weber's *Freischutz*, the first real German opera.

Jon Smith stood in the shadows near the long-dead Saxon king's statue, carefully observing Dresden's self-anointed aficionados of high culture stream across the square. Impatiently, he shook the wet snowflakes out of his dark hair. He hunched his shoulders, feeling the cold bite through his thin windbreaker and black turtleneck.

He had arrived on the city's outskirts roughly an hour before, dropped off by a Hamburg-based truck driver from whom he had bummed a ride all the way from Prague across the Czech-German border. Two hundred euros in cold, hard cash had more than satisfied the trucker's curiosity about why an American businessman needed so long a lift. He had allowed Smith to ride in the sleeping berth at the back of his cab, safe from any prying official eyes. Fortunately, crossing the frontier had proved uneventful. Now that the Czech Republic was part of the European Union, there were very few active checkpoints between the two countries.

But moving any deeper into Germany or getting a plane back to the States or anywhere else would take a lot more than luck. The murderous ambush on the road to Prague's airport had cost him both his laptop computer and his carry-on bag. European hotelkeepers and airport security officials alike frowned on people arriving without luggage. More important, he needed new identification. Sooner or later, the Czech authorities would start casting a wider net for the American doctor and army officer who had missed his plane to London and vanished so mysteriously. They might even tie him to the bullet-riddled corpses found near the road to the airport.

Smith spotted a short, bearded man in evening dress and a bright red scarf walking slowly toward the statue. He wore a pair of thick glasses that reflected the dazzling lights silhouetting the Opera House. The newcomer also carried a colorful program for Mozart's *Don Giovanni* conspicuously beneath one arm.

Jon moved out to intercept him. "Are you here for the performance?" he asked quietly in German. "They say the maestro is in top form."

He noticed the little man relax slightly. *Maestro* was the recognition word Fred Klein had given him when Smith called to arrange this emergency rendezvous.

"So I understand," the short, bearded man replied. He tapped the program under his arm. "But I prefer Mozart to Weber myself."

"That's quite a coincidence," Smith said pointedly. "So do I."

The little man smiled tightly. His blue eyes were bright behind the thick lenses of his glasses. "Those of us who love Europe's greatest composer must stick together, my friend. So take this, with my compliments." He handed the taller American his *Don Giovanni* program. Then, without another word, he turned on his heel and walked away, vanishing into the crowds milling around outside the Semper's arched entrance.

Smith headed in the opposite direction. While on the move, he flipped open the program and found a thick manila envelope clipped to one of the pages. Inside it, he found another American passport, this one made out in the name of John Martin. It bore a current German customs stamp and his picture. The envelope also contained a credit and debit card in the mythical John Martin's name, a train ticket to Berlin, and a numbered tag from the left luggage kiosk at Dresden's Neustadt station.

Jon grinned to himself, reassured all over again by this evidence of Fred Klein's levelheaded thoroughness. He pocketed the various documents, discarded the opera program in a trash bin, and then strode briskly toward the gleaming lights of a nearby tram stop.

Half an hour later, Smith jumped lightly down from the rear door of a yellow electric tram. He was just across from the

Neustadt Bahnhof. A pyramid of modern steel girders and glass rose high above the weathered, pollution-stained stone facade of the original railway station. He dodged a pair of taxicabs that were crawling along the snow-choked street looking for fares, and entered the almost-deserted station.

At the left luggage kiosk, a sour-faced night clerk took the tag from him, rummaged through the back room, and came grumbling back carrying a brand-new overnight bag and a laptop computer case. Jon signed for them and moved off to the side of the counter to inspect his new acquisitions. The overnight bag contained an assortment of clothing in his sizes, including a warmer black wool coat. Gratefully, he shrugged out of his battered windbreaker and donned the heavier coat. The computer case included both a rugged, high-speed laptop and a portable scanner.

Smith glanced up at the departure board. He had almost an hour before the next train to Berlin was scheduled to leave Dresden. His stomach growled, reminding him that it had been far too many hours since his last meal — a couple of pieces of dry toast and jam at the police station in Prague. He closed both cases, slung them over his shoulder, and walked through the station to a small café located near the platforms. A sign in German, French, and

136

English invited patrons to make use of the restaurant's wireless Internet connection while enjoying coffee, soup, and sandwiches.

He had just enough time to kill two birds with one stone, he thought gratefully. He seated himself at an empty table in the corner and ordered black coffee and a bowl of *Kartoffelsuppe*, creamy potato soup flavored with marjoram and slices of pork sausage.

Smith waited for the waitress to leave and then powered up the new laptop and scanner. While sipping his coffee, he pulled out the identity card he had retrieved from the corpse of the broken-nosed man in the Divoká Sárka and studied it closely. The name on the ID card meant nothing, he suspected. But in the right hands the photograph might yield useful information.

He flipped open his phone and hit the preset code for Covert-One's Washington, D.C., headquarters.

"Go ahead, Colonel," Klein's calm voice said.

"The RV went off without a hitch," Smith reported. "I'm at the station waiting for my train now."

"Good," the head of Covert-One said quietly. "You're booked into the Hotel Askanischer Hof, right on the Ku'damm. You should be able to rest up there inconspicuously for a day or so while we consider how to proceed."

Smith nodded to himself. The Kurfürstendamm, once the heart of West Berlin, was still a bustling center of commerce and tourism. Even in the winter, it should be easy enough to blend in discreetly with the other travelers who would be thronging the district's streets and restaurants. "What's my cover as this John Martin character?" he asked.

"Ostensibly, you're a pharmaceuticals salesman spending a few days in Berlin after attending a sales conference," Klein told him. "Think you'll have any problems fitting into that?"

"Nope," Smith said confidently. "There's just one more thing for now."

"Go ahead."

"I have an image to scan and send you," Smith said. "A picture of the guy who murdered Valentin Petrenko and who tried to kill me twice. He's dead now, but his photo might be worth running through various databases."

"Quite probably, Colonel," Klein said drily. "Very well. Send it along. We'll be standing by."

Near the Russo-Georgian Border
The isolated town of Alagir sits at the northern end of the Ardon Valley, deep in

the rugged foothills of the Caucasus Mountains. Roughly seventy kilometers to the south lies the snow-choked, nine-thousand-foot-high Roki Pass into the disputed Georgian territory of South Ossetia. The mountains themselves, jagged masses of stone, snow, and ice that gleamed palely beneath a rising moon, climb in a solid wall across the entire southern horizon.

Bright arc lights flared across the Alagir railroad yard, turning the black night into an eerie, sharp-edged mimicry of day. Sweating despite the freezing cold, Russian combat engineers clad in winter-pattern camouflage uniforms swarmed around the long freight train crowding the yard. They worked in teams, quickly unchaining the tarpaulin-shrouded shapes of T-72 tanks, self-propelled 122mm howitzers, and wheeled BTR-90 and tracked BMP-2 infantry fighting vehicles that were bolted onto flat cars behind the train's three powerful locomotives.

Other troops worked fast to guide the newly unloaded armored vehicles onto ramps leading to a long row of enormous flatbed trucks. These were specialized tank transporters, which would ferry them farther up the cliff-lined valley. Vehicles fitted with snowplows and salt and sand dispensers waited at the head of the convoy, ready to lead the heavily laden trucks up the winding, ice-covered roads into the mountains.

Bundled in his own greatcoat, Colonel-General Vasily Sevalkin, commander of Russia's Northern Caucasus Military District, stood near his staff car, watching the operation with undisguised satisfaction. He checked his watch and then raised a single gloved hand to signal one of his subordinates, an engineer officer.

The engineer major hurried over, snapped to attention, and saluted.

"Well?" Sevalkin asked.

"We will be finished here in less than an hour, sir," the major reported crisply.

"Very good," Sevalkin murmured, pleased to hear his own estimate confirmed. This new convoy of tanks, self-propelled guns, and infantry carriers would be long gone from Alagir before the next American satellite pass. And the freight train itself, now loaded with prefabricated decoy vehicles, would be plainly visible moving through the rail junction near Beslan — to all appearances only another routine shipment of military equipment to the Russian forces fighting Chechen rebels west of here.

The Russian general smiled thinly. Soon he would have the arms, ammunition, and men of two full-strength motor-rifle divisions, the 27th Guards and the 56th, securely hidden within striking range of the small Republic of Georgia. Although both divisions were largely equipped with older, second-line tanks and other military hardware, their weapons were far superior to anything that could be mustered by the rag-tag Georgian armed forces just across the border.

With a casual wave, Sevalkin dismissed the major back to his duties and climbed into his car. "Take me to the forward HQ at Vladikavkaz," he told his driver. Then he sat back against the seat, pondering the likely events of the next several days and weeks. His orders from Moscow for this top-secret deployment claimed it was only a "special mobility and readiness exercise." The general snorted softly. Only a fool would believe the Kremlin really intended so large a movement of troops and equipment — nearly forty thousand men and more than a thousand armored fighting vehicles — as a simple field maneuver. Certainly not in the middle of the notoriously harsh Caucasian mountain winter, with its howling winds, subzero temperatures, and blinding snowstorms.

No, Sevalkin thought, Dudarev and the others had to be planning something bold, some decisive action that would rock the world back on its heels in wonder. May it come soon, he decided grimly. For too long now, he and others like him had watched in depressed silence while Russia's strength and influence faded, diminishing with every passing year. But soon that would all change. When the orders were at last issued to begin restoring his country to its rightful place on the world stage, he and the soldiers under his command would be ready to do their duty.

CHAPTER NINE

The White House

Sam Castilla sat at the big ranch-style table made of New Mexico pine that served as his desk, briskly working his way through more than a dozen, multi-page legislative and policy analysis papers marked *Urgent*. Even with a top-notch White House staff serving as a filter, the amount of paperwork that required his personal attention was staggering. He scrawled a few quick comments on one memo and then turned immediately to the next. His eyes, neck, and shoulders all ached.

One corner of his mouth twisted upward in a wry grin. It was the age-old problem of the presidency. Delegate too much power and responsibility and you wound up derided by the press as a "caretaker chief executive" or tangled up in some damned foolish scandal sparked by over-eager subordinates. Try to exercise too much control and you found yourself drowning in a sea of meaningless memoranda better handled by a junior clerk —

or wasting precious time setting the daily schedule of the White House tennis courts, like poor Jimmy Carter. The trick was to find the right balance. The dilemma was that the right balance was always shifting.

There was a soft rap on the open door of the Oval Office.

Castilla took off his titanium-frame reading glasses. He rubbed briefly at his tired eyes and then looked up. "Yes?"

His executive secretary stood in the doorway. "It's nearly six o'clock, Mr. President. And Mr. Klein is here," she said pointedly, not bothering to hide the look of disapproval on her waspish face. "I've put him in your private study, just as you asked."

Castilla hid a smile. Ms. Pike, his long-suffering personal assistant, took her role as the dragon guarding his schedule seriously — very seriously. She made no secret of the fact that she thought he worked too long, exercised too little, and allowed his limited free time to be wasted by far too many political cronies presuming on old friendships. Like the rest of the White House staff, she was not privy to the Covert-One secret. That was his burden alone. And so, not knowing how else to classify Fred Klein, she lumped the pale, long-nosed spy chief in with the rest of the "good-time Charlie" time-wasters.

"Thank you, Estelle," he said gravely.

144

"The First Lady is expecting you for dinner in the residence tonight," she reminded him sharply. "Promptly at seven."

Castilla nodded with a slow, easy grin. "Never fear. You can tell Cassie that I'll be there come hell or high water."

Estelle Pike sniffed. "I certainly hope so, sir."

Castilla waited until she left. His smile faded. Then he rose quickly from behind his big desk and strode across the Oval Office to the adjoining study. It was filled with comfortable furniture and crowded bookcases. Like his den upstairs in the White House family quarters, this small room was one of the few that fully reflected his own tastes. A balding, medium-tall man in a rumpled blue suit stood next to the fireplace, admiring one of the several paintings of the Old West hanging on the study's walls. He held a battered leather briefcase in one hand.

Hearing the door open, Nathaniel Frederick Klein turned away from his contemplation of a Remington original on loan from the National Gallery. It showed a small, ragged, and weary U.S. Cavalry patrol making a last stand around a dried-up desert waterhole, desperately firing their single-shot, black powder Springfield carbines from behind a rough barricade of their dead horses.

"Seems kind of familiar, doesn't it?" Castilla said quietly. "Too many hostiles and not enough help."

"Maybe so, Sam," the head of Covert-One replied. He shrugged his narrow shoulders. "Then again, nobody rational ever claimed that being the world's only superpower was going to be easy. Or particularly popular."

The president grimaced. "True enough. And it beats the alternative. I guess I'd rather we were the decent, but unloved, five-hundred-pound gorilla than the pitied and hapless ninety-eight-pound weakling." He nodded his head toward a nearby black leather couch. "Go ahead and sit down, Fred. We're facing one hell of a situation, and I need your input."

Castilla waited while Klein sat and then lowered himself stiffly into an upholstered armchair on the other side of a low coffee table. "Have you seen the list of sick intelligence and policy analysts?" he asked.

Klein nodded grimly. Over the past two weeks, more than a dozen of the government's top experts on Russian and former Soviet bloc military, political, and economic affairs had collapsed, falling deathly ill either at home or at work.

"Well, I've been getting updates all through the day," the president said somberly. "Three of our people have already

146

died. The rest are in intensive care and fading fast. That's bad enough. What's worse is that nobody — not at the hospitals, the Centers for Disease Control, or USAMRIID — has been able to identify this disease they've got, much less how to treat it successfully. So far the doctors have been trying every combination of treatments they can think of — antibiotics, antiviral agents, anti-toxins, and chemo- and radiation therapy — without any positive results. Whatever is killing our people is completely outside our medical experience."

"Nasty," Klein murmured. Behind his wire-rimmed glasses, his eyes were troubled. "But this isn't the first time this mystery illness has popped up, Sam."

Castilla raised an eyebrow. "Oh?"

"Over the past forty-eight hours or so, we've picked up reports of several other people who died of a previously unknown disease, one with identical symptoms," Klein told him quietly. "In Moscow. More than two months ago. No details leaked out to the West because the Kremlin clamped a tight security lid on any news of the outbreak."

The president's square jaw tightened. "Go on."

"Two of my best Covert-One field operatives, Fiona Devin and Jon Smith, were separately approached by Russian doctors

147

who had been involved in treating the victims. Unfortunately, both men were silenced before they could provide us with copies of the relevant medical records and other evidence. The first died on a Moscow street two nights ago, supposedly of a heart attack. The second was murdered in Prague yesterday."

"By the Russians?"

Klein frowned. "Perhaps." He snapped open his briefcase and handed Castilla a black-and-white print of the ID card photo transmitted earlier by Smith. It showed the image of a narrow-faced man with cold, dead eyes. "This fellow commanded the hit team in Prague. When I ran this picture through our computers, he turned up in half a dozen intelligence and law enforcement databases, usually with a 'Most Wanted/Apprehend with Utmost Caution' tag attached."

The president read the name printed at the bottom of the photo. "Georg Dietrich Liss? A German?" he asked in surprise.

"An East German," the head of Covert-One corrected. "When the Berlin Wall came crashing down, his father was a high-ranking officer in the communist government's Ministry for State Security, the Stasi. The elder Liss is currently serving a long prison sentence for various crimes against the German people."

Castilla nodded. He tapped the photo in his hand. "What about the son?"

"Also a member of the secret police," Klein answered. "He served as a junior officer in the Stasi's 'Filiks Dzierzynski' regiment, a sort of elite Praetorian Guard force for the East German government. And there are rumors that he was part of a 'black ops' death squad used by the regime to murder political dissidents and even foreign journalists whose reporting proved too embarrassing."

"Charming," the president said in disgust.

Klein nodded. "Liss was a very nasty piece of work. By all accounts, he was a cold-blooded sociopath of the first order. Berlin issued a warrant for his arrest not long after reunification, but he fled Germany before the local police could take him into custody."

"So who's been paying his keep for the past fifteen years?" Castilla asked.

"Most recently, we think he was employed by an organization called the Brandt Group," Klein said. "They're a very shadowy, freelance intelligence and security outfit based in Moscow."

"Moscow again." The president tossed the photo down onto the coffee table. "And just who pulls the strings on this Brandt Group?"

"Our data is very sketchy," Klein admitted. "We don't know much about the organization or its real sources of funding, though they appear to have considerable resources. But there is a lot of back channel chatter claiming that Brandt Group agents sometimes work for the Russian government on a contract basis, conducting deniable surveillance and even assassination operations against Chechen exiles and other troublemakers living outside the Kremlin's immediate reach."

"Hell," Castilla growled.

"And there's more," Klein said. He leaned forward in his chair. The expression on his face was grave. "I've been making discreet inquiries. What looks very much like this same illness is apparently affecting the top Russian specialists in every major Western intelligence agency — the UK's MI6, Germany's BND, the French DGSE, and others."

"We're being blinded," Castilla realized suddenly. "This disease is being used as a weapon. By killing our best intelligence analysts, someone is hoping we'll find it more and more difficult to understand exactly what's happening inside Russia."

"It's possible, even probable," Klein agreed. He opened his briefcase again and held a single sheet of paper filled with names and locations. "We also started scanning news services and medical databases around the world, looking for other reported cases showing similar symptoms. It's taken some digging, but this is what we've found so far."

The president took the new list and studied it in silence. He whistled softly. "The Ukraine. Georgia. Armenia. Azerbaijan. Kazakhstan. All former Soviet republics bordering Russia."

Klein nodded again. "And in each and every case, the men and women getting sick are among the key military and political leaders in those countries. From what I can see, most of those replacing them are significantly less competent — or more closely aligned with Russian interests."

"Son of a bitch," Castilla swore out loud. He scowled. "That sly son of a bitch Viktor Dudarev. The Russians already tried to screw around with the last Ukrainian presidential election — and failed. Having to back down so publicly must have rankled something fierce. Well, maybe the Kremlin is playing the same game again, but this time on a much bigger scale."

"The pattern is certainly suggestive," Klein said slowly.

The president glanced at his old friend. The ghost of a crooked smile crossed his broad face. "Meaning, don't go off half-cocked, because we don't have any real evidence yet, right?"

"That is ultimately your call," Klein pointed out. He cleared his throat softly. "But I submit that we are very long on theory and very short on hard facts at the moment. In the present world circumstances, I'm not sure how an unsupported American suggestion of Russian dirty work would be received."

"No kidding," Castilla said. His broad shoulders slumped, as though they were being weighed down by an immense burden. "Fairly or unfairly, we're perceived as having cried 'wolf' too often over the past few years. As a result, our old friends and NATO allies are ready to believe we're prone to exaggerating dangers — and equally ready to cut and run from us at the first whiff of controversy. We managed to rebuild some of our credibility in the aftermath of the Lazarus crisis, but it's still an uphill fight."

The president frowned. "One thing's certain. Nobody in London, Paris, Berlin, or Warsaw is going to thank us for risking a new round of the Cold War." His eyes fell on an antique globe in the corner of the room. "And with our troops, ships, and aircraft tied down all around the damned planet, we're sure as hell not in good shape for any open conflict with the Russians. Not on our own, anyway."

Castilla sat silently for a few moments

more, contemplating the situation. Then he shook his head sharply. "So be it. We can't undo the recent past. Which means we'll just have to find the proof we need to convince our allies to act with us, if necessary." He sat up straighter. "That first disease outbreak in Moscow seems likely to be the key."

"Agreed," Klein said. His eyes were cold. "Someone is certainly determined to eliminate anyone who tries to tell us about it."

"One more thing is clear," Castilla continued. "I can't rely on the CIA to take the lead on this. They're not prepared to operate effectively in Moscow — at least not clandestinely." He snorted. "We've been so focused on trying to play nice with the Russians these days, trying to keep them as our allies in the war on terror. Langley has spent its time and energy building working relationships with their security services, instead of recruiting networks of deep-cover agents inside the Kremlin. If I ask the Agency's Moscow Station to reverse gears now, at such short notice, the odds are that they'll only muff it. And then we'll end up with so much diplomatic egg dripping down our faces that no one will believe a word we say."

His eyes gleamed for an instant. "That leaves you and your outfit, Fred. Front and center. I want a priority investigation by Covert-One. But it's got to be quick, and it's got to be quiet."

Klein nodded his understanding. "I have a small but excellent team already in place in Moscow," he agreed. Thinking hard, he drew a handkerchief out of his coat pocket, took off his glasses, and polished them. Then he slipped the wire-rims back over his ears and looked up. "Plus, I have another top-notch field operative on standby. He's tough, resourceful, and he's worked in Russia before. Best of all, he has the medical training and scientific expertise to make some sense out of whatever information they uncover."

"Who have you got in mind?" Castilla asked curiously.

"Lieutenant Colonel Jonathan Smith," Klein said softly.

February 17
Poltava, Ukraine

Halfway between the industrial city of Kharkiv and the capital of Kiev, Poltava occupied three hills in the middle of the vast and otherwise almost featureless Ukrainian steppe. Its central streets and avenues radiated outward from a circular plaza. And set in the very center of this open expanse lay the Iron Column of

Glory, ringed by small cannons and topped by a golden imperial eagle. Erected in 1809, this towering monument commemorated Czar Peter the Great's decisive victory over the invading Swedes and their Cossack allies a century before, a victory that had ensured Russia's lasting domination over the region.

Large neoclassical government buildings constructed during the nineteenth century ringed this round park. Their upper-floor windows looked out toward the Iron Column.

Leonid Akhmetov, chairman of Poltava's regional group of parliamentary deputies, stood staring out the window of his office. The burly, white-haired politician and business oligarch glowered out at the golden eagle and then swung away. He shut the blinds with a muttered curse.

"You do not approve of the view?" his visitor, a slender, thin-faced man in a drab suit, asked sardonically. He was sitting in a chair on the other side of Akhmetov's ornate desk.

Akhmetov frowned. "Once I rejoiced in it," he grunted dourly. "But now that column is only a reminder of our shame, of our abandonment to the effete West."

Both men were speaking in Russian — the first language of nearly half of Ukraine's people, most of them concen-

155

trated in the country's eastern industrial regions. Two recent presidential elections, the first of them overturned by allegations of fraud, had split the country into rival factions, one heavily authoritarian and favoring renewed ties to Moscow, the other more democratic and more oriented toward Europe and the West. Akhmetov and his cronies were among the local leaders of the pro-Russian faction. They controlled most of Poltava's industries and businesses.

"Mother Russia never truly abandons her loyal sons," the thin-faced man said quietly. His eyes hardened. "Just as she never forgives those who betray her."

The taller, heavier oligarch flushed red. "I am no traitor," he growled. "My people and I were ready to move against Kiev months ago, right up to the moment that your President Dudarev reached his 'accommodation' with the new government. When the Kremlin pulled the rug out from under us so suddenly, what real choice did we have but to make our own peace with the new order?"

The other man shrugged. "The accommodation you condemn was only a minor tactical retreat. We decided the time was not yet right for an open confrontation with the Americans and the Europeans."

Akhmetov's eyes narrowed. "And now it is?"

"Soon," the other man told him quietly. "Very soon. And you must do your part."

"What must I do?"

"First? We want you to organize a public demonstration, one coinciding with Defenders of the Motherland Day, February 23," the thin-faced man said. "This must be a mass rally demanding full autonomy from Kiev and closer ties to Mother Russia —"

The oligarch listened closely and with mounting excitement while the visitor from Moscow outlined his orders from the Kremlin.

An hour later, the man from Moscow left the Poltava Region Administrative building and strolled calmly toward the Iron Column of Glory. Another man, taller, with a broad, friendly face and a camera slung around his neck, detached himself from a small group of schoolchildren studying the monument and joined his shorter colleague from the Russian FSB's Thirteenth Directorate.

"So?" he asked.

"Our friend Akhmetov has agreed. In six days, he and his supporters will gather here in this plaza, at the base of the column," the thin-faced man reported.

"How many?"

"At least twenty thousand. Perhaps twice

that number, depending on how many of his workers and their families obey their orders."

"Very good," the broad-faced man said, smiling openly. "Then we can assure them a warm reception — and a demonstration to a horrified world of just how far Kiev will go to suppress peaceful unrest among its troublesome ethnic Russians."

"And you have all the information you require?"

The bigger man nodded coolly. He tapped his digital camera. "The images I need for detailed planning are stored in here. The rest is a mere matter of mathematics."

"You're sure?" the thin-faced man asked. "Ivanov will insist on absolute certainty and precision. He wants a cold-blooded massacre, not a pathetic fizzle."

The other man grinned back. "Relax, Gennady Arkad'yevich. Relax. Our masters will have the excuse they need. Give me enough explosive — especially RDX — and I could send that so-called Iron Column flying to the moon."

CHAPTER TEN

Near Orvieto, Italy

The ancient and beautiful Umbrian town of Orvieto perched high on a volcanic plateau above the broad Paglia valley, roughly halfway between Rome and Florence. The sheer cliffs ringing the town had acted as a natural fortification for millennia.

Below those cliffs, a side road broke away from the main highway, the *autostrada,* and wound west up the flanks of a low ridge facing Orvieto. Several ultramodern steel-and-glass buildings sprawled across the ridge, surrounded by a chain-link fence topped with tight rolls of razor wire.

Signs at the main gate identified the complex as the headquarters of the European Center for Population Research. The Center's stated purpose was the study of historical European population movements and genetic drift. Scientists assigned to the different labs inside the compound routinely fanned out across the continent and North America, sampling the DNA of various communities and ethnic groups for a wide array of historical, genetic, and medical research projects.

Early in the gray, damp morning, a black Mercedes sedan passed through the gate and parked near a large building set slightly apart from the others. Two men wearing fur hats and dark-colored coats got out. Both were tall and broad-shouldered. One, blue-eyed with high Slavic cheekbones, stood waiting impassively near the car while the second man strode toward the building's locked main entrance.

"Name?" a voice asked in thickly accented Italian from an intercom set beside the solid steel door.

"Brandt," the big man said clearly. He turned slightly toward the security cameras set to cover the entrance, letting them scan first his face and then his profile.

There was a brief pause while the images captured by the cameras were matched against those on file in the security system computer. Abruptly, the intercom crackled to life again. "You are cleared to proceed, Signor Brandt," the voice said. "Please enter your identifier code."

The big man entered a ten-digit code sequence on the keypad next to the door and heard the multiple locks sealing it click open, one after another. Once inside, he found himself in a gleaming, brightly lit corridor. Two hard-faced men, both cradling submachine guns, stood watching him closely from the adjacent guard station. One of them nodded politely toward a coat rack. "You may leave your coat, hat, and weapon there, Signor."

He smiled thinly, faintly pleased to find that the rigorous security procedures he had decreed were applied even to him. He found that a reassuring contrast to the bad news he had received earlier from Prague. He shrugged out of his coat and then stripped off the shoulder holster containing his Walther pistol. He hung both of them on a hook and then doffed his fur hat, revealing a shock of pale blond hair.

"We've informed Dr. Renke of your arrival," one of the armed guards told him. "He is waiting for you in the main lab."

Erich Brandt, the man code-named Moscow One, nodded calmly. "Very well."

The main lab took up nearly half of the building. Computers, boxlike DNA sequencers and synthesizers, chromatography cells, coffee-grinder-sized electroporation machines, and sealed tubes of reagents, enzymes, and other chemicals crowded a line of black-topped benches. Other doors led into isolation chambers used to culture the required viral and bacteriological materials. Technicians and scientists wearing sterile gowns, gloves, surgical masks, and clear

161

plastic face shields hovered around the equipment, carefully moving through the rigidly prescribed set of steps necessary to produce each unique HYDRA variant.

Brandt stopped near the door and stood watching the complicated process with interest, but very little real comprehension. Although Wulf Renke had tried explaining the intricacies involved several times before, Brandt had always found himself lost in a sea of scientific jargon.

The tall, blond-haired man shrugged. Did it really matter? He had the skills necessary to kill coldly and precisely, and HYDRA was a weapon much like any other. Boiled down to its non-scientific essentials, the mechanisms of HYDRA's manufacture and killing power were cruelly simple in theory, though complicated in execution.

First, one obtained a sample of the intended victim's DNA — from a piece of hair, a fragment of skin, a bit of mucus, or even from the oils left in a fingerprint. Then came the painstaking process of sorting through key sections of the gene-filled chromosomes, looking for specific patches of the genetic sequence that were unique to each individual and also associated with cell replication. Once that was done, one prepared single strands of so-called cDNA — complimentary DNA —

creating precise mirror images of the chosen target patches.

The next step required altering a relatively small, single-stranded DNA virus active in humans. Using various chemical processes, it was possible to strip out everything except the genes associated with its protective protein coat and those that allowed the virus to penetrate into the very heart, the nuclei, of human cells. The carefully crafted patches of cDNA obtained from the victim's genome were added and the altered virus was looped into a ring, creating a self-replicating plasmid.

After that, these viral plasmids could be inserted into a benign strain of *E. coli*, bacteria, one found commonly in the human gut. Then all that remained was to culture and concentrate these modified strains of *E. coli*, building up a useful amount of the material, and the HYDRA variant was ready for delivery to the selected target.

Essentially, invisible, odorless, and tasteless, these bacteria could easily be administered to the person marked for death through any combination of food or drink. Once ingested, the modified bacteria would lodge in the gut and begin multiplying rapidly. As they grew, they would constantly throw off the genetically altered viral particles, which would be carried by the bloodstream throughout the body.

Brandt knew that these viral particles were the key killing component in HYDRA. By their very nature they were designed to pierce the walls of human cells. Once inside a cell, each particle would inject the edited patches of cDNA into the nucleus. In anyone but the intended target, nothing else would happen. But inside the selected victim, a far deadlier process would begin unfolding. As soon as the cell nucleus began replicating itself, those mirror-image patches would automatically attach to the pre-selected portions of chromosomal DNA, blocking any further replication. The whole intricate process of cell division and reproduction — absolutely essential to life — would come to a screeching halt — much like a zipper jammed by a piece of cloth.

As more and more cells became infected and stopped reproducing, HYDRA victims would suffer aches, high fevers, and skin rashes. The failure of the fastest-replicating cells — hair follicles and bone marrow — produced symptoms resembling the wasting and anemia seen in radiation poisoning. Ultimately, of course, the cascading destruction extended to whole organs and systems, leading inevitably to a lingering and painful death.

There was no cure. Nor could HYDRA be detected by any practical means. Doctors, trying desperately to isolate the cause of this unknown disease, would never think to look at the ultra-common, seemingly harmless, and non-infectious bacteria hidden away inside each victim's gut.

Brandt smiled with pleasure at the thought. Undetectable, unstoppable, and incurable, HYDRA was the perfect assassin's weapon. In many ways, he thought sardonically, Renke and his team were crafting microscopic versions of the precision-guided bombs and missiles of which the Americans were so fond of boasting, with the exception that HYDRA would never create any embarrassing collateral damage.

Wulf Renke, a much shorter, thinner man, turned away from one of the DNA sequencers and came toward Brandt. He stripped off his gloves, face shield, and then his surgical mask, revealing a head of short-cropped white hair and a carefully trimmed Vandyke beard and mustache. From a distance, he appeared jovial, even kind. It was only up close that one could see the callous, unblinking fanaticism in Renke's dark brown eyes. The scientist divided all of humanity into two very unequal parts: those who sponsored his research and those on whom he could test the advanced biological and chemical horrors that were his forte.

He extended his hand with a slight smile

of his own. "Erich! Welcome! Come to collect our new batch of toys in person?" He nodded toward an insulated cooler filled with carefully labeled small clear vials. Packs containing dry ice lined the cooler. To reduce the risk that their bacterial hosts would run out of nutrients and start dying off, the HYDRA variants were kept frozen for as long as possible. "There they are, all packed up and ready for transport."

"I am here to collect the Phase II variants, Herr Professor," Brandt agreed quietly, shaking hands. "But we have other matters to discuss as well. Private matters," he said meaningfully.

Renke raised a single, thin white eyebrow. "Oh?" He glanced over his shoulder at the other technicians and scientists busy in the lab before turning back to look up at the bigger man. "Then perhaps we should adjourn to my office."

Brandt followed him to a windowless room just down the central hallway. Shelves of books and other reference materials crowded one wall. Besides a desk and a computer, the tall, blond-haired man was not surprised to see a narrow cot and an untidy pile of blankets in one corner of the small room. Renke was famous for his lack of interest in the material comforts so important to others. He lived almost entirely for his research.

Once the door was closed behind them, Renke swung around to face his much larger colleague. "Well?" he demanded. "Apart from collecting the next HYDRA variants, what else brings you here from Moscow so urgently?"

"Two things," Brandt told him. "First we face a significant security breach."

Renke's face froze. "Where?"

"In Prague, tracing back to Moscow," the bigger man said flatly. He ran through what he had learned about the successful attack on Petrenko and the second failed attempt to kill the American doctor, Lieutenant Colonel Smith. The frantic emergency signals from the shocked survivors of his Prague team had reached him shortly after his arrival in Rome the night before.

As Renke listened closely, his lips curled downward in a frown of displeasure. He shook his head in disgust. "Liss was sloppy," he said. "Unpardonably sloppy."

"True. He was both imprecise and overconfident." Brandt's gray eyes were ice-cold. "At least his death at the hands of the American saves me the effort of eliminating him as an example to Ilionescu and the others."

"Has this man Smith turned up yet?"

"Not yet," Brandt said shortly. He shrugged his massive shoulders. "But he missed his scheduled flight to London and now the Czech authorities are searching for him, too. If they find him, I have other sources in Prague who will alert me."

"It's been nearly twenty-four hours," the scientist pointed out. "By now Smith could easily be across the Czech border. In fact, he could be almost anywhere in the world."

Brandt nodded grimly. "I am well aware of that."

Renke frowned again. He stroked his neat white beard. "What do you know about this American?" he asked at length. "Despite their appalling errors, Liss and his men were professionals. How could an ordinary doctor have disposed of them so easily?"

"I do not know," the taller man admitted slowly. "But clearly Smith is far more than he appears on the surface."

"An agent, you mean? For one of the American military intelligence organizations?"

Brandt shrugged. "Perhaps." The blond-haired man scowled. "I've had people digging into Smith's background, military service record, and medical credentials ever since Liss first reported his meeting with Petrenko, but the work is necessarily slow. If he is connected to one of the American intelligence agencies, I don't want to risk revealing our interest in him. That could tip our hand prematurely."

"If he is a spy, your caution may come too late," Renke said coldly. "The Americans could already be probing deeper into our field tests in Moscow."

Brandt stayed silent, holding his temper in check. No useful purpose would be served by reminding the scientist of his own role in pushing for those first experiments.

"Have you notified Alexei Ivanov?" Renke asked after a moment. "After all, the Thirteenth Directorate may have a file on Smith. At a minimum, our friends in the FSB should be alerted to tighten their security in and around Moscow."

Brandt shook his head. "I've told Ivanov nothing about the American thus far," he said quietly. "He knows that Petrenko and Kiryanov are dead, nothing more."

The scientist raised an eyebrow. "Keeping Ivanov in the dark? Is that wise, Erich? As you say, this is a very serious breach of operational secrecy. Surely that overrides any question of professional jealousy or embarrassment?"

"And direct orders from our patron trump all other considerations," Brandt reminded him coolly. "He expects us to clean up our own messes without running to the Kremlin like frightened children. In this case I feel inclined to obey him. The

Russians are too heavy-handed. Their intervention might only make matters worse. As it is, I have enough manpower to handle the situation if the Americans start poking and prying."

Renke pursed his lips. "What do you need from me, then?"

"A complete list of those in Moscow whose knowledge of the first HYDRA outbreak could prove dangerous to us or to the project. With Smith still on the loose, we can't take the chance that Petrenko and Kiryanov were the only ones inclined to disobey the orders to keep silent."

Renke nodded slowly. "I can prepare such a list."

"Good. Send the names to me as soon as possible." Brandt flashed his perfect teeth in a tight, cold smile. "We must be ready to remove any remaining loose ends, should the need arise."

"Yes, that is true," Renke agreed. He looked up at the bigger man. "And the second development you wanted to discuss?"

Brandt hesitated. He turned slowly, suspiciously examining the crowded bookshelves and plain furniture around him. Then he glanced back at the scientist. "You're sure this office is clean?"

"My security team sweeps it every day," Renke said calmly. "They are loyal to me and to no other. You may speak freely." He smiled primly. "From your uneasiness, I presume you have news concerning our secondary venture? This so-called 'insurance policy' against treachery that our Russian friends are so interested in possessing?"

Brandt nodded. "That's right." Despite the scientist's assurance, he lowered his voice slightly. "Zurich has confirmed the first payment to our accounts. But I need to have the special material we promised him in hand before Ivanov will approve the second funds transfer."

Renke shrugged. "That isn't a problem. I finished the required variant weeks ago." He crossed the room and touched a stud on one of the bookcases. It swung back noiselessly, revealing a hidden wall safe and freezer. He entered a code and then pressed his right thumb to a fingerprint scanner built into the safe door. It cycled open in a puff of condensation. The scientist put on an insulated glove and then reached inside. He drew out a single clear vial. "Here it is. You can pick up a carrier and some more dry ice on your way out."

Brandt noticed a rack containing other vials inside the safe. His gray eyes narrowed.

Renke saw him looking and smiled. "Come now, Erich. We have known each other for years. Surely by now you have realized that I always take precautions to assure my own safety — no matter for whom I work."

CHAPTER ELEVEN

Berlin

Jon Smith drained the last of his coffee and set the cup back down on the round, cloth-covered table. Out of habit, he discreetly studied the people seated around him in the Hotel Askanischer Hof's quiet, tastefully furnished breakfast lounge. This was his first real chance since arriving late last night to take a closer look at some of his fellow guests. Most were somber-faced business travelers, busy reading the morning newspapers or jotting down notes between distracted bites of toast, muesli, or soft sweet rolls, for upcoming meetings. There were two older couples sitting together, tourists taking advantage of reduced winter rates in the German capital. No one in the elegant little room raised any warning bells in his mind.

Momentarily reassured, he left a couple of euros on the table as a tip, rose to his feet, and walked toward the door. Black-and-white-framed photos of the famous authors and actors who had stayed at the

Askanischer Hof during its long history — including Arthur Miller and Franz Kafka — stared down at him from the wall behind a highly polished bar.

Outside in the lobby, the desk clerk intercepted him. "A package has just arrived for you, Herr Martin," he murmured politely. "By special courier."

Smith signed for the sealed legal-size envelope and took it back up to his room. The address label showed that it had been sent from Brussels by Waldmann Investments, LLC, one of a number of front companies Covert-One used for clandestine shipments around the world. He whistled softly at the sight of the time stamp on the envelope. Although it had been shipped well before dawn, somebody still had to have been really hustling to get this package to Berlin so early in the morning.

Jon sat down on a comfortable blue sofa next to the window, ripped open the security seals, and spread the documents it contained across the surface of an ornate 1920s-style coffee table. One was a Canadian passport, also made out in the John Martin name with his picture. Scuffed, travel-stained, and well worn, it included smudged exit and entry stamps showing that he had visited a number of different countries in Europe — Germany, France,

Italy, Poland, Bulgaria, and Romania — over the past several years. A packet of business cards identified him, in the Martin persona, as a resident scholar at an organization called the Burnett Institute, a privately held public-policy think tank based in Vancouver, British Columbia. A single piece of paper headed DESTROY AFTER READING held a brief biography of the fictional John Martin.

The envelope also contained a valid business visa for Russia, attesting that he had been invited to Moscow by a private firm for "consultations on comparative national health and social insurance systems." And an enclosed itinerary showed that he was booked on a Lufthansa flight to the Russian capital later that morning.

For a moment longer, Smith sat staring at the array of forged travel documents spread before him. Moscow? They were sending him to Moscow? Well, Daniel, old pal, he thought wryly, how do you like your first look at the lions' den? Then he flipped open his cell phone.

Klein answered his call on the first ring. "Good morning, Jon," the head of Covert-One said. "I assume that you've just received your new identity package?"

"Sound assumption, Chief," Smith said drily. "Now, do you mind telling me exactly what the hell is going on?"

"Not in the least," Klein replied. His voice was deadly serious. "Consider this a mission briefing. But before we begin, you should know that your orders come straight from the highest level."

Meaning the president himself, Smith realized. Unconsciously, he sat up straighter. "Go ahead."

He listened in growing astonishment while Klein ran through the list of dead or dying intelligence specialists, military leaders, and politicians in the U.S., its Western allies, and the smaller countries surrounding Russia. "My God," he said when the other man finished. "No wonder my meeting with Petrenko stirred up such a hornet's nest."

"Yes," Klein agreed. "That's our evaluation, too."

"And now you want me to dig into the first cases of this disease — the ones Petrenko told me about," Smith guessed.

"Correct. If possible, we need hard data on its origin, mechanics, and methods of transmission," Klein said. "And we need it soon. I have the unpleasant sensation that events are moving very fast just now."

"That's a pretty tall order, Fred," Smith said quietly.

"I realize that. But you won't be alone on this mission, Colonel," Klein promised. "We already have a team in place — a very good one. They're standing by for your arrival."

"How do I make contact with them?"

"You have a reservation at the Hotel Budapest, not far from the Bolshoi Theater," the head of Covert-One told him. "Check in and be at the bar there by seven this evening, local time. You should be approached before seven-thirty."

"And how do I spot my counterpart?" Smith asked.

"You don't," Klein replied softly. "This will be a strictly one-way RV. You sit tight and wait. Your contact will identify you. The recognition word is *tangent*."

Jon felt his mouth go dry. A one-way rendezvous meant that he would fly into Russia without the names, covers, or even physical descriptions of the Covert-One agents based there. Klein was not taking any chances — even though Smith would be using the John Martin cover identity and not his own name. That way, if the Russian security services arrested him at the airport, he could not be forced to betray any other operative. In the circumstances, the procedure was a sensible precaution, but that somehow struck him as rather cold comfort.

"How solid is this Martin cover?" he asked tersely.

"Pretty solid under the circumstances,"

the other man said. "If things go sour, it might hold up under pressure for around twenty-four hours, given decent luck."

"So I guess the real trick is to avoid giving the boys in the Kremlin any reason to start chipping away at Mr. Martin's fake Canadian résumé?"

"That would be best," Klein agreed levelly. "But remember that we'll be standing by, ready to provide you with as much help as we can from this end."

Smith nodded. "Understood."

"Then good luck, Jon," Klein said. "Report from Moscow as soon as possible."

Kiev, Ukraine

Captain Carlos Parilla, U.S. Army, kept his face carefully blank as he listened intently to the troubled voice on the other end of the phone. "Yes, yes, I understand, Vitaly," he said when the caller finished speaking. "I will relay the news to my superiors at once. Yes, you're absolutely right, this is a horrible development."

He hung up and exhaled. "Jesus!"

His boss in the U.S. Embassy's Defense Attaché Office, a colonel in the U.S. Marine Corps, looked up from his computer in surprise. The straight-laced Parilla was known throughout the Kiev-based embassy staff for his refusal to swear or blaspheme,

178

even under extreme stress. "What's up, Carlos?"

"That was Vitaly Chechilo from the Ukrainian Defense Ministry," Parilla reported grimly. "He says General Engler is in the hospital up in Chernihiv — in intensive care. It looks as though he's contracted the same unknown bug that killed General Marchuk yesterday."

The Marine colonel's eyes widened. Brigadier General Bernard Engler was the head of the Special U.S. Military Mission, a team of American officers assigned to assist Ukraine in modernizing and reforming its defense forces. Still worried by the scattered intelligence reports they had been receiving of unusual Russian military maneuvers near the border, Engler had gone up to Chernihiv yesterday to try to prod Marchuk's lackluster successor, Lieutenant General Eduard Tymoshenko, into taking sensible precautionary measures.

The colonel picked up the phone and punched in a number. "Patch me through to the ambassador. Now." He put one hand over the receiver and looked across the room at Parilla. "Contact the hospital in Chernihiv directly and get a confirmation on the general's condition. Then pass the word along to the duty officer in Washington. We're going to need a replacement out here pronto!"

Parilla nodded. With its commander ill and possibly dying, the American military mission here would be largely paralyzed. As a one-star general, Engler commanded a significant level of attention and respect inside Ukraine's government and armed forces. His subordinates, mostly junior officers, did not carry the same amount of clout with their rank-conscious counterparts. With potential trouble brewing along the Russo-Ukraine frontier, it was imperative that the Pentagon send someone else to fill the general's post as soon as possible.

The Army captain frowned, checking the time in Washington, D.C. It was still the middle of the night there. Even under the best possible circumstances, the Pentagon bureaucracy might take days to sift through all the candidates and name a replacement for Bernard Engler. Even a successor of the same rank and skill would need days, perhaps even weeks, to begin absorbing all the ins and outs of this country's complicated military and civil affairs. And until the new man found his feet, the job of coordinating U.S. and Ukrainian defense policies would be significantly more difficult.

CHAPTER TWELVE

Baghdad

CIA officer Randi Russell sat wearily at the head of a large table deep inside the fortified U.S. Embassy in the Iraqi capital's Green Zone. She fought down the sudden urge to rub her tired eyes. A secure satellite-link videoconference with the top brass at Langley was not a wise time to reveal ordinary human frailty. Phil Andriessen, the head honcho at the Agency's Baghdad Station, slouched in the stiff-backed chair next to hers. Both of them faced a video projection screen. It showed the image of several serious-looking men wearing business suits, starched dress shirts, and carefully knotted ties seated at a similar table in a conference room on the seventh-floor of the CIA's Langley, Virginia, headquarters.

Behold one of the miracles of modern technology, Randi thought caustically. We bounce signals off satellites orbiting high above the earth, erasing a gulf of thousands of miles and hours of relative time with remarkable ease — and we do it all only so

181

we can hold yet another interminable, indecisive meeting.

On the Virginia end of the conference, Nicholas Kaye, the Director of Central Intelligence, leaned slowly forward in his seat. Now in his sixties, Kaye was a jowly, heavyset man. Decades ago, he had served briefly in the Agency before retreating to the calmer waters of academia and high-priced Beltway Bandit think tanks. Brought in largely as a caretaker replacement for David Hanson, his over-aggressive, scandal-plagued predecessor, the DCI's mannerisms were sometimes as ponderous and ill defined as his decision-making process. "I understand that this former Iraqi Mukhabarat officer you've captured, General Hussain al-Douri, is still refusing to cooperate?"

Andriessen nodded tiredly. "That's correct, sir. So far, he's stone-walling our interrogation team pretty successfully."

One of the other men at Langley, the deputy director for Operations, interjected, "At the moment, I think we're all rather more interested in those Eighth Directorate files you captured with General al-Douri. Your first reports indicated they seemed to contain critical intelligence on a top-secret biological weapons program. One previously unknown to us. Is that still your assessment?"

"Yes, sir, it is," Andriessen said. He indicated Randi. "Ms. Russell here can brief you more fully on what we've learned. Since her special-ops team snatched al-Douri in the first place, she's been in charge of exploiting the information we collected at his safe house."

The head of the Baghdad Station leaned over and murmured a *sotto voce* warning in her ear. "Now play it cool, Randi. Don't piss these guys off — not when you're angling for permission to go hunting so far out of our theater of operations."

She nodded tightly. "Don't worry, Phil. I promise I'll be a good little girl."

Andriessen grinned at her. "Sure. And maybe the moon *is* made of green cheese." He turned on her mike. "Go ahead."

"We've been able to decode and read almost every file on the hard drive of his personal computer," Randi told the CIA senior managers watching and listening to her from thousands of miles away. "Naturally, we've already funneled the day-to-day insurgent operations material to III Corps and the Iraqi Special Forces. And for once, our friends in uniform have been very grateful."

That drew nods of appreciation and pleased smiles. Al-Douri had been far more than just another high-ranking Saddam Hussein loyalist on the run. He had also commanded a particularly brutal and effective Sunni insurgent cell, one that had masterminded several dozen car-bombings, murders, and assassinations. Taken together, the lists of names, police payoffs, phone numbers, and weapons caches they had found on his computer should enable the U.S. military and its Iraqi allies to rip his terrorist organization apart at the seams.

"The files we were especially interested in were buried much deeper," Randi went on. "They were also encrypted using a more sophisticated system — one based on high-level KGB codes from the late 1980s."

"Codes the Soviets passed on to their friends in the Mukhabarat," the Operations director commented.

She nodded. "Yes, sir."

"And what have you found so far?"

"References to a highly classified biological weapons program," Randi said flatly. "One apparently so secret that it was set up outside the Baathist regime's ordinary chain-of-command structures."

"How far outside?"

"Almost entirely," Randi said. She laid down her next bombshell with quiet assurance. "There are firm indications that this research was being kept hidden from Saddam Hussein himself. General al-Douri made sure that any reports about it passed solely through his hands . . . and stayed in his hands. They were never sent any higher in the Mukhabarat hierarchy."

That drew low whistles of surprise. The ex–Iraqi dictator had been a believer in absolute one-man rule, with all the strands of significant power held tightly in his own grip. Throughout Saddam's thirty-year reign, those who thwarted his will or even who might someday pose a threat to his safety were casually butchered. By keeping secrets from his master, the one-time head of the Eighth Directorate had been playing a very dangerous game.

"Was this bio war program intended to produce weapons capable of causing mass casualties?" one of the senior CIA officials asked.

She shook her head. "Apparently not. The Eighth Directorate was set up to develop weapons for use on a smaller, though no less deadly, scale. Its primary mission was supplying the regime with nerve agents, specialized biotoxins, and other poisons to assassinate opponents both here in Iraq and around the world."

"What sort of scope are we talking about here?" the same man asked. "A small lab and a few researchers? Or a much bigger effort?"

Randi shrugged. "My guess would be that this program was on the smaller end of things — at least in terms of logistics and lab space."

"What about its cost?"

"Substantial," she said tersely. "From what we can see now, probably somewhere on the order of tens of millions of dollars over a one- or two-year period."

Eyebrows went up around the conference table in Virginia. Even in a regime awash in illicit cash, that was serious money. "And the sources of this funding?" the head of Operations asked grimly. "Diverted from the UN oil-for-food fiasco, I suppose."

"No, sir," Randi said quietly. "The money for this program appears to have arrived directly, wired in from a number of anonymous bank accounts around the world. Roughly a million dollars ended up lining our friend al-Douri's own pocket, but the rest seems to have paid for scientific equipment, supplies, and salaries."

Nicholas Kaye frowned. "I hardly consider any of this earth-shaking news," the heavyset CIA chief grumbled peevishly. "What difference does our uncovering one more outlawed Iraqi science project make?"

Randi smiled sweetly. "Because, sir, this particular secret weapons project does not seem to have been an Iraqi-sponsored program at all."

There was a moment of stunned silence.

"Explain that," Kaye demanded at last.

"Al-Douri's notes are fragmentary and incomplete," Randi said. "But they clearly indicate that all of the researchers involved were, quote, foreigners, unquote."

"Then where are these foreign scientists now?" the head of the CIA wondered.

"Long gone," Randi told him. "Several entries show that they packed up all their equipment and left Iraq before our troops reached Baghdad. Probably via Syria."

"Let me be sure I understand your theory on this, Ms. Russell," the Agency's Operations director said carefully. "Are you suggesting that someone else was using Iraq as a cover for their own illegal biological weapons program?"

Randi nodded. "Yes, I am." She smiled wryly. "After all, where better to hide a dirty needle than in a haystack already filled with other dirty needles that don't belong to you."

"Any strong suspects?"

"Based on the material we found in al-Douri's computer?" She shrugged. "Not really. If he knew who was paying him to set up this bio-weapons lab inside his organization, al-Douri was very careful not to record that fact. My hunch, though, is that he didn't know and didn't much care."

"Then all we're left with is another useless, fading, will-o'-the-wisp," Kaye complained.

"Not quite, sir," Randi said with forced patience. Behind his back, the heavyset CIA chief was known as "Dr. No" throughout the Agency, both for his general pessimism and his near-automatic impulse to reject any proposal that involved risk or contravened conventional wisdom.

"Go on, Ms. Russell," the Operations director told her gently, with a faint smile of his own. "For some strange reason, I suspect you have an ace hidden up your sleeve."

Almost against her will, Randi grinned back at the projection screen. "Not exactly an ace, sir. More like a joker — a real wild card." She held up a single sheet of paper, a printout from one of the files concealed on their prisoner's computer hard drive. "After his first meeting with the scientist in charge of this secret program, our friend al-Douri made this rather cryptic entry in his private diary: 'This man is more a jackal than the noble Teutonic wolf he so proudly claims to be. And like the jackal, he feasts greedily on the carrion abandoned by those who were once his masters.' "

Kaye snorted loudly. "What are we supposed to learn from that sort of Arab poetical gibberish?" he scoffed.

"Not gibberish," Randi said coolly. "Just a bad pun. He was playing off this foreign scientist's name. A German scientist. A German biological weapons scientist whose name suggests the word *wolf*."

She waited.

"Christ!" one of the other CIA officials said abruptly. "You're talking about Wulf Renke."

Randi nodded. "Yes, I am."

"That's impossible," Kaye snapped. "Renke is dead. He's been dead for years. Probably since not long after he disappeared from Berlin."

"So the German government insists now. But no one has ever seen his corpse," she pointed out grimly. "And given what we've just learned from these computer files, I think we should do our damnedest to find out the truth."

There were murmurs of agreement around the two video-linked conference tables. Wulf Renke stood very high up in the ranks of the world's "most wanted" Cold War criminals. Once a member of the East German scientific elite, Renke had been famous for his brilliant research and infamous for his eagerness to test his deadly creations on unwilling human subjects, usually political dissidents and common criminals. Not long after the Wall fell, he disappeared without a trace, vanishing be-

189

fore the German federal criminal police could arrest him.

For years since, the West's intelligence services had tracked him, chasing down rumors that put the renegade scientist squarely in the middle of various global hot spots or serving a range of unsavory regimes and causes. He was said to have worked for North Korea, Libya, Serbia, and al-Qaeda and other terror networks. But none of those tantalizing and frightening rumors had ever panned out. A growing number of governments were ready to accept Berlin's contention that Renke was dead — and no longer any threat to the civilized world.

At least until now.

"What are you proposing, Ms. Russell?" the head of the CIA at last asked stiffly.

"That you send me out on a hunt," Randi said. She bared her own teeth in a tight, amused grin. "A wolf hunt."

Kaye sighed. "And just where do you propose to begin this search of yours? Syria? Deep in the Hindu Kush? Or somewhere out in the wilds of Timbuktu?"

"No, sir," she told him quietly. "I think it's time we started right back at the very beginning."

CHAPTER THIRTEEN

Moscow
Despite the bitter cold outside, the Irish Bar on the second floor of the Hotel Budapest was crowded. People were standing two-deep along the polished cherrywood bar, signaling the busy, white-coated barman for another beer or glass of wine or whiskey. Smiling waitresses circulated through the rest of the room with trays of drinks. Around the smaller tables and in the plush, cushioned booths there was a constant buzz of lively conversation, liberally peppered with gusts of boisterous laughter whenever anyone told a particularly funny joke.

Jon Smith sat off in a quieter corner by himself, silently nursing a pint of dark Baltika beer. Listening to the loud, good-humored snatches of Russian, English, French, and German wafting past, he felt strangely disconnected from his fellow patrons, almost as if he were listening to them from a thousand miles away. He had forced a polite smile onto his face, but the expression felt subtly wrong, as though it might abruptly shatter into a thousand pieces. His nerves, he realized suddenly, must be stretched near the breaking point.

At every stage of his journey here — the flight from Berlin, clearing customs at Sheremetevo-2, the cab ride in, and even registering at the hotel's front desk — he had braced himself for a dangerously raised official eyebrow or for the feel of a policeman's heavy hand gripping his shoulder. But nothing ominous had happened. Instead, he had been ushered through passport control and then shown to his room at the Budapest with a quiet, disinterested courtesy. There seemed to be more uniformed militia on the streets than he remembered from his previous trips to post–Cold War Moscow, but otherwise there were no obvious signs of any trouble brewing in the capital of the Russian Federation.

Smith forced down another cautious sip of beer and surreptitiously checked his new watch. It was already well past seven-thirty, closer to eight at night. His Covert-One contact was late. Had something fouled up? Fred Klein had been confident that his Moscow-based team was still safely operating below the radar of the Russian security services, but what if he was wrong? For an instant, he considered leaving. Maybe he should duck out and find a sheltered spot so that he could make a secure call to Washington, D.C., reporting the failed rendezvous.

Jon looked up from his beer and again noticed a lithe, attractive woman with curling, shoulder-length dark hair and bright eyes that appeared more green than blue in the bar's soft lighting. He had spotted her earlier, holding a tall glass of sparkling wine while talking animatedly with a circle of grinning male admirers. But now she was moving slowly, but surely, in his general direction, stopping along the way to greet other men with a smile, a brief kiss on the cheek, or a murmured endearment. The woman wore a striking, sleeveless, midnight-blue dress; one that seemed molded to the supple curves of her figure. An elegant, fur-trimmed coat lay draped over one arm.

Probably a paid professional, he thought dispassionately, deliberately looking away before she could make eye contact. There was no point in drawing any unwanted attention. The best of the elite escorts flocked to whichever bars and restaurants drew the greatest number of wealthy foreign businessmen. He had noticed several other young women, all of them quite beautiful, slipping away earlier with paunchy German or British or American executives for what he presumed were discreet trysts upstairs in their rooms. The Hotel Budapest's Irish Bar appeared to be ground-zero for Moscow's high-class prostitutes.

"You seem very lonely. And very sad," a pleasant voice purred softly in Russian. "May I join you for a drink?"

Smith glanced up. The slender, dark-haired woman stood there, smiling engagingly at him. He shook his head quickly. "No, thank you," he replied. "Believe me, I'm not looking for any company right now. I was just about to leave."

Still smiling, she sat down unhurriedly next to him. He caught a faint whiff of her perfume, something delicate, fresh, and floral. She raised an eyebrow in mock surprise. "Really? So soon? Such a pity when the night is still so young."

Jon frowned slightly. "Look, miss," he said stiffly. "I think there's been some mistake —"

"A mistake? Yes, quite possibly," the dark-haired woman said, now speaking in English with just the faintest trace of an Irish lilt. Her green eyes twinkled, openly amused. "But if so, I believe you are the one who is in error, Mr. Martin. Where I am concerned, you seem to have gone haring off on the wrong *tangent* entirely."

Tangent? Jesus, Smith thought wildly. That was the recognition word for this RV.

That, plus the fact that she knew his cover name without being told, meant she had to be his Covert-One contact, the leader of Klein's small team of operatives in the Russian capital. He felt his face turn bright red. "Hell," he mumbled, embarrassed. "Now I'm in trouble."

"Very likely," the dark-haired woman said quietly. Then she relented and extended her hand. "My name is Fiona Devin. I'm a freelance journalist. Our mutual friend, Mr. Klein, insisted that I welcome you to Moscow."

"Thanks," he said gratefully. He cleared his throat. "Look, Ms. Devin, I'm very sorry about the mix-up. It's just that I was beginning to sweat. I thought something had gone wrong."

She nodded. "I had that impression." She shrugged. "I apologize for the long delay, but I thought it was for the best. This place is like a little bit of home ground to me, and I wanted to make very sure that there weren't any unwelcome visitors tagging along behind you. I know most of the regulars quite well, and strangers intruding on my patch tend to stand out."

"FSB agents or informers, you mean?" he asked, using the acronym for the Russian Federal Security Service.

Fiona Devin nodded again. "The hard-faced lads up at Lubyanka Square are not

195

yet quite so active and all-powerful as when they called themselves the KGB, but they do get around all the same."

"And now President Dudarev is doing his best to restore the bad old order," Smith commented.

"Too true," she agreed somberly. "Czar Viktor has certainly surrounded himself with a very nasty bunch of cronies. The Russians call them the *siloviki*, the men of power. Like Dudarev himself, they're all ex-KGB with a taste for absolute control and a real knack for putting the fear of Stalin into anyone foolish enough to get in their way."

"No kidding," Smith said grimly, thinking back to the bridge in Prague and Valentin Petrenko's murder. "Plus, they use surrogates like this so-called Brandt Group for some of their dirty work."

"So it seems, Colonel," she said coolly. "But keep in mind that the Brandt Group also works for the highest bidder, not just the Kremlin."

"Oh?"

Her eyes grew colder. "I've done a bit of investigative work on the Group. Oh, I admit that they're a fine match for Dudarev and his *siloviki*. Mostly ex-Stasi, like their boss, a vicious creature named Erich Brandt — with a smattering of Romanian Securitate and Serbian secret police thugs thrown in for good measure. But they'll take any assignment, no matter how dirty, if the fee is big enough."

Her mouth tightened into a thin line. "Rumor has it that the Brandt Group provides security for some of the biggest drug lords and *Mafiya* crime bosses in Moscow. One set of parasites guarding another. The Group's ties to the Kremlin keep the police conveniently looking the other way, no matter how many innocents are murdered by the *Mafiya* bosses they protect."

Smith heard the deep anger and pain in her voice. "Including someone you knew?" he guessed.

"My husband," Fiona said simply. "Sergei was a Russian. One of the optimistic entrepreneurs who believed this country could remake itself as a prosperous democracy. He worked hard, built up his business — and then the hard men arrived, demanding the lion's share of his profits. When he refused, the *Mafiya* bastards shot him down in the street."

She fell silent, plainly unwilling to say more now.

Smith nodded, recognizing a boundary he should not cross. Not yet. To fill the silence, he stopped a passing waitress to order a glass of *shampanskae,* a sweet sparkling wine from Moldova, for Fiona and another beer for himself and then turned

197

back to her. He hesitated briefly, not knowing quite how to proceed. "I'm assuming Fred Klein told you why I'm here, Ms. Devin," he said at last, and then winced inwardly, hearing suddenly how pompous that sounded.

"I've been thoroughly briefed by Mr. Klein," she confirmed easily, choosing to show mercy by ignoring this second gaffe. "Besides, I've had my own brush with the news of these mysterious deaths. Three nights ago, Dr. Nikolai Kiryanov was on his way to meet me when he disappeared. Now I suspect he was trying to pass on the same sort of information your friend Petrenko brought to Prague."

"And I understand that Kiryanov turned up in the morgue the next morning?" he asked, recovering.

Fiona frowned. "Not quite. I never saw his body. The poor man had already been cremated."

Smith raised an eyebrow. "That quickly?"

She nodded. "Well now, the cause of death was listed as 'heart attack.' I suppose cremation must have seemed a convenient way to make sure no one could check up on that."

"And since then?"

"I've been poking and prying and asking pointed questions wherever and whenever I can," she told him.

"Sounds pretty dangerous — in the present circumstances," he commented.

One side of Fiona Devin's generous mouth ticked upward in a lopsided smile. "The authorities here may not like it much," she said. "But remember that asking awkward questions is precisely what they expect a Western reporter like me to do. And they know that Kiryanov could have told me at least a tiny bit of what happened with those poor people. If I got wind of a juicy story like those deaths and then simply sat back on my hands, they'd grow more suspicious still."

"Have you had any luck?" Jon asked.

She shook her head disgustedly. "Not a bit. I've haunted the corridors of the Central Clinical Hospital until I can smell the disinfectant they use in my sleep, and all to no avail. I've run straight into a solid wall of obstruction and evasion. Naturally, the staff there all deny that any mysterious disease outbreak ever took place."

"Naturally," Smith said drily. "What about prowling through their medical records?"

"Strictly forbidden," Fiona Devin said flatly. "The hospital director insists that the medical records of all current or former patients are strictly off-limits. Going over his head to get the necessary authorizations from the Ministry of Health could take weeks."

"Or forever."

She nodded. "Far more likely. One thing is quite clear, though: The doctors and nurses there are all utterly on edge. You can sense the fear rolling off them under all that horrid carbolic soap. Believe me, they aren't going to talk to a foreigner or anyone else about what happened, no matter what kind of inducement is offered to them."

Smith thought that over. If the hospital was a dead end, he was going to have to explore other angles. From what Petrenko had said, it sounded as though the Kremlin orders quashing talk about the strange deaths came later — after the mini-epidemic had run its lethal course. Before then, the hospital's doctors had been trying everything in their power to diagnose and treat their sick patients. Even though the Russian hadn't explicitly mentioned doing so, he was willing to bet that Petrenko and his colleagues had shared the data they had gathered with other medical professionals. At least until the Kremlin clamped a lid on the situation. One of the first principles for anyone fighting an unknown disease was to spread the information across a wide spectrum, bringing as much competent brainpower and lab time as possible to bear on solving its deadly mysteries.

Well, Smith knew people in some of the leading Russian medical and scientific institutions — top-notch scientists who were sure to have been consulted about this illness. Sure, they would have received the same cease-and-desist orders from on high, but with luck he might be able to persuade one or more of them to give him access to their case records or lab test results.

Fiona Devin nodded slowly when he ran that idea past her. "Approaching them could be risky, though," she pointed out. "You're masquerading as John Martin, a harmless and inconsequential Canadian social scientist. But you won't be able to use your cover when dealing with people who already know you by sight and reputation. If just one of them panics and runs off screaming about being approached by Colonel Jonathan Smith, the American military disease specialist, some very loud alarm bells will start ringing inside the Kremlin."

"True," Smith agreed quietly. "But I don't see many other real options, Ms. Devin." He pushed his untouched second beer to the side. "You've seen the lists of those who've been hit with this illness. We really don't have time for anything subtle or indirect. Somehow I *must* find a way to make contact with the Russian experts who are likely to have the information we need."

"Then at least let us run some quick checks on these possible sources first," she said. "My team and I know the ground here better than you do. Maybe we can weed out those who are too close to Dudarev's regime — or too openly frightened by it — to be worth questioning."

"How long will you need for this vetting process?" he asked.

"Several hours, starting from the moment you give me the names and institutional affiliations of those you're interested in," Fiona said firmly.

Smith raised a skeptical eyebrow. "That fast?"

She grinned at him. "I really am very good at my job, Colonel. And I've got some decent sources, both inside the government and out of it."

Almost against his will, he found himself grinning back at her. Now that her earlier mood of tightly repressed anger and sorrow had faded, her natural air of buoyant self-confidence had come bubbling back to the surface. It was infectious. "So, how do I get in touch with you again?"

Fiona pulled a business card out of her small handbag and quickly jotted down a telephone number on the back. "You can safely reach me through that secure number, day or night."

He slipped the card into his shirt pocket.

"In the meantime, I'll keep the pressure on the Russian medical bureaucracy from my end," she promised. "I have an interview set up tomorrow morning largely for that very purpose. With Konstantin Malkovic."

Smith whistled softly. "The financier? The guy who made billions in commodities and currency speculation?"

Fiona nodded. "The very one."

"He's an American, isn't he?"

"A naturalized American," she agreed. "Much as I am myself, for that matter. But Malkovic is Serbian by birth, and he's invested heavily in Russian industries over the last several years. He also donates large sums to the charities trying to rebuild this country's antiquated health care systems. And all of that investing and donating has bought him close ties to these new lads in the Kremlin. No matter how much Dudarev and the other 'men of power' long to bring back the old ways, they're not utter fools. They walk softly around a man with so much money to throw around."

"And you hope to persuade Malkovic to start asking a few awkward questions of his own about this disease?" Smith guessed.

"Indeed, I do," Fiona agreed. "He's said to have quite a temper, and he's used to getting his own way." A look of devilish delight danced in her bright blue-green eyes. "So I would very much hate to be the first Russian official forced to refuse his requests."

CHAPTER FOURTEEN

Near the Russo-Ukrainian Border
Four requisitioned passenger buses crammed full of Russian soldiers crawled along a narrow, deeply rutted track, an old logging road, slowly winding their way deeper into the pitch-black forest. Overhanging branches scraped loudly along the sides and windows of the darkened vehicles.

Up at the front, Captain Andrei Yudenich crouched beside the driver, holding on to the back of the man's seat to keep his balance. He peered out through the cracked and dirty windshield, again trying vainly to get a better idea of just where he and the crews of his tank company were being sent. He grimaced, deeply disquieted by recent events.

So far, this twenty-four-hour-long journey from their barracks outside Moscow had been a nightmare of misdirection. Their original orders had sent them south by rail toward Voronezh, ostensibly as the first stage of a battalion-sized deployment to Chechnya. But once there, they had been switched onto another train, this one heading back west to Bryansk. From there, Yudenich and his tank crews had been bundled onto these old buses and sent lumbering off into the woods, following a confusing succession of newly plowed country roads.

A soldier in a white camouflage smock suddenly loomed up ahead, illuminated by the wavering beams of the headlights. He was standing on a mound of snow piled up by the side of the logging road. A bright red armband and glowing baton identified him as a member of the Commandant's Service — a special Army-level unit that served as field security and traffic control troops.

The white-smocked soldier waved his baton abruptly, pointing imperiously to the right. Obeying his signaled order, the buses turned off the logging track one after the other and rumbled up an even narrower path, one newly hacked out of the forest, judging by the fresh-cut stumps visible on either side. Frowning openly now, Yudenich clung tighter to the back of the driver's seat, swaying up and down as the heavy vehicle bounced through deep ruts.

Several minutes later, they pulled into a clearing and stopped.

More field security troops in red armbands, with assault rifles held ready, swarmed around the buses, shouting, "All out! Everyone out! Move! Move!"

Yudenich was the first one through the open doors. He dropped lightly onto the rock-hard, frozen earth of the clearing and then saluted the nearest officer — a captain like himself. His tank crews tumbled out of the buses behind him, hurriedly forming up in ranks under the chivvying of their sergeants and his lieutenants.

"Your orders?" the other man snapped.

Wordlessly, Yudenich dug the thick sheaf of papers out of the breast pocket of his field jacket.

The other captain flipped them open and studied them in the light of a small shielded flashlight held by an orderly. "I see that you're part of the Fourth Guards Tank Division," he commented. He handed the orders back and then studied a list on his clipboard. "Right. You and your company are posted to Cantonment Fifteen, Barracks Tents Four through Eight."

"Cantonment Fifteen?" Yudenich asked, not bothering to hide his surprise.

"Off through the trees over there, Captain," the other man said tiredly, nodding toward the forest beyond the clearing. "You'll be guided."

Obediently, Yudenich looked in that direction. His mouth fell open. Now that his eyes were adjusting to the darkness, he could see that they were standing on the outskirts of an enormous military encampment, one built right in among the trees. Huge panels of infrared- and radar-absorbent camouflage netting were strung overhead, and coils of barbed wire stretched as far as the eye could see, apparently encircling the whole camp. Teams of heavily armed guards — Interior Ministry troops by their uniforms — and growling dogs nervously prowled the perimeter.

"What the devil is going on here?" he asked quietly.

"You'll be briefed when you need to know," the captain told him. He shrugged. "Until then, you communicate only through your own chain-of-command. Clear?"

Yudenich nodded.

"Good," the other man said grimly. "And make sure your boys don't go wandering off. Anyone who crosses the perimeter without authorization gets a bullet in the neck and a shallow grave hacked out of the snow and frozen mud. No formal court-martial. No appeals. No mercy. Understand?"

Yudenich nodded again, shivering suddenly under his heavy camouflage jacket.

Moscow

Erich Brandt stepped off the steep escalator and walked into the vast, echoing underground hall of the Novokuznetskaya Metro station. Throngs of tired-looking shift workers heading home surged around him. Even this late at night, subway trains rumbled loudly through the tunnels, arriving and departing in warm gusts of oil-scented air every two or three minutes. Moscow's underground railway system was the best in the world, carrying nearly nine million passengers a day — more than the London Underground and New York's subways put together. And in contrast to the dreary utilitarian hubs of the West, many of the Metro stations were gems of art and architecture. As a means of demonstrating the growing power and culture of the now-dead Soviet Union, each had been built in marble and decorated with sculptures, carved reliefs, mosaics, and enormous hanging chandeliers.

For an instant, Brandt stood still, eyeing the khaki-colored bas-reliefs lining the walls. They depicted soldiers and military leaders, ranging from stout Marshal Kutusov, who had fought Napoleon at Austerlitz and Borodino, to panels carved to show heroic Second World War Soviet Naval Infantrymen leaping ashore from assault boats to join the climactic battle at Stalingrad. On the high curved ceiling overhead, occasional mosaics showed smiling factory workers and farmers reveling in their happy, idyllic lives as servants of the Communist State.

The big, blond-haired man snorted wryly. The Novokuznetskaya station had been constructed in 1943, at the height of the brutal Soviet struggle against Nazi Germany. Its art celebrated certain victory over Hitler and his fascist minions. Trust Alexei Ivanov to choose this as a place to meet his unwelcome East German colleague. For all his reputed subtlety as a spymaster, the head of the Thirteenth Directorate had a blunt, heavy-handed sense of humor.

After a moment, Brandt spotted the gray-haired Russian intelligence chief sitting calmly on a marble bench and went straight over to sit beside him. Both men were much the same height.

"Herr Brandt," Ivanov said quietly.

"I have the special HYDRA variant you requested," Brandt told him.

"Show me."

The blond-haired man opened his briefcase, revealing a small, soda-can-sized thermos. With his thick leather gloves still on, he unsealed the metal cylinder in a puff of vapor, pulled out a small vial full of clear frozen liquid, and then handed it over.

Ivanov held the vial up to the light. "A lingering death with so innocent an appearance. Remarkable," he murmured. Then he glanced at his companion. "But how can I be sure that this tube contains anything more lethal than ordinary tap water?"

"In all candor, you cannot. Not without using it against the intended target. You will have to trust me."

The head of the Thirteenth Directorate smiled grimly. "Trust is not something I grant easily to anyone, Herr Brandt. Especially not with more than a million euros' worth of state funds involved."

The ex–Stasis officer returned the same thin, cold smile. "That is understandable, but unavoidable. You asked for a means of ensuring the continued cooperation of my employer — or for taking vengeance on him should that prove necessary. Renke and I have met your request. Whether you believe us or not is up to you. Under the circumstances, our price is entirely reasonable."

Ivanov grunted. "Very well, you'll have your money. I'll authorize the second wire transfer to Switzerland tonight." He held the vial up to the light again and then looked narrowly at Brandt. "What if our scientists instead used the material this contains to reverse-engineer the HYDRA technology? Then we would no longer need you, Professor Renke, or your master."

"You could try that, I suppose." The blond-haired man shrugged his massive shoulders. "But Renke assures me that such an attempt would inevitably fail. Your researchers would only recover a few broken fragments of unusable genetic material drifting in a sea of dying bacteria."

The head of the Thirteenth Directorate nodded slowly. "A pity." He slid the vial back into the thermos. The thermos itself went into his own coat pocket.

Brandt said nothing.

"One thing more, Herr Brandt," Ivanov said abruptly. "I want your personal assurance that your security for HYDRA is still intact. Now that we are entering the final phases of our own military preparations, absolute secrecy is vital. The Americans and their allies must not discover what is about to happen."

"Both Kiryanov and Petrenko are dead," Brandt said flatly, hiding his concerns about the missing Colonel Jon Smith. "There are no other outstanding threats to HYDRA," he lied.

"Good." Ivanov smiled again, but his dark brown eyes were completely devoid of any warmth or amusement. "And you understand that we will hold you personally responsible for any failure?"

Brandt nodded tightly, feeling droplets of sweat beginning to form on his forehead. "Yes."

"Then I bid you good night, my friend."

The gray-haired chief of the Thirteenth Directorate rose heavily to his feet. "For now we have nothing more to discuss."

CHAPTER FIFTEEN

February 18
Warm in her full-length, fur-lined coat, Fiona Devin came out of the Borovitskaya Metro station and turned south. She walked carefully along the icy pavement, moving gracefully around the other pedestrians on their way to work in the lingering darkness. Though it was morning by the clock, the long winter night still gripped the city. Not far ahead, a large mansion rose above the street, set on a massive stone base. Pillars and ornate carvings decorated the building's white facade and a perfectly proportioned rotunda topped its roof. To the east, Moscow's streets and other buildings fell away, sloping downhill toward the red walls and towers of the Kremlin.

She smiled narrowly to herself. She was not surprised that Konstantin Malkovic had set up shop in one of the Russian capital's most beautiful and conspicuous locations. The Serbian-born billionaire was famous for both his self-aggrandizement and his lavish spending. This mansion,

213

Pashkov House, had been built in the late eighteenth century for a fantastically wealthy Russian officer, Captain Pyotr Pashkov, a man determined to own the grandest private home in all of Moscow, one perched on a hillside overlooking the Kremlin itself. After the Bolshevik Revolution in 1917, the building had become an annex of the adjoining Russian State Library, the repository of roughly forty million precious books, periodicals, and photographs.

Shortly after deciding to make Moscow one of the centers of his global business empire, Malkovic had donated more than twenty million dollars to help restore the sagging fortunes of the aging and antiquated Russian archives. One of the strings attached to his grant had been permission to set up a suite of offices on the top floor of the Pashkov House. Protests by a few architectural purists had fallen on newly rich and newly deaf official ears.

Bells from the nearby Cathedral of Christ the Redeemer, recently rebuilt after its destruction by Stalin, began pealing, echoing across the surrounding neighborhoods. It was just after nine. Her interview with the billionaire was scheduled to begin in ten minutes.

Moving faster now, Fiona strode up the broad stone steps and into the main hallway. There a bored-looking functionary checked her name against the register and directed her up the main interior staircase. Two unsmiling security guards waiting at the top carefully examined her identification, closely studied her camera and tape recorder, and then motioned her through a set of detectors, checking her for weapons and traces of explosives.

A second pair of employees, both pretty young women, took her in tow. Speaking politely in hushed tones, they briskly ushered her through the busy semi-chaos of a large outer office full of desks, computers, and people entering data or issuing buy and sell orders for stock markets across Europe. One of the women took her coat and vanished. The other escorted her into a slightly smaller, immaculately decorated room — Konstantin Malkovic's private office.

Along one wall, three tall windows offered a spectacular view of the Kremlin's floodlit walls, turrets, and golden domes. Centuries-old Russian Orthodox religious icons, priceless originals, stood in niches built around the rest of the room, carefully lit by recessed lights shining down from the high, intricately painted ceiling. A thick Persian rug covered the floor in muted splendor. Malkovic's elegant eighteenth-century desk faced away from the windows.

A flat-screen computer and a set of slim, ultra-modern phones seemed to be the room's only concession to the twenty-first century.

The billionaire himself rose to his feet from behind his desk and came around it to greet her with an outstretched hand. "Welcome, Ms. Devin! Welcome!" he said, smiling broadly, revealing a full set of perfect white teeth. "I'm a great admirer of your work. That last article in *The Economist* — the one on the competitive advantages of Russia's flat tax system — was particularly good."

"You're far too kind, Mr. Malkovic," she said calmly, taking the offered hand and smiling back. She recognized this effusiveness as one of the routine tactics he employed on those whom he hoped to influence. "After all, I only wrote a few thousand words of analysis about its likely effects. But I've been told that you had a hand in crafting the new tax code itself?"

He shrugged. "A hand? Nothing so direct." His eyes twinkled. "Oh, perhaps I spoke a word here. And perhaps another small word there. Nothing excessive, though. As a mere man of business, I never interfere too deeply in any nation's domestic politics."

Fiona let the polite fiction pass unchallenged. According to her sources, this man could no more resist meddling in political affairs than could a starving lion lie down quietly beside a nice fat lamb.

Malkovic was taller than she had expected, with a mane of thick white hair left long on top but cropped short at the sides and neck. High cheekbones and pale blue eyes marked his Slavic ancestry. The clipped tones and slightly flattened vowels of his English reflected the years he had spent in Britain and America, first as a student at Oxford and Harvard and later as a wildly successful businessman, investor, and commodities speculator.

"Please, do sit down," he told her, indicating one of the two embroidered armchairs set at angles in front of his desk.

When Fiona took one, Malkovic sat down casually in the other. "Some tea first, perhaps?" he asked. "It's still quite cold outside, or so I understand. I came in very early this morning myself — several hours ago, actually. The world financial markets, alas, follow an unholy schedule in our day and age."

"Thank you, yes. Tea would be lovely," she said, hiding her amusement at hearing his scarcely veiled boast about the long hours that he worked.

Almost immediately, another of Malkovic's secretaries brought in a tray with a sterling silver samovar, two tall clear glasses, and two small crystal bowls, one containing slices of fresh lemon, the other a dollop of jam to sweeten the strong tea. The woman poured for them and then left quietly and quickly.

"And now to business, Ms. Devin," he said amiably, after they had both taken a few cautious sips of steaming tea. "My staff tells me that you are especially interested in the role I see for myself and my companies here in the new Russia."

Fiona nodded again. "That's quite right, Mr. Malkovic," she replied, settling down into a familiar role, that of a journalist in search of a good story. It was not difficult. Over the past several years, she had built a well-deserved reputation as a talented, hard-hitting reporter. She specialized in following and explaining the often-complicated interaction of Russian politics and economics. Her work appeared regularly in leading newspapers and business journals around the globe. Conducting this interview — with the largest and most influential private investor in Russian industry — would have been a natural for her, even without her ultimate interest in using the billionaire as one more means of prying open the secrets of the state medical bureaucracy for Covert-One.

And, on the surface at least, Malkovic himself was an easy man to interview.

Ever-charming and apparently perfectly relaxed, he answered her questions about his plans and business dealings readily and without evident evasion, choosing only to dodge a few probes that even she realized were too personally intrusive or that might reveal closely held proprietary information useful to his competitors.

Nevertheless, Fiona sensed that the billionaire was always in full control of himself. He chose his words with precision, plainly determined to influence the way she saw him and the way he would appear to her readers whenever this interview was published. She shrugged inwardly. This was the great game, the eternal dance for any journalist — especially a freelancer working without the clout provided by a major newspaper, magazine, or television network. Ask too many tough questions and your subjects refused to speak to you again. Ask too few and you wound up writing puff pieces that could have been churned out by any second-rate public relations firm.

Slowly and carefully she brought the conversation around toward politics, focusing delicately on the growing authoritarianism of the Dudarev government. "Surely you see the risks of arbitrary rule to any investor, especially a foreign investor?" Fiona said at last. "I mean, you've seen what happened to the owners of the Yukos oil cartel — prison for some, disgrace for the rest, and the forced sale of all their holdings. Every dollar or euro you invest here could be snatched away by Kremlin decree in the blink of an eye. If laws or regulations can be made and unmade at the whim of a few, how can you plan rationally for the future?"

Malkovic shrugged expansively. "There are always risks in any venture, Ms. Devin," he said genially. "Believe me, I know that very well. But I am a man who looks to the long-term, beyond the shallow day-to-day twists and turns of fortune. For all its many faults, Russia remains a land of great opportunity. When Communism collapsed, this country gave itself over to capitalist excess — to its own Gilded Age of greedy tycoons and business oligarchs. So now, quite naturally, the pendulum has swung back a bit in reaction, toward tighter state control over life and politics. But that same pendulum will eventually swing back toward the moderate middle. And those of us who were wise enough to stand by Russia through the difficult times will reap enormous rewards when that day comes."

"You seem very confident of that," she said quietly.

"I am confident," the billionaire agreed.

"Remember, I know President Dudarev personally. He is no saint, but I believe that he is a man determined to give this country the law and order it craves. To restore a sense of discipline and decency. To break the power of the *Mafiya* and make the streets of Moscow and other cities safe again."

He raised a quizzical eyebrow. "I would have thought that you, of all people, would appreciate the vital importance of that, Ms. Devin. Your husband's untimely death was a great tragedy. It would not have occurred in a society better able to safeguard the lives and property of its citizens — the kind of society I believe Russia's new leaders honestly hope to build here."

For a moment, Fiona stared back at Malkovic without speaking, aware of a wave of cold anger rising behind her tightly controlled features. Even after two years, the memories of Sergei's murder were still very much a raw wound in her psyche. To hear the subject raised so casually, especially as a rhetorical prop for Dudarev's growing tyranny, seemed a kind of grotesque sacrilege.

"I helped bring my husband's killers to justice myself," she said at last, speaking with a calm, even voice that masked her true feelings. For months, she had hunted those who ordered her husband's death, piecing together evidence of their crimes at considerable risk to her own life. In the end, the public outcry she raised by her articles had forced the authorities to take action. The men most responsible were now serving long prison sentences.

"So you did," Malkovic agreed. "And I followed your courageous crusade against the *Mafiya* with great admiration. But even you must admit that your task would have been easier if the police here were less corrupt, more efficient, and better disciplined."

Fiona hid a frown. Why was the billionaire suddenly throwing her husband's murder back in her face? This man never said anything without a purpose, so what was his goal in trying to force her off-balance now? Was this his way of warning her off the uncomfortable subject of Russia's gradual slide back to a police state? Was he trying to distract her from asking any more inconvenient or embarrassing questions about his business connections to the Dudarev regime?

If so, she would have to move quickly, before he decided to cut this interview short on one pretense or another. "There may be worse things than police corruption and incompetence," she told him. "This growing cult of official secrecy, for example — secrecy I consider to be obsessive, unnecessary, and even dangerous. Especially when it concerns a serious matter of public health and safety."

He raised an eyebrow. "I'm not quite following you, Ms. Devin. To what 'cult of secrecy' are you referring?"

Fiona shrugged. "What else would you call trying to hide the news of a deadly new disease, not only from the Russian people themselves, but also from the world's public health agencies?"

"A new disease?" Malklovic leaned forward, suddenly wholly intent. His eyes were troubled. "Go on," he said quietly.

He listened carefully while she ran through the gist of what she and Smith had learned separately from Kiryanov and Petrenko, though she concealed her knowledge that the two doctors had been murdered. Or that this mysterious ailment was now spreading outside Russia itself. When she finished, he pursed his lips in dismay. "Do you have any evidence to confirm these rumors of a strange new illness?"

"Evidence? Not yet. None of the other doctors involved will talk to me and all of the important records are under lock and key," Fiona said, shaking her head. She frowned again. "But you see the danger, I hope. One way or another the word is bound to leak out. If the Kremlin — or even just an official in the Ministry of

Health — is covering up the beginning of a new epidemic in a foolish attempt to avoid public panic or international embarrassment, the consequences could be catastrophic."

Malkovic grimaced. "Indeed. The economic and political costs could be horrendous. The world community and the financial markets would not easily forgive a nation caught hiding something that might turn out to be another epidemic as bad as AIDS — or worse."

"I was thinking more of the possible cost in human lives," Fiona said softly.

A wintry smile touched his lips. "Touché, Ms. Devin," he said. "I stand, or rather, sit rebuked." He looked at her with a new measure of respect. "So what is it that you really want of me? I assume all of your questions earlier were simply window dressing, a means of maneuvering our conversation onto the question of this apparent medical cover-up."

"Not entirely," she said, blushing very slightly. "But yes, I am hoping that you'll exert your influence with the appropriate ministries to shed some light on this mystery disease."

"So you expect me to help you break open this story, this news scoop of yours?" Malkovic asked drily. "Out of the pure goodness of my own heart?"

Fiona smiled back at him, intentionally matching the billionaire's wry expression. "You are famous for your philanthropy, Mr. Malkovic," she said. "But even if you were not, I suspect that you are quite adept at measuring the value of good publicity."

"And the cost of bad publicity, too," he said with a brief, sardonic laugh. Then he shook his large head slowly in a gesture of surrender. "Very well, Ms. Devin, I will do what I can to pry open a few official doors for you, even if only in my own best interests."

"Thank you," she told him, closing her notebook and rising gracefully to her feet. "That would be most kind. Your staff knows how to contact me."

"No thanks are necessary," Malkovic said, politely standing up with her. A dour expression settled on his face. "If what you have told me this morning is true, we may both be acting in time to remedy a terrible, almost unforgivable mistake."

Jon Smith followed a path heading deeper into the quiet, tree-lined square called Patriarch's Pond. His shoes crunched softly on the icy snow still covering the walkway. There were very few other sounds. This far in among the trees the roar of traffic from the busy Sadovaya Ring road was muted, reduced to a faint hum. In the distance, children laughed and shouted, busy building forts and hurling clumps of snow at each other among the white-covered shapes of playground equipment. Strange sculptures, distorted images of creatures popular in nineteenth-century Russian fables, peered out at him from between tree trunks and bare, twisted branches.

He reached the edge of the large, shallow ice-covered pond at the center of the square and stopped for a moment, standing with his hands in his pockets as some protection against the below-zero temperatures. In the summer, this small, secluded patch of parkland was a favorite picnic spot for Muscovites, full of smiling crowds, sunlight, and singing. On this gray, overcast winter day, it showed a gloomier, more desolate face.

"The devil appeared here once, you know," a woman's voice said lightly from behind him.

Smith turned his head.

Fiona Devin stood not far away, framed between two leafless lime trees. Her cheeks were flushed in the cold and she wore a stylish fur hat atop her dark hair. She drew nearer.

"The devil?" Smith asked. "Literally or figuratively?"

Amusement glinted in her blue-green eyes. "Fictionally, only. Or so one hopes." She nodded toward the pond. "The writer Mikhail Bulgakov set the first scene of his classic *The Master and Margarita* at this place. In it, Satan himself arrives right here, ready for a romp through the atheist Moscow of Stalin's era."

Smith shivered suddenly, from the cold seeping through the lining of his black wool coat, or so he hoped. "What a great place for a rendezvous, then," he said with a quick grin. "Frozen, bleak, *and* cursed. We've hit the perfect Russian trifecta. Now all that's missing is a sleigh and a pack of howling wolves hot on our trail."

Fiona chuckled. "Soulful pessimism complete with gallows humor, Colonel? You may fit in here better than I thought." She moved closer, coming right up to stand beside him at the edge of the snow-covered pavement. The top of her head came up to his shoulder. "My people have finished vetting that list of doctors and scientists you gave me," she said abruptly, lowering her voice. "Now I'm ready to brief you."

Surprised, Smith whistled tunelessly under his breath. "And?"

"Your safest and surest bet is Dr. Elena Vedenskaya," she said firmly.

Smith nodded slowly. Just as with

Petrenko, he had met Vedenskaya at different medical conferences over the past several years. He had a vague memory of a rather plain, prim woman somewhere in her early fifties — a woman whose skill, dedication, and competence had carried her right to the top of her male-dominated profession. Vedenskaya now headed the Cytology, Genetics, and Molecular Biology department at the Central Research Institute of Epidemiology. Since that was one of Russia's top scientific institutions for the study of infectious disease, she was sure to have been involved in trying to identify the mystery illness whose origins they were now tracking.

"Is there any particular reason that you think I can trust her?" he asked.

"There is," Fiona told him. "Dr. Vedenskaya has a good record as a friend of democracy and political reform," she said quietly. "Going all the way back to her student days when Brezhnev and the other Communist Party bosses ruled the Kremlin roost."

Smith looked at her sharply. "Then she must have a KGB/FSB security dossier as long as my arm. With the Kremlin keeping tabs on suspect scientists, she'll be right at the head of their surveillance list."

"She would be," Fiona agreed. Then she shrugged her shoulders. "Fortunately, her file no longer reflects reality. As far as the FSB is now aware, Elena Vedenskaya is a thoroughly reliable and apolitical servant of the State."

Smith raised an eyebrow. "Somebody cleaned out her dossier? Mind telling me how that little miracle of excision took place?"

"I'm afraid that's on a strictly need-to-know basis, Colonel," Fiona told him calmly. "And you do not need to know. For quite obvious reasons."

He nodded, accepting the mild reproof. "Fair enough," he said. "How do you suggest I contact her? Through the Institute?"

"Definitely not," she said. "It's highly likely that all land-line calls into Moscow hospitals and research facilities are being monitored." She passed him a small slip of paper with a ten-digit number written in a neat, feminine hand. "Fortunately, Vedenskaya has an unlisted cell phone."

"I'll call her this afternoon," Smith decided. "And try to set up a dinner meeting for tonight, at some restaurant well away from her lab. Making this look like a purely social call between old colleagues seems the safest way to approach her."

"Sensible," Fiona agreed. "But make the reservation for three."

"You're planning on coming?"

"I am," she said. One side of her mouth

tilted upward in an impish smile. "Unless, that is, you were hoping to woo the good doctor with your masculine charm."

Smith reddened. "Not exactly."

Her smile grew wider. "Very wise, Colonel."

One hundred meters away, two men sat in the front seat of a silver BMW parked along the side of a narrow street. One, a German named Wegner, leaned forward, taking pictures through the dark, tinted windshield with a digital camera equipped with a high-powered telephoto lens. The other entered a series of commands into the small portable computer perched on his lap.

"I've got a connection," the second man announced. His name was Chernov and he had served as a junior officer in the old KGB. "I can send the images whenever you're ready."

"Good," his companion grunted. He snapped another quick set of pictures and then lowered the camera. "That should do it."

"Any idea who the man is?"

The cameraman shrugged. "None. But we'll let someone else puzzle that out. In the meantime, we stick to our orders: Follow the woman Devin and report any and all contacts she makes."

Chernov nodded sourly. "I know. I know. But this is getting too risky. I thought you'd lost her for good on the Metro this morning. I had to drive like a madman just to pick up your trail and hers." He frowned. "I don't like it. She's asking too many questions. We should just terminate her."

"Kill a journalist? An American?" the man with the camera said coldly. "Herr Brandt will have to make that decision himself — when the time comes."

Not far away, a tall, barrel-chested man stood, slowly rocking back and forth in the shelter of a doorway. He wrapped his arms around himself, hugging his shabby coat tighter for warmth. His pants were faded and patched. At first glance, he seemed to be nothing more than one of the many poverty-stricken old-age pensioners who often wandered Moscow's streets in an alcoholic daze. But beneath his bushy, silver eyebrows, the tall man's gaze was clear, even penetrating. He frowned, carefully memorizing the BMW's license plate. This situation was growing more complicated and dangerous at a dizzying pace, he thought grimly.

CHAPTER SIXTEEN

Thick clouds rolled west through the slowly darkening skies above the elaborate spires of the Kotelnicheskaya high-rise. A few fresh flakes of snow spun through the air, brushing gently against the windows of the Brandt Group's penthouse office suite. Erich Brandt himself stood at the window, looking down through the lightly falling snow at the busy city streets far below.

He could feel the tension growing in his thick neck and powerful shoulders. He had always disliked these periods of enforced idleness — the time spent waiting for subordinates to report or for superiors to issue new orders. Part of him craved the physical and emotional release of action, reveling in sudden violence as though it were a drug. But years spent stalking enemies, first for the Stasi and then later for his own pleasure and profit, had taught him both the necessity and the means of controlling those cruder instincts.

He swung around at the sound of a rap

232

on his open door. "Yes!" he snapped. "What is it?"

One of his subordinates, like him a former Stasi officer, came in carrying a file folder. The slim, hatchet-faced man looked worried. "I think we have a new security breach," he said tightly. "A serious one."

Brandt frowned slightly. Gerhard Lange was not ordinarily a man prone to a show of nerves. "In what way?"

"These were transmitted by the team conducting surveillance on that American reporter," Lange told him, opening the folder and fanning out a set of black-and-white images across his desk. They showed the American woman talking animatedly with a lean, dark-haired man. "Those pictures were taken roughly two hours ago, during what appeared to be a clandestine rendezvous at Patriarch's Pond."

"And?"

"See for yourself." Lange slid another document across the desk. "This was just faxed by one of our informants."

The sheet was a summary of a U.S. Army service record — that of Lieutenant Colonel Jonathan Smith, M.D. It included a blurry, slightly-out-of-focus photograph.

Brandt stared down at the picture. Silently, he compared it to the images taken by his surveillance team. He scowled. There was no possible doubt. This was the same man. Smith was in Moscow — and he was in contact with the freelance journalist whose persistent inquiries were causing them concern.

The blond-haired man shivered slightly. Despite his solemn pledge to Alexei Ivanov, HYDRA's operational security was continuing to fray around the edges.

He looked up from the damning pictures. "Where is Smith staying?"

Lange shook his head wearily. "That is our first problem. We don't know. We've checked the passenger manifests from every airport and railway station in the Moscow region. His name does not appear on any of them."

Brandt sat down behind his desk. "So Smith arrived here under a cover identity," he mused. "And he is using forged documents that were solid enough to deceive the Russian immigration authorities."

"Almost certainly," Lange agreed. "Which makes him a spy, either for the CIA or for one of the other American intelligence organizations."

The blond-haired man nodded grimly. "So it seems."

"The FSB could help us," Lange suggested tentatively. "If we had access to the Interior Ministry's passport registration forms for the past couple of days, we could run a search program to cross-index

Smith's picture with —"

"And hand our Russian friends the excuse they need to take over this end of the HYDRA operation?" Brandt shook his head. "No, Gerhard. We'll manage this matter ourselves. I do not want the FSB, especially Ivanov's Thirteenth Directorate, involved in any way, shape, or form. Not yet. Clear?"

Lange nodded reluctantly. "Clear enough."

"Good." Brandt glanced through the photos taken by his surveillance team again. He tapped one showing the two Americans deep in conversation. "This journalist, Ms. Devin, is the key to finding Smith. He's contacted her once. He's almost sure to do so again. Where is she right now?"

The other man shrugged gloomily. "That's our second problem. We've lost her."

Brandt stared back at him. "Lost her? How?"

"After meeting Smith, she led Wegner and Chernov on a merry chase across half of Moscow," Lange reported. "First by doubling back on different Metro lines a couple of times, and then finally by ducking into the shops inside the Petrovskiy Passage. They think she may have changed her hat or coat to alter her appearance and then slipped away unnoticed in the crowds."

Brandt nodded stiffly. In a city this size, there were any number of ways to shake off a tail — if you knew you were being followed and if you knew what you were doing.

"They're headed back to her flat, hoping to regain contact," Lange went on carefully. "But she may have gone to ground."

"Quite probably," Brandt growled. He frowned. "Two years ago, she managed to elude several *Mafiya* hit teams, all while operating on her own. This woman may be an amateur, but she is most assuredly not a fool. She probably spotted Wegner and Chernov following her. By now, she's undoubtedly safely tucked away in a hotel somewhere, or staying with friends."

Lange sighed. "If so, we're left with no effective way to track down Smith. Whether you like it or not, we will have to request assistance from the Thirteenth Directorate."

"Don't be too sure of that," Brandt said, thinking hard. "We have an alternative."

The other man looked puzzled.

"Smith is here for a purpose," Brandt reminded him. "And we know what that purpose must be, correct?"

Lange nodded slowly. "He's trying to learn what Petrenko wanted to tell him in Prague. Or worse, gather evidence to verify what Petrenko *did* tell him."

"Exactly." Brandt showed his teeth. "Tell me, Gerhard, what is the best way to hunt a wild animal, especially a dangerous predator?"

His subordinate said nothing.

"Water is the key," Brandt told him. "All animals must drink. So you find its watering place and then you wait, with your rifle at the ready, for the creature to come to you."

He pushed aside the surveillance photos and Smith's service record and paged through the materials stacked neatly on his desk, looking for a printout of the most recent message from Wulf Renke. The scientist had sent him the list he had asked for at their last meeting — the names of the other doctors and scientists in Moscow whose knowledge of the first HYDRA outbreak could prove dangerous.

Brandt handed Renke's list to Lange with a thin-lipped smile. "Somewhere on here is the American's watering hole. Focus first on anyone who attended international conferences where they might have met Colonel Smith. Sooner or later, he will have to contact one of those men or women. And when he does, we'll be there ahead of him, waiting to make our kill."

Located on the shared border of the

New Arbat and Tverskaya districts, the Kafe Karetny Dvor occupied a charming older building, a rare survivor of the drab concrete excesses of Soviet-era urban redevelopment. The Moscow Zoo and another of Stalin's mammoth "Seven Sisters," the Kudrinskaya apartment high-rise, were close by, just on the other side of the wide Sadovaya Ring road. On hot summer evenings, the restaurant's patrons sat outside in its shaded interior courtyard, eating salads and drinking wine or vodka or beer. In colder weather, customers savored the spicy Azerbaijani cuisine served in its intimate, warm, and cheerful dining rooms filled with green, hanging plants.

Seated in a booth in a far corner of the main room, Smith saw Fiona Devin come through the front door. She stood poised there for a moment, brushing the snow off her coat while gracefully turning her head, first in one direction and then another, obviously looking for him. Relieved, he rose to his feet. With a casual nod, she headed in his direction, striding nimbly through the crowded, smoke-filled restaurant.

"I presume this is your companion, at long last," Elena Vedenskaya said calmly, watching this attractive, elegantly dressed woman approach with dark, expressionless eyes. She stubbed out her cigarette in an ashtray and stood up to greet Fiona just as she joined them.

In appearance, the Russian research scientist was as plain as Smith had remembered. Her narrow, lined face, pallid skin, and stiff, iron-gray hair pinned up in a tight bun made her look at least ten years older than she really was. Her drab skirt and blouse were clearly chosen more for comfort and convenience than for style. Still, her mind was just as sharp and incisive as he had recalled, and here in her home city she showed few traces of the reserved shyness he had observed at their last encounter — a molecular biology conference in Madrid.

"Ms. Devin, this is Dr. Elena Borisovna Vedenskaya," Smith said, carefully introducing them formally.

The two women nodded to each other coolly, but politely, and then sat down, choosing opposite ends of the semicircular booth. After a brief hesitation, Smith slid into the side closest to Vedenskaya. Without demur she moved over to the middle, making room for him.

"I'm sorry I'm late, Jon," Fiona said quietly. "I ran into a few . . . complications. Somewhere along the way I picked up a pair of unwelcome guests — door-to-door salesmen, I think — that I wanted to avoid."

Smith raised an eyebrow. In Covert-One voice code the term "door-to-door salesmen" was used to describe a hostile surveillance operation aimed at the agent. "These guys weren't selling anything you were interested in?" he asked, choosing his words carefully to avoid spooking the Russian doctor sitting beside him.

"No. At least, I don't think so," Fiona told him. Her voice betrayed just the slightest hint of uncertainty. "It's possible they were only paying me a routine visit. There are a lot of pushy salesmen around Moscow these days."

Smith nodded his understanding. As Dudarev and his cronies tightened their control over Russia, journalists, especially foreign journalists, were increasingly subject to random, and often painfully obvious, police and FSB surveillance. It was a method the authorities used to distract and intimidate the media without imposing more overt restrictions that might draw protests from the outside world.

They all fell silent as a youthful pair of smiling waiters arrived, each bearing a tray of plates and bowls heaped with food. Working with practiced efficiency, the servers set these dishes out across the table and departed. A third waiter, older than the others, followed right on his companions' heels bringing their drinks: a bottle of slightly fizzy Moskovskaya vodka and another containing sweetened apple juice.

"To save time, we ordered before you arrived," Dr. Vedenskaya told Fiona. The gray-haired woman raised a quizzical eyebrow. "I hope this was all right?"

"Quite all right," Fiona replied with an answering smile. "I don't know about anyone else, but personally I'm absolutely famished."

Delicious aromas wafted up from the array of dishes laid before them. Suddenly ferociously hungry, the three of them took turns serving themselves, choosing from a wide assortment of Azeri specialties. Some plates held steaming slivers of *satsivi*, chicken breasts marinated in a creamy garlic sauce. Others were piled with sweet peppers stuffed with a mixture of minced lamb, mint, fennel, and cinnamon. There were also small bowls of *dovgra*, a thick, hot soup made with yogurt, rice, and spinach. While they were finishing these starters, more dishes arrived, mostly various *shasliks*, skewers of lamb, veal, and chicken soaked in onion, vinegar, and pomegranate juice, grilled over glowing embers, and served with thin sheets of *lavash*, a form of unleavened bread.

With the edge taken off their appetites, Elena Vedenskaya held up a glass of vodka. "*Za vashe zdarov'e!* Your health!" she said and downed the clear, cold liquor in one large gulp, following it immediately with a chaser of apple juice.

Smith and Fiona followed her example, savoring a combination of sharply contrasting flavors that perfectly complemented the highly spiced food they were eating.

"So now," the Russian scientist said quietly when they set their empty glasses down. "To business." She looked narrowly at Fiona. "Our mutual friend here," she nodded at Jon, "tells me that you are a journalist."

"I am."

"Then let us understand one another, Ms. Devin," Vedenskaya said firmly. "I do not wish my name to appear splashed across the front pages of some lurid tabloid." She smiled thinly. "Or even a respectable newspaper."

Fiona nodded easily. "That's perfectly reasonable."

"Although I do not like the government that pays my salary, I am very good at my job," the gray-haired woman continued. "And it is important work. Work that saves lives. So I have no great desire to lose my position unnecessarily."

Fiona looked across the table at the scientist. "Then I give you my word that I will leave your name out of any story I write," she said seriously. "Believe me, Dr. Vedenskaya, I'm far more interested in learning the truth about this mysterious disease than I am in selling the story to a newspaper or magazine."

"If so, we have at least one thing in common," the Russian woman said drily. She turned back to Smith. "On the telephone you said that you believed this same illness was now spreading outside Russia."

He nodded grimly. "Without more data on the first outbreak here, I can't be absolutely sure, but the symptoms appear identical. And if it is the same unidentified disease, this news blackout ordered by the Kremlin is essentially killing people."

"Fools! Dolts!" Vedenskaya swore acidly. She pushed her half-filled plate to the side and lit another cigarette, plainly trying to buy a few moments to regain her composure. "This cover-up is an act of criminal folly. I warned the government about the dangers of its decision to keep these strange deaths a secret. So did my colleagues."

She scowled. "We should have been allowed to consult with the other international health authorities as soon as the first four cases were recognized." Her narrow shoulders slumped. "And I should have said something, or *done* something, to pass the warning on myself. But, then, as weeks passed without anyone else falling ill, I allowed myself to hope that my initial fears of a larger epidemic had been exaggerated."

"There haven't been any new cases here in Moscow?" Fiona asked.

The Russian research scientist shook her head firmly. "None."

"You're sure?" Smith asked, surprised.

"Quite sure, Jonathan," Vedenskaya said. "True, the government has forbidden us to reveal the facts of the outbreak to the outside world. But we remain under explicit instructions to continue our own research. The Kremlin is still deeply interested in learning more about this disease: what causes it, how it is transmitted, the methods by which it kills its victims, and for some way to slow or reverse its cruel and inexorable progression."

"But Valentin Petrenko told me that he'd been ordered to call off his probe into those first four deaths," Smith said with a frown.

"Yes, that is so," Vedenskaya agreed. "The hospital investigative teams were shut down, probably to control the flow of information. Instead, all research work surrounding this illness is being conducted in other, higher-level facilities, my BIO-CGM section at the Institute among them."

"Including the Bioaparat labs?" Smith

asked quietly, referring to the collection of heavily guarded science complexes that were said to be the center of Russia's top-secret biological weapons research. If, as Klein and President Castilla suspected, the Russians *were* using this strange disease as a weapon, the scientists and technicians working for Bioaparat had to be involved in some way.

The gray-haired woman shook her head gravely. "I do not know what goes on behind the barbed wire at Yekaterinburg, Kirov, Sergiyev Posad, or Strizhi." Her mouth tightened. "My security clearances do not reach that high."

Smith nodded his understanding. He frowned, trying vainly to make these new pieces of information fit into the puzzle. If this new illness was a Russian-made weapon, and it was already being used against important people in the West and other countries, why was the Kremlin so insistent that its own top civilian scientists continue their research?

There was a short, uncomfortable silence.

"I brought copies of my case notes as you requested," Vedenskaya told Smith at last. She prodded the heavy winter coat bundled beside her on the seat. "They're there, hidden inside a selection of old medical journals. I will give them to you after we leave. It is too public here."

"Thank you, Elena," Smith said gravely, with genuine gratitude. He looked sidelong at her. "But what about the blood or tissue specimens taken from the victims? Is there any way you could smuggle samples of those out to us?"

"It would be impossible," she answered shortly. "Your friends Petrenko and Kiryanov saw to that. All biological specimens are now kept under strict lock and key. No one can obtain them without a signature and signed forms from the Ministry authorizing specific experiments or tests."

"Is there anything else you can tell us?" Fiona asked at last. "Anything at all?"

Vedenskaya hesitated briefly, looked sideways to make sure no one else was in earshot, and then answered in a lower voice, one that could barely be heard over the loud clatter of dishes and conversation from the rest of the restaurant. "I heard a rumor, a rumor that greatly disturbed me —"

The two Americans stayed silent, waiting for her to go on.

The Russian woman sighed. "One of the hospital orderlies, a man who had spent many years as a political prisoner in a labor camp, claimed that he saw that madman Wulf Renke examining one of the dying patients."

Startled, Smith sat up straighter. "Renke?" he muttered in disbelief.

"Wulf Renke? Who is he?" Fiona asked.

"An East German scientist. Basically, a biological weapons expert with a very ugly reputation for coming up with new and especially nasty ways to kill people," Smith told her. He shook his head. "But it couldn't have been him. Not really. That bastard has been dead for years."

"So it is said," Vedenskaya said softly. "But this orderly knew the German well . . . painfully well. While a prisoner, he was forced to witness a series of vicious experiments Renke conducted on other inmates at his camp."

"Where is this man now?" Fiona pressed her. "Can we talk to him?"

"Only if you can summon the spirits of the dead," the gray-haired woman told her curtly. "Unfortunately, he fell beneath the wheels of a tram — shortly after he began telling the story of what he had seen in the hospital."

"He fell? Or was he pushed?" Smith wondered grimly.

Vedenskaya shrugged. "They say he was drunk when it happened. For all I know, that could be true. Almost all Russians are drunk at one time or another." She smiled bitterly through the smoke curling from her cigarette and then tapped her empty vodka glass with a single, tobacco-stained finger.

Outside, the snow flurries were coming down harder now, beginning to cover the heaped mounds of older, smog-blackened snow and ice. Fresh flakes dusted the streets and parked cars, steadily accumulating in a layer of white powder that sparkled faintly under the street lamps and in the wavering beams of passing cars.

Still fastening his thick parka, a young-looking man with a long, slightly crooked nose left the Kafe Karetny Dvor. He stood motionless for a moment, waiting for a break in the evening traffic, and then crossed the street at an angle. Once there, he walked rapidly east along Povarskaya Street, brushing through throngs of pedestrians hurrying along the pavement beneath bobbing umbrellas. Most were loaded down with purchases made during an evening's shopping among the Arbat District's trendy boutiques and galleries. He carried his own furled umbrella cradled casually under one arm.

A couple of hundred meters up the street, he paused to light a cigarette, standing right next to a large black luxury sedan idling along the curb.

Instantly, the car's rear side window slid silently down, revealing little of the darkened interior.

"Vedenskaya is still inside the restaurant," the young man muttered.

"And she is with the two Americans?" a voice from inside the sedan asked quietly.

"Yes. I've left one of my men in there to keep an eye on them. He'll report the moment they get up to leave. From the look of things, I'd say that will be soon."

"Your team is ready?"

The young man nodded. He took a deep drag on his cigarette. The tip glowed bright red in the darkness. "Perfectly ready."

Erich Brandt leaned forward slightly, just far enough so that a tiny bit of light from the street lamps fell across the harsh lines of his square-jawed face. "Good." His icy gray eyes gleamed briefly. "Then let us hope Colonel Smith and his friends have enjoyed their meal. After all, it will be their last."

CHAPTER SEVENTEEN

Smith held the door open for Fiona Devin and Elena Vedenskaya and then followed them out of the Kafe Karetny Dvor. After the warmth inside the Azeri restaurant, the freezing night air cut deep, biting through every layer of his clothing. He gritted his teeth to stop them from chattering and hunched his shoulders, grateful at least for his thick wool coat.

Together they walked a short distance up Povorskaya Street and then stopped in a small huddle on the sidewalk to make their farewells. Other pedestrians edged around them, hurrying onward toward their homes or errands. Occasionally, cars drove past on the street, rumbling by in a procession of bright headlights mixed in with the occasional blare of an angrily honked horn and the faint crunch of studded tires rolling over fresh drifts of new-fallen snow.

"This is for you, Jonathan," Vedenskaya murmured, reaching into the recesses of her coat and pulling out a thick plastic binder. "Use the information it contains wisely."

Silently, Smith took the binder and opened it. It was full of dog-eared medical journals, some in English, others in Russian and German. He flipped open the cover of one, a months-old copy of *The Lancet*. Neatly folded inside were several pages crowded with Cyrillic typescript, evidently a selection of the gray-haired Russian scientist's case notes. He looked up with a quick, grateful nod, knowing how much she was risking by smuggling these out to him. "Thanks. I'll make sure this data gets to the right people."

"That is good. With luck, lives can still be saved." She looked fiercely at Fiona Devin. "You remember our agreement?"

"I do," Fiona told her quietly. "No names will be used in any news article I write, Dr. Vedenskaya. Of that you may be sure."

The other woman nodded back, this time with an austere smile. "In that case, I shall wish you well —"

Suddenly she reeled forward, almost knocked off her feet by a man who crashed straight into her from behind. He had been walking too fast, striding with his head well down and his collar turned up against the falling snow. She only saved herself from falling by grabbing Smith's arm. Angrily,

251

she let go and whirled around. "You there! Watch where you're going, why don't you?"

Abashed, the man — young, with a slightly crooked nose — stepped back quickly. "*Izvinite!* Excuse me!" he muttered. Grinning foolishly, he retrieved the umbrella he had dropped in the collision and reeled off down the street, walking now with exaggerated care.

Vedenskaya sniffed, disgusted. "Drunk!" she said. "And this early in the evening! Bah. Alcohol is our national curse. Even the young poison themselves."

"Are you all right?" Smith asked.

Still tight-lipped with anger, she nodded. "Yes. Though I think the lout must have poked me in the leg with that damned umbrella of his," she said, rubbing at the back of her left thigh. Then she shrugged. "But it's nothing serious."

"Still, I think it's high time we all went our separate ways," Fiona said worriedly, following the apparent drunk with her own narrowed eyes. "We have what we need. There's not much point in standing around out here in the open, risking more unwanted attention."

Smith nodded. "Makes sense." He turned back to Vedenskaya, patting the binder she had given him. "Look, I'll keep you posted by private e-mail on what we learn —"

Smith stopped in midsentence. The Russian woman was staring at him with an expression full of horror. "Elena? What is it?" he asked quickly. "What's wrong?"

She drew in a single deep, shuddering breath and then choked, gasping for air. Jon could see the muscles in her neck straining as she struggled to speak. Her eyes were wide open, grotesquely bulging almost out of their sockets, but her pupils were constricted, reduced to tiny black pinpoints. Her knees sagged.

Shocked, Smith reached out.

But before he could catch her, Elena Vedenskaya collapsed, crumpling to the snow-covered pavement like a rag doll. Her arms and legs jerked wildly, flailing and twitching as she writhed, apparently gripped by a series of eerily silent convulsions.

"Call an ambulance! Now!" Smith snapped to Fiona.

"I'm on it." She nodded crisply, pulled out her phone, and punched in 03, Moscow's medical emergency number.

Jon dropped to his knees beside the stricken woman. The wild, frenetic spasms were fading, leaving her lying contorted on her back. He set aside the plastic binder, yanked off one of his gloves, and then laid two fingers against her neck, feeling for her pulse. It was very fast and very weak, fluttering like a broken-winged bird. Not good. He leaned forward, putting his ear to her nose and mouth. She was not breathing.

Christ, he thought bleakly. What the hell had just happened to her? A heart attack? Not likely, given what he was seeing. A stroke or seizure? Maybe. Another, infinitely more frightening possibility flickered vaguely at the back of his mind, but he shook his head, knowing he did not have the time or the information he needed to chase down that fugitive thought. A firm diagnosis would have to wait until later. In the meantime, he had to do his best to keep her alive until the Russian paramedics could arrive.

"One of the hospitals is dispatching an emergency medical team, Colonel," he heard Fiona Devin report over the babble of shocked voices from a rapidly gathering circle of onlookers. "But it might take five minutes or more to reach us."

Smith nodded, frowning. Five minutes. For most medical situations, that was a good response time — very good, in fact. But under these circumstances, it might as well be an eternity.

Working fast, he stripped off his coat, bundled it up, and shoved it under the older, gray-haired woman's shoulders, tilting her head back to help open her airway. Then he pulled her jaw forward with one thumb, shifting her tongue out of the way. He listened again. She was still not breathing. Gently, he turned her head to the side and probed the back of her throat with his fingers, searching for any obstruction, any lump of mucus or bit of food, that could be choking her. There was nothing.

Grim-faced, Smith cradled Elena Vedenskaya's head in his arms, pinched her nose shut with his fingers, and began rapid mouth-to-mouth resuscitation, blowing hard enough to see her chest rise. Every so often, he paused and put his ear to her mouth and nose again, checking to see if the Russian woman was breathing on her own yet. But she still lay paralyzed, staring up at the sky with eyes that never blinked.

He kept working, forcing air into her lungs. *Breathe,* Jon willed silently. *Come on, Elena, breathe.* Two or three minutes went by in a blur of frantic activity. A siren keened in the distance, drawing closer.

Under his fingertips, Vedenskaya's pulse faded, staggered on for a few more irregular beats, and then stopped. Hell. He switched to CPR, cardiopulmonary resuscitation, alternating mouth-to-mouth breathing with short, powerful compressions on her sternum in an increasingly frantic effort to restore her breathing and restart her heart. Nothing worked.

Fiona knelt beside him. "Any good?" she asked somberly, carefully speaking in Russian.

Smith shook his head in frustration. "I think she's gone."

Several of the bystanders staring down at Vedenskaya overheard them and crossed themselves rapidly, from right to left in the Russian Orthodox manner. One or two took off their hats in a show of respect for the dead woman. Others began edging away. The drama was over.

"If so, we should leave, Colonel," Fiona suggested softly. "We really can't afford any official complications." She picked up the binder containing Vedenskaya's case notes from the pavement. "Not now."

Smith shook his head again, still continuing his CPR. Rationally, he knew that Devin was right. By now, Elena was almost certainly beyond anyone's help. And getting embroiled in a militia investigation of her death would put them both at risk. For one thing, his John Martin cover was not designed to stand up to intense scrutiny. But he was a doctor first, before he was an intelligence agent. He had an ethical duty to aid this stricken woman. So long as he kept pushing oxygen into her lungs and doing his best to restart her stopped heart, she still had a chance, however slim.

And then, suddenly, it was too late to duck out anyway.

With its siren still wailing, a red-and-white ambulance braked to a stop along the curb. As the siren died away, the rear doors of the vehicle popped open and a slim, sallow-faced man in a rumpled white doctor's coat jumped out with a black medical bag clutched under one arm. Two burly paramedics scrambled out in his wake.

The doctor waved Smith aside with one dismissive hand and bent down beside the body to conduct his own quick, almost cursory, examination.

Wearily, Jon stood up, brushing the snow off his knees. He looked away from Vedenskaya's contorted corpse, fighting down a sense of failure and abiding sorrow. Patients died. It happened. But it never got any easier. It always felt like a defeat.

The sallow-faced Russian doctor felt for a pulse. Then he sat back on his heels and shrugged. "Poor woman. It's much too late. There's nothing I can do for her." He nodded to the paramedics standing nearby with a portable stretcher they had pulled out of the ambulance. "Well, go ahead, boys. Get her into the ambulance. Let's at least get her away from the prying eyes of the morbidly curious."

The two big men nodded silently and

clumsily bent down to begin preparing the body for transport.

Still shaking his head, the white-coated doctor climbed back to his feet. He turned slowly, contemptuously surveying the small and rapidly shrinking crowd of onlookers. His gaze swung toward the two Americans. "Which of you can tell me what happened to her? A heart attack, I suppose?"

"I don't think so," Smith said flatly.

"Why not?"

"She collapsed quite suddenly, suffering convulsions and muscle spasms — within a second or so after experiencing what appeared to be complete respiratory failure," Smith answered rapidly, running through the symptoms he had noted. "Her pupillary muscles also showed signs of extreme contraction. I tried mouth-to-mouth first, and then CPR when her heart stopped, but unfortunately neither technique produced any beneficial result."

The doctor raised an eyebrow. "Cogently summarized. I gather you have medical training, Mr. — ?"

"Martin. John Martin," Smith replied stiffly, mentally kicking himself for slipping so naturally and unconsciously into medical jargon that did not fit his cover identity. Clearly, Elena Vedenskaya's horrifying death had rattled him more than he realized. He shrugged. "No, no medical

258

training. But I have taken a couple of first-aid courses."

"Only first-aid courses? Really? You show remarkable aptitude." The doctor smiled in polite disbelief. "Still, it is fortunate that you are here."

"Oh? In what way?" Smith asked carefully.

"Your training and your observations will be very helpful in filling out my report on this tragic incident, Mr. Martin," the other man said calmly. He nodded at Fiona Devin. "That is why I must ask you and this charming companion of yours to accompany us to the hospital."

Fiona frowned.

"Don't worry, this is only a matter of routine," the doctor said, holding up a hand to stifle any protests. "I assure you that any inconvenience will be temporary."

The two paramedics finished strapping the dead woman onto their stretcher and heaved her up between them. "Watch out for her left leg," Smith heard one of them mutter brusquely to the other. "You don't want to get any of that stuff on your hands."

Stuff? Jon felt his blood run ice-cold. He remembered the young "drunk" who had collided with Vedenskaya, "accidentally" jabbing her with the tip of his rolled-up umbrella. Suddenly all the damning symptoms he had cataloged fell into place: respiratory collapse, convulsions, her constricted pupils, and finally, complete heart failure.

Jesus, he thought grimly. She must have been injected with some kind of deadly, fast-acting nerve agent, probably a variant of Sarin or VX. Even a drop of either toxic compound on bare skin could kill. Pumping VX or Sarin directly into the bloodstream would be even more lethal. He looked up quickly and saw the sallow-faced doctor watching him with a cold, calculating expression.

Smith took a step back.

With a slight smile, the white-coated man pulled a small, compact pistol out of his white coat — a Makarov PSM, a Russian-made knockoff of the Walther PPK. He held the weapon down low at his side, aiming straight at the American's heart. Slowly he shook his head. "I hope that you will resist the temptation to act unwisely, Colonel Smith. Otherwise, we will be forced to kill both you and the lovely Ms. Devin. And that would be a terrible shame, would it not?"

Bitterly angry with himself for missing the warning signs of this ambush, Smith grimaced. The other man was just outside his reach. Out of the corner of his eye, he saw that the ambulance driver, as big and hard-eyed as the others, had climbed down out of the cab. This man now stood close behind Fiona Devin, holding a pistol pressed hard into the small of her back.

Her face had gone pale, either with anger or fear or a mixture of both emotions.

Smith forced himself to stand very still. Carefully, he showed his open, empty hands. "I'm unarmed," he said tightly.

"A rational decision, Colonel," the doctor said approvingly. "No one would benefit from any useless heroics."

The first two paramedics roughly slid Elena Vedenskaya's blanket-wrapped body into the back of the ambulance. They swung away and stood waiting for further orders.

"Into the vehicle, please," the sallow-faced man said quietly. "Ms. Devin first."

Numbly, Fiona climbed into the ambulance. The stretcher occupied the central aisle, leaving two narrow benches, one on either side. She scooted down the left-hand bench, going all the way to the end. One of the burly paramedics crowded in after her, dropping heavily onto the bench on the far side. Once seated, he drew his own pistol to keep her covered.

"And now you, Colonel." The white-coated man nodded inside. "Sit next to Ms. Devin. But make sure you keep your hands in sight at all times. Otherwise, I fear Dmitri might get jumpy and then, sadly, you would end up as dead as poor Dr. Vedenskaya there."

Still coldly furious with himself, Jon obeyed. He slid down the bench toward Fiona. The dark-haired woman glanced at him with an unreadable expression in her blue-green eyes. She still held the binder containing Vedenskaya's notes.

"No talking," the paramedic growled in thickly accented English, emphasizing his order with the muzzle of his pistol.

She shrugged slightly and looked away, saying nothing further.

Smith winced inwardly. Their predicament was largely his fault. If he had not stayed so long in his futile effort to save Elena Vedenskaya's life, they might have been able to evade this trap before it snapped shut on them.

The slender, sallow-faced doctor scrambled up into the cramped interior and sat down facing the two Americans, squashed up next to his much bigger subordinate. With a slight, cynical smile, he kept his own pistol aimed at Jon's chest.

The second paramedic and the big, hard-eyed driver slammed the doors shut, sealing the four of them inside.

Moments later, the ambulance lurched into motion. They were pulling out from the curb. The siren and flashing blue light came on again, clearing a path through the light evening traffic. Slowly, the emergency vehicle swung through a wide U-turn, evidently heading back toward the much-busier Sadovaya Ring road.

Smith could feel ice-cold sweat trickling down his ribs. Somehow he had to find a way to break them out of this moving prison — and soon. He had no illusions about their fate if he failed. Once they arrived wherever they were being taken, he and Fiona Devin were as good as dead.

CHAPTER EIGHTEEN

Not far down Povarskaya Street, the tall, silver-haired man sitting hunched over behind the wheel of a boxy dark blue Russian-made Niva 4x4 utility vehicle cursed softly as he watched the two Americans being bundled unceremoniously into the back of the ambulance. His jaw tightened.

Sighing, he made sure his shoulder belt was tightly fastened, and then reached down to turn on the ignition. There were said to be patron saints for fools and madmen. If so, he earnestly hoped they would look down with favor on him, because there was certainly no time left to do anything subtle or sensible.

The Niva's powerful engine roared to life. Without hesitating any longer, he shoved the vehicle into gear, stamped down on the gas pedal, and accelerated away from the curb, aiming straight for the front side of the ambulance just as it turned across Povorskaya Street.

Inside the ambulance, Smith sat rigidly

still, carefully eyeing the pistol aimed in his direction. His mind raced, rapidly concocting and then discarding a series of wild-eyed schemes to escape from their captors. Unfortunately, every plan he came up with only seemed likely to get them killed sooner rather than later.

Suddenly the driver up front shouted something in alarm. Jon felt Fiona Devin tense up.

An engine roared close by, growing ever louder. Brakes squealed piercingly. Car and truck horns blared out panicked warnings. And then Smith felt an enormous, jolting bang as some other vehicle slammed into the ambulance at high speed. The impact hurled him right off the bench. He fell forward across Vedenskaya's body. There were more startled shouts from the others around him.

Hit broadside, they were sliding across the road, spinning out of control amid an ear-splitting shriek of tearing metal and the tinkling crash of shattering glass. First-aid kits and other medical gear tumbled out of storage compartments. A sharp, stinging reek of spilled gasoline and the acrid stench of torn and burning rubber rolled through the cramped interior.

Still spinning, the ambulance crashed into the side of an old, rust-eaten Volga sedan parked along the street and rocked to a stop, lying canted over at an odd angle with its blown front tires propped up high on the curb. The deafening noise died away.

Smith looked up.

The first sudden impact had tossed the doctor backward, smashing his head hard against the metal interior. He looked dazed. Rivulets of blood dripped down the side of his lean, pale face. But he still held onto his Makarov PSM.

Reacting fast, Jon shoved himself upright onto his knees.

The doctor's eyes widened. Snarling, he raised the pistol. His fingers curled around the trigger, already starting to squeeze it.

And then Smith lashed out, chopping down with the edge of his right hand to knock the barrel away just as the Makarov fired. At such close quarters, the sound was shattering. In a spurt of flame, the small-caliber 5.45mm bullet punched a hole in the floorboards, smacked dully into the road below, and ricocheted away.

In that same instant, Jon drove his left fist into the other man's face.

The punch slammed the Russian doctor's skull back against the wall with tremendous force. More blood spattered across the metal. The white-coated man groaned in agony. His eyes rolled up into the back of their sockets and he slumped forward, starting to lose consciousness.

The small pistol thudded onto the bench beside him.

Smith reached for it and then froze.

With the back of one big hand, the burly paramedic had already knocked Fiona Devin sprawling. She lay curled up at his feet, with the red mark left by his hand plainly visible on her pale cheek. Now he sighted carefully down the barrel of his own pistol, a larger, 9mm Makarov. He was aiming right at Smith's face.

And then the dark-haired woman moved, uncoiling with astonishing speed.

While rising to her knees, she yanked a slender, black-handled switchblade out of a sheath concealed in one of her elegant leather boots. At the touch of a button on its hilt, a four-inch stainless-steel blade flicked out, glinting cruelly in the light. Acting with cold determination, she stabbed the big man in the neck. The long, narrow blade plunged deep, severing his trachea and one of his carotid arteries in a single powerful thrust.

Horrified, the Russian paramedic dropped his pistol. His hands pawed frantically at the terrible wound. Jets of bright-red blood spurted across the ambulance, pulsing wildly at first with every heartbeat but diminishing fast as his life force ebbed away. Still clutching desperately at the gaping hole in his neck, the dying man slid slowly sideways. He sagged to the floor beside Elena Vedenskaya's blanket-wrapped corpse. The blood stopped pumping from between his locked fingers. He quivered once and then at last was still.

White-faced herself, Fiona quickly wiped her knife on the back of the dead man's coat. Her hands shook slightly as she retracted the blade and slipped the knife back into her boot.

"You've never killed anyone before?" Smith asked quietly.

She shook her head. "No." She forced a sickly smile. "But I'll worry about it later . . . assuming, of course, that we live through the next few minutes."

He nodded. The doctor and one of the two paramedics were down, but they were still facing at least two more enemies. "Can you handle a gun?"

"I can."

Smith scooped up both pistols and handed her the smaller Makarov PSM. Quickly, he checked the 9mm pistol, making sure the safety was off and that it had a round chambered. Fiona did the same with hers.

There was a loud rap on one of the closed rear doors. "Fiona?" a deep voice boomed from outside the wrecked ambulance. "This is Oleg. Are you and Dr. Smith unharmed?"

Jon whirled around with the Makarov raised, ready to open fire. But the dark-haired woman laid a hand gently on his wrist, pushing the weapon down. "Don't shoot," she said quietly. "He's a friend." Then Fiona raised her own voice. "Yes, we're fine. And free."

"What of the others? Those who took you captive?"

"They're out of commission," Fiona reported shortly. "One permanently. The other is still alive, but he'll have the devil of a headache later on."

"That is good!" The doors were yanked open. A tall, broad-shouldered man with a full head of silver hair stood there. In one hand, he held a pistol fitted with a silencer. With the other, he motioned them out. "Come! Quickly! We have very little time before the militia arrives."

Smith stared at the other man in astonishment. There was no mistaking that haughty, large-nosed profile, one that could easily have appeared on an ancient Roman coin. "Kirov. Well, I'll be damned," he said quietly. "Major General Oleg Kirov of the Russian Federal Security Service."

"Not anymore, Doctor." Kirov shrugged his powerful shoulders. "I have been retired, put out to pasture, as you Americans say," he said drily. "The men in the Kremlin decided that I was not sufficiently

269

loyal to their dreams of restoring the old order."

Jon nodded tersely. A few years before he had worked closely with the tall, barrel-chested FSB officer, joining in a desperate hunt to track down a container full of deadly smallpox stolen from one of Russia's biological weapons facilities. Since then he had often wondered how Kirov, so closely tied to his country's political reformers, was faring under the rule of President Dudarev and his hard-line cronies.

Now he knew.

"Small talk and career news will have to wait until later," Fiona broke in. "Right now we should be moving." She waved a hand at the street. "As it is, we're drawing a crowd."

"True," Kirov agreed, glancing briefly over his shoulder. Cars that had braked hard to avoid the crash he had caused were scattered randomly across the street. A few of the drivers were climbing out of their stalled vehicles to stare at the tangled wreckage. Others who had heard all the noise were spilling out of the neighboring apartment buildings, restaurants, and cafés. Several of the onlookers were speaking excitedly into their cell phones, presumably summoning the militia and emergency medical assistance.

Kirov looked back at the two Americans.

"You have what you came for? Those notes Dr. Vedenskaya brought for you?"

"They're right here," Fiona said, gingerly retrieving the bloodstained plastic binder from where it had fallen during the crash.

Smith turned grimly toward the dazed white-coated man huddled in one corner of the ambulance. The doctor was groaning softly now, drifting right on the edge of full consciousness. "Let's take that son of a bitch with us. I have a few questions to ask him. For one thing, just how the hell he knew my real name and rank."

The former FSB officer nodded. "An excellent question. If nothing else, it would also be useful to learn who issued his orders and where he was taking you."

Together he and Smith dragged the sallow-faced man out onto the street. Clotting blood matted the sparse hair on the back of their prisoner's head. His eyes were half-closed and clearly unable to focus. Propping the injured man up between them, Smith and Kirov half-carried, half-dragged him around the side of the ambulance. Fiona walked beside them, still keeping a wary eye on the small, but growing crowd of the curious drawn to what must have seemed a terrible accident.

Jon whistled softly. The collision had smashed in the whole front end of the emergency vehicle, reducing it to a mangled mass of twisted steel and broken glass. Still tangled in their seat belts, the two men who had been riding in front were slumped back against the seat. Both held weapons in their hands. Both had been shot dead at point-blank range.

He glanced at Kirov. "Your work, I presume?"

The other man nodded somberly. "It was regrettable, but necessary. I had no time for half-measures." He indicated the dark blue Niva slewed across the street beside the wrecked ambulance. "Come. Our chariot awaits."

Smith stared at the small SUV, noting the 4×4's smashed grill, dented hood, and broken headlights. He arched an eyebrow. "You think that piece of junk is still in good running condition?"

"Let us hope so, Jon," Kirov said with a bleak smile. "Otherwise we could be in for a very long, cold, and conspicuous walk."

The Russian propped their dazed captive up against the Niva's side. He tugged the rear passenger side door open. "Let's get him inside. Ms. Devin will sit up front by me. You take the back seat and keep your weapon aimed at our guest here. Make sure he stays down on the floor and out of sight."

Smith nodded. He turned toward the bleary-eyed ambulance doctor. "In you go, pal," he growled, using the barrel of his Makarov to prod the wavering man toward the open door.

Crack.

Their prisoner's head exploded, torn open by a high-velocity rifle round. Blood and bits of shattered bone sprayed across the Niva's upholstered interior. The dead man slid slowly down the side of the truck.

"Get down! Take cover!" Smith roared. He dived for the snow-covered asphalt just as another rifle bullet smashed the window right above his head. Splinters and shards of broken glass cascaded across the back of his neck and bounced off the street beside him.

Kirov and Fiona Devin raced for cover and dropped flat behind the boxy Russian-manufactured 4x4.

Panicked by the sudden burst of gunfire, the civilians who had been drawn to the accident scene fled, scattering in all directions like a flock of terrified geese. Some ducked out of sight behind the cars parked along the street. Others stumbled back inside the surrounding buildings.

Caught out in the open, on the wrong side of Kirov's vehicle, Smith rolled away to the right, heading for the shelter offered by the wrecked ambulance. A third 7.62mm round slapped into the street only inches away. It sent chunks of torn asphalt flying and then tumbled away past his ear, buzzing loudly like a malevolent, lethal wasp.

Panting with fear and exertion, Jon threw himself off to the side, rolling even faster now. He made it back to the mangled emergency vehicle and stopped moving. A fourth rifle bullet punched through torn metal and caromed off the ambulance's steel frame, showering him with sparks and tiny, jagged pieces of near-molten steel. Wincing, he brushed them away.

Smith thought fast, considering their options. Now what? So long as they stayed hidden behind solid cover, they were relatively safe from this unseen sniper. But that left them pinned down, unable to move or fight back effectively, and he could hear sirens closing in on them from several different directions.

He shook his head. Staying to surrender to the Moscow militia was not an option, not with Elena Vedenskaya's case notes in their possession and four enemy agents sprawled dead across the street. He shifted his grip on the 9mm Makarov, mentally preparing himself to make a quick dash back to where Kirov and Fiona Devin were taking cover.

One hundred and fifty meters up Povorskaya Street, Erich Brandt knelt down beside the open door of his black Mercedes sedan. Another man lay prone on the road next to him, peering intently through the telescopic sight of a long-barreled Dragunov SVD sniper rifle.

"They're all in good cover," the marksman reported coolly. "But at least I managed to nail Sorokin."

Brandt scowled. The "doctor," an ex–KGB officer named Mikhail Sorokin, had been one of his most reliable agents, a coldly professional killer who had never muffed an assignment. Up until now, that was. Then he shrugged, pushing away the momentary sense of regret. Although it had irked him to order Sorokin terminated, he had not been given any real choice. He would not risk leaving any of his operatives alive in enemy hands. "Can you flush the Americans out into the open?"

The other man shook his head slightly. "Not soon enough." He shrugged. "If they move anywhere on the street, I will kill them, but I cannot hit what I cannot see."

Brandt nodded tightly.

The sniper pulled his eye away from the scope and looked toward his superior. "Do we wait for the militia to arrest them? Their first squad cars will be here in a matter of minutes."

Brandt pondered that. Thanks to Alexei Ivanov, he carried official credentials that would pass muster with the local police. If the militia took any prisoners, they could certainly be cowed into handing them over to him. But whatever the immediate outcome, the surly, suspicious chief of the Thirteenth Directorate would discover that he had been lied to, and that at least one American intelligence officer was already exploiting the Moscow-based breach in HYDRA's operational security.

The blond-haired man grimaced. If so, it would be better by far to present the Russian spymaster with a fait accompli in the form of Smith, Fiona Devin, and their unknown accomplice — dead if necessary, alive and under interrogation if possible. He glanced down at the sniper waiting patiently for his orders. "We'll cut off their first avenue of retreat," he decided. "Disable their get-away vehicle."

The other man nodded calmly. "Easily done, Herr Brandt."

He put his right eye back against the telescopic sight, shifted his aim slightly, and squeezed the trigger. The SVD sniper rifle fired, barely kicking up as its long, well-balanced barrel recoiled gently against his shoulder.

Smith scrambled to his feet and crossed the short open space between the ambulance and Kirov's all-wheel drive SUV at a dead run. Another shot rang out. Still running flat-out, he dived forward, rolled on his shoulder, and came up crouching behind the Niva's battered front end. He held the Makarov in a two-handed shooter's grip, ready to fire immediately if any target presented itself in range.

"Very acrobatic, Doctor," Kirov called wryly. The silver-haired Russian and Fiona Devin were lying prone a couple of meters away. "I envy you your youthful agility."

Smith forced himself to grin back, mainly conscious of the pulse pounding in his ears. The sniper zeroing in on them was too damned good. And he was close enough to put his rounds almost anywhere he chose with absolute precision.

The 4x4 rocked suddenly, hit by yet another 7.62mm round. It tore into the engine compartment, hit the block, and ricocheted up and out through the crumpled hood. Within seconds, the marksman switched targets and fired again, this time sending a heavy slug straight into the Niva's fuel tank. Gasoline spilled out through the punctured metal, dripping onto the street at an ever-increasing rate. The next bullet hit the dashboard, smashing instruments and tearing through wiring.

The rifleman was destroying the Niva, Smith realized abruptly — methodically putting rounds into every key system and component. "They're trying to make sure we can't bug out," he told the others grimly. "We're being held in check here for the militia to deal with."

Fiona nodded. She bit her lip. "Does anyone have any bright ideas?"

"We leave," Kirov said simply. "Right now."

Fiona stared at him in disbelief. "And just how, precisely, do you propose that we do that?" she demanded. "This street will be swarming with militia in a minute or two. We won't get two blocks on foot. And the closest Metro station is at least a kilometer away."

"We liberate a car," Kirov replied, almost smugly. He jerked a thumb over his shoulder. "Take a look. We have plenty of options to choose from."

Smith and Fiona turned around. The Russian was right. There were at least half a dozen vehicles scattered across the road, deserted by their panicked owners when all the shooting started. Most had been abandoned so hurriedly that the keys were still in the ignition. Some still had their engines running.

Jon nodded quickly. "Good idea." He glanced back at Kirov. "But we'll need a distraction, something big. Otherwise that sniper out there will drop us one by one before we've gone even ten meters."

The Niva shuddered again, hammered by another high-velocity round into the fuel tank. The sickly sweet stench of gasoline grew stronger. Leaking fuel spilled out from under the vehicle, slowly melting a meandering path through the dirty snow piled up around its tires.

"Very true," Kirov agreed. He reached into his coat pocket and calmly pulled out a packet of matches. He bared his teeth in a quick, predatory grin. "Fortunately, the means for such a distraction are close at hand."

He struck a single match and used it to light the whole book, which blazed up in an instant. Then, without hesitating, the former FSB officer tossed the flaming matchbook under the Niva, right into the biggest puddle of gasoline. It went up with a soft *whoosh*. Bright white flames leaped high, igniting the gallons of fuel still sloshing in the bullet-torn tank. In seconds, the whole back end of the dark blue 4x4 was fully engulfed in fire.

From his position up the street, Brandt saw the flames erupt suddenly beneath the Niva, spreading fast until the whole vehicle was alight. Black smoke boiled outward from the pyre. "Excellent work, Fadayev," he told his marksman.

Smith and the others were trapped. With luck, that fire would flush them out of cover, right into the sights of his waiting sniper. If not, the loss of their get-away car at least robbed the Americans of any real chance to escape the militia speeding to the scene.

But then, as the cloud of smoke began spreading fast, Brandt's smile faded. Buildings and whole swathes of the street behind the burning sport utility vehicle were disappearing from view, shrouded in smoke. The pall created by the fire was acting as a screen, hiding the fugitives from view. "Do you have any targets yet?" he demanded.

"Negative. The smoke is too thick," the prone marksman said. He took his eye away from the scope on his rifle and looked up. "What are your orders?"

Brandt listened to the sirens growing louder. His face darkened. The Russians would be here in moments. At last he snapped, "We'll leave them for the militia and pick them up once they're in custody. Smith and his friends won't get far on foot."

Smith lay flat behind the blazing 4x4. This close to the flames, he could feel the heat searing his face. Smoke from the inferno stung his eyes. He breathed shallowly, trying hard not to drag too much of the acrid fumes into his lungs. Visibility around them dropped to just a few meters as the smoke cloud billowed across the street. He glanced at Kirov and Fiona.

The Russian nodded in satisfaction. "Now we go."

Without waiting any longer, they turned and loped away. Kirov led them toward a small two-door car, a dingy, off-white Moskvitsh that had clearly seen more than its share of accidents and harsh winters. Its worn-out, lawn-mower-sized engine sputtered and coughed, left stuck in idle when its driver fled.

Jon nodded to himself, approving the other man's choice. Of all the cars left abandoned on the street, the Moskvitsh was the cheapest, the least colorful, and the least noticeable. There were tens of thousands just like it on Moscow's streets. Even if someone spotted them commandeering the little car, the militia would have a very difficult time picking it out among all the rest.

Fiona climbed into the narrow back seat, while Smith and Kirov settled themselves in front, with the older man in the driver's seat. The Russian slammed the gearshift into reverse and backed up fast, cranking the steering wheel hard over. The Moskvitsh swung round through an arc and ended up facing away from the direction it had been going.

Kirov drove east at an easy clip, deliberately staying below the posted speed limit.

"Oleg," Fiona warned suddenly, leaning forward over the Russian's big shoulder. She pointed ahead through the dirty windshield. Flashing blue lights were coming into view, rushing up the road toward them at high speed. "We have company."

The first militia squad cars were converging on the scene of the reported accident and gun battle.

Kirov nodded coolly. "I see them." He spun the steering wheel again, turning right onto a narrower side street. He drove on a bit farther and then pulled over to the curb, parking right next to the Mongolian embassy. The elegant nineteenth-century building now housing Lithuania's embassy was just across the street. The ex–FSB officer reached down and flicked the little car's headlights off. He left the engine running.

Smith shifted around in the cramped seat, craning his neck to peer out through the Moskvitsh's small rear window.

In seconds, the first militia squad car flashed past their side street without slowing, still racing west up Povorskaya Street. Others followed in its wake, one after another, tearing along with their sirens wailing.

They all breathed out in relief. Slowly,

Kirov reached down and put the Moskvitsh in gear again. Then he pulled out and drove away, heading south, deeper into the Arbat district.

"What's our next move?" Smith asked quietly.

The older man shrugged. "First, we look for a place to ditch this stolen car, discreetly if possible. And then we find a safe house for you and Ms. Devin."

"And after that?"

"I try to think of some way to smuggle the two of you out of Russia as soon as possible," Kirov said flatly. "After what happened tonight, the Kremlin will mobilize every element of the state security apparatus to hunt you down."

"We're not leaving, Oleg," Fiona Devin said firmly. "Not yet, anyway."

"Fiona!" Kirov protested. "Don't be a fool! What can you possibly hope to accomplish by staying in Moscow?"

"I don't know yet," she said stubbornly. "But I do know that we still have a job to do here. And so long as that is true, I have no intention of tucking my tail between my legs and running."

Fiona held up the bloodstained binder. "Those bastards back there murdered Elena Vedenskaya to prevent her from passing these medical records to us. Right?"

283

Both men nodded slowly.

"Well, then," the dark-haired woman told them grimly. "As I see it, that means that Colonel Smith and I had better do our best to uncover the secrets they contain."

PART THREE

CHAPTER NINETEEN

Berlin

The Bundeskriminalamt (BKA) — the Federal Criminal Police — served as the German equivalent of the American FBI. Like the FBI, its several thousand law enforcement officers and forensic experts provided assistance and coordination for the separate police forces of the sixteen individual German states. And like the FBI, the BKA was also responsible for investigating a wide range of high-level crimes, among them, international arms and narcotics trafficking, money laundering, and terrorism.

The agency was in the middle of a large-scale reorganization. The bulk of its personnel and facilities were being gradually relocated to Berlin, with the predictable result being a certain amount of chaos and confusion as BKA units settled into unfamiliar locations around the city.

The State Security Division — charged with investigating high-level political crimes that threatened the Federal Republic — was no exception. Its Berlin-based officers and clerical staff now occupied a five-story building in the Nikolaiviertel, St. Nicholas' Quarter, a labyrinth of crowded streets, alleys, restaurants, and small museums along the brick-lined banks of the River Spree. The building itself was a modern reconstruction of a centuries-old structure that had once housed medieval merchants and artisans.

Inside the foyer, Otto Fromm sat behind a long counter, manning the front desk at the beginning of the long, dull night shift. He yawned, already bored with the tabloid newspaper he'd brought to keep himself occupied. As a young man straight out of technical school, he had joined the BKA as a lowly uniformed security guard, imagining himself one day promoted to chief detective on the basis of sheer merit. Twenty years later, he was still trapped in the same dead-end position, though at least with substantially higher pay and six weeks of vacation time.

The door from the outside opened in a quick gust of clean, cold air.

He looked up from his paper. A tall, long-legged young woman with fashionably short, almost spiky, auburn hair, a straight nose, firm chin, and very bright, deep blue eyes crossed the foyer, coming straight toward his desk. She was already unbuttoning her long winter coat, revealing a slender figure with small but firm breasts that set his pulse racing.

Fromm's eyes brightened at the sight of such an attractive woman, especially one without a wedding band on her left hand. His last live-in girlfriend had kicked him out of her apartment just six months ago and now his drinking pals were all urging him to "get back in the hunt." Unconsciously, he sat up straighter and smoothed back his unruly, thinning hair. "Yes, Fraulein?" he asked politely. "Can I help you?"

She handed him her Bundeskriminalamt identity card with a dazzling smile. "I'm sure you can. My name's Vogel. Petra Vogel. I'm with the Information Technology Division in Wiesbaden." Then she swung her leather attaché case lightly onto the top of the counter and unsnapped its flap, revealing an array of CD-ROMs nestled in separate compartments. "I'm here to install new software upgrades for your local-area network."

Fromm looked up at her, unable to conceal his bewilderment. "Now? But almost everyone here has already gone home for the night."

"That's precisely the point," the young woman said pleasantly, still smiling. "You see, to run the upgrades, it's possible that I'll have to shut down parts of your system for an hour or two. This way nobody is seriously inconvenienced or loses too much valuable computer time."

"But you still need an official authorization for that," Fromm muttered, fumbling quickly through the papers piled on his desk. He looked up at her in confusion. "And I don't see any approval for this software upgrade. There's nothing listed here. Plus, Herr Zentner, our IT specialist, is away on vacation for the next three weeks. Somewhere on the beach in Thailand, I think."

"Lucky for him," the auburn-haired woman said enviously. "I wish I could get away to the sun and sand, too." She sighed. "Look, I don't know why you don't have the right paperwork. Someone, somewhere, must have fouled things up. Wiesbaden was supposed to have faxed all that here yesterday."

She rummaged through one of the inner compartments of her attaché case and pulled out a folded sheet of paper. "Here's my copy. See?"

Chewing his lower lip nervously, the security guard got up from his chair. He read quickly through the copy that she handed him. Written on official letterhead and signed by the director of the Information Technology Division, it ordered Computer Specialist Petra Vogel to conduct a systems software upgrade at the

Bundeskriminalamt's Nikolaiviertel office.

Fromm's eyes brightened as he saw a discrepancy. "Here's the problem!" he said, pointing to a telephone number appearing at the top of the document. "This was sent to the wrong place. Our fax number here ends in 46 46. But your office in Wiesbaden sent this to 46 47 instead. That's probably the number of a local bakery or a flower shop or something."

The young woman leaned forward to take a look herself, bringing her face very close to his. He swallowed hard, suddenly feeling as though his shirt collar and tie were choking him. The fresh, clean floral scent of her perfume wafted into his flared nostrils.

"Unbelievable," she murmured. "They muffed it. And now the office in Wiesbaden is closed until tomorrow morning." She sighed. "So now what am I supposed to do? Go back to my hotel and kick up my heels while waiting for my director's slow-witted secretary to untangle the mess he's made?"

Fromm shrugged helplessly. "I'm sorry," he said. "But I don't see what else you can do."

The auburn-haired woman sighed in regret. "That's a shame." With a slight pout, she began closing her attaché case. "You see, I really wanted to finish this project tonight, so that I could take a day's leave tomorrow, to explore more of Berlin."

Fromm caught what he thought might be a subtle nuance in her words. He cleared his throat. "You have friends here to visit? Or family, perhaps?"

"As a matter of fact, no." She looked meaningfully up at him from under her long, half-lowered eyelashes. "I had hoped to find a new friend. Someone who knows all the ins and outs here in Berlin. Someone who could show me around . . . maybe even take me to the most exciting new clubs." Then she sighed. "But I guess I'll be tied up here instead, just trying to finish the job before my train leaves —"

"No, no, Fraulein," Fromm said in a strangled voice. "That won't be necessary." He held up her authorization letter. "Look, it's simple enough. What I'll do is make another copy of this for our records. Then we'll just pretend it arrived by fax, as it should have. And then you can go ahead and finish your work this evening, as planned."

"You could do that? Bend the rules that way for me, I mean?" the young woman asked.

"Oh, yes," Fromm said expansively, puffing out his chest. "Absolutely. I'm the senior security officer on duty. So it's not a problem. Not a problem at all."

"That would be wonderful," she said delightedly, smiling directly at him in a way that made his mouth go dry.

Twenty minutes later, at a landing on the building's deserted fifth floor, the woman who called herself Petra Vogel stood watching Fromm clomp heavily back down the central staircase running all the way to the ground level. Once he was well out of sight, CIA officer Randi Russell wrinkled her nose in disgust. "What an idiot," she murmured. "Luckily for me."

Then she took a deep breath, mentally preparing herself for the risky work ahead. Now that she had vamped her way in through the castle gates, it was time to storm the inner keep. She dipped her hand into her coat and came out with a pair of skintight surgical gloves.

She slipped the gloves on, then turned and entered the room unlocked for her by the ever-helpful Otto Fromm. She carried a set of lockpicks that would have done the job, but it was nice not to have needed them. Even the most sophisticated picks left small scratches inside locks that would show up under close investigation. This operation depended on her getting in and out of the Nikolaiviertel building without leaving hard evidence behind that could tie the CIA to the strange and unexplained actions of the phony Petra Vogel.

Randi closed the door firmly behind her and then carefully examined the layout of the room. Humming and clicking softly, various pieces of compact electronic equipment — sophisticated servers, a modular hub, and routers — lined the walls, connected by a maze of cabling. This was the heart of the State Security Division's local-area network. Every workstation, printer, and personal computer in the building was tied together by the hardware contained in this one room. Also from here, high-speed, high-security connections linked each office to the main computer systems, databases, and archives inside the BKA's Wiesbaden headquarters.

She nodded in satisfaction. This was exactly where she needed to be. With Karl Zentner, the division's IT specialist, still off on his long holiday in Thailand, it was unlikely that anyone else here in Berlin would waste much time poking around inside the computer network that he was responsible for maintaining. In the meantime, thanks to her forged ID card, fake paperwork, and Fromm's over-inflated sexual ego, she had a free pass to try some in-depth digging of her own.

Randi checked her watch. At best, she would only have an hour or so before the balding BKA security guard took his next coffee break and came tromping up the stairs to pester her. It was time to get busy. She moved quickly to a workstation set up in one corner. Rows of well-thumbed software and hardware tech manuals stuffed full of yellow Post-it notes indicated that this must be where Zentner spent most of his time. She pulled up the nearest swivel chair, sat down at the machine, and opened her attaché case.

Three of the six CD-ROMs it contained stored legitimate variations of the same information management, access, and retrieval programs used by the Bundeskriminalamt. Two were blanks. The sixth disc held something very different indeed, a piece of highly specialized and extremely advanced software prepared by the CIA's Office of Research and Development.

Humming quietly to herself, she tapped the keyboard space bar, kicking Zentner's flat-screen display out of sleep mode. A page topped by the BKA's logo — a stylized German heraldic eagle with outstretched wings — appeared, welcoming her to the State Security Division's local-area network. She slid the special CD-ROM into the appropriate drive. The computer whined softly, rapidly transferring information from the disc to its main hard drive. The default screen vanished.

For nearly a minute, Randi held her breath, waiting. Suddenly a small text box flashed onto the blank screen in front of her: DOWNLOAD COMPLETE. SYSTEM READY.

Her shoulder muscles tightened. Her eyes narrowed. Now to find out whether the Agency programmers who had written this code were worth more than their very modest government salaries and pensions. If not, what she was about to do would set off top-level computer security alarms from here to Wiesbaden and back again.

Frowning now as she concentrated, Randi leaned forward and carefully typed in a command of her own: ACTIVATE JANUS.

JANUS, code-named for the Roman god of gates, doors, and beginnings was a top-secret program devised by the CIA's technical experts to surreptitiously break past or bypass the defenses and alarm systems of a targeted computer network. Once inside those defenses, it was designed to identify, retrieve, and decrypt all of the user identities and passwords stored in the system. And then, by allowing her to masquerade as any BKA staffer — from the lowliest file clerk right up to the agency director himself — the JANUS software should make it possible for Randi to snoop through any file contained in the Bundeskriminalamt's most secret archives.

Or so ran the theory anyway.

But to the best of her knowledge, this was the program's first operational test. If there were any bugs in the JANUS code, Randi Russell knew she was about to find out about them the hard way.

For what felt like an eternity, the machine only seemed to whir and click and beep softly to itself. JANUS was busy spreading itself through the entire BKA computer system, rummaging first through the servers and workstations in this building and then rippling outward to those in the rest of Berlin, to Bonn, and the headquarters complex in Wiesbaden.

Randi fought the urge to stand and pace off some of the nervous energy she felt building up inside her. Though she understood the need in this case to rely on the competence of the CIA's technical people, she did not enjoy the sensation of dependence. She had always resented not being fully in control of her own fate and this was not a personality trait she had been able to hide. There were several memos to that effect in her Agency personnel file noting, with appropriate bureaucratic concern, both her "lone wolf" tendencies and willingness to bend rules and regulations whenever she believed it to be necessary.

A new text box flashed onto the display: SECURITY PENETRATION COMPLETE. ALL

FILES ACCESSIBLE. NO ALARMS DETECTED.

She sat back with a soft sigh of relief, feeling her shoulders and neck starting to unkink. She was safely inside the BKA system. Then she leaned forward again, intent on the necessary next step in this operation. Her fingers flashed over the keyboard, sending her next commands to JANUS. She ordered the program to retrieve every single report, dossier, and piece of correspondence that so much as mentioned Wulf Renke's name.

Again, she was forced to sit waiting for JANUS to work its black magic, matching the required passwords to classification levels and then sifting through hundreds of thousands of archived files, some of them digitized copies of paper records dating back as far as thirty years. One-line summaries of the relevant documents began crowding the screen, scrolling upward at a faster and faster pace. Most were from the BKA itself, but others appeared to be classified East German government documents obtained after German reunification.

Randi waited until the enormously long list came to an end and then punched in another order: COPY ALL TO DISC. Controlled by the imperatives laid down in JANUS, the Bundeskriminalamt computer system complied, obediently duplicating every file involving Renke onto the blank

CD-ROMs she inserted one after another. With that done, one last command purged the system of the CIA spy program, effectively erasing the most obvious traces of what she had done.

As soon as the BKA default screen popped back up on Zentner's display, she stood up, slid the various discs into her case, and headed for the door. Once she was away from this building, she could head to an Agency-owned safe house and get out of this disguise. The man-hungry Computer Specialist Petra Vogel would vanish forever, to the certain dismay of the unfortunate Otto Fromm.

Randi would then take the discs to the CIA's Berlin Station, where intelligence analysts would begin hunting for anomalies or for other clues. For anything that might explain Wulf Renke's mysterious ability to evade arrest by the German authorities.

One hour later, a small subroutine hidden deep inside the software which managed the Bundeskriminalamt's computer systems began its regular daily scan through certain tagged files, examining them for any signs of tampering or unexpected access. Almost immediately, the scan detected significant anomalies and began recording them. The information it collected activated previously unused sections of code within the concealed subroutine, triggering an emergency alert that was e-mailed to a personal computer outside the official BKA network.

From there, the encrypted e-mail went racing eastward, shunted through a succession of Internet servers until it reached its final destination — the Moscow offices of the Brandt Group.

Gerhard Lange read through the auto-generated report in worried silence. He pursed his thin lips, thinking through the implications of the information it contained. Coming as it did right on top of tonight's total failure to capture Smith and Fiona Devin, this latest development was deeply disturbing.

The slim ex–Stasi officer picked up his phone and dialed Brandt's direct cell number.

"Yes?" Erich Brandt snapped, answering on the first ring. "What is it now?"

"Someone is sniffing around the Renke files," Lange warned him quietly.

"Who?"

Lange sighed. "That is the difficulty. According to the sentry subroutine we planted inside the BKA computer system, several hundred separate files concerning Herr Professor Renke were just accessed by more than twenty different users, including the director himself, and all within a ten-minute period. What is more, all of those document requests were made from the same workstation, one assigned to the system administrator for a local-area network in Berlin."

For a moment, there was silence on the line. Then Brandt growled, "That's impossible."

"So I would think," Lange said softly.

"You believe this is the work of the Americans," Brandt said.

"That seems the likely answer," Lange agreed. "Certainly both the CIA and the NSA possess the technological means to conduct such a large-scale penetration of the Bundeskriminalamt archives."

"And the Americans have a motive," Brandt realized, speaking slowly and reluctantly.

Lange nodded. "Yes. If, that is, one accepts the probability that our security for HYDRA has been compromised to a much greater degree than we had first assumed."

"So it appears," Brandt said through gritted teeth. "Well, then, let us hope this latest news escapes the Russians."

Lange chose his next words very carefully. "If the Americans *are* probing Renke's past history, they could begin tracing our clandestine sources and assets inside the German government —"

"I am well aware of what they may learn," Brandt interrupted. "Listen closely, Gerhard. I want you to assemble a hunter-killer team and fly to Berlin. Leave tonight, if possible."

"And my orders?"

"You and your team will find and close this new security breach," Brandt said icily. "At any cost."

CHAPTER TWENTY

Washington, D.C.
Located on Lafayette Square across from the White House, the Hay-Adams Hotel was a Washington landmark. For nearly eighty years, American movers and shakers of all kinds — powerful politicians, federal cabinet officers, top White House aides, famous actors, and wealthy corporate executives among them — had been drawn to its beautifully decorated private rooms and public spaces.

The hotel's premier restaurant, the Lafayette Room, was famous for its award-winning cuisine and superb wine list. For nearly a year, it had also been the favorite haunt of a group of senior staffers for the House and Senate intelligence and armed services committees. Once every week, they met in the Lafayette Room for a "working lunch" with ranking analysts and advisors from the Pentagon, CIA, and State Department. These regular gatherings were seen as an opportunity to exchange information, hash through policy disputes, and smooth over occasional personality clashes in a friendlier, more collegial setting, one far removed from the usual political posturing up on Capitol Hill.

Inside the restaurant's pristine kitchen, one of the Lafayette Room's newest sous-chefs, a Romanian immigrant named Dragos Bratianu, worked deftly, swiftly combining snow peas, asparagus, and fresh green beans in a large, shallow bowl with several tablespoons of freshly minced chives and tarragon. He was putting the finishing touches on the special salad ordered by one of the State Department's most highly regarded experts on Russian foreign policy.

Bratianu risked a cautious, sidelong glance over his shoulder. The other white-coated men and women crowding the kitchen were all busy preparing their own dishes for the weekday lunch crowd. No one was paying close attention to him. This was his opportunity.

Dry-mouthed now, the short, stocky man dipped his right hand into a pocket of his apron and pulled out a small clear glass vial. With one quick, decisive gesture, he unsealed the vial and poured the clear, colorless liquid it contained into the salad he had just made. With that done, he lightly drizzled fresh walnut oil dressing over the bowl, tossed the ingredients to blend their flavors together, and then tapped a bell.

A waitress appeared at the summons. "Yes, Chef?"

"Your *Salade de Printemps* for Table Five," Bratianu told her calmly.

Without demur, she slid the salad bowl onto her silver tray, picked it up, and made her way out through the swinging doors into the elegant dining room beyond. The Romanian-born sous-chef breathed out in relief as the waitress disappeared. He had just earned another twenty thousand American dollars — tax-free money that would appear in his private Panamanian bank account as soon as he reported this latest success to his controller. Meanwhile, yet another deadly HYDRA variant was moving toward its intended victim.

Moscow

The Vodootvnodny Canal curved through a great arc from east to west before rejoining the Moscow River just a kilometer or so south of the Kremlin. The canal also marked the northern boundary of the Zamoskvoreche district, home to a growing population of foreigners, mostly European and American businessmen and their families. A row of pale yellow three- and four-story buildings lined the southern bank of the frozen canal. First built as luxurious town homes, they had long since been divided up into smaller flats.

Inside the living room of one of those apartments, Lieutenant Colonel Jonathan Smith turned away from the window. It was very late, near midnight, and the darkened streets outside were almost completely empty. A blue-and-white militia car drove slowly past and then turned left onto a bridge that ultimately ran straight to the Kremlin. Its glowing red taillights vanished in the solid winter blackness. He let the heavy drapes fall back behind him and looked narrowly at Kirov. "You're sure this place is safe?"

The Russian shrugged. "Absolutely safe? No, I cannot promise that. But this is certainly the most secure shelter I could find at such short notice." He smiled. "The landlord is an old friend of mine, a man who owes me many favors — including his life and freedom. Best of all, most of his other tenants are corporate executives rotating through Moscow on short-term assignments, so at least you and Fiona will not stand out as strangers."

Smith nodded. Kirov had a good point. In a city as crowded as Moscow, neighbors seeing anything or anyone out of the ordinary grew suspicious easily, and they were likely to report strangers to the authorities. But if the other residents in this apartment building were newcomers themselves, he and Fiona were less likely to draw unwanted attention. "So how long can we stay here without causing too much trouble for you or for your friend the landlord?"

"Certainly for two or three days," Kirov replied. "Perhaps longer. After that, it might be wise to move you to another safe house — possibly one outside the city."

"And what about you?" Fiona asked quietly. Pale and drawn-looking after the bloody close-quarters melee in the ambulance, she was sitting on a sofa, watching the two men closely. Elena Vedenskaya's case notes were spread out across a coffee table in front of her, along with a pad of notepaper she and Smith had been using to jot down rough translations of the obscure medical jargon and terminology they contained. Their work had been interrupted when the silver-haired Russian returned from a quick trip to purchase food, a few other staples, and some necessary toiletries. Acquiring new clothes would have to wait until the next morning.

"Me?" Kirov shook his head. "I am in no real danger. I'm quite certain that the men hunting for you and Jon never got a real look at my face." His eyes were bleak. "At least none of those who are still alive."

"But what about that SUV you abandoned? Can they trace it back to you?"

"No," Kirov told her confidently. "I bought the Niva for cash, through a series of go-betweens. The registration will not lead anyone to me."

"There's still a problem," Smith broke in.

Kirov raised an eyebrow. "Oh?"

"You and I have a past history of working together, both here and in Washington during the Cassandra smallpox crisis," Jon pointed out. "And these people, whoever they are, know my name and at least some of my background. They might start asking awkward questions about Oleg Kirov, formerly a general in the Federal Security Service."

"That is extremely unlikely," the Russian said simply. His teeth flashed in a quick, wry grin. "You see, before I left the FSB, I made sure that certain top-secret files were . . . erased. I can assure you that no one searching the records at the Lubyanka headquarters will find any information connecting me to the notorious Colonel Jonathan Smith." He shrugged his large shoulders again. "If you recall, even then the details of our temporary association were kept hidden from all but a select few."

Smith nodded, remembering.

Suddenly aware of his own enormous fatigue, Jon crossed the room and dropped into a battered old armchair across from Fiona. The adrenaline surge during their escape had faded away, leaving him feeling weak and weary. It was a relief to get off his feet, even if only for a few brief moments. He glanced back at the other man. "Okay, so you're in the clear for now. That's a relief and a big one. But I'd still like to know exactly what role you're playing in all of this mess." He grinned tiredly. "Not that I'm complaining, mind you — not after you saved both our necks. I'm just kind of curious about how you just happened to show up in the nick of time. Especially armed and driving a conveniently untraceable vehicle."

"Fiona asked me to provide distant cover for her during your rendezvous with Dr. Vedenskaya," the Russian said quietly. "I was glad to oblige her."

"Oleg runs a private security consulting firm, mostly advising companies interested in doing business here in Moscow," Fiona Devin explained. For the first time since their capture and narrow escape, her large eyes twinkled with mild amusement. "But he has a rather wide range of clients."

"Including your mysterious Mr. Klein," Kirov interjected calmly. He smiled broadly at Jon. "So once again we are colleagues."

Smith nodded slowly again as the pieces

began falling into place. The retired Russian officer was one of Fiona Devin's Moscow assets, a member of her handpicked Covert-One team. Pensioned off or not, it was a safe bet that Kirov still had reliable friends and trusted colleagues at every level of the Russian government. No wonder she had been so confident that she could vet his list of potential sources so quickly. And no wonder she had been so sure that Elena Vedenskaya's FSB security file had been scrubbed clean of any damaging information. How many other files had Kirov doctored before allowing himself to be purged by the Dudarev regime?

Jon studied the taller man silently for a few moments, wondering how he squared working for an American intelligence organization with the lifetime he had already spent as a faithful high-ranking officer in Russia's army and security services. Cases of divided loyalty all too often turned sour. Men, even the best men, cracked under the strain of deciding between abstract ideals and the closer ties of blood and nationality. Without thinking about how that might sound, he said as much out loud.

"I am still a Russian patriot, Doctor," Kirov shot back. The muscles around his jaw visibly tightened. "But I am not a blind or unthinking patriot. Dudarev and his supporters are leading the Motherland back into darkness, down an old, tyrannical path that will only bring us to disaster. So long as that is true and so long as the real interests of my country are not damaged, I see no harm in doing what I can to help you in this matter." He looked steadily at the American, and when he spoke again there was a distinct edge in his voice. "In the past, we have fought side by side and shed blood together, Jon. And now I ask you to put your trust in me one more time. Is that too much to expect, after all I have already risked for you — and for Ms. Devin?"

"No, it's not," Smith admitted, realizing abruptly that he had pushed the other man too hard. He rose to his feet so that he could look Kirov directly in the eyes. "I'm sorry, Oleg," he said quietly, offering his hand. "It was wrong of me to doubt either your honor or your integrity."

"In your place, I, too, would have such questions," the Russian assured him. "Suspicion and doubt are inherent perils in this game we play — the game of spies."

Both plainly abashed, the two men shook hands.

"Now that you and Oleg have decided that you're both loyal, noble, trustworthy, and paragons of all the other virtues, do you think you could finish helping me with Dr. Vedenskaya's notes?" Fiona asked Smith, unable to hide a bemused half-smile. She indicated the papers scattered across the coffee table. "My Russian is very good. But my knowledge of high-tech medical terminology is almost nonexistent. So unless you can explain what all these phrases mean, I'm not going to get very far in turning this material into comprehensible English."

Smith grinned back ruefully, acknowledging the justice of her complaint. Still faintly red with embarrassment, he sat back down on the sofa and picked up the next set of case notes. "You may fire when ready, Ms. Devin," he told her. "My brain is at your service."

With a barely suppressed chuckle, Kirov moved into the apartment's tiny kitchen to stow their supplies. He poked his head back into the living room only long enough to ask whether anyone wanted him to make tea to help them stay awake. Both did. Once that was done, he joined them, and together they fought their way through small, dense columns of Cyrillic typescript, struggling to make sense out of the various abbreviations and bits of medical shorthand Vedenskaya and the other doctors on her team had used.

This dreary, painstaking work took hours, lasting until well into the early morning. Though difficult to read and occasionally cryptic, Vedenskaya's notes were remarkably thorough. She had listed every conceivable particular of the first four victims — their names, ages, sex, socioeconomic status, and significant physical and mental characteristics. She had included detailed observations on the course of this mysterious disease in each person, from the first moment they were admitted to the hospital up to the very second they died. Every test result and autopsy report was there, with all the relevant data broken out and analyzed in dozens of different ways.

At last, Smith sat back with a discouraged sigh. His reddened eyes felt as though he had been rubbing them with sandpaper, and his neck and shoulders were so sore and stiff that they ached at the slightest movement.

"Well, what do you think?" Fiona asked softly.

"That we're no closer to understanding this puzzle than we were when we started," he said bluntly. "These notes essentially confirm everything Petrenko told me before he died. None of the victims knew each other. They all lived in widely separated sections of Moscow or the outer suburbs. They didn't have any common friends or acquaintances. Hell, they didn't seem to even share any of the same kinds of life or work experiences. There's absolutely nothing here that I can see operating as a natural vector for this illness."

"A vector?"

"A vector is any person, animal, or microorganism that transmits a given disease," Smith explained.

Kirov looked at him closely. "And that's important?"

Smith nodded. "It could be very important, since it strongly suggests this disease does not have its origins in nature. Which means that whatever killed those people could have been something cooked up in a lab, either accidentally or intentionally —"

He broke off suddenly, thinking hard. His mouth compressed into a thin, grim line.

"What is it, Colonel?" Fiona asked.

"A very ugly thought," Smith said quietly. He frowned. "Look, those affected by this outbreak seem to have been as different as any four human beings could possibly be, right?"

The other two nodded, puzzled.

"Well, it's almost as if they were selected as experimental subjects — chosen to test the action of some deadly organism or process on humans of varying ages, genders, and metabolisms."

"That *is* an ugly thought," Fiona agreed soberly. Her eyebrows rose. "You're thinking of that rumor Vedenskaya repeated, the one about that East German scientist, aren't you?"

"Yes, I am," Smith said. "If Wulf Renke is still alive, this first outbreak is just the sort of gruesome bioweapons test that sick son of a bitch would love to conduct." Then his shoulders slumped. "But even considering that possibility doesn't get us much further. I still haven't been able to zero in on a useful pattern in these case notes. They don't seem to contain any data that would give us a clearer idea of exactly where this illness comes from, or how it kills its victims, or even how the damned thing is transmitted."

"Which confronts us with a disturbing paradox," Kirov pointed out quietly. His eyes were cold. "If these records are so useless, then why have so many been murdered to prevent you from studying them?"

CHAPTER TWENTY-ONE

February 19
Berlin
Eighteen kilometers south of the city center, Berlin's Brandenburg International Airport was still shrouded in early morning fog when a small corporate jet touched down on Runway Twenty-Five-R. Its twin engines howled as the aircraft decelerated smoothly, rolling past rows of paired red and green lights that bordered the long strip of concrete. Halfway toward the brightly-lit terminal buildings, the jet turned off the runway, taxied to a freight apron near a huge Lufthansa maintenance hangar, and then rolled to a stop.

A black BMW sedan sat parked close by on the gleaming, wet tarmac.

Four lean, fit men wearing heavy overcoats and fur hats disembarked from the aircraft and strode quickly toward the waiting automobile. Each of them carried a lightweight overnight bag, but no other luggage. Their cold, hard eyes were constantly in motion, checking and rechecking their surroundings for potential threats or any other signs of trouble.

A fifth man, this one shorter, heavier-set, and somewhat older, came forward from the BMW to meet them. He offered their leader a cool, correct nod. "Welcome to Germany, *mein Herr*. How is Moscow these days?"

"Cold and dark," Gerhard Lange said bleakly. "Just like here." He looked down at the older man. "Have our immigration and customs clearances been granted?"

"Everything is arranged. The authorities will make no difficulties," the other man assured him.

"Excellent." The slim, ex–Stasi officer nodded in satisfaction. "And the special equipment we will need? You have it?"

"In the trunk," the heavyset man told him.

"Show me."

The older man led Lange and the three members of his team around to the back of the BMW. He unlocked the large trunk with a flourish and stood aside, allowing them to examine the contents of the five metal cases stacked inside.

Lange smiled grimly as he noted the array of lethal weaponry secured in four of the five carrying cases: Heckler & Koch submachine guns, H&K and Walther-manufactured pistols, spare ammunition, blocks of plastic explosives, detonators, and timing devices. The fifth contained sets of body armor, communications gear, black jumpsuits, assault vests, and forest-green berets similar to those worn by Germany's elite GSG-9 antiterrorist detachment. Clearly, Brandt was taking no chances. His hunter-killer team would be equipped for almost every conceivable contingency.

"Do you have a target yet?" the heavyset man asked curiously.

Lange's thin mouth tightened. "Not yet." Frowning, he closed the trunk and stepped back. "But I expect to receive our next set of orders from Moscow very soon."

Near the Kazakhstan-Russo Border

A range of low, barren hills rose north of the Derkul River. There were a few scattered stands of stunted trees crowning the heights, but most of the shallow slopes were open ground, covered only by a carpet of long dry grass. Across the river, the terrain flattened out, spreading south and east beyond the distant horizon. This was the northwestern edge of the vast steppes that made up so much of Kazakhstan.

Spetsnaz Senior Lieutenant Yuri Timofeyev lay concealed in the tall dead grass just below the crest of one of the low hills. The muted tan and brown patterns of his camouflage smock and hood blended almost perfectly with the natural cover, rendering him effectively invisible to anyone more than twenty meters away. He peered through his binoculars, again scanning the highway and railroad running parallel to the river below them.

After a minute, he lowered his binoculars and glanced at the man next to him. "Time: 0700 hours. I see two ten-ton trucks, both civilian, and one bus, mostly full. There is also a black Volga sedan, probably an official vehicle of some sort. They are all moving east toward Ural'sk at around eighty kilometers an hour. There is nothing coming west just now."

His companion, Warrant Officer Pausin, obediently jotted down his findings in a small notebook, adding them to the long list detailing the vehicle and rail traffic they had observed over the past forty-eight hours. "Got it, sir," he muttered.

"How much longer do we have to sit on our asses here, counting goddamned cars and locomotives?" groused a third Spetsnaz soldier, this one concealed a few meters off to the side. He cradled a short-barreled AKSU-74 submachine gun, a cut-down variant of the standard Russian assault rifle.

"As long as I say so, Ivan," Timofeyev told him bluntly. Then he shrugged. "And I say we stay here until headquarters sends me new orders on this little machine." He gently patted the long-range portable radio set up beside him in the withered grass.

The three Russian commandos, all hard-bitten veterans of the endless fighting in Chechnya, were members of a special long-range reconnaissance group. They had slipped across the border with Kazakhstan two nights ago and established this hidden observation post overlooking the junction of two major roads and the only major stretch of railroad along the northwest Kazakh frontier. Their orders were to monitor all traffic moving on those lines of communication, paying special attention to any military or border patrol units. So far they had seen very few. Most of Kazakhstan's small, poorly equipped army was stationed far to the east, along its border with the People's Republic of China.

"It's still a waste of time," the third soldier, a sergeant named Belukov complained, still clearly unhappy and bored.

"Would you rather be out chasing after the Mujs?" Pausin asked with a grin, referring to the tough Chechen guerrilla fighters.

"Christ, no," Belukov admitted with a

shiver. Their last combat tour in Chechnya had been a prolonged nightmare, full of sudden, vicious ambushes and costly hit-and-run raids by both warring sides. "But I don't see the point of this reconnaissance. The only way this crap makes sense is if we're going to invade. And why should we bother fighting over this dump?" He waved a hand over the desolate, empty steppe stretching off into the gray, half-lit distance.

"Because Kazakhstan once was ours. Nearly half of those who live here are ethnic Russians, people of our own kindred," Timofeyev said quietly. "And because it is sitting on huge deposits of oil, natural gas, bauxite, gold, chrome ore, and uranium — all the precious stuff President Dudarev's dreams are made of —"

He broke off suddenly, hearing a horse whinny behind them. The Spetsnaz lieutenant and his two men swung round in surprise — and saw a young boy staring down at them in astonishment from the top of the hill.

The boy, no more than twelve or thirteen years old, wore the long wool coat, loose white shirt, and baggy brown trousers tied at the waist of a typical Kazakh herdsman. He held the reins of a shaggy steppe pony, which was busy nuzzling the withered grass. A bedroll, tent, and supplies were piled up behind the pony's saddle.

Carefully, Timofeyev and his men rose to their feet. "What are you doing here?" the Russian snapped. His hand edged slowly, almost imperceptibly, toward the holster at his side. "Well?"

"My father and I are scouting the land, preparing for the spring," the boy said quickly, still staring with wide eyes at the three camouflage-smocked soldiers. "When we move our herds out of their winter pens around Ural'sk, we need to know where the best forage and water will be found."

"Your father is with you?" Timofeyev asked gently.

"Oh, no." The boy shook his head proudly. "He is riding the land to the west. This stretch of hill country is my responsibility."

"You are a good son," the Spetsnaz lieutenant agreed absentmindedly. Smoothly, he drew his pistol — a silenced P6 Makarov — worked the slide to chamber a round, aimed, and pulled the trigger.

Hit high in the chest, the boy rocked back under the impact. His eyes widened even further, now in horror, as he stared down at the blood running down his torn white shirt. Then, slowly, he fell to his knees.

Timofeyev chambered another round

and shot him again, this time in the head. The Kazakh boy crumpled and went down. He lay curled up among the tall stalks of dead grass.

His pony whinnied in alarm. Panicked by the hot, coppery smell of fresh blood, the small sturdy horse reared up on its hind legs and then broke free, galloping back over the hill and out of sight. Belukov, the Spetsnaz sergeant, snarled and sprinted toward the crest, followed a second later by his two comrades.

At the top, he tucked the AKSU-74 against his shoulder and sighted down the barrel, drawing a bead on the steppe pony racing away down the reverse slope. He flipped the firing selector to full automatic.

"No!" Timofeyev knocked the submachine gun down before the sergeant could open fire. "Shooting the beast now would make too much noise. Let it go. The farther that horse runs the better for us. This way, when the Kazakhs come looking for the boy, they won't know where to start."

Belukov nodded sullenly, accepting the reproof.

"You and Pausin dig a hole over there," the lieutenant continued, jerking his thumb toward the closest stand of trees. "While you're burying the body, I'll signal headquarters that we're moving to our alternate position."

"Shouldn't we head back across the border?" Belukov asked in surprise. "Before the Kazakhs start their search for the kid?"

"We have our orders," Timofeyev reminded him icily. He shrugged. "One regrettable death makes no difference to our mission. After all, when the balloon goes up, other innocents will die. That is the nature of war."

CHAPTER TWENTY-TWO

Berlin

Randi Russell took the steps up to the embassy's third-floor two at a time. She paused briefly at the landing to clip her Central Intelligence Agency photo ID card to the breast pocket of her navy blue jacket. Then she pushed open a fire door and turned left, marching fast down a wide corridor. Harried-looking embassy file clerks carrying armloads of visa applications and reams of other official correspondence from one busy office to another saw her coming and moved quickly out of her way.

The tall, square-jawed Marine corporal on duty outside the secure conference room stepped forward to meet her. With one hand on his holstered sidearm, he peered closely at her ID and then nodded. "You can go right on in, Ms. Russell. Mr. Bennett is expecting you."

Inside the conference room itself, Curt Bennett, the head of the technical team sent out from the CIA's Langley headquarters, barely glanced up when she came in.

Red-eyed with fatigue, unshaven, and thoroughly disheveled, he sat hunched over a pair of linked personal computers set up at one end of a long table. He and his team had spent all of last night and the morning so far dissecting the material she had copied from the Bundeskriminalamt archives. Cups of cold coffee and half-full soda cans were scattered around the room, some on the table, some on the floor, and some perched precariously on chairs. Even the air smelled stale.

Randi pulled up a chair and sat down beside him. "I got your page, Curt," she told the senior analyst — a short, fidgety man with very little hair and a pair of thick, wire-rimmed spectacles. "What can you tell me?"

"That your wild-eyed guess was on target," he replied, with a quick, toothy grin. "Someone inside the BKA has been a bad, bad boy — at least where Herr Professor Wulf Renke is concerned."

Randi breathed out, feeling very much as though an enormous weight had been lifted off her shoulders. The more she had studied Renke's past, the more she had become convinced that someone high up in German law enforcement was protecting him. How else had the biological weapons scientist so easily avoided capture after the Wall came down? And how else was he

326

able to travel, seemingly at will, to so many of the world's rogue states — Iraq, North Korea, Syria, and Libya, among others?

Of course, being sure of her hunch was one thing. Risking her career and the Agency's relationship with its German ally by breaking into the BKA's archives was quite another. Hearing that her gamble had paid off was a huge relief. If this operation went sour, the CIA brass at Langley could still toss her to the wolves, but at least they could no longer do it while claiming she was wrong on the facts.

Randi leaned forward. "Show me."

"Most of the files JANUS picked up were innocuous," Bennett said. His fingers flew over the keyboard of one of the linked computers while he talked, rapidly bringing documents onto its display screen and then just as rapidly whisking them back into virtual electronic oblivion. "Standard stuff, really. Pretty much the same kind of thing we have on Renke in our databases — reports of rumors heard by field agents, mentions of possible sightings that didn't pan out, routine follow-up queries from senior officials . . . all that jazz."

"So what's different?" she asked.

"What's different, Randi," Bennett told her with another big grin, "is that the BKA computer system is full of ghosts."

"Ghosts?" Randi asked steadily.

"Deleted files and e-mails," the CIA computer expert explained. "See, most word processing and database management programs have a common flaw, at least from the vantage point of anyone trying to erase incriminating documents or records."

"Which is?"

Bennett shrugged. "You can hit the delete key and see a file go 'poof.' But that doesn't really mean that it's gone forever, shredded into unreadable bits and bytes. It's actually just been shuffled away, ready to be overwritten when the system needs the space. But since e-mails and most files don't take up that much room — especially on huge, interconnected systems — they're usually still there, waiting to be retrieved by the right recovery software."

"Gee, Curt, let me guess," Randi said drily. "That's something you included in JANUS."

"Yep. That we did."

"But aren't there programs designed to wipe deleted files permanently?" she asked after a moment's thought.

Bennett nodded. "Sure. And a lot of private companies and government agencies use them routinely these days. But almost no one ever bothers going back through their systems to scrub out all the old, supposedly deleted, material that's been accumulating in various nooks and crannies."

"Like these ghost files you discovered," Randi realized.

"Exactly," the CIA technical expert confirmed. "And that's how we spotted the way someone inside the BKA has been shielding Wulf Renke. Check out some of his early handiwork." With a few quick commands, he pulled up a file on one of the computers.

Randi studied the displayed document in silence for a few moments, watching as Bennett clicked from page to page. It was a digitized version of Renke's official East German government personnel dossier, complete with a black-and-white photograph of the scientist's face, his fingerprints, a detailed physical description, and brief records of his birth, education, and research. The picture showed a jowly, round-faced man with wavy, dark hair and thick, bushy eyebrows.

"That's the one the Bundeskriminalamt has in its current archives," Bennett said flatly. "The data they send out whenever some other law-enforcement or intelligence agency — say us, or the FBI, or MI6 — gets interested in tracking down Renke and requests information from the German government."

"But there's another version of the dossier?" Randi guessed. "An earlier copy of the original that someone erased?"

Bennett nodded. "Watch this." Again, his fingers danced across the keys. Another set of digitized images from Renke's East German personnel file appeared on the second computer screen.

Randi glanced from one to the other, comparing them. Her eyebrows rose in dismay. "Jesus," she muttered.

The original version of the file showed a different photograph of a very different-looking man, this one much slimmer, with short white hair, and a neatly trimmed beard and mustache. The typed physical description matched this photograph, and it was clear, even on a quick inspection, that the fingerprints in this dossier were not the same ones appended to the newer file.

"No wonder no one ever lays a glove on Renke," Randi said bitterly. "Thanks to that forged dossier, we've been looking for the wrong guy, probably somebody who's been dead since at least 1989. Meanwhile, the real Wulf Renke can waltz in and out of just about any country he chooses, confident that his fingerprints and face won't set off any warning bells."

"Yep," Bennett agreed. He gently patted the side of one of the computers. "And the more we dig into the material you swiped, the more we find evidence of a continuing pattern of protection for Herr Professor Renke. For pretty much the past fifteen years, any genuine sightings of Renke have been routinely altered by the same BKA source. And anyone trying to follow up on those forged reports must have found themselves tearing off on a series of really wild-goose chases."

For a moment, Randi eyed the shorter man carefully. Then she grinned. "Okay, Curt. I know you're itching to dazzle me with your knowledge. So spill it. Who is the traitor inside the Bundeskriminalamt? Who's been covering up for Renke all these years."

"His name is Ulrich Kessler," Bennett said matter-of-factly. "Basically, the guy's electronic fingerprints — his network user ID and his passwords — are all over those deleted files. Plus, he was perfectly positioned to help Renke evade arrest when the Wall went down."

"How so?"

"Kessler was the ranking BKA officer in charge of the original investigation," Bennett told her bluntly. "The Renke case was almost entirely his show, right from its promising start all the way to its inglorious and frustrating finish."

"Swell. Just swell." Randi stared at the "ghost" dossier for a few seconds more and then shook her head in disgust. "And where is this son of a bitch Kessler stationed now?"

"Right here in Berlin," Bennett replied. "But he's been promoted a long way up through the ranks." He smiled cynically. "Probably as a reward for his first big failure, at least if the Germans work the same way we do."

Randi snorted. "Go on. Give me the bad news."

"Ulrich Kessler is one of the BKA's most senior administrators," Bennett said quietly. He shrugged. "In fact, he's basically one of the right-hand men for Germany's Minister of the Interior."

CHAPTER TWENTY-THREE

Strike Force Lead, 164th Guards Bomber Aviation Regiment

The twin-tailed Su-34 fighter-bomber raced low over the gently rolling countryside, roaring southwest through the pitch-black night at nearly eight hundred kilometers an hour. The aircraft shuddered and bounced sporadically, buffeted by turbulent currents of warmer and colder air.

The Su-34's two-man crew sat side-by-side in its large cockpit, with the pilot/commander on the left and the navigator/weapons officer on the right. Both crewmen were sweating now in their G-suits, intensely focused on the mission at hand. Softly glowing multi-function displays allowed each man to monitor the critical systems under his control. But the pilot, a sturdy, middle-aged Russian Air Force major, spent almost every moment peering intently through his infrared heads-up display, or HUD, carefully scanning the sky and ground ahead.

To help avoid detection by enemy radar,

they were flying at an altitude of less than two hundred meters — and at this speed that left no room for pilot error or inattention. Small pools of white light, signs of isolated villages and lone farm compounds, streaked toward them out of the green-tinted darkness and then vanished just as quickly astern.

"Twenty kilometers to primary target," the navigator, a younger captain, announced quietly at last. He pushed a button on one of the displays set at his right knee. "Cue up."

"Understood," the major muttered, impatiently blinking away a small droplet of sweat that stung his right eye. A small box appeared on his HUD, above and just a few degrees to the left of the Su-34's current flight path. The box was a navigation cue supplied by their onboard computer — a visual guide to their primary ground attack target. He pulled back on the stick, climbing steeply to two thousand meters or so and turning slightly until the target box was centered on his display.

The brighter glow of city lights appeared ahead, spreading across the horizon as they closed in. A web of roads and rail lines converged on the growing sea of lights, cutting straight across the darkened landscape. The darker ribbon of a wide river, the Dnipro, came into view to the east.

Days and weeks of intensive map study paid off as he recognized the outer eastern suburbs of Kiev, Ukraine's capital.

"Fifteen kilometers," the Su-34's navigator reported. He touched another set of buttons. "Ordnance guidance systems active. Coordinates downloaded."

Suddenly a warning tone sounded in the major's headset.

"Search radar spike!" the navigator snapped, scanning his defense displays frantically. "Detection alert! Right rear quadrant!"

"Jam it," the major growled. They had been picked up by Ukrainian radar, probably those sited at the large air defense complex outside Konotop. He snorted softly in disgust. According to the mission brief, covertly inserted Spetsnaz teams were supposed to have destroyed those radars fifteen minutes ago. So much for the Army's arrogant, fawned-over commandos, he thought coldly.

Then he shrugged. Even in these days of high-tech combat, of satellites and precision-guided weaponry, the old adage that no plan ever fully survived contact with the enemy was still true. War was always the province of random chance, uncertainty, and human and machine error.

Beside him the navigator was busy with the controls on his console, trying to jam the powerful Ukrainian search radar with the Su-34's built-in electronic countermeasures systems. It would be a miracle if he managed it, but every extra second he bought them was valuable. The range-to-target indicator on the HUD now showed twelve kilometers. The target cue box flashed red. They were almost in range of their primary target, the wartime headquarters for the Ukrainian Defense Council.

A new, shriller tone sounded in the major's earphones.

"Weapons radar lock-on!" his crewmate warned. "SAM launch detected! Two missiles inbound. Pattern indicates they are S-300s. Commencing active and passive defense measures now!"

"Shit," the major said under his breath. The S-300 was one of the most modern long-range surface-to-air missiles in the Ukrainian arsenal, the equivalent of the American Patriot missile.

The Su-34 shuddered briefly as onboard chaff dispensers fired. Cartridges popped out and detonated behind the speeding fighter-bomber. Within a second, clouds of thousands of tiny Mylar strips blossomed in the air. Each ultra-thin strip of chaff was precisely cut to match the wavelength used by the enemy radar locked on to them. With luck, the rapidly widening chaff blooms would decoy the incoming

SAMs away from them.

"Come on. Come on!" the major heard himself muttering under his breath, still grimly holding his aircraft on course despite the temptation to begin immediate evasive maneuvers. The target box turned green. They were in range.

"Weapons away!" he snarled, punching the release button on his stick. Immediately, the Su-34 jolted upward, several thousands of kilos lighter as four precision-guided bombs tumbled away from under its wings. Without waiting any longer, the colonel yanked the stick hard left, rolled the aircraft upside down, and dove for the ground in a tight, hard, multiple-G turn.

He rolled out of the dive barely a hundred meters off the deck — so close to the ground that trees, barns, houses, and electric power pylons appeared out of the darkness and disappeared almost before they even registered as solid objects in his vision. The warning tone in his headphones fell silent.

"Radar lock broken!" his navigator confirmed, breathing easier. "We're below their horizon."

The major yanked his head around, craning his neck to look through the clear canopy behind them. A succession of dazzling white flashes cascaded across the horizon, momentarily turning the black night into brilliant day.

"Bomb impact," the navigator said quietly. "The computer predicts that all weapons hit the designated target."

Suddenly everything outside the Su-34's cockpit went black.

A new voice sounded in their headsets. "Attack simulation complete. Stand-by."

With a shrill hydraulic whine, the canopy swung up, revealing a cavernous hangar filled with several other large box-like Su-34 flight simulators. The other machines were still in motion, twisting and tilting rapidly while computer-driven displays provided crews with realistic views of the sky and ground outside their wildly maneuvering aircraft.

The major frowned, thinking back over the events of the past hour. "Reset the mission, Controller," he said, speaking into his throat mike. "This time I want to try a slightly different flight path to see if we can avoid detection from Konotop when we pop up to drop our bombs."

His navigator glanced across the cockpit at him with a weary grin. "That was our fifth time through this attack run today, Sergei Nikolayevich. We've been in the simulators twelve hours a day for three days now, running through every possible permutation and wrinkle. Couldn't we take a break for a bit, at least just to stretch our legs?"

The major shook his head. "Not yet, Vladimir," he told the other man firmly. He shrugged. "You've seen the warning orders from Moscow. We've only got two more days to train here before the whole regiment deploys to Bryansk. And I don't buy any of the nonsense about this being just a so-called emergency readiness exercise."

The Su-34 squadron commander looked seriously at his subordinate. "Remember, if we do wind up carrying out this air strike on Kiev, there won't be any room for serious mistakes or miscalculations. There won't be any second chances if we screw up during the real mission. We'd better be damned ready, or we're going to end up dead."

CHAPTER TWENTY-FOUR

The Kremlin

Russian President Viktor Dudarev maintained his private office in the central section of the triangular, yellow-and-white Senate building. In sharp contrast to the incredibly ornate ceremonial audience chambers that were scattered throughout the other Kremlin palaces, this small, rectangular room was furnished simply and practically, with only a few touches of classical elegance.

The elaborate coat of arms of the Russian Federation hung on the wall behind Dudarev's malachite-topped desk. Two flags flanked the desk — on the left, Russia's white, blue, and red national banner, and on the right, the more intricate and colorful Presidential Standard. These banners were the only traces of bright color in the entire office, which was otherwise marked by dark oak paneling, a high molded ceiling painted in muted yellows and eggshell whites, and the faded green, red, and ochre geometric designs of a centuries-old Astrakhan rug. Along the interior walls stood bookcases filled with rare volumes and up-to-date reference works. Between the room's two windows stood a long oak table surrounded by straight-backed chairs.

Konstantin Malkovic occupied one of those chairs. He glanced across the table at Dudarev and then quickly at the stocky, gray-haired man seated next to the Russian president. The Serbian-born billionaire hid a frown. The unexpected presence of Alexei Ivanov, the dour head of the FSB's Thirteenth Directorate, at this critical meeting disturbed him.

He sensed the same uneasy mood in the man sitting on his own right, Erich Brandt. Before they arrived at the Kremlin, the former Stasi officer had notified him that Ivanov was likely to make trouble for them over HYDRA's unfortunate security lapses. Studying the Russian spy chief's sternly impassive face, Malkovic decided Brandt was probably correct. Something about Ivanov's hooded look reminded him of a big cat — a tiger or a leopard — lazily eyeing those whom it considered potential prey.

It was an image he found unsettling.

When he had first opened negotiations with the Russians, the German had warned him of the potential dangers, reminding him that, "When you try to ride the tiger, sometimes the tiger eats you." At the time, Malkovic had dismissed Brandt's concerns, judging them far too pessimistic. Now, sitting across the table from the grim head of the Thirteenth Directorate, the billionaire began to understand his subordinate's warnings.

With an effort, Malkovic forced those unwelcome thoughts away. Perhaps his nerves were only playing tricks on him. This was a moment of imminent triumph, the payoff for years of risky, expensive research and intricate planning. This was not a time to fret. He turned his attention back to the large screen set up at the head of the table. Colonel Piotr Kirichenko, Dudarev's military aide stood there, using a hand-held controller to display the different map slides and charts that comprised this Most-Secret briefing.

"The tank, motor rifle, Spetsnaz, and combat aviation units earmarked for Operation ZHUKOV continue to deploy from their peacetime bases to their designated war concentration areas," Kirichenko said, using the controller to highlight key points along Russia's borders with Ukraine, Georgia, Azerbaijan, and Kazakhstan. "So far, there are no indications that the United States or its allies have detected the magnitude of these troop transfers. Or that they understand their real significance."

"The West's ignorance is thanks largely to HYDRA, the special weapon I have supplied," Malkovic interjected. Whatever Ivanov's purpose here today, it was always best to remind these Russians of just how much they owed him. "By killing so many of their best intelligence analysts, my agents have made it almost impossible for the CIA, MI6, or any of their counterparts to pierce the more conventional veil of secrecy you have drawn over these movements." He smiled pleasantly. "Naturally, the same holds true for the countries which are your intended victims. Once HYDRA has run its course, too few of their key military commanders and political leaders will remain alive to coordinate any effective opposition to your operations."

"Yes, it is quite clear that this viral assassination weapon of yours has proved its worth . . . thus far," Dudarev agreed coolly.

Ivanov simply shrugged. His broad face showed no real emotion.

The Russian president nodded to Kirichenko. "Continue, Piotr."

"Sir." The colonel obeyed. "Once ZHUKOV commences, our long-range aviation regiments will conduct simultaneous strikes against a wide range of targets — command and control facilities, air defense sites, airfields, and enemy troop concentrations." He touched a button on the controller. Dozens of red stars appeared on the map, identifying targets scattered widely across the former Soviet republics slated for reconquest.

"At the same time, our tanks and motorized infantry units will advance, moving rapidly to secure their designated objectives," Kirichenko went on enthusiastically. Arrows slashed across the map, driving hundreds of kilometers deep into hostile territory to secure important cities, bridges, road and rail junctions, and vital industrial areas. Whole swathes of the map turned red, indicating their planned occupation and forcible return to Russian control — all of Kazakhstan, Georgia, Azerbaijan, and Armenia, and the entire eastern half of Ukraine.

Malkovic nodded, paying less and less attention as Dudarev's aide began a detailed appreciation of the precise units involved, their strengths and equipment, and their specific orders. To his way of thinking, these were mere tactical details, important only to the generals and other military men involved. He was more interested in the bigger picture, in contemplating how this operation would shift the balance of power around the globe.

The ZHUKOV plan made excellent strategic, political, and economic sense. For

Russia, it meant securing more defensible borders, reclaiming vast regions rich in natural resources and heavy industry, and bringing tens of millions of ethnic Russians back under the Kremlin's authority and protection. In the long run, it would mark the beginning of a grand effort to reclaim Russia's rightful place as one of the world's great powers, as an imperial nation whose strength would someday again rival that of the United States. In the short term, crushing the most successful of the new democracies surrounding Russia was vital to Dudarev's own political survival. For now, a majority of Russia's citizens supported his authoritarian rule, but there were signs of rising discontent — discontent he blamed on the democratic examples set by its one-time subject peoples.

For Malkovic himself, ZHUKOV represented the opportunity to become one of the richest and most powerful men in all of human history. That was a dream he had nurtured from his childhood as a despised, poverty-stricken refugee drifting around Europe. As he grew older and began to realize the extent of his skills — especially his uncanny ability to predict the future movements of financial and commodities markets — the dream had turned into a burning desire, a driving passion above all others.

Now fantastically wealthy, he exercised a substantial measure of influence over several governments in Europe, Africa, and Asia — both through his overall economic clout and through direct bribes to susceptible politicians and bureaucrats. His enormous holdings also allowed him to subtly manipulate the operations of banks, brokerage houses, investment firms, pharmaceutical labs, oil companies, arms manufacturers, and other industries around the world. Through the Brandt Group, he commanded a force of hired killers and spies, enabling him to act clandestinely and violently if necessary against his personal enemies and business rivals. But, of late, he had discovered there were still limits to his power. To his dismay, there were politicians he could not bribe or threaten, corporations he could not buy, and laws and regulations he could not yet overturn or safely ignore.

And so Malkovic had begun scheming to find a way to increase his personal wealth and power at least ten-fold. Long ago, in the immediate aftermath of the Cold War, he had secured the services of various Soviet-bloc weapons scientists — Wulf Renke among them. At the time he had only imagined developing a discreet side venture for one of his shell companies, the business of supplying unconventional armaments to the world's richest rogue states in return for huge sums of thoroughly illegal cash.

But when Renke came to him with the HYDRA breakthrough — the ultimate precision-guided assassin's weapon — the Serbian-born billionaire had seen its potential in a single shattering instant. Control over this undetectable, unstoppable, and incurable weapon would give him the power he had long desired. With it, he could break nations whose leaders opposed him, and reward those who allied themselves with his purposes.

Under Viktor Dudarev, Russia had chosen the path of wisdom.

As payment for use of the HYDRA weapon to soften up their enemies in the West and the former Soviet republics, Dudarev and his allies in the Kremlin had signed solemn and secret agreements with Malkovic, sealing a bargain that benefited both sides. By crippling the West's intelligence services, HYDRA was making it possible for Russia to plan, organize, and conduct its military campaign without interference from America and its allies. Once the shooting started, the Europeans and Americans were sure to protest fiercely, but if they were caught by surprise it was extremely unlikely that they would risk a wider war by intervening. Presented with the hard fact of Russian troops on the ground and firmly in control, the Americans would blink, reluctantly accepting reality.

In turn, when Russia's conquests were complete, the billionaire would own the lion's share of the captured oil, natural gas, mining, armaments, and other industries. Within a short time, the profits from these new holdings would make him the richest man in the world, far eclipsing any possible rival.

Malkovic gloried in that approaching prospect. Fools argued that wealth was the root of all evil. Wise men knew better: Money was only a lever, a tool that could be used to remake the world as one saw fit.

"When will you attack?" he heard Brandt ask.

Kirichenko looked at Dudarev, received a brief nod, and answered the question. "ZHUKOV will commence in less than five days," he replied. "The first Spetsnaz raids and air strikes will begin a few minutes after midnight on February 24. Our tanks and other troops will cross the frontier shortly after that."

"Without prior provocation?" Brandt said cynically. "Forgive me, Colonel, but that seems somewhat . . . unsubtle."

Ivanov leaned forward in his seat with a thin, humorless smile. "There will be ample provocation, Herr Brandt." His eyes were cold. "For example, in Ukraine, special intelligence strongly suggests there may soon be a regrettable terrorist incident, one that will kill a great many innocent ethnic Russians."

Brandt nodded coolly. "I see. That is certainly convenient. And naturally this terrorist attack would demand an immediate military response by your forces."

"Naturally," Ivanov agreed laconically. "If the Kiev government cannot protect our people from its own Ukrainian ultra-nationalists, then we must do it for them."

Listening, Malkovic snorted. He turned to Dudarev. "And what excuse will you find to intervene in Georgia and the other countries?"

The Russian president shrugged. "In Georgia and the rest of the former republics, there are already signs of growing political instability." He inclined his head toward the billionaire with a dry, ironic smile. "Thanks, of course, to the civilian and military leadership deaths inflicted by your HYDRA virus."

Malkovic nodded.

But now Ivanov pounced. "Unfortunately, Mr. Malkovic, HYDRA itself may now present the greatest threat to our success." Coldly, the head of the Thirteenth Directorate looked across the table at Brandt. "Herr Brandt's failure to eliminate

Dr. Petrenko before he talked was a serious mistake. But his continuing failure to capture or kill this Colonel Smith and his associates is a potential disaster. The longer Smith runs free here in Moscow, the greater the chance that he will penetrate the HYDRA secret. Put bluntly, that is a chance we cannot take."

"Very true, Alexei," Dudarev agreed. The Russian president pointed to the screen depicting armored spearheads thrusting deep into Ukraine, Georgia, and the others. "ZHUKOV's success depends entirely on our achieving almost complete surprise. But if the Americans learn of our involvement in the deaths caused by your viral weapon, everything we hope to achieve is put at risk."

"What do you propose?" Malkovic asked stiffly.

"First, that my directorate assume full control over the search for Smith and the American journalist, Ms. Devin," Ivanov told him. He turned back to Brandt. "But I want total cooperation this time. Nothing must be held back or concealed from me. Nothing. Is that clearly understood?"

For a moment, the former Stasi officer said nothing. His jaw tightened as he tried to hide his anger. Then he shrugged elaborately, feigning almost total indifference. "As you wish."

Malkovic kept his gaze fixed on Dudarev. For all his ruthlessness, Ivanov, like Brandt, was merely a servant. The Russian president was the man who pulled the strings. He raised a single eyebrow. "Well, Viktor, is that all?"

Dudarev shook his head. "Not quite, my friend." His fingers drummed softly on the table. "This American intelligence effort troubles me. Despite its real successes, so far, at least, it appears that HYDRA has not yet sufficiently blinded Washington. I also worry that President Castilla may prove more stubborn than wise. If, in the end, he proves unwilling to accept our conquests, the risk of an unwanted direct confrontation with the United States grows exponentially. Given our strategic advantages in Ukraine and central Asia, we should still prevail, but the costs, in troops, equipment, and money, might be excessive."

The other men in the room nodded slowly.

"For that reason," Dudarev continued, "I have decided to make sure that this particular American president no longer threatens us." He focused his eyes on Malkovic. "You will instruct your people to hand over the appropriate HYDRA variant to one of Ivanov's couriers as soon as possible."

Malkovic stiffened in surprise. "But the risks of killing Castilla are —"

"Manageable," the Russian leader said calmly. He glanced at Ivanov. "Correct?"

The head of the Thirteenth Directorate nodded coldly. "We have a mole in place, inside the White House," he confirmed. "Deploying HYDRA successfully should present no particular problems."

Malkovic felt cold. "There will be hell to pay if the United States ever suspects what we have done," he said tightly.

Dudarev shrugged. "Let the Americans suspect what they will, so long as they cannot prove anything." He smiled thinly. "Which brings me to another concern. In the circumstances, with American agents on the prowl, have you considered the possible dangers to your HYDRA facility?"

"The lab is secure," Malkovic told him flatly. "The Americans will not discover it."

Beside him, Brandt nodded in agreement.

Dudarev eyed them both with amused cynicism. "That is good news," he said after a moment, delaying just long enough to make it clear that he did not believe them. "Still, it might be safer for all of us if Dr. Renke and his scientific team were transferred here — to one of our special maximum-security Bioaparat complexes, for example. Don't you agree?"

Malkovic grimaced. Now he could see the game the Russian president was playing. Complete control over HYDRA and the secret of its creation was his high card in this high-stakes gamble. The unique viral weapon created by Renke made the billionaire an irreplaceable ally, a man with whom Dudarev must deal as an equal. But if he ever lost his monopoly on this lethal technology, the men in the Kremlin would be free to act as they saw fit. For that reason, he had kept all knowledge of Renke's whereabouts a closely guarded secret, especially from the Russians.

"The facility is safe," he repeated coldly. "Of that you have my most solemn word."

Dudarev nodded slowly. "Very well, I am willing to accept your pledge." Then, quite abruptly, his seemingly mild, half-amused expression hardened. "But one thing must be made absolutely explicit, Mr. Malkovic: Since you will not allow us to protect the secret of this weapon ourselves, we will hold you personally responsible for any further failures. Five days remain before we can launch ZHUKOV. Five short days. But until our soldiers and combat aircraft are in action, the Americans must not learn of HYDRA's existence. If they do, your life is forfeit. Remember that fact."

★ ★ ★

Later, during the brief limousine ride back to his Pashkov House office, Malkovic moodily considered the Russian president's threat. So the tiger has shown me its teeth and claws, he thought grimly. He scowled. All the more reason then to make sure that he kept a firm grip around its throat.

He looked across at Brandt. The tall, blond-haired German was sitting on the rear-facing seat, staring blindly out the window.

"Will Ivanov succeed in capturing or killing the Americans?" Malkovic asked quietly.

Brandt snorted. "I doubt it."

"Why?"

"Because the militia and the security services are fundamentally unreliable," the German explained slowly through gritted teeth. "For all of Dudarev's vaunted purges, both still contain too many officers who are either corrupt and willing to sell information or protection to fugitives with enough money — or else who are tainted by so-called 'reformist' ideals. The chances are too great that Smith and Devin will find officials willing to help them, or at least to turn a blind eye while they escape. If Ivanov thinks otherwise, he's a fool."

Malkovic pondered his subordinate's bitter, cynical assessment in silence. With his own neck very much on the line, hearing Brandt's low opinion of the FSB and militia was deeply worrying.

The billionaire came to a decision. "Then you will continue your own hunt for Smith and Devin," he told Brandt. "I want them found, and found quickly. Preferably by your men, and not by the Russians."

"What about the Thirteenth Directorate?" the other man wondered. "You heard Ivanov. He'll want every scrap of information we dig up. It will be hard enough tracking down the Americans without tripping over FSB agents at every turn."

Malkovic nodded. "I understand." He shrugged. "Give the Russians enough of the data you have obtained on this man Smith to keep them happy. In the meantime, press your own search as far and as fast as possible."

"Capturing the two Americans under Ivanov's nose will be difficult," Brandt warned. "But I promise you that my men and I will."

"I am not paying you to *try*, Herr Brandt," the billionaire said icily. "I am paying you to *succeed*. I strongly suggest that you remember the difference."

"And if I take Smith and Ms. Devin alive?" the German asked calmly, ignoring the implied threat. "Without Ivanov finding out, I mean. What are your orders then?"

"Squeeze them dry," Malkovic said brutally. "Find out who they're working for and how much information on HYDRA they have already relayed to the United States —"

"And after that?"

"Kill them," Malkovic snapped. "Quickly, if necessary. But slowly, if possible. Colonel Smith and Ms. Devin have caused me a great deal of trouble and anxiety. That is something I would dearly like them to regret."

CHAPTER TWENTY-FIVE

Moscow

Jon Smith reacted instantly to the sound of a soft knock on the apartment's front door. Rising from the sofa where he had been trying to catch up on his sleep, he scooped up the 9mm Makarov from the coffee table, thumbed the safety off, and yanked back on the slide to chamber a round. Then he swung around with the pistol extended in both hands, ready to fire. He breathed out, calming himself as he steadied his aim. The Makarov's front and rear sights settled on the center of the door and stayed there.

With her own weapon held at the ready, Fiona Devin came ghosting in from the bedroom, moving cat-quiet on her bare feet across the scuffed hardwood floor. "Who is it?" she called out in Russian, altering the tenor of her voice to imitate the quaver of an old woman.

A man answered her, his voice muffled by the heavy wood door. "It's me, Oleg."

Smith relaxed slightly. He recognized Kirov's voice. More important, by using

only his first name the Russian had signaled them that it was safe. If he had identified himself fully, he would have been
warning them that he was acting under du-
ress, as a prisoner of either the Moscow
militia or of anyone else who might be
hunting for them.

Slowly, Smith lowered his Makarov and
put the safety back on. Fiona did the same
with her weapon and then went forward to
unlock and unbolt the door.

The tall, barrel-chested Russian came in
quickly, carrying a pair of heavy suitcases.
His silver eyebrows rose when he saw the
pistols in their hands. "You are nervous?"
he asked. Then he nodded grimly. "And so
you should be."

"What's up?"

Kirov set the suitcases down and moved
to the nearest window. He pulled back the
drapes a bit. "Come and see for yourselves," he suggested, nodding at the street
below.

Smith and Fiona joined him.

Cars and delivery trucks were backed
up all along the bridge across the
Vodootvodny Canal. Militiamen in gray
overcoats and peaked caps were moving in
pairs from vehicle to vehicle, bending down
to examine papers and ask questions of
each driver. A squad of soldiers armed with
assault rifles and clad in winter-pattern

camouflage uniforms stood guard at the nearest intersection.

"Ministry of the Interior troops," Kirov said coolly. "From what I've seen, there are checkpoints going up at most of the key intersections and outside the more important Metro transfer stations."

"Damn," Smith muttered. He glanced at the other man. "What's the official reason they're giving?"

Kirov shrugged. "According to the news, this is just part of a routine security sweep for suspected Chechen terrorists. But I managed to get close enough to one of the checkpoints to see what they were using to sift through the crowds." He looked back at the two Americans. "The militia have copies of your passport photos."

Fiona sighed. "It was only a matter of time, I suppose."

"Yes," Kirov said soberly. "And now we must face facts. We cannot delay any longer. Both of you need new papers — with new faces and new names."

Smith stared back at him, struck by something the other man had just said. A faint possibility stirred far back in his mind, something that was more the vague hint of an idea than anything really solid. But then, as other small fragments of evidence started tumbling neatly into place, this new theory of his began taking on a dazzling form and substance, like a smoldering ember whipped into flame by the wind.

His eyes widened. "Names," he said abruptly. "That's the link we've been missing. We've all been wondering why so many people were killed to prevent us from getting our hands on those case notes. Well, maybe the answer has been staring us right in the face all along."

"Exactly what are you talking about, Colonel?" Fiona asked quietly. Kirov's face mirrored her incomprehension.

On fire with his new theory, Jon led them back to the coffee table. "Names," he said again, fanning out the sheaf of typed papers and their scrawled translations. With a red pencil, he swiftly circled certain sections of the papers. "See for yourselves. That's what Elena's notes contain . . . the names of the victims of the first outbreak. And their families. And their addresses. Right?"

The other two nodded slowly, still clearly unsure of where he was leading them.

"Look," Smith explained. "Somehow, somewhere, there has to be a connection between those who died and between their families. A connection that could give us a better understanding of how this new disease works and where it comes from."

Fiona frowned. "I don't see it, Colonel." She shook her head. "You've already pointed out that there isn't any clear link between those poor people — no friendships, no family ties, nothing that would explain why they fell ill and died so horribly."

Smith nodded. "That's true. Elena, Valentin Petrenko, and the other Russian scientists studying the outbreak were completely unable to identify any ordinary connection between the four victims." He tapped the notes again. "But what if the link between them is something more subtle, maybe a shared genetic or other biochemical trait — some weakness or pre-existing condition that made them especially vulnerable to this new disease?"

"Do you really believe it might be possible to discover this shared trait?" Kirov asked. "Even now?"

Smith nodded again. "Yes, I do." He looked at the other man. "But it won't be easy. First, we'll have to find a way to interview the families of the victims. If we can persuade them to let us take blood, tissue, and DNA samples, a series of lab tests ought to be able to pinpoint any areas of similarity."

"And somehow you plan to do all of these things while you and Ms. Devin are on the Kremlin's Most Wanted list?" Kirov commented drily.

"Yep, that's about the size of it." Smith forced a grin onto his lean face. "What's that old saying? Something like 'If you can't take a joke, you shouldn't have signed on to be a soldier'? Well, we all signed on the dotted line, so I guess this is where we start earning our pay."

Berlin

Set in and around a forest and several small but beautiful lakes, the Grunewald district was one of Berlin's most elite and expensive suburbs. The older houses here were set far apart from each other, surrounded by immaculately landscaped grounds, stone walls, hedges, and patches of woodland.

A small utility truck in the red-and-white colors of Deutsche Telekom, the German telephone company, was parked along Hagenstrasse, one of the wider residential streets in the Grunewald. It was very late in the afternoon and the pale winter sun, already low on the horizon, threw long black shadows across the road. It was bitterly cold and very few people were out and about in the frosty air. A paunchy jogger, wrapped up in the rhythms of the music pulsing through his headphones, puffed across the street in front of the truck and kept going, grimly focused on finishing his doctor-ordered exercise. He soon vanished in the growing darkness among the trees. An elderly couple, out for an afternoon stroll, tottered past, tugging their unhappy, shivering terrier behind them. Then they too turned a corner and were gone.

Inside the truck cab, Randi Russell sat slouched behind the steering wheel. She wore thin leather gloves, a plain black baseball cap to hide her short blond hair, and drab gray workman's coveralls that concealed her slender figure. She checked her watch impatiently. How much longer was she going to have to wait?

One side of Randi's generous mouth twisted upward in a wry grin as she looked down at her gloves. If she had to sit here idly much longer, she might just be tempted to start chewing through the leather just to get at her fingernails.

"The servants are on the move," a young woman's voice reported suddenly in her headset. "Looks like they're finally heading out for the day."

Randi sat up straighter, watching an old, dented Audi pull slowly out of the driveway not far ahead of her. The pair of illegal Slovak immigrants that Ulrich Kessler paid to clean his house, cook his meals, and maintain his garden were on their way home to their own flea-ridden flat on the far side of Berlin. The Audi turned left on Hagenstrasse and drove off past her truck.

Her eyes followed its taillights in her side mirror until they disappeared.

"What about our boy Kessler himself?" she asked, speaking softly into the mike clipped to her coveralls.

"Still in his office," another voice, this one male and older, reported. It belonged to the CIA officer assigned to keep an eye on the BKA building in which Kessler worked. "But he's definitely confirmed as one of the guests for a big shindig the Chancellor is throwing at the Staatsbibliothek this evening. According to our file, Kessler is a champion brown-noser. He won't miss the chance to mingle with the Who's Who of German politics, so you should be clear to go in."

"On my way," Randi said coolly. Now that she was free to act, her nerves were noticeably steadier. "I'm moving onto the grounds now."

Without waiting any longer, she put the utility truck in gear and turned into the driveway that curved through the tall trees surrounding Kessler's villa. The house itself, built in the early 1900s, was a replica of an Edwardian-era English country manor, all the way from its gleaming white, ivy-cloaked walls to the wide veranda running the length of its second story.

Randi pulled around to the side of the house and parked next to a large garage that must have once served as both a carriage house and stables. She slid out of the truck and stood still for a moment, watching and listening. Nothing stirred either inside the house or outside among the trees.

Reassured, she quickly fastened an SAS-pattern assault vest over her gray coveralls. This vest's Velcro-sealed pouches and pockets contained a collection of small tools and electronics gear, not the usual assortment of weapons and spare ammunition. With that done, she walked back around the house, heading straight for the front door. It was the only way in that she could be sure was not on a security latch or a deadbolt.

Randi stopped, knelt down to briefly examine the lock, and then fished the appropriate set of lockpicks out of one of her vest pockets. She slipped them into the tiny opening and stopped. "I'm at the door, Carla," she murmured into her radio, speaking to her lookout. "Once I give you the word, I want to hear a running thirty-second countdown. Clear?"

"Understood," the younger woman answered. "The thirty-second clock is set."

"You with me, Mike?" Randi asked, this time addressing the electronics specialist assigned to her forced-entry team.

"Standing by, Randi," the technician replied calmly.

"Good." She risked a quick glance over her shoulder. Anyone passing by on the street would be able to spot her, though only if they looked carefully. All the more reason to stop fussing around, Randi told herself sternly. She took a deep breath, felt the crisp, clean oxygen flood her system, and then breathed out. "Here goes."

Using both hands, she delicately maneuvered the picks into the lock mechanism. After several seconds of careful jimmying, she felt it click open. With a soft sigh of satisfaction, she slid the pick set back into her vest and stood up. "Listen closely, guys," Randi said quietly. "My forced-entry is commencing . . . now!"

Without hesitating any longer, she pushed the door open, walked inside Kessler's house, and immediately pulled the door closed behind her. She was in a broad entry hall lit by a chandelier high overhead. Doors opened off the hall on either side, leading into other rooms — a lounge or sitting area on the left and what might be a formal living room on the right. A wide, curving staircase swept up to the second floor.

"Thirty seconds," the lookout's voice said through her headset, distinctly and steadily repeating the numbers flickering past on her digital stopwatch.

Randi swiftly scanned the hallway,

searching for the burglar alarm control panel. There it was! She spotted a small gray plastic box fixed at eye level, just to the right of the door. A tiny red light blinked on the front face above a ten-digit keypad, indicating that the alarm had been triggered as soon as she came through the front door. Her eyes narrowed. At best, she had thirty seconds while the alarm system cycled through a hold period designed to give the homeowner enough time to enter his security code on the keypad. After that, the alarm would go off, immediately alerting the closest Berlin police unit that a break-in was in progress.

Instantly, she tugged open another Velcro pocket and brought out a small power screwdriver. With the quick press of a button on the side, it whirred into motion, swiftly spinning in reverse to pull out the first of the two screws holding the front plastic panel closed.

"Twenty-five seconds."

The first screw dropped into Randi's gloved hand. She shifted the screwdriver to the next. It spun back out easily. She popped off the front panel and peered inside past a tangle of colored cables connected to a circuit board, looking for the tiny printed strip that would identify the alarm system.

"Twenty seconds."

Randi felt her mouth drying out. Where was that damned ID tag? She was running out of time here. At last, she spotted the small box of text, glued to the rear wall of the control box. "Mike! The system is a TÜRING 3000."

"Understood, Randi," the CIA technician told her. "Go with Card Five. Detach the green cable you see and plug it into the new card at Position One. Then do the same with the black cable at Position Two. Got it?"

"Got it," she confirmed, pulling a specially preconfigured system card out of one of her vest pouches.

"Ten seconds."

Moving rapidly, Randi followed the directions she had been given, shifting cables from the old circuit board to the new one she had brought with her. Her pulse was racing now, thudding wildly in her ears. A fear-filled voice inside her own head began complaining that she wasn't working fast enough, that the alarm was about to go off no matter what she did. She did her best to ignore it, concentrating instead on the task at hand.

"Five seconds. Four. Three —"

The second cable snapped into the card held in her gloved hand. New commands flowed immediately from the card to the alarm control box, mimicking instructions that would have been sent remotely by Kessler's security company to reset the system after any false alarm. The red light shifted to green.

Randi breathed out in relief. Now, when she was finished inside the house, she could simply reverse the process, replace the panel, and exit through the front door, without leaving any obvious evidence that the alarm had ever been tampered with.

"I'm clear," she reported quietly. "Commencing my recon now."

Moving confidently, Randi began a thorough search of Kessler's villa, starting with the rooms at ground level and then continuing up the stairs to the second floor. One thing struck her right away. Ulrich Kessler was an art collector, a serious collector with a taste for extremely expensive original works of modern art. Unless she missed her guess, he had pieces by Diebenkorn, Kandinsky, Klee, Pollock, Mondrian, Picasso, and several other famous twentieth-century painters hanging in places of honor on the walls of various rooms.

She paused at each one and took a digital picture. "Not bad for a simple civil servant, Herr Kessler," she murmured, recording the image of what looked very much like an original de Kooning. Although it was difficult to pin down precisely how much these paintings were worth, she was willing to bet their total value was somewhere well above ten million dollars. No wonder he was so widely known for his unwillingness to invite work colleagues to his home.

Randi shook her head in disgust. From all appearances, the Bundeskriminalamt official had been remarkably well paid for his role in protecting Professor Wulf Renke. Close examination of the images she was photographing for CIA-retained art experts should provide an intriguing look at the details of Kessler's finances. And those were details that she knew he would be very, very unhappy to have dragged out into the open.

Replacing the camera in her vest, she moved on, prowling carefully first through the German's bedroom and then through a connecting door into what appeared to be his private study. Set at the very back of the villa, this was a large, lavishly furnished room with windows that looked out over the surrounding trees toward the bright lights of Berlin's busy city center.

From the doorway, Randi surveyed the study through narrowed eyes, quickly noting the computer and telephone sitting on an elaborately carved antique desk, the walls lined with bookcases, and another expensive painting — one that she strongly suspected concealed a small safe. She resisted the urge to begin rummaging through desk drawers or trying to break into the safe.

The BKA official was corrupt, but he was not an idiot. The odds were very much against discovering any hidden document conveniently labeled "My Secret Life and Wulf Renke." She was also sure that Kessler would have set hard-to-find telltales and possibly even other electronic alarms to protect his most prized information. Disturbing those would only put him instantly on his guard.

Instead, Randi began pulling open various pouches on her equipment vest, revealing an assortment of miniaturized listening devices. She smiled coldly. Suspicious or not, Herr Ulrich Kessler was about to discover that there were other ways to learn his most closely held secrets.

CHAPTER TWENTY-SIX

Moscow
It was the evening rush hour and hundreds of Muscovites worn out after a long day's work packed the steep escalators serving the Smolenskaya Metro Station. Among them were three people, one of them a tall, strong-looking man in his mid-fifties. He carried a heavy canvas duffel bag slung over one shoulder and wore a martyred expression as he patiently shepherded his doddering, elderly mother and his equally ancient father off the escalator.

"We're almost outside, little mother," he said gently. "Just a little farther now." He looked back over his shoulder at the older man. "Come now, Papa. You must do your best to keep up."

Up at the top, a growing crowd of increasingly unhappy Metro riders were pressing up against the barriers leading to the street, restlessly waiting for a chance to run their magnetic tickets through the machines and leave the station. But most of the ticket-readers were shut down, forcing everyone in the crowd to funnel through the three barriers that were still in service. Exasperated murmurs swept through those milling in line when they saw the reason for the slowdown. Squads of gray-coated militiamen were deployed at every entrance and exit. They were busy carefully checking the faces of everyone entering and leaving the Smolenskaya station. From time to time, they pulled people away in ones and twos for closer questioning — often, but not always, lean, dark-haired men or slender and attractive, black-haired women.

After scrutinizing the identity papers of the most recent pair hauled before him, Militia Lieutenant Grigor Pronin tossed the cards back and then waved the worried-looking man and woman away. "Fine," he growled. "Everything's fine. Now move along!"

He grimaced. He and his entire unit had been tied up in this ridiculous manhunt for hours, stuck here on pointless, glorified sentry duty on orders from the Kremlin. No Chechen terrorist had ever looked anything like the photographs he had been shown. Meanwhile, he thought bitterly, Moscow's real criminals must be having a field day — mugging, shoplifting, and stealing cars to their black hearts' content.

Pronin swung round in irritation at a

sudden outbreak of loud cursing and swearing from the barrier. People were pushing and shoving one another near one of the ticket machines. He scowled. What the devil was wrong now? The militia officer stalked closer, angrily laying one hand on his holstered sidearm.

The crowd at the barrier saw him coming and fell silent. Most stepped back a pace or two, leaving three people still gathered around the machine. One, a tall, silver-haired man, seemed to be trying to gently urge a plump, much-older woman through the narrow opening. Stooped over a cane, an elderly man with long whiskers and dirty, matted white hair leaned heavily against the railing on the other side, feebly motioning the woman on. Two medals pinned to his dirty coat proclaimed him a veteran of The Great Patriotic War against Fascism.

"What's the trouble here?" Pronin demanded grimly.

"It's my mother, sir," the silver-haired man said apologetically. "She's having trouble with her ticket. She keeps sticking it in the wrong way round." He turned back to the woman. "Now see what you've done, little mother? The militia have come to see what the fuss is about."

"Never mind that," Pronin said brusquely. He reached across the barrier, grabbed the magnetic card from the old woman's shaking hand, and inserted it himself. The barrier slid aside, allowing her to hobble through, followed soon after by her son. Almost immediately, a horrid odor assailed the militia lieutenant's nose, a rank, acrid stench that made him gag.

He stepped back, astonished by the smell. "Good God," he muttered in shock. "What's that stink?"

The other man shrugged sadly. "I'm afraid it's her bladder," he confided. "She doesn't have very much control over it these days. I try to get her to change her diaper more often, but she's very stubborn, you see — much like a little child, really."

Disgusted, Pronin waved the trio through his waiting men. So that was what old age could be like, he thought darkly. Then he turned back to survey the crowds, already dismissing the depressing incident from his mind.

Once they were safely outside the Metro station, the old woman painfully made her way over to a bench and sat down. The two men followed her.

"I swear to God, Oleg," Fiona Devin muttered crossly to the tall man masquerading as her son. "I'm going to be sick all over myself if I don't get out of these foul-smelling clothes and all this damned padding . . . and soon!"

"I am sorry," Kirov said ruefully. "But it is necessary." One of his bushy eyebrows rose in wry amusement. "On the other hand, my dear, you must admit that a bit of vomit would add a very nice touch of authenticity to your disguise."

Leaning hunched over on his cane, Jon Smith tried hard not to laugh. The glued-on theatrical whiskers and wig he was wearing itched abominably, but at least his coat and worn trousers were only stained with machine oil and ground-in dirt and not anything worse. Fiona, swaddled in layers to make her look fat and then stuffed into horribly soiled garments, had it a lot worse.

Smith noticed other shoppers and pedestrians giving them a wide berth, quickly walking away with wrinkled noses and averted eyes. Even in the open air, the smells emanating from them were still pungent. He nodded. These get-ups, uncomfortable and demeaning though they were, were proving remarkably effective.

"Come, Fiona," Kirov urged. "We're almost there. It's only a hundred meters or so farther on, just down that next little side street."

Still grumbling under her breath, Fiona forced herself back onto her feet, which were stuffed into boots that were at least a size too small for her, and shuffled off in the direction Kirov indicated. Together they hobbled and limped east along the Ulitsa Arbat and turned into an alley lined with small shops selling books, new and used clothing, perfumes, and antiques.

Patiently, the Russian led them to a narrow door halfway down the alley. Next to the door, a dirty window displayed a poorly lit selection of antique samovars, *matryoshka* dolls, lacquer boxes and bowls, crystal, Soviet-era porcelain, and old lamps. Faded gold lettering above the window read ANTIKVAZ-AVIABARI.

If anything, the tiny shop behind the door was even more of a jumble, full of items heaped together on dusty shelves and counters without any apparent rhyme or reason. There were replicas of famous religious icons, Red Army belt buckles and fleece-lined fabric tanker's helmets, gold-plated candle sticks, chipped China tea sets, costume jewelry, and framed and faded Soviet propaganda posters.

When they came in, the proprietor, a large, ponderous man with just a fringe of curly gray hair around his bald pate, looked up from the cracked teacup he was gluing back together. His dark eyes brightened at the sight of Kirov and he came lumbering around the counter to greet them.

"Oleg!" he boomed, in a baritone voice that carried the hint of a Georgian accent. "I assume these are the *friends* of whom you spoke on the phone?"

Kirov nodded coolly. "They are." He turned to Fiona and Smith. "And this overfed villain is Lado Iashvili, the self-described bane of Moscow's legitimate antique dealers."

"What the general here says is very true," Iashvili admitted with a tolerant shrug. He grinned widely, revealing a worn set of tobacco-stained teeth. "But then I have my poor living to make, and they have theirs, eh? We each prosper in our own way."

"So I hear," Kirov agreed.

"But now to business, correct?" Iashvili said expansively. "Do not worry, Oleg. I think you and your friends will be very pleased by the quality of my merchandise."

"Will we?" Fiona said carefully, eyeing the clutter around them with barely concealed disdain.

Iashvili chuckled. "Ah, *Babushka,* there you misunderstand the nature of my business." He waved a dismissive hand at the bric-a-brac scattered around his shop. "These things are largely for show. They are only a hobby, something to deceive the curious policeman or the occasional nosy tax inspector.

Come! I will show you my true passion!"

With that, the burly Georgian swung round and ushered them through another door at the back of his shop. It opened into a storeroom piled high with the same mix of genuine antiques and useless junk. Off in the far corner, a steep flight of stairs led down into the basement. This staircase ended at a locked steel door.

Iashvili unlocked the door and pushed it open with an extravagant, sweeping gesture. "Take a look for yourselves," he said grandly. "Here you see my studio, the little temple of my art."

Smith and Fiona stared around them in wonder. They were standing in a large, brightly lit chamber. It was filled with expensive photography equipment, computers, several different types of color laser printers and photocopiers, engraving machines, and rack upon rack containing what appeared to be almost every imaginable kind of paper, inks, and chemicals used to artificially age documents. One whole side of the room was set up as a photo studio, complete with different backdrops, a wash basin with soap, shampoos, and towels, and a privacy screen.

With another broad grin, the Georgian patted himself on the chest. "Speaking with all due modesty, of course, I, Lado Iashvili, am the very best in my chosen profession — certainly in Moscow, and perhaps in all of Russia. The general here understands this fact, which is why he has brought you to me."

"You are definitely a gifted forger," Kirov agreed tersely. He shot a glance at Smith and Fiona. "In the old days, the KGB held a monopoly on Iashvili's rather unique services. But now that he's branched out into the private sector, he has proved himself quite the entrepreneur."

The Georgian nodded matter-of-factly. "I do have a wide range of clients," he admitted. "Those who would like to leave their unfortunate pasts behind for any number of reasons have learned to rely on me for help."

"Including members of the *Mafiya?*" Fiona guessed. Her face was expressionless, but Smith could hear the anger in her voice. She had no love for anyone who aided members of Moscow's criminal underworld.

Iashvili shrugged. "Who knows? It may be so. But I never ask awkward questions of those who pay me." He smiled drily. "For that, I think you two should be grateful, eh?"

Fiona looked back at Kirov. "How far can we trust this man?" she asked bluntly.

The Russian smiled coldly. "Quite far, actually. First, because he is a man whose livelihood depends entirely on his reputation for absolute discretion. And second, because he values his own skin." He turned toward Iashvili. "You know what will happen if news of the work you're going to do for my friends leaks out?"

For the first time, the effusive Georgian seemed at a loss for words. His fleshy face turned pale. "You will kill me, Oleg."

"So I will, Lado," Kirov said quietly. "Or, if I could not, there are others who would do it for me. In either case, your death would not be quick. Do you understand me?"

Iashvili nervously licked his lips. He nodded quickly. "Yes, I understand."

Satisfied, Kirov dumped the canvas duffel bag he was carrying on a nearby table and began quickly removing items from it. Within moments, the table was covered with shoes and sets of clean, stylish clothing in sizes that would fit the two Americans, different-colored wigs and hairpieces, dyes, and a kit containing other items that would help them alter their appearance in any one of several ways.

"And you still want all of the documents we discussed earlier?" Iashvili asked tentatively, watching the growing piles of clothing and gear through narrowed eyes.

Kirov nodded. "My friends will need new foreign passports . . . Swedish, I think.

Also, photocopies of appropriate business visas and immigration cards — ones issued at St. Petersburg would probably be best. Plus, they'll need paperwork confirming their employment by the World Health Organization. They'll also want a set of local identity papers as a fallback, documents with good, solid Russian names on them. Will any of that present a problem?"

The Georgian shook his head rapidly, beginning to recover his customary poise. "Not a bit," he promised.

"How long will you need?"

Iashvili shrugged. "Three hours. Maybe four at the outside."

"And the price?" Kirov asked.

"One million rubles," the other man said flatly. "In cash."

Smith whistled softly. At the present rate of exchange, that came to more than thirty thousand U.S. dollars. Still, it was probably a fair price for the high-grade forged papers he and Fiona Devin would need if they were stopped at a militia checkpoint.

Kirov shrugged. "Very well. Half now." He pulled a large stack of Russian bank notes out of the duffel bag and handed them to Iashvili. "And half later, when the work is finished to my friends' satisfaction."

While the suddenly much-happier Georgian forger took the money upstairs for safekeeping, Kirov spoke quietly to Smith and Fiona. "Join me when Iashvili is done here. The rest of his money is in the bag," he said. "I'll wait for you in the bar in the Hotel Belgrade, just on this side of the Borodinsky Bridge." He grinned at them. "With luck, of course, I won't recognize either of you."

"You're not staying?" Fiona asked in surprise.

Kirov shook his head regretfully. "I have a rendezvous I must keep," he explained softly. "A private meeting with another old friend. A man who may have some of the answers we need."

"An old friend in uniform?" Smith guessed.

"Perhaps from time to time, Jon," the other man agreed with a slight smile. "Though senior officers in the Federal Security Service often prefer a simple business suit for social occasions."

CHAPTER TWENTY-SEVEN

It was well after ten at night when Smith and Fiona Devin entered the Lobby Bar at the Hotel Belgrade, but the place was still hopping. Men and women in business attire, mostly Russians, though with a scattering of foreigners, occupied most of the booths and tables or stood elbow-to-elbow at the bar. Soft jazz played in the background, but the music was almost completely drowned out by the clamor of loud conversation. Although the Belgrade was a big, boxy hotel without much architectural charm, its convenient location, close to the Metro and the Arbat, and its reasonable prices kept its occupancy rates high even in the winter.

Oleg Kirov sat by himself in one corner of the noisy room, silently smoking a cigarette. Two shot glasses and a half-empty bottle of vodka stood on the table in front of him. He had a pensive look about him.

Together, Smith and Fiona made their way over through the crowds. "May we join you?" Jon asked in accented Russian.

Kirov looked up at them with a grave,

welcoming nod. "Of course. It would be a pleasure." He stood up, pulled out a chair for Fiona, and then signaled a waitress to bring fresh glasses. "Shall I ask your names? Or would that be considered rude on so brief an acquaintance?"

"Not at all," Smith answered smoothly. He sat down and slid his new Swedish passport across the table. True to his boasts, Iashvili had done superb work. The forged passport looked as though he had carried it around for several years and it included entry and exit stamps for a number of different countries. "I'm Dr. Kalle Strand, an epidemiologist assigned to the World Health Organization."

"And my name is Berit Lindkvist," Fiona said with an impish grin. "Dr. Strand's personal assistant."

Kirov arched an eyebrow. "With the emphasis on *personal?*"

She wagged a stern finger at him. "Not all Swedes are sex-crazed, Mr. Kirov. My relationship with Dr. Strand is strictly business."

"I stand corrected, Ms. Lindkvist," the Russian replied with an answering smile. He sat quietly a while longer, studying their changed appearance. Then he nodded. "A good job. It should suffice."

"Let's hope so," Smith said. He resisted the urge to rub at his eyebrows. A blond wig covered his dark hair, but he'd had to bleach his eyebrows to match and now they were itching like crazy. A pair of cheek inserts broadened his face, and padding around his waist added fifteen or twenty pounds to his apparent weight. And a pair of heavy black-frame eyeglasses with clear lenses should draw attention away from his blue eyes. None of it was very comfortable, but, taken together, the various changes altered his looks enough to give him a decent shot at passing through any militia checkpoint without being spotted.

Fiona Devin had undergone a similar transformation. She had cut her shoulder-length hair shorter and dyed it a dark red. Heels added an inch to her height while new undergarments changed her figure subtly, but enough so that she seemed a very different woman.

Jon fell silent while the waitress cleared away the old vodka glasses and replaced them with new ones. Then he asked, "Did your friend in the FSB give you any information worth sharing?"

"He did," Kirov said heavily. His eyes were troubled. "First, he confirmed that the manhunt for you was set in motion by orders from the very highest levels of the Kremlin. The militia and Ministry of the Interior units involved have instructions to report directly to Alexei Ivanov."

"Ivanov?" Fiona repeated with a frown. "That's not good."

Smith leaned forward. "Who exactly is this Ivanov character?"

"He's the head of the FSB's Thirteenth Directorate," Kirov told him. "He takes his orders from President Dudarev and no one else. For all practical purposes, his section operates independently of the regular FSB command structure. It is said that his men violate the law and our constitution with total impunity. And I believe those rumors."

Fiona nodded. "The man is ruthless and completely amoral. But he's also extremely competent." Her face darkened. "Which leaves me wondering how we managed to escape that first ambush at all. Why murder Vedenskaya on the street and then try to kidnap us using a fake ambulance crew? Why not just call out the militia and have them snap us up?"

"Because that was not Ivanov's show," Kirov said quietly. "At least not completely. My former colleague managed to get a look at the first militia reports of the incident — before the Kremlin ordered a halt to any further investigation."

"And?" Smith asked.

"The militia managed to identify two of the dead men," Kirov said. "Both were former KGB, men who were used chiefly for 'wet work' against dissidents and sus-pected traitors."

Smith nodded grimly. "Wet work" was a euphemism for State-sanctioned murder. "You said 'former' KGB?"

"Correct," Kirov said. "For the past sev-eral years, they have been employed by the Brandt Group." He shrugged. "The same people who tried to eliminate you in Prague."

"But Brandt and his thugs work for the highest bidder, not on their own whim," Fiona pointed out. "So who was paying the bills to have us kidnapped? The Kremlin, through Ivanov? Or someone else?"

"That is still unclear," Kirov admitted. "But my colleague did learn that the am-bulance was registered to the Saint Cyril Medical Center."

Fiona saw Smith's questioning look and explained. "The center is a sort of joint Western/Russian teaching hospital set up to improve the standard of health care in this country." She turned to Kirov. "Was the ambulance stolen?"

"If so," the Russian said flatly, "the theft does not seem to have been reported to the authorities."

"How very curious," Smith said drily. "And who funds this medical clinic?"

"It's a public-private consortium," Fiona told him. "Roughly a third of its budget comes from the Ministry of Health. But the rest of its money comes from a network of foreign charities and foundations —" She stopped abruptly, apparently deep in thought. Then her jaw tightened. She looked up at them in dismay. "Including a very substantial percentage from a foundation controlled by Konstantin Malkovic."

"Curiouser and curiouser," Smith said, contemplating the chain of events over the past two days from a new perspective. An ugly possibility now reared its head, one they could not afford to ignore. He gestured toward Fiona. "Consider this: You tell Malkovic about this disease outbreak and the official cover-up. He says that he's horrified and promises that he'll do whatever he can to help you learn the truth. But hey, presto, within just a couple of hours, you're under close surveillance by a professional tag team. Are you with me so far?"

She nodded.

"Okay," Smith continued. "You manage to shake the tail, but probably not until after they spot us together at the Patriarch's Pond. Right then all sorts of alarm bells must have started going off in various places. Later that same night, the Brandt Group swoops in to nail us both. And now it turns out that the ambulance they used just happens to belong to a hospital that gets a ton of money from good old Konstantin Malkovic."

"You believe that he may be involved in this conspiracy, together with Dudarev?" Kirov asked, frowning.

"Beyond a shadow of a doubt?" Smith said. He shook his head. "No. All of this stuff could be just pure coincidence. But there sure seems to be a hell of a lot of smoke drifting around Mr. Malkovic, doesn't there?"

"So there does," Fiona agreed bitterly. "Enough to imagine there may well be some very bright flames dancing about beneath the smoke." Her face was flushed with anger as she recalled the details of her interview with Malkovic and put a new spin on what he had said to her. She gritted her teeth in frustration. "Not that we stand much chance of pinning anything on him right now."

"That is so," Kirov said, equally grimly. "If this billionaire is in league with the Kremlin, he will take every conceivable precaution so long as you and Colonel Smith are still alive. No one unknown to him will be allowed anywhere near his person, let alone near any incriminating evidence. Pursuing Malkovic directly would only mean putting our own heads in a noose."

Smith nodded. "You're right. It still

makes more sense to contact the families of the victims while we can. Obtaining solid data on this new disease is our first priority. But we should brief Fred Klein on what we suspect before we make our next move."

"There is one more thing I think Mr. Klein should know," Kirov said slowly. "According to my colleague in the security service, there are signs of an even greater danger stirring in this country, a danger that may well be connected in some way to this mysterious illness, but eclipsing it in size and scope."

As he talked, Smith and Fiona sat silently, listening with growing concern while Kirov recounted the rumors of intensive military preparation that were beginning to circulate through the upper levels of the FSB headquarters at Lubyanka Square. There were whispers of secret troop movements and military exercises, the movement of vast stockpiles of ammunition, food, and fuel to camouflaged supply dumps on Russia's borders, and ever-tighter security around the Kremlin and the Ministry of Defense. And they all seemed to point toward the unthinkable — a campaign of conquest aimed at the former Soviet republics.

CHAPTER TWENTY-EIGHT

The White House

"Mr. Klein, sir," Estelle Pike said tartly, ushering the pale, long-nosed man into the Oval Office. "He insists on seeing you."

With a wry, welcoming smile, President Sam Castilla looked up from the pile of briefing folders crowding his pine table desk. There were shadows under his eyes, showing the effects of several long days and as many sleepless nights. He nodded toward one of the chairs in front of the desk. "Take a seat, Fred. I'll be with you in a second."

Klein obeyed, watching in silence while his old friend finished skimming a memo. Large, bold red letters stamped across the top indicated that it included top-secret intelligence obtained from U.S. spy satellites. Castilla came to the end, snorted in disgust, and stuffed the document back into one of the folders.

"More trouble?" the head of Covert-One asked carefully.

"In spades." Castilla ran his big hands

distractedly through his hair and then indicated the folders stacked in front of him. "Our satellites and signals intercept stations seem to be picking up signs of Russian military moves and increasing readiness in several frontier districts — those bordering Ukraine, Georgia, Azerbaijan, and Kazakhstan. But the intelligence is damned sketchy, and no one in the Pentagon or the CIA seems willing to place any bets on what may be going on."

"Because of problems with the data?" Klein wondered. "Or because they're having trouble analyzing the facts they've got?"

"Both," Castilla growled. He shuffled through the various folders, picked one out, and shoved it across the desk. "There's an example of what I'm getting. Take a look for yourself."

It was a Defense Intelligence Agency report on the possible buildup of Russian divisions stationed in Chechnya and along the Caucasus Mountains. Relying largely on satellite photos showing large amounts of military equipment moving by rail into the areas around Grozny, some analysts speculated that the Russians were building up forces for yet another all-out offensive on the region's Islamic rebels. Others disputed this conclusion, claiming the rail shipments were only part of a normal troop rotation. A small minority claimed that the tank and motor rifle formations ostensibly being transferred to Chechnya were actually being diverted to other areas, though no one could say exactly where.

Klein flipped through the folder quickly, reading with growing disapproval. By its very nature, intelligence analysis was an imperfect, imprecise business. But this report was fuzzier than most. The competing theories were couched in remarkably vague terms, loaded down with so many qualifiers that they lacked any semblance of conviction, and were presented in a jumble, without making any attempt to rank them in order of probability. From the standpoint of a senior policymaker, especially one at the president's level, the analysis was essentially useless.

He looked up in dismay. "This is second-string material, Sam."

"Try third-string," Castilla said grimly. "Our best Russia analysts are either dead or running scared that they're next. The folks who are next in line just don't have the same level of experience . . . and it shows."

Klein nodded. Sorting out the wheat from the chaff of modern intelligence — garbled fragments of intercepted communications, satellite photos that were difficult to interpret, stray rumors passed along by agents and embassy staffs, and all the rest — was a skill that took years of training and practice to fully develop.

Still frowning, the president took off his reading glasses and tossed them onto his desk. He looked across at Klein. "Which brings us to Covert-One's assignment, pinning down the cause of this illness. What have you learned so far?"

"Less than I would like," the other man admitted. "But I have just received an urgent signal from Colonel Smith and Ms. Devin."

"And?"

"They've definitely run into something very nasty going on in Moscow," Klein said quietly. He grimaced, resisting the temptation to fiddle with the battered briarwood pipe tucked away inside his suit coat. "Some of their news ties into those reports you just showed me. Unfortunately, precisely what it may all mean is not yet completely clear to me."

Castilla listened intently while Klein summarized what his team had reported, including their suspicions about the possible involvement of Konstantin Malkovic and the rumors of impending military action passed on by Oleg Kirov's contact inside the Russian security service.

The lines on the president's face grew deeper. "I don't like the sound of this,

Fred. Not one little bit." He sat back in his chair. "So there's no doubt that what killed those people in Moscow two months ago is the same disease we're confronting now?"

"No doubt at all," Klein told him bleakly. "Smith confirms that the symptoms and test results he saw correlate perfectly with those reported by the CDC and other researchers. But . . ." His voice trailed off.

"But what?"

"Without solid evidence of official Russian involvement in spreading this mystery illness as a weapon, we can't expect anyone else — whether in NATO or in the other countries around Russia — to agree to any serious countermeasures," Klein continued. He shrugged his narrow shoulders apologetically. "The Kremlin's efforts to cover up an epidemic may be regarded as criminally stupid, but our European allies are not going to see that as a justification for possible economic sanctions or for raising NATO's alert status."

"No kidding," Castilla said drily. "I can just imagine the howls of anguish from Paris or Berlin or Kiev if I asked them to take a serious stand against Dudarev and his regime on the basis of one dead doctor's notes. And they're sure not going to be convinced by seeing a few iffy satellite photos or hearing second-hand gossip about a possible Russian military mobilization."

He sighed. "Damn it, Fred! We need facts. Right now we're just punching at shadows."

Klein nodded silently.

"I'm going to call an emergency meeting of the National Security Council when we're through here," the president decided at last. "We've got to tighten our surveillance of the Russian armed forces. At a minimum, we can retarget our satellites and conduct more reconnaissance missions along the border areas."

Unable to sit still any longer, Castilla pushed back his chair and strode over to the tall windows overlooking the South Lawn. The capital's evening rush hour was in full swing. In the gathering darkness, the cars inching along distant Constitution Avenue looked like small, crawling beads of brightly colored light. He glanced back over his shoulder. "Have you ever met Konstantin Malkovic?"

"No, I haven't," Klein admitted. He smiled slowly. "Hobnobbing with billionaires is well above my pay grade, Mr. President."

"Well, I have," Castilla said quietly. "He's a powerful man. A forceful man. An ambitious man."

"How ambitious?"

Castilla smiled thinly. "Ambitious enough to be sitting at this desk in my place — if he had been born here in the United States instead of Serbia."

Klein nodded soberly. "We'll start digging into Malkovic and his business empire. If he is secretly working with the Russians, we might be able to find connections between them that would give us a lead on what they're planning."

"You do that, Fred," the president agreed. Then he shook his head. "But I'm not sure how far you'll get. The IRS tried to go after him a few years ago — on some question of possible tax evasion as I recall. They ran into a solid wall and had to back off. Apparently he's arranged his finances as an incredible labyrinth of offshore holding companies and private foundations. The Treasury and Commerce departments suspect that he also controls a large number of other businesses on the sly, using third-party surrogates to avoid any overt ties that might prove embarrassing or illegal. The trouble is that no one seems able to prove anything."

Klein frowned. "It sounds like a perfect set-up for running deniable clandestine operations."

"Doesn't it just," Castilla agreed sourly. He swung away from the windows to face his old friend directly. "Let's talk about your team in Moscow."

"Yes, sir."

"Well, now that their cover is blown, I assume you've ordered Colonel Smith and Ms. Devin out of Russia?"

Klein chose his words carefully. "I have strongly suggested that they leave as soon as possible."

Castilla raised an eyebrow in surprise. "Only suggested? Hell, Fred, from what you've told me, every cop in Moscow is out chasing after them. What on earth can they hope to achieve in those conditions?"

The head of Covert-One shot him a lop-sided grin. "You've met Jon Smith before, Sam. You haven't yet met Fiona Devin. But I can assure you that they are both re-markably stubborn." He shook his head slowly. "In fact, almost as stubborn as you are sometimes. And right now, neither one of them is willing to admit that they're licked."

"I admire guts and persistence," Castilla said quietly. "But do Smith and Ms. Devin understand that if they are arrested, we'll throw them to the wolves?" His face was deadly serious. "That we'll deny any knowledge of them and wash our hands of any responsibility for their actions?"

"Yes, they do, Mr. President," Klein said somberly. "That's part of working for Covert-One and both of them knew the risks when they signed up. Should it prove necessary, I'm confident they will pay any price that is demanded of them."

CHAPTER TWENTY-NINE

February 20
Berlin
Ripped unwillingly from the bleary depths of a bad night's sleep, Ulrich Kessler first tried to ignore the phone ringing by his bed. Then he opened one eye a slit. The luminous numbers on his alarm clock told him it was just after six in the morning. Appalled, he groaned, rolled over, and tried to muffle the maddening, chirping noise the phone made by pulling his pillow over his head. Let the damned answering machine get it, he told himself drowsily. There would be time enough at a more reasonable hour to handle whatever crisis needed his attention.

Crisis. His eyes opened again. Even thinking the word was enough to force him all the way back to full consciousness. His position inside the highest circles of the Ministry of the Interior depended on his being seen by his superiors as the hard-working, ever reliable, indispensable man — the senior Bundeskriminalamt official they could trust with any predicament.

Groaning again with the effort, Kessler pushed himself up into a sitting position. He winced at the stabbing pain in his temples and the horrid taste in his mouth. He had drunk too much at the Chancellor's reception the night before, and then made things worse by drinking cup after cup of thick Turkish coffee in a failed bid to fully sober up before he drove home. By the time his sour, heaving stomach had finally settled itself, it must have been well after three.

He fumbled blindly for the receiver. *"Ja? Kessler hier."*

"Good morning, Herr Kessler," a woman said to him in crisp, clear German, sounding almost obscenely cheerful considering the early hour. "My name is Isabelle Stahn. I'm a special prosecutor for the Ministry of Justice, working in the public corruption division, and I'm calling to request an immediate appointment with you to discuss a special case —"

Kessler's headache flared up. He had been woken up before dawn by some over-zealous underling from the Ministry of Justice? He gripped the receiver tighter in irritation. "Look, what the devil are you doing calling me at home like this? You know the normal procedures. If your ministry wants Bundeskriminalamt assistance on some investigation, first you need to apply through the proper channels! Fax whatever paperwork you have to our liaison office and the appropriate officer will get back to you in due time."

"You misunderstand me, Herr Kessler," the woman said, now with a hint of open amusement in her voice. "You see, *you* are the target of the official corruption case I'm calling about."

"What?" Kessler snapped, suddenly wide awake.

"Some very troubling allegations have been made about your conduct, Herr Kessler," the woman continued. "Allegations concerning the escape of Professor Wulf Renke sixteen years ago —"

"That's utter nonsense!" Kessler blurted out angrily.

"Is it?" the woman asked. Her voice grew colder, taking on a tone filled with contempt. "Then I look forward to hearing your explanation for the following purchases of very expensive works of art — purchases made strictly in cash, it seems — which we have, with some difficulty, traced to you. First, in 1990, a painting by Kandinsky, bought from a gallery in Antwerp for the sum of 250,000 euros at today's rates of exchange. Then, in 1991, a collage by Matisse —"

Listening in mounting horror, Kessler broke out in a cold sweat while she ran through a painstakingly accurate list of the paintings so dear to him, paintings acquired with the money he had been paid for keeping Renke safe for so many years. He swallowed hard, trying desperately not to throw up. How could this investigator from the Ministry of Justice know so much? He had been so careful, always buying through a different agent and always using a different name and address. It should have been impossible for anyone to follow a paper trail from the various art dealers and galleries back to him.

His mind raced. Could he apply pressure to block this investigation? His own boss, the Minister of the Interior, owed him many favors. Instantly, he discarded the notion. The minister would never compromise himself by trying to conceal a scandal of this magnitude.

No, he realized desperately, he would have to flee, abandoning the possessions for which he had mortgaged his integrity and his honor. But to do so safely, he would need assistance from another source.

Inside a dark green Ford panel van parked several blocks away from Kessler's villa, Randi Russell finished her call and hung up. "That ought to send a well-deserved chill down the bastard's spine," she said, with a satisfied grin. "Ten-to-one he screams for help right away."

One of the two CIA audio-operations technicians sitting beside her in the van's cramped equipment-filled interior shook his head. "I'm not taking that bet." He nodded toward a display that showed the stress patterns they had recorded in Kessler's voice during the call. "The guy was skating right on the edge of total panic as soon as you started talking about his paintings."

"Stand by," the second technician said suddenly, holding up a hand for quiet while listening carefully to the sounds coming through her earphones. She flicked through a series of switches on the console in front of her, pausing just long enough to listen briefly to the signals transmitted by each of the listening devices Randi had planted in Kessler's house during her break-in the day before. Then she looked up. "The subject is on the move. He's left his bedroom. I think he's heading for the study."

"He'll use the telephone in there," Randi predicted. "The one in his bedroom is cordless and he won't want to risk inadvertently broadcasting anything he's about to say."

Her companions both nodded. All cordless phones acted as small radio transmitters, allowing the easy interception of conversations made using them. No one in his or her right mind ever used a cordless phone to discuss anything confidential.

The first CIA tech entered a series of commands on the keyboard in front of him. "I'm linked into the Deutsche Telekom network," he said calmly. "Ready to initiate a trace."

Still sweating, Kessler sat slowly down at the beautiful antique desk in his study. In silence, he contemplated the phone for a moment. Did he dare make contact? The number he had been given was for emergency use only. Then he laughed harshly. An emergency! he thought bleakly. Well, what else was he facing?

With a shaking hand, he picked up the receiver and slowly and carefully punched in the long international telephone code. Despite the early hour, the phone on the other end rang only three times before being answered.

"Yes?" a cold voice said brusquely. It was a voice from which he had taken occasional orders for nearly two decades.

The BKA official swallowed before speaking. "This is Kessler."

"I am well aware of who is calling me, Ulrich," Professor Wulf Renke replied. "Do not waste my time with pleasantries. What is it that you want?"

"I need immediate extraction and a new identity."

"Explain."

Trying his best to sound calm, Kessler quickly relayed the substance of the call he had received. "So you see, I need to get out of Germany as soon as possible," he said. "I've bought a few hours by agreeing to meet with the Ministry of Justice prosecutor later today, but she already knows far too much about my financial affairs. I cannot risk appearing before her."

"You believe this woman Stahn was genuine?" Renke asked icily.

Kessler was bewildered. "What else could she be?"

"You are a fool, Ulrich," the other man said flatly. "Did you even bother to confirm her story before you came running to me in fear?"

"What difference does it make?" Kessler asked. "Whoever she may be, she knows too much. I am not safe here." He felt a flicker of resentment ripple through him. "You owe me this, Herr Professor."

"I *owe* you nothing," Renke said coldly. "You have already been amply rewarded for your services. The fact that others have learned of your transgressions is unfortunate, but it gives you no special claim on me."

"Then you will do nothing for me?"

Kessler asked, appalled.

"That was not what I said," Renke retorted. "As it happens, I will honor your request for my own purposes. Now, listen carefully and follow my instructions to the letter. Stay where you are. Do not make any more calls — for any reason. When the arrangements for your escape are complete, I will telephone you with further instructions. Is that clear?"

Kessler nodded his head rapidly. "Yes, yes, that's clear."

"Good. Are you alone?"

"For now," Kessler glanced at the clock on his desk. "But my handyman and cook will be here in an hour or so."

"Send them away," Renke told him. "Tell them you are ill. There must be no witnesses to your disappearance."

"I will make sure of that," Kessler said quickly.

"I am very glad to hear it, Ulrich," Renke said, sounding genuinely pleased. "It will make everything much easier in the end."

Inside the CIA surveillance van, the first tech turned to Randi with a rueful look on his face. He took off his headset and held it out to her. "This is what we picked up from our tap on the phone line during Kessler's call."

Randi slid the earphones on and listened closely while the tech replayed the signals they had intercepted. She heard only a shrill, high-pitched whine broken by patches of static. One eyebrow rose. "Encrypted?"

"Highly encrypted," the tech told her. "At a guess, whatever encryption software these guys are using is more sophisticated than anything I've ever heard before — with the possible exception of our own stuff."

"Interesting," Randi commented.

He grinned. "Yeah, isn't it, though? I suppose the NSA might be able to break that noise apart into the clear, but doing it could take weeks."

"Did you at least manage to trace the telephone number Kessler called?" Randi asked him.

The tech shook his head. "Nope, I'm afraid not. Whoever set up the communications network he dialed into sure knows how to play the game. Every time we started getting close, the signal skipped over to a new number, automatically resetting our trace."

Randi frowned. "Could you set up a system like that?"

"Me?" He nodded slowly. "Sure." Then he shrugged. "But I'd need several weeks, a ton of money, and almost unlimited access to the proprietary switching software

409

for several different telecom corporations."

"Which means our Professor Renke has some other very influential friends watching his back," Randi said slowly.

The second CIA technician glanced at Randi with a wry smile of her own. "I guess you knew what you were doing when you planted all those other bugs in Kessler's study."

Randi nodded easily. "Let's just say I had a hunch that it would be useful to have a fallback when dealing with these people — whoever they are."

"Well, the audio-pickups worked beautifully," the second tech assured her. "I've got recordings of the whole call from Kessler's end. And once I clean up some of the ambient noise and enhance the sound, we'll be able to hear everything the other man said, too."

"Can you isolate and play back the sounds you picked up when he punched in that first telephone number?" her male colleague asked.

"No sweat."

"Outstanding." He swiveled back to face Randi. "Then we're in business. See, every time Kessler pushed one of the buttons on his phone it generated a unique tone. Once we put all those tones together in the right order, we'll know that first number he called."

Randi nodded her understanding.

"And that gives us a little piece of string that we can follow through the telecommunications maze these guys have created," the tech went on seriously. "It'll take some time, but by using that first number we can start tracking back through that maze, eventually tracing all the way to the real number hidden at its core."

"Which must belong to a telephone line tied directly to Wulf Renke," Randi said coolly. Her eyes hardened. "And then the professor and I will have a private little chat about these powerful backers of his, right before we toss him into a cell for the rest of his miserable life."

"What about Kessler?" the second CIA technician asked.

Randi smiled thinly. "Herr Kessler can sit and stew a while longer. He's already hit the panic button. Now we'll wait and see just who shows up on the doorstep to collect him."

Moscow

Impatiently, Erich Brandt prowled back and forth across his office. He was on a secure line to Berlin. "You have your orders, Lange," he snapped. "Now carry them out."

"With respect," the other man said quietly, "my men and I did not come here to commit suicide."

"Go on."

"The Americans are surely watching Kessler's house," Lange explained. "And as soon as we make our move, they will close in on us."

"You are convinced this is a CIA operation?" Brandt asked, forcing himself to restrain his anger.

"I am," Lange said. "As soon as I received your alert, I began checking with some of our other sources inside the government here."

"And?"

"There is a real Isabelle Stahn and she is a special prosecutor for the Ministry of Justice," Lange said. "But Frau Stahn is currently on maternity leave and not expected back for duty until sometime next month. Nor is there any record of an internal investigation with Kessler as the focus."

"So you think the Americans tricked him into pleading for our help," Brandt said grimly.

"Yes," Lange agreed. "And by now they will be trying to trace that call he made to Renke."

Brandt stopped pacing. If the Americans found Renke, they would also discover the HYDRA facility. And if that happened, the length of Brandt's own life would be measured in hours at best. "Will they succeed?"

"I do not know," Lange said slowly. Brandt could almost hear the other man shrug. "But that is precisely the sort of technical intelligence task at which both the NSA and CIA excel."

Brandt nodded reluctantly, knowing that his subordinate's assessment was accurate. As a rule, Americans made pitiful field agents, but their skill with machines and electronics was almost unsurpassed. His gray eyes turned ice-cold. "Then you must destroy this CIA surveillance unit before it is too late."

"We cannot destroy what we cannot find," Lange told him bluntly. "The Americans could be working from a vehicle or building anywhere within a mile radius of Kessler's villa. My team and I do not have the time to drive aimlessly all over Grunewald in the hopes of stumbling across them. To focus on a valid target, we must have more information on the CIA operations here in Berlin, and we must have it soon."

Brandt nodded. Again, Lange was right. "Very well," he said coldly. "I will contact Malkovic immediately. Our patron has a special contact in Cologne, a man who should prove most useful in this matter."

CHAPTER THIRTY

Huge housing projects lined Moscow's Outer Ring Road, surrounding the city with row after row of drab gray blocks — soulless hives built by Communist bureaucrats as lodging for the faceless masses drawn to the Soviet capital in search of work. Nearly two decades after the death of the system that created them, these housing projects were still home to hundreds of thousands of Moscow's poorest citizens.

Jon Smith and Fiona Devin made their way carefully up the interior stairwell of one of these apartment buildings. A few bare lightbulbs dangled from wiring, providing small, irregularly spaced patches of wavering light in the darkness. The concrete stairs were cracked and chipped and horribly stained. In several places along the staircase, whole sections of rusty iron railing had sheared away from their supports.

The air was thick with unpleasant smells — the eye-stinging odor of cheap disinfectant, the scent of boiled cabbage from apartment kitchens, and the odor of urine and dirty diapers from darker corners piled high with sacks of uncollected garbage. Over everything there hung the sour reek of far too many people forced to live cheek-by-jowl without enough hot water to stay truly clean.

The tiny two-room flat they were seeking was on the fourth floor, at the far end of the building, past row upon row of identically grimy and battered doors. Smith and Fiona were here to visit the parents of Mikhail Voronov, the seven-year-old boy who had first contracted the terrible disease they were tracking.

At first glance, Jon found it difficult to believe that the silent, withdrawn woman who opened the door at their knock could possibly be the boy's real mother. She seemed far too old, more a grandmother than the comparatively young woman she must be. Her hair had gone gray. Her face, probably already thin, was now horribly gaunt and deeply lined. But then he saw her eyes, full of ever-renewed sorrow and left raw and red by constant weeping. They were the eyes of a woman, always poor, who had now been robbed of her one real treasure — her only child. Even two months later, she was still clad all in black, still in mourning.

"Yes?" she asked, plainly surprised to

find two well-dressed foreigners standing on her doorstep. "How can I help you?"

"Please accept our deepest sympathies on your tragic loss, Mrs. Voronova. And please accept our most sincere apologies for intruding in this difficult time," Smith said quietly. "If it were not absolutely necessary, we would not dream of bothering you this way."

He showed her his forged UN identity card. "My name is Strand, Dr. Kalle Strand. I'm with the World Health Organization. And this is Ms. Lindkvist." He indicated Fiona. "My assistant."

"I do not understand," the woman said, still puzzled. "Why are you here?"

"We're investigating the illness that killed your son," Fiona explained gently. "We're trying to find out exactly what happened to Mikhail, so that others may someday be saved."

Slowly, comprehension dawned on the woman's grief-ravaged face. "Oh! Of course. Come in! Come in! Please, enter my home." She stepped back from the door and motioned them inside.

It was a bright winter morning outside, but the outer room she showed them into was only dimly lit, illuminated by a single, overhead fixture. Thick drapes blocked the lone window. A single-burner electric stove and a washbasin occupied one corner of the tiny room, while a threadbare sofa, a pair of battered wooden chairs, and a low table took up most of the rest.

"Please, sit down," the woman said, indicating the sofa. "I will bring my husband, Yuri." She reddened. "He is trying to sleep. You must excuse him. He is not fully himself. Not since our son —"

Clearly unable to say anything more without weeping, she turned and bustled away through a door into the flat's only other room.

Fiona silently nudged Smith, indicating the framed picture of a small, smiling boy propped up on the low table. It was wreathed in black ribbon. Two small candles flickered on either side of it.

He nodded tightly, regretting the need to deceive these poor, sad people in any way — even for a good cause. But it was necessary. From what Fred Klein had said last night, it was more urgent than ever that they obtain hard evidence about the origins of this cruel disease. One by one, the props were being knocked out from under the West's intelligence services right at a time when their best work was most needed. And one by one, the new republics surrounding Russia were being fatally weakened by the loss of their most talented political and military leaders.

The dead boy's mother came back into

417

the room, now accompanied by her husband. Like his wife, Yuri Voronov was more a shambling grief-ridden shadow than a living being. His bloodshot eyes were sunk deep in their sockets and his hands trembled constantly. His clothes, smelling of stale sweat and alcohol, hung loose on a stooped frame that seemed to be visibly wasting away.

Seeing Smith and Fiona waiting for them, Voronov slowly straightened up. With an embarrassed smile, he smoothed down his sparse, spiky hair and made a painfully correct and polite effort to welcome these two foreigners to his home, offering them tea in lieu of anything stronger. While his wife began heating water in a kettle on their small stove, he sat down across from them.

"Tatyana has told me you are scientists," Voronov said slowly. "With the United Nations? And that you are studying the illness that took our little boy?"

Smith nodded. "That's right, sir. If possible, we would very much like to ask you and your wife questions about your son's life and about his overall health. Your answers may help us learn how to fight this disease before it kills other children in other parts of the world."

"Da," the other man said simply. "We will do whatever we can." He blinked back

tears and then went on. "No one else should have to suffer as Mischka did."

"Thank you," Smith said quietly.

Then, while Fiona took detailed notes, Jon led the two Russians through a painstaking inquiry into their son's past medical history and theirs, trying to find some angle that Petrenko, Vedenskaya, and the others might have missed. For their part, the boy's parents answered patiently, even when most of Smith's questions turned out to duplicate those they had already been asked a dozen times.

Yes, Mikhail had suffered the usual childhood ailments in Russia, measles, mumps, and occasional bouts of the common flu. For the most part, though, he had been a healthy, reasonably happy child. Neither of his parents had ever used illegal drugs, although his father shamefacedly admitted to drinking too much "now and then." No, no one in the Voronovs' immediate or extended family had a history of serious chronic illness — no strange cancers or birth defects or other crippling disorders. One grandfather had died relatively young in a tractor accident on a collective farm. But the other grandparents had lived well into their late seventies before finally succumbing to a mixture of common, garden-variety ailments among the elderly — a heart attack, a stroke, and a case of severe pneumonia.

At length, Smith sat back feeling completely frustrated. So far, he could see nothing that might explain how or why Mikhail Voronov had contracted the previously unknown disease that had killed him. What linked this boy to the others who had also fallen ill in Moscow?

Jon frowned. He strongly suspected that the answer, if there was one, lay buried somewhere in their genetic makeup or in their biochemistry. Checking his theory meant obtaining DNA, blood, and tissue samples from the victims' surviving relatives. It would require unfettered access to sophisticated science labs capable of running the necessary tests. Although Oleg Kirov was sure he could safely smuggle anything they collected back to the United States, doing so would take time. And conducting those tests would require even more time — time they might not be given.

Smith sighed. If you've only got one shot left, he told himself, you'd better take it while you can and hope for the best.

To his relief, both of Mikhail Voronov's parents were eager to give him the blood and other samples he wanted. Somehow he had feared more resistance to the idea of being poked and prodded by needles.

"What else can these poor people do now that would give more meaning to their lives?" Fiona murmured softly, while she helped him sort out the test kits, syringes, Dacron-tipped swabs, and other pieces of medical equipment provided by one of Kirov's contacts in the black market. She looked up at Smith with a serious expression. "You're offering them another chance to fight back against the disease that murdered their child. Most parents I know would gladly walk through fire for that opportunity. Wouldn't you?"

Smith nodded slowly. Humbled, he turned back to the Voronovs. "Let's start by obtaining samples of your DNA." He offered them each a long swab. "Now, what I'd like you to do —"

To his surprise, before he could give them any instructions, both Russians began using the swabs to scrape away at the insides of their mouths, collecting the soft tissue cells that were the most useful for DNA analysis. Jon stared at them in astonishment. "Have you done this before?" he asked quietly.

Both of them nodded.

"Oh, yes," the boy's father told him. He shrugged. "For the big study."

"And so did little Mischka," his wife recalled softly. Tears welled up in her eyes. "He was so proud that day." She looked across at her husband. "Do you remember, Yuri? How proud he was?"

"I do." Voronov wiped at his own eyes. "Our boy was a brave little man that day."

"Pardon me?" Fiona said carefully. "But which study was this?"

"I will show you." Voronov rose to his feet and went into the back bedroom.

For a moment, they heard him rummaging around among some papers, and then he returned, holding out a large, handsomely embossed certificate of appreciation. He offered it to Smith.

With Fiona reading over his shoulder, Jon scanned the ornate script. Essentially, the certificate thanked the Voronov family for their "vital participation in the Slavic Genesis study conducted by the European Center for Population Research." It was dated the year before.

He exchanged a startled glance with Fiona. She nodded slowly in dawning comprehension. So someone had been collecting DNA from these people; and collecting it only months before the Voronov's seven-year-old son contracted a previously unknown disease — a fatal disease that destroyed systems and organs throughout the body.

For a moment longer, Smith sat still, staring down at the certificate in his hands. His eyes narrowed. Now, at last, he knew what they might be looking for.

Zurich Airport

Nikolai Nimerovsky paused briefly at the door to the Alpenblick Bar, looking for his contact. His gaze roved over the mostly solitary business travelers seated at different tables and stopped when he saw a pale, gray-haired man sitting with a copy of yesterday's International *Herald Tribune* conspicuously open before him. He moved closer, noting the man's black leather briefcase — virtually identical to the one in his own hands — and the small, double-helix lapel pin in his plain blue sport coat.

The Russian drew even nearer, conscious that his pulse was speeding up. Years of service as a clandestine agent for Ivanov's Thirteenth Directorate had taught him caution. He stopped in front of the gray-haired man and motioned to the empty chair. "Do you mind?" he asked in American-accented English.

The other man looked up from his newspaper. His eyes were appraising. "Not at all," he said slowly. "My flight is almost ready to leave. I'm only in *transit*."

Sign, Nimerovsky thought, hearing the slight emphasis on the last word. He sat down and set his briefcase on the floor next to its counterpart. "So am I. My flight has only a short layover here in Zurich. The world grows ever more *connected*, does it not?"

Countersign.

The gray-haired man smiled slightly. "So it does, friend." He folded his newspaper, stood, picked up one of the two briefcases, and then left with a polite, disinterested nod.

Nimerovsky waited a few moments more before retrieving the briefcase the other man had left behind from under the table. He opened it quickly. It contained a sheaf of papers, business magazines, and a small gray plastic box marked "SC-1." Inside that heavily insulated box, the Russian knew, nestled a tiny glass tube. He closed the briefcase.

"Ladies and gentlemen," a woman's voice said politely over the public-address system, speaking first in German, then French, Italian, and English. "SwissAir announces that its Flight 3000, with nonstop service to New York's John F. Kennedy International Airport, is now ready for passenger boarding."

The Russian stood up and left the bar, carrying with him the unique HYDRA variant destined for President Samuel Adams Castilla.

CHAPTER THIRTY-ONE

Cologne, Germany

It was midmorning. Sheets of freezing rain spattered against the towering twin spires of Cologne's massive Gothic cathedral, hiding them from the view of people hurrying along the paved streets far below. Inside the cathedral, a few hardy tourists milled around the enormous nave, staring in awe at its many priceless treasures — among them, beautiful stained-glass windows, finely sculpted stone and marble statues, and an ancient wood-carved crucifix, the Cross of Gero, which dated back more than a thousand years. Here and there, lone worshippers either knelt in private prayer or paused briefly to light small candles on their way back out to take up the ordinary burdens of the work-aday world. Otherwise, the vast, shadow-filled space was almost deserted, seemingly frozen in an ethereal, eternal silence.

Gray-faced with fear and wearing a gray raincoat, Bernhard Heichler genuflected before the high altar. He crossed himself, entered one of the nearby pews, and then laboriously went to his knees. He bowed his head as though deep in meditation.

Footsteps echoed across the stone floor, drawing ever closer. Heichler closed his eyes, feeling his heart pounding wildly in fear. Please, God, he thought desperately, let this cup pass me by. Then he bit his lip, suddenly appalled by the grotesque blasphemy of his own thoughts. Of all men in this sacred place, he had no right to echo the agonized plea made by Christ in the Garden. He was a Judas, a betrayer.

And Bernhard Heichler knew that he had much to betray. He was a senior officer in the Bundesamtes für Verfassunsschutz, the Federal Office for the Protection of the Constitution. The BfV was Germany's principal counterintelligence agency, its equivalent of the British MI5. His security clearances gave him unfettered access to some of his government's most closely held secrets.

Someone slid into the next pew behind him.

Heichler raised his head.

"Do not turn around, Herr Heichler," a man's voice said quietly. "You are prompt. I congratulate you."

"I had no choice," Heichler replied stiffly.

"That is true," the other man agreed. "You became our man the moment you

426

took our money. You will remain our man until the day you die."

Heichler winced. For six long years he had waited in fear for his benefactors to collect the debt he owed them. For six long years he had hoped that horrible day would never come.

But now it had.

"What is it that you want of me?" Heichler muttered.

"A gift," the other man replied. He sounded amused. "The Shrine of the Magi lies just behind that altar, correct?"

The BfV official nodded uneasily. The Shrine, a golden box encrusted with precious gems, was said to contain relics of the three Magi, the wise men who had come from the east bearing gifts for the Christ child. Brought from Milan in the twelfth century, the reliquary was the cathedral's greatest treasure, the very reason it had been built.

"You can rest quietly," the other man told him. "You need not bring us gold or frankincense or myrrh — only that which is already yours to command. Information, Herr Heichler. We want information."

A missal thudded onto the pew beside Heichler, startling him.

"Open it."

Trembling, he obeyed. The prayer book contained a single slip of paper bearing a twelve-digit telephone number.

"You will fax the information we require to that number. And you will do so within the next two hours. Is that clear?"

Heichler nodded. Reluctantly, he took the slip of paper and tucked it away inside his raincoat. "But what is this information you need?"

"The registration and license numbers of all vehicles currently operated by the Berlin Station of the American Central Intelligence Agency."

Heichler felt the blood drain from his face. "But that is impossible!" he stammered.

"On the contrary," the man behind him said coldly, "it is perfectly possible — for a high-ranking officer in Section V. For someone like you, in fact, Herr Heichler." With implacable precision, the man went on. "Section V oversees all foreign intelligence organizations operating on German soil, including those of allied countries like the United States. Liaison officers from these organizations provide your staff with regular updates on the equipment they are using, the names of their field agents, and other aspects of their clandestine work within our borders. Isn't that so?"

Slowly, the BfV official nodded.

"Then you can obtain the data we need, and you will follow our instructions."

"The risk is too great!" Heichler whined. He was ashamed to hear the note of panic in his voice and desperately fought to regain some measure of control over himself. "Accessing the information you require so quickly will inevitably mean leaving traces that might incriminate me. And if the Americans ever find out what I have done —"

"You must choose which you fear more," the other man said harshly. "The Americans or us. A sensible man would weigh the odds carefully."

Heichler squirmed under the awful knowledge that he had no real choice. He must obey these orders, or pay the terrible price for his earlier crimes and betrayals. His shoulders slumped in surrender, and he nodded drearily. "Very well. I will do what I can."

"You have chosen wisely," the other man commended him sardonically. "Remember, you have just two hours. And failure will not be tolerated."

Near Orvieto, Italy

Professor Wulf Renke ran a magnifier slowly over the printout of the results of his most recent DNA sequencer run. Carefully, he studied the intricate patterns the printout showed, hunting for the unique patches of the genetic sequence — rare single-nucleotide polymorphisms — that were needed to continue sculpting this next HYDRA variant. But then his watch beeped insistently, reminding him that it would soon be time to inspect the next batch of *E. coli* cultures. He had only a few more minutes to complete an analysis that should take at least another hour.

The German weapons scientist frowned, irked by this latest evidence of excessive haste. Constant demands from Moscow for faster production were forcing him to run the lab, his staff, and their equipment at a dizzying, breakneck pace. Each HYDRA variant was a miniature work of art, one ideally requiring ample time to design and craft with loving precision. Instead, Malkovic and Viktor Dudarev expected him to churn out new lethal strands on an assembly-line basis, as though this facility was only an old-fashioned armaments factory mass-producing high-explosive artillery shells.

Renke thought it would have been wiser to wait longer before unleashing his creation on the world. With only a few more months of preparation, none of this rushing about would have been necessary. He could have had all the necessary HYDRA variants stockpiled and ready for use on command. Unfortunately, his employers were impetuous and angry men. Worse, from his viewpoint, the men in Moscow were still wedded to an outdated belief in the power of massed armor, infantry, and bombers. As a result, their timetable for ZHUKOV revolved entirely around considerations of the weather, Russia's ability to deploy military forces by rail and road, and how long it might take those Russian troops to capture their objectives once the shooting started.

He sniffed in contempt. Neither Malkovic nor the Russian president had any real appreciation of the subtler and more lasting power conveyed by their control over a weapon like HYDRA. His creations could have been used to terrify prospective opponents, frightening them into toeing the Russian line without the need for any wasteful, large-scale violence. But instead, his employers saw HYDRA as just one more means of killing. Typical Slavs, Renke thought derisively. They understood the application of power only in its most brutal and obvious guise.

Renke shrugged. Error compounding error. And folly feeding on folly. It was an old story in his career — whether in East Germany, the Soviet Union, or in Iraq. One could never trust laymen to think and act with clarity. Their greed and basic ignorance always interfered with rational decision-making. Fortunately, he was immune to such weaknesses.

"Professore?" one of his assistants called, holding out a phone. "Signor Brandt is on the secure line."

Impatiently, Renke yanked off his face shield, surgical mask, and gloves. He tossed them into a bin and then took the phone. "Yes?" the white-haired scientist snapped. "What is it, Erich?"

"An update on our two most troubling security problems," Brandt said tersely. "The ones we face in Berlin and here in Moscow."

Renke nodded to himself. In this case, the other man was right to interrupt him. "Go ahead."

He listened intently while Brandt filled him in on recent events. The news from Berlin reassured him. Once Lange and his hit team had the information they needed, their success seemed certain. The news from Moscow was far less pleasing. "There's still no sign of these Americans?" he asked in disbelief.

"None," Brandt said. "None of Alexei Ivanov's vaunted militia checkpoints have turned up so much as a hint of their whereabouts. He believes Smith and Devin may have gone to ground at a safe house outside the city — or that they have already escaped from Russia."

"And what do you think?"

"I think Ivanov is too optimistic," Brandt replied. "Ms. Devin may only be an amateur spy, but Colonel Smith is most certainly a hardened professional. He will not abandon a mission so easily."

Renke contemplated that. The former Stasi officer's evaluation of his opponent seemed accurate. "So? What is your next move, then?" he asked coolly.

Brandt hesitated. "I am not sure."

The scientist raised an eyebrow in disbelief. "Come now, Erich," he snapped. "Smith and Devin are not fools. Surely you know what they will find in Vedenskaya's notes?"

"Herr Professor," the other man said through gritted teeth, "you forget that I am not a scientist. My skills lie in other directions."

"The names," Renke said in exasperation. "The Americans will learn the names of those we used as the first test subjects for HYDRA. Whatever else Colonel Smith is, he is also a scientist, a medical researcher. Faced with a strange disease, he'll try to determine the vector. Now, all you have to do is bait the proper trap, and then wait for them to walk right into it."

CHAPTER THIRTY-TWO

Berlin
Deep in the interior of a multistory public parking garage a few kilometers from the Grunewald district, Gerhard Lange heard a static-laden voice squawk over his radio. Between the interference and the man's obvious excitement, it was impossible to make out what he was trying to report. Frowning, Lange straightened up slowly and pushed the tiny receiver deeper into his ear. "What was that, Mueller?" he demanded. "Say again."

This time, Mueller, the heavyset man who had met his team at the airport the day before, spoke more slowly and clearly. "I have your targets," he said. "Repeat: I have your targets confirmed."

Lange breathed out. The waiting game was over. He leaned in through the open driver's side window of their black BMW and retrieved a copy of the faxed list they had received two hours ago. "Read them back to me."

While Mueller fed him the license plates and makes of vehicles he had spotted during his reconnaissance, the ex–Stasi officer checked them against the list of CIA-registered cars and trucks in Berlin. They matched perfectly. He folded the fax and slid it inside his jacket. Then he unfolded a detailed map of the local streets. "Excellent work. Now, where exactly are these Americans deployed?"

Lange listened closely, using a red pen to circle the positions given to him by the heavyset man. He studied them briefly, noting relative distances and alternate approach and escape routes. A plan began taking shape in his mind. Quick and dirty, he thought coldly. And the quicker, the better.

He turned to his companions. *"Pripremiti. Nama imati jedan cilj!"* he growled in Serbian. "Get ready. We have a target!"

At his command, the three hard-faced men, all veterans of Serbian State Security and of the brutal ethnic cleansing campaigns in Bosnia and Kosovo, put out their cigarettes and scrambled to their feet. Lange opened the BMW's trunk and swiftly handed out equipment and ammunition. When he was through, the ex–Stasi officer and the members of his handpicked hunter-killer team began donning their gear and checking their weapons.

Although it was only midafternoon, it

435

was growing dark fast. Solid masses of leaden clouds covered the sky. Whipped up by a strong wind from the east, occasional flurries of fresh snow danced across the Grunewald's nearly deserted streets and sidewalks. The rising wind howled through the nearby woods and sent more snow sliding off the steep slate roofs of houses nestled among the trees.

To keep warm, Randi Russell walked at a brisk pace, heading south along Clayallee. This wide avenue, which ran here along the urban forest preserve's eastern border, was named for the American general, Lucius Clay, who had ordered the Berlin Airlift to save the city from starvation during the opening rounds of the Cold War. Wearing a fashionable ski jacket, black turtleneck sweater, and jeans, she was returning to the CIA surveillance van after making a cautious prowl through the quiet neighborhood around Ulrich Kessler's villa.

So far, nothing much was happening. Her lookout outside the villa reported only normal traffic through the area. The BKA official himself was still inside his home. As the day wore on without further contact from Wulf Renke, though, Kessler was growing increasingly edgy. The listening devices she had planted earlier were picking up sounds of constant pacing, sporadic cursing, and the frequent clink of bottles and glassware from around his well-stocked liquor cabinet.

Randi thought again about this strange silence from Renke. Had the renegade weapons scientist decided to cut his losses and leave Kessler to his fate? The more time that went by without any sign of movement in or out of the house, the more likely that began to seem. Above all else, Renke was a survivor. He had never demonstrated real loyalty to any other person, country, or ideology. The scientist would save Kessler only if he saw some advantage to himself in doing so. And by now, Renke must suspect that his longtime protector inside the BKA was under close surveillance. If so, Randi wondered, was it worth snatching Kessler herself? Could she squeeze any useful information out of the guy before Langley got nervous and ordered her to hand him over to his own people?

She grinned, imagining the likely reaction of the risk-averse CIA bureaucrats if one of their field officers kidnapped a German federal criminal police official. No, Randi decided wryly, grabbing Kessler was not going to fly. Instead, her best bet might be to back off for now. Later she could look for a discreet way to let his superiors know about his criminal conduct.

Of course, she would also have to manage that without revealing that she had hacked into one of their high-security computer networks.

In the meantime, her audio-operations technicians were busy trying to trace that first emergency number Kessler had dialed. So far, they had linked it to a cell phone registered in Switzerland. Where the trail would lead from there was still anyone's guess.

A big yellow BVG transit bus roared past with only a handful of passengers on board. Randi looked up, getting her bearings. On her right, to the west, lay the quiet, snow-cloaked forest. On her left, across the road, there were houses and a row of small shops. There were more vehicles moving on this stretch of the avenue — a few private cars and a couple of delivery trucks out making their rounds despite the slowly worsening weather. A block ahead, she could see the surveillance team's Ford panel van parked between an older Audi and a brand-new Opel station wagon.

She tapped a button on what looked like a silver iPod hooked to her belt. Designed for undercover operations, this iPod actually contained a sophisticated tactical radio set with several secure channels. "Base, this is Lead. I'm coming in."

"Understood, Lead," one of the techs working in the van replied. Suddenly his voice sharpened. "Wait one, Randi. We're picking up an incoming call to Kessler's house. Someone's telling him to be ready to leave, that an extraction unit is on its way!"

Yes! Randi enthusiastically pounded her clenched right fist into the open palm of her left hand. It was about time. "Okay, Base. Get ready to saddle up. When these guys swoop in and scoop Kessler up, we'll tag along behind to see where they take him."

"Got it," the CIA tech said. Over the radio link, she could hear him awkwardly clambering from the back of the window-less van into the driver's seat.

Still walking toward the Ford, Randi switched frequencies to speak directly to the young Berlin Station field officer posted down the street from Kessler's villa. "Watcher, this is Lead. Did you copy that?"

Silence.

She frowned. "Carla, this is Randi. Come in."

There was no answer. Only the faint hiss of static over dead airwaves. Randi swung round in alarm, feeling a cold chill run down her spine. Something was going wrong. Very wrong. She unzipped her

439

jacket just far enough so that she could draw the 9mm Beretta pistol in her shoulder holster without snagging it on her clothes — in case she needed the weapon out in a hurry.

At that moment, she saw a black BMW sedan racing down Clayallee at high speed, with its powerful engine revving as it wove in and out around slower-moving cars and trucks. Instinctively, her hand dove inside her jacket, reaching for her pistol. But the speeding car drove on past her surveillance van. She breathed out in relief.

Then, suddenly, the BMW braked hard. The black sedan slewed around through a tire-squealing, rubber-burning, 180-degree turn, and rocked to a full stop just a few meters away from the parked Ford.

Three of the BMW's four doors flew open, and three lean, cold-eyed men jumped out onto the street. They moved rapidly, fanning out in an arc around the CIA-owned van. Each man held a submachine gun — Heckler & Koch MP5SDs equipped with integral noise suppressors — tucked against his shoulder in a shooting stance. Randi's eyes widened as she recognized the black jumpsuits and dark green, eagle-badge berets worn by Germany's elite counterterrorist unit, GSG-9, Grenzschutz-gruppe-9.

"Oh, shit," she muttered. One of the

area residents or local shopkeepers must have spotted her surveillance team, started getting suspicious, and then called the authorities with a warning. After 9/11 and the horror of the Madrid commuter train massacre, Germany, France, Spain, and others now kept elements of their rapid-reaction forces on permanent alert. Randi quickly took her hand off the butt of the Beretta. There was no point in spooking these heavily armed commandos. If they thought they were going up against terrorists, their nerves and reflexes were sure to be set on a hair-trigger.

Instead, carefully reaching inside her jacket for her Agency identity card, she started walking even faster, heading straight for the GSG-9 unit. Maybe she could intervene before these overeager German soldiers blew her whole clandestine operation sky-high. Once they roused her people out onto the sidewalk in full view of every curious onlooker, there would be no way to keep the story off the airwaves. And the local media would have a field day running breathless updates about the foolhardy American intelligence agents caught spying on peaceful German citizens.

"Lead, this is Base," one of the two technicians inside the van radioed, sounding rattled. "What should we do?"

Randi switched back to her primary channel. "Just sit tight, guys. I'm coming. Let me handle this."

She was still at least fifty meters away when the three black-clad gunmen suddenly opened fire, shooting without any warning or provocation.

Their submachine guns stuttered on full automatic, raking the van from back to front at point-blank range. Showers of sparks cascaded high in the air as dozens of 9mm rounds ripped through the vehicle, puncturing metal, shattering fragile electronics gear, and shredding human flesh. Most of the bullets punched straight through and came out on the other side still moving at close to the speed of sound. But enough hit home to turn the interior of the Ford into a blood-drenched slaughterhouse. Through her earphones, Randi heard agonized screams that were mercifully cut short as the hail of submachine gun fire went on and on.

These must be Renke's men, she realized in horror. They had not come to rescue Kessler. Instead, they had come to kill those who were keeping watch on him.

Snarling in rage, Randi drew her Beretta, aimed rapidly at the nearest gunman, and squeezed off two shots. One round missed. The other hit the man high in the chest. But instead of dropping him, the impact only knocked him backward a couple of paces. He grunted, doubled over for a brief moment, and then straightened back up. She could see the hole torn in his clothing, but there was no sign of any blood.

Christ, she realized suddenly, these bastards are wearing body armor. Her survival instincts kicked in and she threw herself sideways, diving for cover behind a Volvo parked along the side of Clayallee.

The man turned fast in her direction, bringing his submachine gun up in the same, whirling movement. He fired a long burst, spraying bullets toward the Volvo.

Lying prone behind the parked car, Randi buried her head in her hands as the Volvo shuddered and rocked above her, hit repeatedly at close range. Bits and pieces of shredded metal, glass, and plastic spun away across the street. Ricochets and near misses cracked by low overhead. They tore into other parked vehicles or spun away off the pavement, hurling shards of shattered concrete in all directions. Earsplitting car alarms began going off up and down the avenue, triggered by the barrage of sudden impacts.

The shooting stopped suddenly.

Breathing hard, Randi rolled back out onto the sidewalk with her Beretta held out in front of her and ready to fire. She saw two of the black-clad gunmen scrambling back into the BMW. The third had slung his submachine gun across one shoulder and stood hunched over, fiddling with what looked like a small green canvas bag.

This time, she took careful aim, extending the Beretta in a two-handed marksman's grip. She waited until her pistol's sights settled on the third gunman and held steady. Then she squeezed the trigger. The Beretta barked once, recoiling back against her tight grip. Nothing. A miss. Randi's eyes narrowed, focusing on her target. She steadied the pistol again and took another shot.

This 9mm round slammed into the gunman's upper right leg, shattered his femur, and exploded out the other side in a spray of blood and bone fragments. He sat down suddenly, staring in disbelief at his mangled leg. The canvas bag tumbled out of his hands and fell to the street.

A look of desperation flashed across the wounded man's face. He lashed out with his left foot, kicking the bag away from him. It spun wildly across the ground and ended up under the bullet-riddled CIA surveillance van.

Randi heard the crippled gunman shout a panicked warning in what sounded like some kind of guttural Slavic language. Immediately, one of his comrades leaned out of the BMW, grabbed him under the arms, and hauled him inside, leaving a pool of bright red blood smeared across the street.

Without waiting any longer, the driver of the black sedan hit the gas pedal and peeled out, accelerating back up Clayallee the way they had come. Pistol in hand, Randi scrambled to her feet. She swung the Beretta through a wild, wide arc, leading the BMW as it flashed past her at well over eighty kilometers an hour. She squeezed the trigger repeatedly, trying to fire as many shots as she could at the fast-moving target.

One of her rounds smashed the car's rear window. A second hit punched a hole in the trunk. But the others went wide. Cursing under her breath, she stopped shooting, not willing to risk hitting innocent bystanders by mistake.

The BMW kept going, heading north along the avenue until at last it disappeared in the gathering twilight.

For a moment longer, Randi stood staring along the street in sheer disbelief. She felt stunned by the magnitude of this unhesitating and utterly murderous assault on her surveillance team. How in God's name had this happened? she wondered bitterly. How could Wulf Renke's men have zeroed in on them with such unerring precision?

Slowly, she lowered the Beretta and

forced herself to flip the safety catch on. It was not easy. Her hands were starting to shake as the wild exhilaration of close combat ebbed away, leaving only sorrow and a deep, abiding anger in its place. Then Randi glanced back over her shoulder at the bullet-shattered Ford van.

The small canvas bag was just visible. It was lying on its side beside one of the rear wheels.

A bag, her mind said. Then, a split-second later, her mind corrected itself. No, she thought coldly. That's a bomb — a satchel charge.

Run, Randi told herself. Run away now! Her mind suddenly in overdrive, she turned and fled, sprinting away from the van as fast as she could move. Gun in hand, she raced past stalled cars whose drivers were still staring in shock at the mangled van.

"Get out! Get out!" she yelled at them in German, gesturing with the Beretta. "There's a bomb!"

And then the satchel charge exploded.

A sudden flash of blinding white light ripped through the darkness behind Randi. Still running flat-out, she hurled herself down, curling up for protection just as the shock wave, roaring outward from the very center of the powerful blast, rolled over her. The massive wall of superheated air bounced her high off the pavement and then tossed her tumbling end over end across the ground. At the same time, a giant fist — the overpressure caused by the blast — seemed to squeeze every ounce of oxygen out of her lungs.

Slowly, the flaring white light faded. Everything went pitch-black. The world around her vanished as she fell out and away from consciousness.

She came to only seconds later, lying curled up against the side of a car thrown sideways across the road by the blast. Half deafened, with her ears still ringing, Randi forced herself first to sit up and then to climb back to her feet, wincing unwillingly at the pain from tortured muscles and bruised and bleeding patches of skin.

All around her on the street, other dazed and injured people were pulling themselves out of vehicles that had been hammered by the shock wave or hit by flying debris. Others, streaked with blood or cradling broken limbs, were stumbling blindly out of their bomb-damaged homes and businesses. The enormous explosion had torn open roofs, toppled chimneys, and shattered every window facing the street, sending shards of broken glass sleeting through living rooms, kitchens, bedrooms, and storefronts.

Slowly, Randi turned and stared back at

the place where the surveillance van had been.

The Ford was gone, replaced by an ugly tangle of twisted, burning wreckage. All of the other cars that had been parked within fifty meters of the shattered van now lay canted across Clayallee — crumpled, smashed, and wreathed in billowing orange and flame. Thick black smoke drifted across the road.

Randi blinked away tears. There was no time now for sorrow, she decided coldly. If she lived long enough, that would have to come later.

Forcing herself to focus, she quickly checked over her equipment. Her radio was dead, probably wrecked beyond repair when the explosion sent her skittering across the pavement. Well, it doesn't really matter, she thought bleakly. After all, she had no one left to contact. She spotted her Beretta lying on the sidewalk a few meters away and awkwardly limped over to pick it up.

Frowning in concentration, Randi carefully examined the pistol. Although the Beretta's grip and barrel were scraped and scarred, its firing pin, trigger spring, hammer, and slide all appeared undamaged. One side of her mouth twitched upward in a bitter, self-mocking grin. From the look of it, the 9mm weapon was in better shape than she was.

She hit the magazine release catch, dumped out the half-empty clip, and dropped it into one of her jacket pockets. Then she slapped in a fresh fifteen-round magazine, pulled back on the slide, and lowered the hammer. She was ready.

Randi slid the pistol back into her shoulder holster and took one last, grim look at the burning wreckage scattered across Clayallee. She could hear police, fire, and ambulance sirens warbling louder and louder as the German authorities began reacting to the disaster.

It was time to go.

She turned away and hobbled to the west, pushing deeper in among the trees of the Grunewald forest preserve until she was well out of sight from the road. There, Randi turned north and forced herself into a painful loping run, moving faster and faster among the shadows and the silent, white-cloaked woods.

CHAPTER THIRTY-THREE

Main Space Command Center, Near Moscow

Colonel-General Leonid Averkovich Nesterenko, the tall, dapper commander-in-chief of the Russian Federation's military space forces, marched briskly down the corridor connecting his quarters with the Operations Control Center. Bright fluorescent lighting overhead and a constant flow of fresh-smelling, cool air from ventilation shafts made it difficult to remember that this massive installation was buried hundreds of meters below ground, shielded from attack by massive slabs of steel-reinforced concrete. Its heavily guarded entrance and exit tunnels were concealed in the dense birch forests north of Moscow.

The two armed sentries on guard outside the Operations Center stiffened to attention as he approached. Nestrenko ignored them. Ordinarily a stickler for the finer points of formal military courtesy, he was far too pressed for time just now.

Nestrenko pushed quickly through the

door and hurried into the vast chamber beyond. As his eyes adjusted to this huge room's subdued lighting, he could see row upon row of control consoles. The officers at each console were either busy monitoring the satellite and early warning radar systems in their charge, or conferring quietly via secure communications equipment with colleagues at launch sites, ground stations, and local command posts across Russia.

At the far end of the Center, an enormous, wall-sized screen showed the world and the key spacecraft and satellites orbiting around it. Bright yellow dotted lines depicted each object's predicted orbital path, while small green vector arrows indicated their current positions.

The duty officer, a much shorter, square-jawed man named Baranov, hurried to Nestrenko's side. "The Americans are maneuvering one of their Lacrosse radar-imaging reconnaissance satellites, sir," he reported.

Nestrenko frowned. "Show me."

The shorter man turned and snapped an order to one of his subordinates at the nearest control console. "Bring up the data on Lacrosse-Five."

One of the blinking arrows on the huge wall screen changed color, flashing from green to red. At the same time, a new dotted line began slowly diverging from the satellite's previously observed orbital track.

"We detected the burn approximately five minutes ago," Baranov told him.

Nestrenko nodded, glowering as he studied Lacrosse-Five's new predicted course. "What are our American friends up to?" he murmured. He turned back to Baranov. "Show me a close-up of that projected track where it first crosses our borders. And put up overlays showing the locations where we can expect the Americans to gain significantly better reconnaissance capability from this new orbital path."

The image on the wall screen flickered and then expanded rapidly, zooming in to focus on a much smaller area — the Ukraine, Belarus, and western Russia. Glowing boxes marked out huge swathes of territory along a diagonal running northeast from Kiev to Moscow and beyond. The assembly areas for the tank and motor rifle divisions slated to invade the Ukraine were right in the middle of one of those boxes.

"Damn," Nestrenko muttered. The Lacrosse satellite carried a powerful synthetic aperture radar imaging system, one that could "see" through clouds, dust, and darkness. The ZHUKOV assembly areas were hidden beneath layers of radar-absorbent camouflage netting, but no one could be sure that this experimental material would successfully deflect such close scrutiny.

"We have a Spider in position," Baranov reminded him quietly, pointing at another vector arrow blinking on the display. "Our targeting computers predict that it will be in effective range for another thirty minutes."

Nestrenko nodded tightly. The Spider was one of Russia's most secret space weapons systems. Disguised as ordinary civilian-use communications, weather, and navigation satellites, each Spider also contained anti-satellite weapons for use against enemy space platforms in low earth orbit. In theory, such an attack could be carried out covertly. But in practice? If detected, any Russian effort to destroy an American spy satellite could easily be construed as an act of war.

Then he shrugged. This decision was beyond his authority. He stepped forward to the nearest console and picked up a red secure phone. "This is Colonel-General Nestrenko. Patch me through to the Kremlin," he told the operator on the other end firmly. "I must speak with the president immediately. Inform him that this is a war priority communication."

In Orbit

Four hundred kilometers above the earth's sun-flecked seas and its great brown, green, and white masses of land, a Russian meteorology satellite officially registered as COSMOS-8B swung through its regular elliptical orbit, moving at twenty-seven thousand kilometers an hour. In reality, the counterfeit satellite was a weapons-carrier code-named Spider Twelve. Now, as it flew high over the coast of Africa, the spacecraft's high-frequency data-relay antenna began receiving coded transmissions containing new programming for its onboard computers.

Within sixty seconds of receiving the last transmission, Spider Twelve went active.

Small altitude rockets fired, spewing small puffs of vapor into space. Slowly, the long cylinder-shaped satellite spun through an arc until its blunt nose aimed at a point in space above the earth's distant curved horizon. When Spider Twelve reached the desired angle, the rockets fired again, arresting its rotation. A relay closed and hatches popped open at the base of the nose.

Six smaller space vehicles — cone-shaped anti-satellite warheads — drifted out through the hatches and slowed slightly, braked by clusters of tiny maneuvering thrusters firing in a preprogrammed sequence. As they decelerated, the warheads began falling toward the earth, arcing downward through a great curve that would bring them within striking range of that distant, precisely calculated point.

When the six warheads were several kilometers away, Spider Twelve performed its last programmed act. Self-destruct charges placed at key points throughout the ten-ton satellite exploded in short, sharp, blinding flashes that were bright enough to be picked up by both American and Russian early-warning sensors orbiting high above the globe. The detonations ripped Spider Twelve to pieces, shearing antennas, solar arrays, and puncturing fuel tanks. Spewing water vapor and fuel, the tangled wreckage began tumbling through space, shedding smaller fragments as it fell slowly toward the upper fringes of the earth's atmosphere.

Covered by the brighter explosions behind them, the six anti-satellite warheads also detonated. Each burst sent a hail of thousands of small, razor-edged pieces of titanium into space. Together, they formed a giant cloud of shrapnel, a deadly cloud flying onward at more than seven kilometers a second.

Forty-five seconds later, and more than three hundred kilometers down-range, the shrapnel cloud intersected the orbital track of Lacrosse-Five, one of only two U.S. radar-imaging reconnaissance satellites circling the globe.

Main Space Command Center

"Our tracking radar confirms multiple shrapnel impacts on Lacrosse-Five," Baranov said jubilantly, listening closely to a report relayed by one of his watch officers. He turned his head toward Nestrenko. "Preliminary damage assessment shows that the American spy satellite has been totally destroyed."

The colonel-general nodded calmly. He picked up the red phone again. "This is Nestrenko," he said calmly. "Connect me with the United States Space Command."

He looked across at Baranov with a slight smile while waiting for his hotline call to go through. "I will have to convey my sincere regrets and deepest apologies for the terrible damage accidentally caused by this catastrophic explosion on board one of our COSMOS-class weather satellites."

"Do you think the Americans will believe you?"

Nestrenko shrugged. "Maybe. Maybe not. What is most important is that they cannot possibly launch a replacement for their wrecked radar spy satellite in time.

Soon, very soon, we will no longer be forced to care so much about what the Americans believe. Or what they may do."

The White House

It was still early in the morning when a uniformed Secret Service agent ushered Fred Klein into the president's den upstairs in the East Wing. The room, full of old books, prints of works by Frederic Remington and Georgia O'Keeffe, and photographs of the rugged New Mexico landscape, was all Castilla's own — his private refuge from the routine frenzy of the White House's more public spaces.

The president himself sat in one of the room's two large recliners, moodily paging through the morning intelligence brief. A tray nearby held his untouched breakfast. He motioned toward the other chair. "Sit down, Fred."

Klein obeyed.

Wearily, Castilla pushed the pile of papers aside and turned to his old friend. "Has there been any more news from Smith or the others in Moscow?"

"Not yet," Klein told him. "But I expect another report in a matter of hours at most."

The president nodded somberly. "Good. Because I'm going to need as much information as I can get — and I'm going to need it very soon. Certainly within the next forty-eight hours."

Klein raised an eyebrow.

"I'm more and more convinced that whatever the Russians are planning is coming up fast," Castilla explained. "Which means that our window for heading them off is closing even faster."

"Yes, sir," the head of Covert-One agreed. If the rumors Smith and Fiona Devin had picked up about the accelerating tempo of Russian military preparations were accurate, the U.S. and its allies would already be hard-pressed to react in time.

"I'm calling a secret meeting with high-level representatives of some of our closest allies," Castilla told him. "Those who still pack a respectable military punch — the UK, France, Germany, and Japan, for a start. I want us to forge a united response to the Kremlin, a series of concrete measures that will force Dudarev to back down *before* he pulls the trigger on whatever operation he's planning."

"When?" Klein asked quietly.

"The morning of February 22," the president said. "I don't see how we can afford to wait any longer than that."

Klein frowned. "That's a very tight deadline," he said at length. "I don't know that I can promise concrete results by then."

458

Castilla nodded. "I understand. But that's all the time we have left, Fred. Believe me, I'm making the same impossible demands of everyone else. At the NSC meeting last night, I ordered the redirection of every other component of our national intelligence capability — spy satellites, signals intercept stations, and whatever agent networks we still have — onto the same mission. When our allies show up in the Oval Office, I need solid and convincing evidence of Russia's aggressive intentions."

"And if we can't get it for you in time?"

The president sighed. "Then I'll go ahead with the meeting anyway, but I won't kid myself. Without something more than my own fears and a few vague hints of trouble, the odds are very much against anyone else being willing to join us in facing down Moscow."

Klein nodded tightly. "I'll relay the critical time frame to Colonel Smith as soon as I can."

"You do that," Castilla said softly. "I hate like hell to ask you to expose your people to more danger, but I don't see any alternative." He broke off, hearing his secure phone ring. He answered it swiftly. "Yes?"

While Klein watched, the president's broad, deeply lined face sagged. Suddenly

459

he looked years older.

"When?" Castilla asked, gripping the phone until his knuckles turned white. He listened to the reply, then nodded his head firmly. "I understand, Admiral," he said quietly.

The president disconnected and then punched in an internal White House number. "This is Sam Castilla, Charlie," he said to his chief of staff. "Round up the NSC pronto. We have an emergency situation on our hands."

Finished, he turned back to Klein. "That was Admiral Brose," he said. His eyes were tired and discouraged. "He just received a flash communication from Space Command headquarters out in Colorado. There's been an explosion in space, and we've lost one of our most sophisticated spy satellites — Lacrosse-Five."

CHAPTER THIRTY-FOUR

North of Moscow

It was pitch-black outside by the time Jon Smith and Fiona Devin reached their next destination, a large dacha once owned by Aleksandr Zakarov, the old man who had been the second victim of the suspicious disease outbreak they were investigating. Before he retired, Zakarov had been both an influential member of the ruling Communist Party and the State manager of a heavy industry complex. During the first, wild years of crony capitalism after the Soviet Union imploded, he had earned a substantial fortune by selling off "shares" in the factories under his control.

The luxurious dacha he had acquired with some of his ill-gotten loot was located over an arduous hour's drive north of the Outer Ring Road. While grinding slowly along narrow, snow-clogged country lanes through gloomy patches of forest and past tiny villages and abandoned churches, Smith had wondered why on earth Zakarov's rich widow would choose to live so far outside Moscow — especially during the long, cold, and dark winter months. For most of the city's wealthy elite, their dachas were chiefly rustic summer retreats, places of escape and relaxation during the sweltering days and nights so common in July and August. Few of them ever bothered leaving the comforts of the capital once the first snows fell, except perhaps for rare weekends and holidays dedicated to cross-country skiing and other winter sports.

Within five minutes after they were ushered into her elegantly furnished sitting room, neither Jon nor Fiona wondered very much about why the former Party boss's widow lived in rural isolation. Their reluctant hostess was a woman who neither wanted nor enjoyed the company of others. She preferred a life of essential solitude with only the handful of paid servants necessary to cook, clean, and otherwise cater to her every petty and eccentric whim.

Madame Irina Zakarova was a tiny woman with a sharp, beaklike nose and small, dark, predatory eyes that seemed always in motion — observing, judging, and then dismissing with contempt. Her narrow, deeply lined face bore the sour, caustic frown of one who never expects much from anyone, and who almost always finds her abysmally low expectations of her fellow humans fully satisfied. With a jaundiced eye, she finished examining Smith's forged World Health Organization credentials and handed the papers back with an indifferent shrug. "Very well. You may ask your questions, Dr. Strand. I do not promise many useful answers. Frankly, I found the whole matter of my husband's last illness a great bore." Her mouth turned downward even more sharply. "All those ridiculous doctors and nurses and health ministry officials asking the same dreary questions: What did he eat last? Had he ever been exposed to radiation? What medications was he taking? On and on they went, in a never-ending interrogation. It was all so absurd."

"Absurd in what way?" Smith asked carefully.

"For the simple reason that Aleksandr was a walking catalogue of ill health and bad habits," Madame Zakarova replied coolly. "He smoked and drank and ate far too much all his life. Anything could have killed him — a heart attack, stroke, some kind of cancer . . . anything at all. So the fact that his body gave out in the end was hardly a matter of special surprise, or of much real interest, to me. I really don't understand all the fuss these doctors made over his death."

"Others were killed by the same strange

illness," Fiona pointed out tersely. "Among them, an innocent little boy who did not share your husband's bad habits."

"Really?" the other woman asked casually. "An otherwise healthy child?"

Smith nodded, doing his best to hide his own dislike for this cold, remarkably selfish, woman.

"How odd," Madame Zakarova said, with yet another emotionally detached shrug. She sighed languidly. "Well, then, I suppose I must do my best to help you, regardless of the inconvenience to myself."

Patiently, more patiently than he would have supposed was possible, Smith led her through the same set of health-related questions he had already asked the Voronovs. As before, Fiona carefully took down her answers, maddeningly incomplete though they were.

At last, when the old woman began to show unmistakable signs that her own limited patience was wearing thin, Jon decided it was time to shift his line of questioning to their chief area of interest — the European Center for Population Research and its DNA sampling around Moscow.

"Thank you for your time, Madame Zakarova. You have been extremely helpful," Smith lied, sitting back in his chair and beginning to gather up his papers. But then he stopped and sat forward again. "Oh, there is just one other small matter."

"Yes?"

"Our records show that you and your husband participated in a major DNA survey last year," Smith said casually, mentally crossing his fingers. "Is that correct?"

"The big genetic study?" The older woman sniffed quietly. "Oh, yes. Swabbing out our mouths for perfect strangers in the name of science. A disgusting ritual, if you ask my opinion. But Aleksandr was very excited about the whole grotesque process." She shook her head in contempt. "My husband was a fool. He actually believed that this so-called Slavic Genesis project would prove one of his own silly pet theories — that we Russians are the pinnacle of European racial and ethnic evolutionary development."

Jon forced himself to smile noncommittally, hiding his own elation. He was now sure that they had uncovered an important part of the origins of this deadly disease.

After he and Fiona Devin finished talking to the Voronovs that morning, they had gone back to their Zamoskvoreche District safe house. Then, while he reviewed his notes and made the careful phone calls necessary to arrange this interview, Fiona had spent several hours on-line digging up whatever she could about the ECPR and its Slavic Genesis project. Since it was too risky for her to contact her regular news sources, the detailed information they needed was hard to come by. Nevertheless, two important pieces of the puzzle had become clear.

First, although Slavic Genesis was a very large, expensive, and ambitious scientific undertaking, its researchers had collected DNA from just one thousand of the roughly nine million people living in the greater Moscow region. For the purposes of evaluating historical shifts in Slavic populations, this sample size was sufficient — especially when combined with the thousands upon thousands of other samples taken in other countries in Eastern Europe and across the former Soviet republics. But it also meant that this link between seven-year-old Mikhail Voronov and seventy-five-year-old Aleksandr Zakarov was more than the blind operation of random chance. The odds against such a coincidence were something on the order of eighty-one million to one.

Second, Konstantin Malkovic's name had popped up yet again. Corporations and foundations that he controlled provided a substantial share of the ECPR's funding. Few specifics of the Center's budget were in the public domain, but Fiona was fairly sure that the billionaire's money was directly underwriting the Slavic Genesis project.

Smith grimaced. One potential connection to Konstantin Malkovic, the ambulance from the Saint Cyril Medical Center, might be dismissed as a fluke. Two could not. Malkovic was involved in this conspiracy, along with his pal in the Kremlin, Viktor Dudarev.

In the woods outside the dacha, Oleg Kirov lay propped up behind a log half-buried in the snow, keeping a careful eye on the deeply rutted track that led up from the nearest country lane. Surplus army-issue night vision goggles turned the surrounding darkness into green-tinted mono-chromatic day. Twenty or so meters behind him, covered in branches and boughs to break up its sharp, boxy silhouette, lay the squat bulk of his GAZ Hunter, a vehicle that was the rough Russian equivalent of the American Jeep Wrangler.

Kirov had driven to the Zakarov dacha ahead of Smith and Fiona Devin. His first task had been to quickly scout the area for signs of possible danger. His second had been to establish this hidden observation post, concealing himself in a spot where he could keep an eye on the most likely approach to the dacha while Jon and Fiona asked their questions. The sides of his mouth turned down. He hoped they would hurry.

The broad-shouldered Russian shivered, chilled to the bone despite the protection offered by his heavy winter coat, hat, and gloves. The temperature, already below zero, was falling fast as the night wore on.

He understood his friends' need to confirm the information the Voronovs had given them, but he had deep misgivings about coming so far outside Moscow. Here in this harsh and forbidding landscape, they were all terribly exposed. There were no convenient crowds to mingle with. There were no handy Metro stations or packed department stores to duck into for evasion and escape. There were just the trees and the snow and a few winding roads that were completely empty once the sun went down.

Sighing, the Russian focused his gaze on the car parked next to the front door. Madame Zakarova kept her Mercedes in a heated garage attached to the house. Her infrequent guests were forced to make do with a small patch of icy gravel. Nothing seemed to be stirring near the dark blue Volga sedan he had obtained for the two Americans.

Then, suddenly, Kirov stiffened. He heard powerful engines echoing among the trees. The sounds were still some distance away, but they were unmistakably drawing nearer. He rose higher to get a better look and then dropped flat, reaching into his pocket in a tearing hurry.

CHAPTER THIRTY-FIVE

Smith's cell phone rang suddenly.

"Excuse me," he told the widow. He flipped the phone open. "Yes?"

It was Kirov. "You've got to leave, Jon. Now!" the Russian said urgently. "Two unmarked cars just turned off the main road. They're heading straight for the dacha. Go now! Out the back!"

"We're on our way," Smith said grimly. He shut the phone and stood up, grabbing his winter coat in the same motion. He felt the bulge of the 9mm Makarov pistol concealed in one of the pockets. For a moment, Jon was tempted to make a stand here in the house, fighting from cover instead of fleeing out into the open. But then he shoved the idea away. With the widow and her servants inside, he could not risk provoking a gun battle. If bullets started flying, too many innocents could easily be hurt or killed.

"Trouble?" Fiona asked quickly, in English. She rose at the same time, already gathering up her coat and gloves.

"We've got company," he murmured in the same language. "We're abandoning the car and bugging out. Oleg will meet us outside."

Pale and tense, she nodded her understanding.

The older Russian woman looked up at them in confusion. "Your questions are finished? You are going?"

Smith nodded. "Yes, Madame Zakarova, we're going. Right now." Ignoring the widow's startled protests, he steered Fiona out of the sitting room and into the dacha's wide central passage. There, they ran into a stout, middle-aged maid carrying a tray with the tea and small cakes her mistress had grudgingly offered when they first arrived. "Where's the back door?" Jon demanded.

Startled, the maid nodded her head down the hallway to their left, back the way she had just come. "It's there," she replied, plainly bewildered by his question. "Through the kitchen."

The two Americans slid around her and moved rapidly down the hall. Behind them, someone began pounding loudly on the dacha's solid front door. *Militsia!* a loud voice boomed. "Open up!"

Jon and Fiona walked on even faster.

The kitchen was quite large and equipped with every modern conve-

471

nience — a gas range, refrigerator, freezer, microwave oven, and all the rest. Mouthwatering smells hung in the warm air. In the corner, another of Madame Zakarova's servants, a young, strongly built man, sat finishing his dinner, a bowl of *pelmeni* — meat dumplings smothered in sour cream and rich butter. He looked up in astonishment as they came hurrying past him. "Hey, where are you — ?"

Smith waved him back to his chair. "This lady is not feeling well," he explained. "She needs some fresh air."

Without hesitating, he pulled the heavy wood door open. Light and warmth spilled out into the icy darkness, illuminating a narrow expanse of deep, white snow. The dacha occupied a small clearing in the forest, and the closest trees were only a few meters away. A small trampled path through the snow led off toward a collection of trash cans set against the rear of the house.

"Quick now," Smith whispered to Fiona. "And once we're in among the trees, run like hell. Circle to the left. Don't stop for anything or anyone until we reach Kirov. Got it?"

Grim-faced, she nodded.

Together, the two Americans headed out toward the forest, crunching up to midcalf in the icy powder. Smith took a quick breath, feeling the clean, arctic bite deep into his lungs. Just a few seconds more, he thought. That's all we need to get clear.

Suddenly three armed men stepped out from among the trees. All three wore snow camouflage parkas and carried Russian-made AKSU submachine guns. Two were shorter than Smith, but they were powerfully muscled and moved with the quiet confidence of trained soldiers. The third man was an inch or so taller than Jon and his eyes were a wintry slate-gray. There were matching strands of gray in his pale blond hair.

Smith and Fiona froze in their tracks.

"Put your hands up, please," the tall man ordered quietly in English. "Otherwise my men and I will be forced to shoot you here and now. And that would be regrettably messy, would it not?"

Slowly, Smith raised his arms, keeping his palms out to show that he was unarmed. Out the corner of his eye, he saw Fiona doing the same thing. All the color had drained out of her face.

"A sensible decision," the blond man approved. He smiled coldly. "I am Erich Brandt. And you are the notorious Colonel Jonathan Smith and the lovely, though equally notorious, Ms. Devin."

"Smith? Devin? I don't know what you're talking about," Jon said stiffly. "My name is Strand, Dr. Kalle Strand. And this is Ms. Lindkvist. We are scientists working for the United Nations." He knew it was a futile gesture, but he wasn't willing to concede everything so easily to the other man. Not yet anyway. "Who are you exactly? Criminals? Thieves? Kidnappers?"

Still smiling, Brandt shook his head. "Come now, Colonel. Let's not play such silly games. You're no more a Swede than I am." He took one step closer. "But I do congratulate you. Very few men have ever evaded me for so long."

Smith said nothing, trying hard to tamp down his anger at having been herded into this trap so easily. The cars coming up to the front of the dacha had mostly been a feint, he realized bitterly — a means of prodding them out here into the open.

Brandt shrugged. "Stoicism is also a trait I admire. But only to a degree." He jerked the barrel of his submachine gun toward the dacha. "Inside. Move."

Slowly, Smith and Fiona backed up.

There were three other gunmen inside the house now. They were holding Madame Zakarova and her three servants — the maid, the young man from the kitchen, and an older man with a few strands of hair plastered across his bald scalp — as prisoners in her sitting room.

Still seated regally in her high-backed

armchair, the older woman stared in outrage at Brandt. "What is this nonsense?" she demanded angrily. "How dare you invade my home!"

The former East German secret policeman shrugged. "A regrettable necessity, Madame," he said smoothly. "Unfortunately, these people" — he indicated Smith and Fiona — "are spies. They are enemies of the State."

"Ridiculous," Zakarova scoffed.

Brandt smiled again. "You think so?" He turned to his men. "Bind their hands. And then search them. Be very thorough."

Conscious of the several weapons pointed straight at him, Smith stood still, reluctantly submitting as his hands were roughly bound behind his back with a length of plastic cable — flex-cuffs of the same kind used on insurgents and terrorists captured by U.S. troops in Iraq. He heard Fiona hiss in pain through her clenched teeth as the same thing was done to her.

Once they were tied up and helpless, Brandt's men frisked them expertly, checking every place a weapon or any other piece of useful equipment might be hidden. Smith bristled, angrier and angrier inside, both with them and at himself, as the search went on, growing ever more intrusive. The blond wig came off, revealing his dark hair, and he was forced to spit out the cheek inserts that had altered the shape of his face. He knew it must be far more humiliating for Fiona than it was for him.

Brandt stood watching without visible reaction as his men first found Jon's 9mm pistol, then Fiona's 5.45mm Makarov PSM, their elements of disguise, their forged passports and other papers, and, finally, their high-tech Covert-One-issue cell phones. They set the weapons and other equipment on a coffee table in front of him. Only when one of the men pulled Fiona's concealed switchblade out of her right boot, did the blond-haired man show any serious interest.

He picked up the knife, touched the button on its slender black hilt, and saw the long, deadly blade flick out. One pale eyebrow went up in surprise. He turned to Fiona with a dry smile. "I saw the gruesome wound this little toy of yours inflicted on one of my men, Ms. Devin. And Dmitri was a trained assassin. Clearly, you are something more than a mere journalist."

She shrugged defiantly. "Think what you like, Herr Brandt. I'm not responsible for your fevered imagination."

Brandt chuckled. "Brave words, Ms. Devin. But empty words, I suspect." He turned back to Madame Zakarova, who sat watching the proceedings with a fierce scowl. "You see?" he said, still smiling.

"Weapons. Disguises. Forged passports. And sophisticated communications devices. Tell me, Madame, are these the normal accoutrements carried by *Swedish* medical researchers — or are they devices better suited to foreign spies?"

"Spies," the older woman admitted quietly, turning paler.

"Just so," Brandt said calmly. He reached into a pocket inside his camouflage smock, took out a pair of thin latex gloves, and then began slowly and methodically putting them on. Everyone in the room watched him in silence, unable to pull their eyes away. "Your late husband was a high-ranking member of the Party in the old days, Madame. You are not a simple member of the uneducated masses. Tell me, what was the penalty for espionage and for treason?"

"Death," she whispered. "It was death."

"Exactly right," the German told her. He finished donning the gloves and then glanced toward the visibly frightened servants sitting lined up on one of the sofas — a slim-legged nineteenth-century antique richly embroidered in a bright fabric of blue and gold. "Which of you is Petr Klimuk?"

The older, bald-headed man hesitantly raised one hand. "I am, sir," he muttered.

Brandt smiled thinly. "And you are the

477

one who contacted us, when you heard that your mistress was going to meet with these foreigners?"

Klimuk nodded, more eagerly now. "That's right," he said. "Just like you asked me to do earlier today. You promised that if I reported anyone snooping around asking questions about her husband, I would get a reward."

"So I did," Brandt admitted coolly. "And so you shall."

Then, without hesitating, the gray-eyed man took Smith's Makarov off the coffee table in front of him, thumbed off the safety, aimed, and shot Klimuk in the forehead at point-blank range. Blood splashed across the back of the sofa, staining its richly colored fabric an ugly red.

While the other servants were still staring at their dead colleague in horror, Brandt swung the pistol slightly and fired two more times. The maid and the younger man both slumped back against the sofa, each killed by a single shot.

The former Stasi officer turned away. There was no expression whatsoever on his face.

Madame Zakarova sat motionless in her high-backed chair, looking at her murdered servants with an ashen face. "Why?" she spat out furiously. "Why kill them? They were not spies. Yes, Klimuk and the others were ignorant and foolish, but they had done nothing to deserve death."

Brandt shrugged. "Very few people ever do." He raised the Makarov and fired again.

Shot through the heart, the older woman fell back in her chair. Her eyes stared up at the ceiling, forever locked in an expression that mingled anger, contempt, and the first horrified realization that she too was marked for death.

Carefully, Brandt set the pistol down on the floor and then kicked it away under the sofa. He glanced at Smith. "When the *militsia* arrive, they should find the fingerprints on that weapon of great interest, don't you think? Your fingerprints, naturally." He shook his head in wry amusement. "You Americans are so violent, so trigger-happy. No wonder you are so widely disliked throughout the world."

"You're nothing but a black-hearted, murdering bastard!" Fiona told him fiercely, speaking through gritted teeth.

"Yes, I suppose that I am," Brandt said calmly. Then he stared back at her with his cold gray eyes. "And now you are my prisoner, Ms. Devin. Think about that, why don't you?"

He swung back to his watching men. "Bring them," he snapped. "Let's go."

With gunmen prodding them from behind and others watching warily from the front, Smith and Fiona were hustled out through the door and shoved into the backseat of one of the three vehicles parked outside the dacha — an all-wheel-drive Ford Explorer. Brandt and one of his men climbed into the front seat. One of the remaining gunmen scrambled into the Volga brought by the Americans, while the others got into the third car, another big four-wheel-drive Ford.

In convoy, with the Explorer transporting Brandt and the two Americans in the lead, the three vehicles turned across the patch of gravel and drove away from the dacha, bumping slowly down the rutted track leading back to the road. Once on the road, they turned right, not left, and sped up.

Ignoring the pain from his abraded wrists, Smith sat up a little straighter. They were heading west through the darkness. Trees, high, mounded snowbanks, and brush-choked turnoffs to old logging tracks appeared briefly in their high beams and then vanished behind them into the night.

He glanced at Fiona to see if she had noticed. She nodded slightly. Brandt and his men were not taking them back to Moscow.

Why not? Smith wondered. If the former Stasi officer was working for Malkovic, and the billionaire was working with the Kremlin, why not simply hand them over to the Russians for interrogation? Were Brandt and his wealthy employer playing a double game of some kind?

Vladik Fadayev lay perfectly still among the clumped birch trees lining the road. Thanks to his snow parka and twig-laced camouflage netting, anyone looking at the lean, hollow-cheeked sniper from more than a couple of meters away would only have seen one more snow hummock among many in the woods.

Despite the bitter cold, Fadayev was content. As a younger man he had spent two years in combat in Afghanistan's rugged mountains and foothills, killing mujahideen warriors at long-range with his much-loved SVD rifle. The experience had taught him to enjoy the difficult and dangerous game of hunting other men. After the Red Army abandoned its long war against the Afghans, peace had come as a tremendous letdown. All in all, the sniper reflected, he was fortunate to have found employment with a man like Erich Brandt — a man who appreciated his special skills and found many different ways in which to employ them.

One by one, the taillights of Brandt's three vehicles disappeared around a bend.

481

The sound of their engines faded into the night.

Fadayev stayed motionless, waiting.

His patience was rewarded.

A big boxy GAZ Hunter lumbered out of the woods ahead of him. Gears shifting noisily, the Russian-made jeep swung sharply west onto the narrow road and accelerated. Snow and broken boughs and branches slid off its roof and hood, tumbling across the lane in its wake.

The sniper smiled. He spoke quietly into his radio mike. "This is Fadayev. You were quite right. The Americans had company. And now you are being followed."

Smith fought to control his expression when he heard the report crackling over the tactical radio hooked to the Explorer's dashboard. Beside him, he heard a soft, indrawn breath from Fiona. They both knew Oleg Kirov had been spotted. And now they were powerless to warn the Russian that he was in danger.

Brandt leaned forward and took the mike. "Understood, Fadayev. We'll deal with the situation from this end. Out." He looked over his shoulder at the two Americans. "That will be your colleague, I imagine."

Neither moved a muscle.

Brandt smiled at the sight of their carefully impassive faces. "I am not a fool," he said calmly. "You are both professionals. I knew that you would never go into a danger zone without support."

To hide his sudden feeling of despair, Smith stared out the window. In the dark, it was difficult to see much of anything, but he thought they were just coming up a little rise, following the road as it wound along a low, densely wooded hill. Off on their left, the ground fell away in a gentle, tree-covered slope, cut here and there by steeper-sided ravines that were choked with boulders, brush, and scrub timber.

In the seat ahead of him, he heard Brandt using the radio again. "All vehicles, halt," the tall man said flatly. "Deploy for action to our rear."

Immediately, the big car they were in slowed, pulled over to the side just past a blind curve, and stopped. The Volga and the second Ford Explorer did the same, pulling up right behind them. Doors slammed open, and Brandt's men spilled out onto the narrow road, rapidly fanning out among the trees with their automatic weapons ready.

In the silence, Jon and Fiona heard the noise of another car coming up the hill behind them. Awkwardly, they swung round in the seat to stare through the back window.

Smith felt his jaw tighten. What could he do? Grimly, he ran through possible courses of action. But, with his hands bound behind his back there seemed very little he could achieve. Sure, he might be able to hurl himself across the front seat at Brandt and the driver, but would that create the kind of distraction needed to give Kirov a real fighting chance? He shrugged mentally. Though the action seemed futile, it was his only real option. Furtively, he flexed his arms and legs, trying to loosen stiff muscles before he made his move.

"Be still, Colonel," Brandt said coldly. "Or I will put a bullet into your brain."

Warily, Smith glanced over his shoulder. The gray-eyed man sat there staring straight at him, aiming a pistol squarely at his head.

Suddenly, sooner than any of them had expected, the oncoming GAZ-manufactured jeep came racing around the corner. It was moving fast in a blaze of headlights.

Brandt's men opened up instantly, firing their submachine guns on full automatic. The stuttering, clattering roar of gunfire shattered the frozen hush of the winter night. Bullets hammered the speeding jeep, punching enormous holes through its chassis and sending pieces of torn metal flying. Its windshield blew inward, shattered into a thousand separate bits by 9mm rounds fired at close range.

Without slowing at all, the bullet-riddled jeep veered sharply off the road and plunged wildly down the wooded slope. Still skidding downhill at high speed, the Hunter slammed into a birch tree with an earsplitting crash, spun away, and then slowly toppled sideways over the edge of a ravine. The pale beam of one headlight lit the overhanging trees and brush for a few seconds longer and then winked out, again leaving the hillside cloaked in absolute darkness.

When the light vanished, Jon and Fiona exchanged horrified glances. Neither of them had any real hope that Kirov could have survived the murderous ambush and crash they had just witnessed.

Brandt waited until the two Americans turned away in sorrow. Still holding his pistol on Smith, he picked up the radio mike. "Fadayev? This is Brandt. We're finished here. Listen, get back in your car and come up the hill after us. I want you to investigate the wreckage of that jeep and to retrieve any documents carried by the driver. See if you can learn the name of the man we just killed. Understand?"

A flat, emotionless voice crackled back across the radio. "I understand."

Brandt nodded. "Good. When you're

finished, report back to Group headquarters in Moscow. The rest of us will proceed to the monastery."

He listened for the sniper's acknowledgment and then signed off.

The gray-eyed man looked across the seat at Smith and Fiona. He shrugged. "So much for your friend." Then he smiled coldly. "And soon we can begin the painful process of finding out just who employs you and how much you have already told them —"

PART FOUR

CHAPTER THIRTY-SIX

Baku, Azerbaijan
The wide boulevards and narrow alleys of
Baku, the largest and most sophisticated city
in the Caucasus region, stretched for miles
along the shore of the Caspian Sea. As billions of euros and dollars poured in to fi-
nance new oil and natural gas ventures,
Baku was more than ever a city of striking
contrasts. It was both a bustling, prosperous
twenty-first-century boomtown of glittering
steel-and-glass skyscrapers, and also an ancient metropolis of mosques, royal palaces,
and bazaars set amid a maze of shaded cob-
blestone lanes.

On a hill rising just outside the walls of
the Old City lay the ugly concrete building
that housed Azerbaijan's president and his
staff. Scowling Azeri soldiers patrolled the
surrounding streets, making sure that visiting oil company representatives and curious tourists looking for the nearby Baku
Philharmonic and the state art museums
kept moving along.

Deep inside the Presidential Administration building, one of the household staff emerged from a central elevator. He was pushing a heavy cart piled high with covered dishes. Troubled by what appeared to be a threatening buildup of Russian troops in neighboring Dagestan, the republic's Defense Council was meeting in emergency session. As the night wore on, the generals and government ministers had ordered food sent in from the kitchen.

Two hard-eyed men in dark suits stepped forward. "Security," one said, showing an identity card. "We'll take that from here. Only authorized personnel go any farther."

The waiter shrugged wearily. "Just make sure you get their orders right," he said, handing over a sheet showing the meals requested by each member of the Defense Council. Yawning, he turned back into the elevator.

Once the doors closed, one of the security service officers quickly lifted the lids of the dishes on the cart, comparing them with the list now held in his hand. He stopped once he found the bowl of *piti*, a stew of mutton, chickpeas, fat, and saffron. He turned to his comrade. "This one," he said quietly.

"Looks delicious," the other man said with a quick, cynical grin.

"So it does," the first man agreed. He

glanced swiftly up and down the corridor to make sure no one was looking. Satisfied, he took a vial out of his pocket and stirred the liquid it contained into the stew. The vial went back into his coat pocket while his colleague slowly trundled the cart up the corridor. Another HYDRA variant was moving toward its chosen target.

The White House

The outlook of those sitting around the crowded White House Situation Room conference table was unreservedly bleak, President Sam Castilla realized, observing the grim, set faces of his national security team. Most were deeply worried that the United States could soon be facing a serious clash with Russia, but no one felt confident enough in the available information to offer any solid suggestions on how to handle the terrifying diplomatic and military crisis they feared might be rushing toward them.

Basically, the president knew, they were all tired of stumbling around in the dark. Right now all they had were tiny bits and pieces of data — the accelerating wave of mysterious deaths both here in the States and abroad, whispers of intensifying Russian military preparation, and the steady drumbeat of Russian propaganda decrying the "dangerous instability" in countries around its borders. Unfortunately, everyone lacked the broader evidence and analysis needed to tie those bits and pieces into a clear-cut pattern, into something that would convincingly reveal what Dudarev and his generals were really planning. Without that clear blueprint, no one in Europe or elsewhere would be willing to confront Moscow.

Castilla turned to William Wexler, his new national intelligence director. "Can we alter the orbit of our surviving Lacrosse satellite to obtain good coverage over these Russian frontier districts we're most concerned about?"

"I'm afraid not, Mr. President," the trim, handsome former senator admitted reluctantly. "Lacrosse-Five was the newer of the two satellites. Lacrosse-Four has been up too long. It just doesn't have enough maneuvering fuel left to reach the required orbit."

"So how long will it take to launch a replacement for Lacrosse-Five?" Castilla asked.

"Too long, sir," Emily Powell-Hill, his national security adviser, interjected flatly. "The CIA says six weeks, at a minimum. If I had to put serious money on it, though, I would bet that three to five months is probably a more realistic time-frame."

"Good God," the president muttered. By that time, the Russians could have marched the troops and tanks they were hunting for all the way to Siberia and back again. He looked across the table at Admiral Stevens Brose, the chairman of the Joint Chiefs of Staff. "What's your evaluation of the destruction of our satellite, Admiral? Was it an accident — or a deliberate attack to blind us?"

"I don't know, sir," the wide, powerfully built Navy officer said carefully. "Space Command has only been able to conduct a preliminary analysis of the images our early-warning satellites picked up. However, General Collins and his staff report that the explosions they observed onboard the Russian COSMOS-8B vehicle were extremely powerful."

"Powerful enough to knock out another satellite hundreds of kilometers away?"

"Frankly, I doubt it, Mr. President. Given their different orbits, the odds against so many fragments from COSMOS-8B hitting Lacrosse-Five seem, well, astronomical," Brose said drily. Then he shrugged. "But I'm only guessing. As of this moment, we don't have the data to prove anything one way or the other."

Castilla nodded grimly, seething inside. Without proof that the Russians had acted intentionally, the United States had no practical recourse but to write off the suspicious loss of a multibillion-dollar spy satellite. His mouth tightened to a thin, angry line. "What about our KH-series photo-recon satellites?" he demanded.

"We're already running significant numbers of orbital passes over the target areas," Emily Powell-Hill replied. "But cloud cover is the big problem. The weather is incredibly bad over most of the Ukraine and the Caucasus right now. Even with our thermal sensors, we're not able to pick up much detail through the heavy cloud masses blanketing those regions."

Left unsaid in all of this, Castilla realized gloomily, was the fact that even the best satellite photographs required skilled interpretation and analysis to reveal usable data, and too many of the best U.S. photo interpreters were fatally ill or already dead.

Charles Ouray, the White House chief of staff, spoke up from his end of the table. "Then why not take a stab at aerial reconnaissance? We have radar-equipped aircraft. Can't we fly them near the Russian border?"

"Physically, yes," Secretary of State Padgett said abruptly. "Diplomatically, no. With so many of their key political and military leaders dead or dying, the governments of the Ukraine, Georgia, Azerbaijan, and the other former Soviet republics are increasingly fragile. In the present circumstances, none of them will risk provoking the Kremlin by allowing us to use their airspace for reconnaissance flights. So far, every request we've made, through every channel, has been rebuffed."

Again Castilla nodded. The nightmare scenario he and Fred Klein had been worrying about over the last few days seemed to be moving closer to reality. If the Russians were behind this new disease, as seemed increasingly likely, they were using it very effectively to sow confusion and chaos. The big question was: How far was Dudarev willing to push his present advantage? Would he be content to weaken the fledgling democracies around Russia? Or did he have something far more ambitious in mind?

The door to the Situation Room opened and an aide, a young, serious woman wearing horn-rimmed glasses, hurried in, moving quickly to where William Wexler sat making notes. She leaned over and whispered something in the intelligence director's ear. His tanned face turned pale.

"Is there something I should know about, Bill?" Castilla asked sharply.

Wexler cleared his throat, looking uncomfortable. "Quite possibly, Mr. President," he admitted. "I'm afraid that the CIA has just lost one of its clandestine action teams, a group of field officers operating in Berlin. The first reports are very sketchy, but it appears that gunmen armed with automatic weapons and explosives ambushed our people on a public street. The head of the CIA's Berlin Station is on his way there right now, but things look very bad. Very bad, indeed. There don't appear to be any survivors."

"Jesus," Charles Ouray whispered.

"Amen, Charlie," Castilla said softly. His shoulders bowed slightly, momentarily feeling the weight of more deaths, of more gold stars for the marble memorial wall at CIA headquarters. Then he frowned. First the Lacrosse satellite and now this vicious massacre of American intelligence officers. Were they connected in some way? He turned back to Wexler. "What was this clandestine action team's mission?"

The national intelligence director looked baffled. "Their mission, Mr. President?" he repeated uncertainly. He shuffled through the papers in front of him, clearly trying to buy time.

An awkward silence followed. No one else sitting around the Situation Room conference table had much respect for the former senator. At best, they considered him a nonentity. At worst, they viewed him as a liability, as one more bureaucratic obstacle for the already-fettered U.S. intelligence community to overcome.

"I'm not sure I have the details of their assignment," Wexler admitted at last, reddening in embarrassment. He turned to his aide, the woman who had first brought him the news. "Did Langley ever relay any of that information to us, Caroline?"

"They were tracking a former East German biological weapons scientist, sir," she said quietly. "A man named Wulf Renke."

Castilla sat back in his chair, feeling as though he had been pole-axed. Renke! Good God, he thought in astonishment. Renke was the renegade son of a bitch that Fred Klein's Moscow-based Covert-One unit suspected of having created the strange illness they were investigating.

Quickly, the president excused himself, put his chief of staff in charge of the meeting, and left the Situation Room. As the door closed behind him, he heard more wrangling break out. He frowned deeply, but kept walking. Taken as a whole, his national security team was remarkably competent, but their tempers and patience were definitely beginning to fray as they faced the nightmare of being forced to act blindly, without adequate intelligence. And right now, he simply could not afford to spend any more time riding herd on them.

Upstairs in the Oval Office, Castilla

picked up one of the phones on his desk and punched in a special number known only to himself.

"Klein, here," the head of Covert-One said somberly, answering the call on the first ring.

"Have you heard the news from Berlin?"

"I have," Klein replied grimly. "I'm scanning the first CIA and local police reports right now."

"And?"

"The link with Wulf Renke is highly significant," Klein agreed slowly. "As is the extremely violent reaction to the CIA probe."

"Meaning the Russians are afraid of what we may learn about him?" Castilla asked.

"Or from him," Klein pointed out. "If Renke was working safely under lock and key in one of their own Bioaparat facilities, they would have far less reason to fear our learning that he is still alive and on the loose."

"You think he's running his own operation at a laboratory outside Russia?"

"Let's say that I consider it a very strong possibility," Klein replied. "I've been studying Renke's file. He strikes me as a man who would never willingly put himself in a position where others held too much power over him. If he is creating a weapon for the Russians, I believe that he will be working for them at a safe distance."

"Have you passed this theory of yours on to Colonel Smith?" Castilla asked.

"No, sir," Klein said quietly. "I'm sorry to say that I have very bad news of my own to report. Sometime over the past hour, we've completely lost contact with our team in Moscow. For all intents and purposes, Jon Smith, Ms. Devin, and Oleg Kirov all seem to have dropped off the face of the earth."

CHAPTER THIRTY-SEVEN

Berlin

The street in front of Ulrich Kessler's villa was deserted. Set at regular intervals, wrought-iron lamps cast pools of soft light across the snow-covered sidewalks and illuminated a handful of silent cars parked along the empty street. Off in the darkness on either side of Hagenstrasse, more lights glowed among the pine, oak, and birch trees, marking the location of other houses that were set well back from the road.

About one hundred meters down the street from the driveway to Kessler's home, CIA officer Randi Russell stood motionless in a patch of deep shadow between two large oak trees. She breathed out slowly and gently, letting her pounding heart settle down after her long, painful sprint through the Grunewald forest. Her pupils were adjusting to the dim light, expanding as she carefully scanned her surroundings, looking for any signs of watchers posted to observe the immediate area. Nothing moved. Nothing stirred. There were no suspicious silhouettes or shapes lurking between the parked cars or among the trees and shrubs bordering the quiet street.

Good enough, she thought coldly. Sometimes even the bad guys made mistakes.

Randi slid the Beretta back inside her concealed shoulder holster. This time, she left her ski jacket almost completely unzipped. Then she stepped out of the shadows and strolled up the sidewalk, walking fast and making no effort to hide her movements. With a bit of luck, anyone spotting her would think she was just another local coming home after work, some light shopping, or a late afternoon walk.

Not far up the street, she passed a silver-colored Audi. It was parked beside the pavement in a spot that offered a good view of the entrance to Kessler's property. From a distance, the car appeared undamaged. It was only when Randi got close that she spotted the small, neat hole blown through the rear window. As she walked past, she used her peripheral vision to check out the interior. Inside the Audi, a brown-haired young woman sat folded over the steering wheel, not moving. Dark smears of dried blood streaked the dashboard and the inside of the windshield.

Randi carefully averted her eyes, pushing away her feelings of sorrow and regret. The dead woman was her lookout, a bright, perky, just-graduated CIA trainee whose name was Carla Voss. From the look of things, the young woman must have died without ever spotting her killer.

The back of Randi's neck tingled, anticipating the impact of a bullet. The muscles around her right eye twitched slightly. Stay cool, she told herself sharply, and forced herself to keep strolling as though she had seen nothing strange at all. If any of the men who had murdered the rest of her team were watching right now, reacting suspiciously would be a dead giveaway. With the emphasis on dead, she thought grimly.

Forty meters from Kessler's driveway, she turned aside while reaching into the pocket of her jeans as though looking for her keys. Then she pushed open a small gate set in the high stone wall and entered the spacious front garden of the neighboring villa. Wide gravel paths meandered between barren flowerbeds now mounded with snow. Up at the house, a light shone over the door, but the rest of the building — built to look like a Renaissance Italian palazzo — was dark. She was in luck. The owners were not yet home.

Now that she was out of sight, it was time to move faster. Randi sprinted across the garden, staying off the gravel paths to avoid making too much noise. She ran straight for the length of wall that marked the edge of Kessler's property. Barely slowing down, she leaped up, caught the edge of the stone wall with her gloved hands, and then swung herself up onto the top. For a moment, Randi lay still, pressed flat against the rough surface of the mortared stones. She was conscious of her pulse pounding in her ears, but ignored it, focusing instead on any faint sounds that might be rising from the grounds next door.

At first she heard nothing, just the wind keening through the tree branches overhead. But then she began to pick up different sounds, first the soft crunch of someone prowling back and forth on gravel and concrete, and next the muffled, static-laden squawk of a brief radio transmission. Her best guess was that these noises were coming from roughly twenty to thirty meters away.

Slowly, Randi swung down off the wall on the other side. She dropped lightly to the ground, spun around to face the direction from which she had heard the sounds, and crouched low, drawing her pistol in the same motion with a quick, fluid, and lethal grace.

Her eyes narrowed. She was in good cover among the tall trees and flowering bushes planted around Kessler's Edwardian-style home. Although lights glowed behind several of the villa's second-floor windows, casting elongated rectangles of faint illumination across the open lawns near the house, this narrow fringe of woods was wrapped in almost total darkness. Staying low, she slid cautiously to the right, edging around broad tree trunks and snow-crusted shrubs, carefully watching where she put her feet to avoid snapping any fallen branches and twigs.

Suddenly Randi froze and crouched even lower, trusting to the shadows to stay hidden. Not far ahead, no more than a few meters away, she had seen something moving, a brief glimpse of a figure outlined by the light from Kessler's house.

She peered intently through the tangle of underbrush and the maze of low-hanging branches. She was looking at a man, a short, heavyset man in a suit and a thick wool overcoat. He was pacing slowly up and down along the driveway. In one big, beefy hand, he held a small tactical radio. In the other, he gripped a pistol fitted with a silencer. He looked nervous. Despite the cold, his forehead glistened with sweat.

Randi looked past him. There were two cars parked in the space between the villa and the garage. One was a dark red Mercedes sedan. The other was the black BMW she had shot up during the brief, brutal action along Clayallee. Another man in black clothes and body armor sat slumped against the side of the BMW. Blood-soaked bandages were wrapped tightly around his extended right leg. He was either unconscious or dead.

She nodded, knowing now that she had guessed right. Renke's assassins must have driven straight here after wiping out her surveillance team. The other black-clad gunmen must still be inside dealing with Ulrich Kessler.

The heavyset man they had left outside on guard turned again on his heel and paced back toward the two cars. He checked his watch, swore worriedly, and then lifted the radio to his mouth. "Lange, this is Mueller," he said tensely. "How much longer?"

A harsh voice crackled over the radio. "Five minutes. Now sit tight and stay off the air. Lange out."

Listening, Randi made up her mind. She was going to have to go in after these bastards. There was no time to call for a new backup team. And waiting here to ambush Renke's men when they came out of the house was a non-starter. If she was lucky, she might be able to drop one or two of them before they nailed her, but those silenced submachine guns they carried gave them too much firepower to face in a stand-up fight out here in the open. Inside, in a close-quarters battle, she would actually have slightly better odds of surviving.

A quick, self-conscious grin flashed across her lean, taut face. "Better" in this case was probably only the difference between "no chance at all" and "one chance in a thousand." Then her grin faded. Any chance at all was still more than the other members of her team had gotten.

Intently, Randi studied the short, paunchy man called Mueller as he nervously paced up and down. Should she try to take him prisoner? No, she decided coldly. That would be far too risky. If he managed to shout or radio a warning to his heavily armed comrades inside Kessler's house, she was as good as dead.

Still watching Mueller parade back and forth in increasing agitation, she put one hand in her coat pocket and pulled out a noise suppressor of her own. It screwed tightly over the muzzle of her Beretta.

Ready now, she took careful aim, sighting coolly down the barrel. *Phut. Phut.* Her pistol coughed twice. The metallic noise of the bolt crashing back as the weapon fired seemed to hang forever in the hushed evening air. In reality, she knew, both sets of sounds would be almost inaudible to anyone more than ten meters away.

One round hit Mueller in the chest. The second tore open his throat. The heavyset man went down in a heap and lay twitching and gurgling, bleeding his life away across the cold concrete. He was dead in seconds.

Randi swiveled rapidly, swinging the Beretta to cover the man she had wounded earlier. Her finger tightened on the trigger, ready to fire, and then gradually eased off. He had not moved. Hurrying now and staying low, she raced out from under the trees and across the open driveway, careful to keep the cars between her and the house. She reached the BMW and dropped to one knee beside the silent, motionless man. He sat as before, propped up against the side of the black car, with his shattered leg stretched out in front of him.

While she held her pistol aimed at his head with one hand, she felt for a pulse with the other. Nothing. And his skin was already growing cold. There, lying on the concrete beside him, Randi saw an empty syringe. Her mouth tightened in disgust. That had undoubtedly contained an overdose of morphine or some other fatal drug. Renke's men must be under orders not to leave any wounded behind them — not even their own.

Then she saw something else, a black angular shape, set on the hard ground next to the dead man. It was his submachine gun. His comrades must have left the weapon beside him, waiting for the lethal drug with which they had injected him to take effect.

Scarcely daring to believe her luck, Randi unscrewed the silencer from her Beretta and shoved the pistol back into her shoulder holster. Then she reached across the corpse and snagged the abandoned submachine gun. Moving quickly and confidently, she examined the weapon, a Heckler & Koch MP5SD, found a nearly full thirty-round magazine, yanked back on the cocking handle to chamber a 9mm round, and set the firing selector for three-round bursts.

Pleased, she patted the weapon with one hand. At least now she had firepower parity with the bad guys. Of course, that still left her outnumbered by at least three-to-one, Randi reminded herself coolly — by trained killers. Trained killers wearing body armor.

Then she shrugged. Waiting longer was not going to make this any easier. She took one more deep breath, counting down inside her own head. Three. Two. One. Now!

Randi jumped to her feet and dashed for the side of Kessler's villa, half-expecting a sudden burst of gunfire from one of the lighted upstairs windows. Instead, there was only silence. She reached the house and flattened her back against the wall, listening hard for the startled shouts that would tell her that she had been spotted.

Still nothing.

With the MP5SD tucked firmly against her shoulder, Randi glided forward again, edging around the corner until she had a view of the front door. She kept going, caught up in an adrenaline rush that made her intensely aware of every nerve ending, and of even the smallest movements around her. Every sense seemed magnified. All the pain from the cuts, scrapes, and bruises she had taken earlier seemed to fade away. She could hear even the tiniest sounds — the crunch of her boots on snow, the faint tick of one of the car engines as it cooled, contracting slowly in the freezing air, and the distant wail of fire, ambulance, and police vehicles speeding toward the carnage on Clayallee.

She reached the front of the house.

The front door was already starting to open. Bright interior light spilled through the rapidly widening crack. For a fraction of a second, time seemed to come to a full stop. What should she do? Then, equally abruptly, the world spun back into motion. She only had time to act, not to think.

Furiously, Randi hurtled forward and hit the door with her right shoulder, slamming it all the way open with enormous force. The heavy door jarred back against her as it crashed into someone on the other side. There was a sudden, loud, surprised grunt as the powerful impact knocked whoever it was backward into the villa's broad entry foyer. Her shoulder went numb for a brief moment and then flared into white-hot agony. Moving too fast to stop easily, she skidded across the tiled floor, rebounded off a wall, and spun around to cover the corridor.

One of Renke's gunmen — lean, dark-eyed, and with dark blond hair — was sprawled just a couple of meters away. Still dazed by the unexpected blow he had taken, the man pushed himself up onto his knees. His submachine gun lay on the floor beside him. Blearily, he glanced up and saw her staring back at him. His mouth fell open in astonishment, and he grabbed for his weapon, trying frantically to aim it in her direction.

Randi shot him first, squeezing off a quick, three-round burst at point-blank range.

Two rounds slammed into the gunman's torso. Unable to penetrate his armor, the copper-jacketed slugs splattered across the bulky vest instead, smashing vital internal organs with enormous impacts that threw the dark-eyed man back against the nearest wall. Her third bullet hit him right in the face and tore his head apart.

"Karic?" a startled voice called out from above.

Caught equally off-guard, Randi swung round and looked up the great curving staircase that led to the villa's upper floor. A second black-clad gunman loomed there, peering over the railing. He raised his weapon first, taking rapid aim.

She threw herself backward just as the submachine gun stuttered. Rounds cracked through air all around her, blowing huge craters in the floor. Pieces of broken tile flew in all directions. Ricochets tumbled wickedly across the corridor.

Desperately, Randi rolled away across the foyer, trying to get out of the line of fire without being hit. A sharp-edged sliver of tile sliced across her cheek, drawing blood. Another burst from the staircase smashed two antique chairs on either side of a gold-framed mirror, turning them into heaps of splintered wood and torn fabric. The mirror itself exploded, sending broken glass flying. More gunfire knocked one of Ulrich Kessler's ill-gotten pieces of art, a Diebenkorn, off the wall and sent the tangled wreckage skidding across the foyer. It had been reduced to a few tattered shreds of stained canvas clinging to a bullet-mangled frame.

"Damn," she muttered grimly. While the gunman above her kept shooting, this wide-open entrance to Kessler's home was quickly becoming a death trap. She had to do something to change the situation, and she had to do it fast.

Abruptly, Randi stopped rolling. Ignoring the bullets lashing the corridor around her, she brought her submachine gun on line, aiming straight up at the large chandelier hanging above the foyer. Frowning in concentration, she squeezed the trigger. The MP5SD hammered back against her shoulder.

The chandelier exploded, smashed into a thousand glittering shards by her burst. Fragments of shattered glass and crystal spiraled away through the air and cascaded down across the tiles. Immediately, the lights went out, plunging the foyer into darkness.

Right away, the gunman at the top of the stairs stopped shooting, holding his fire to avoid giving away his position.

Randi grimaced. This guy was too good. She had been hoping to draw a bead on his muzzle flashes in the dark. Instead, the gunman seemed perfectly content to hold his ground in silence, waiting for her to make the fatal mistake of trying to charge up that staircase.

It was a Mexican standoff, she thought

512

coolly. She could not get up those stairs without getting killed, and Renke's hired killers could not come down without suffering the same fate. Well, maybe she could hold them here long enough for the German police to arrive.

Then Randi shook her head, angry with herself for being overconfident. There were at least two of the gunmen left alive. While one kept her pinned down, the other could easily sneak up behind her. After all, this grand, sweeping staircase was not the only way down from the upper floor.

She sat up cautiously, thinking hard about that.

When Randi had broken into Kessler's house the day before, she had spent more than an hour combing through it from top to bottom, exploring every room and corridor while looking for incriminating evidence against the corrupt BKA official and planting an array of hidden listening devices. In the process, she had come across another staircase toward the back, a much smaller and drabber piece of construction.

These stairs, concealed behind a nondescript door near the kitchen, had originally been intended for use by the servants employed by every upper-class family in the early 1900s. In those days, household staff were expected to go about their daily labors unobtrusively, staying out of the grand public spaces reserved for their masters and their guests whenever possible.

In the darkness, she grinned suddenly. The odds were that Renke's men had not yet found those back stairs. Their whole attention would be fixed here, at the front of the villa.

Randi flipped the firing selector on her submachine gun to safe and slung the weapon across her back. Then she rolled back onto her stomach and crawled quietly away down the pitch-black hallway that led toward the rear of the house. As she glided away across the floor, she carefully brushed the debris of spent shell casings and bits of broken tile and glass out of her path. If her plan was going to work, it was absolutely essential that she avoid making any noise that could betray her movements to that unseen gunman lurking at the top of the stairs.

CHAPTER THIRTY-EIGHT

Upstairs, in Ulrich Kessler's study, Gerhard Lange scowled. "Mueller," he hissed into his radio. "Come in!"

But only static crackled through the small receiver set in his ear. "Mueller," the former Stasi officer said tersely, repeating his attempt to contact the man he had left on guard outside. "Reply!"

Again, there was no answer.

Angrily, Lange abandoned the futile effort. Mueller was either dead, a prisoner, or already fleeing the scene as fast as his fat legs would carry him. In any case, he and Stepanovic were very much on their own.

He glanced across the room to where Kessler's body lay twisted and contorted on the carpet next to an ornate, intricately carved desk. His lips curled in contempt. Against all logic, the weak, cowardly fool had actually imagined that they had come to rescue him.

What now, though? Lange bleakly considered his own options. His orders from

Brandt had been explicit. Destroy the CIA team spying on Kessler. Kill Kessler himself and, after that, destroy the house itself. Leave only ashes for the German police to sift, Brandt had said, destroying any evidence that might link the dead man to Wulf Renke. Everything had seemed to be going according to plan, at least until that maniac crashed through the front door into the foyer, killed Karic, and then managed to survive Stepanovic's return fire.

The former Stasi officer cursed softly. Mueller must have missed one of the American agents watching the perimeter of Kessler's property. Now this unknown American had them trapped up here, trapped with a corpse and a room full of incriminating evidence. But waiting meekly for the police to come and arrest them was not an acceptable option. Erich Brandt had a very long arm and any man who failed him so miserably would not live long enough to regret it, even in the supposed security of a Berlin jail cell.

No, Lange decided coldly, he and Stepanovic would have to break out past this lone American, trusting that their weapons and body armor would help them survive a headlong rush down those stairs. But first he would carry out Brandt's orders to the fullest possible extent. If nothing else, setting the villa on fire should

516

provide a useful distraction when they made their escape. Shrugging, he picked up the heavy petrol can again and continued sloshing the flammable liquid across the carpet, drapes, and desk as he backed out through the open door and into the upstairs corridor. He had already thoroughly drenched Kessler's corpse with petrol. A single match would set the whole room ablaze.

Striding upward through the darkness on cat-quiet feet, Randi Russell reached the top of the servants' staircase. She went prone on a small landing and peered down the barrel of her submachine gun, poised and ready to open fire. The door out into the main second floor corridor was just ahead of her. It was closed, but light glimmered faintly through a narrow gap at the bottom.

Randi frowned. Some of the upstairs lights were still on. That was bad. It meant that once she went through that door, she would be out in the open, lit up and left without any real cover — a sitting duck for anyone who happened to be looking in her direction.

A faint smell eddied under the door, growing stronger with every second. Her nose wrinkled at the familiar, cloying reek. Gasoline fumes? Inside the house? Her eyes widened as understanding dawned. Renke's men must be planning to burn Kessler's villa to the ground to cover their tracks!

Frowning, Randi jumped back to her feet. Whatever she was going to do, she had better do now. Her only chance would be to move fast and keep moving. Still holding the MP5SD's pistol grip with her right hand, she reached out for the doorknob with her left. It turned easily. The latch clicked and the door began slowly swinging open, creaking loudly on hinges that had not been oiled for far too long.

Go! She took a short, sharp breath, kicked the door open all the way, and immediately threw herself out into the hallway. She rolled on her shoulder to get well away from the open door and came up on one knee, already sighting down the long corridor toward the top of the staircase.

There, in the faint glow filtering out into the hall from several of the adjoining rooms, she spotted movement — a squat black shape silhouetted against the deeper black of the unlit foyer. It was a dark-haired man, bulky in body armor, and he was already spinning round to face her. He had a weapon in his hands.

Too late, you son of a bitch, Randi thought icily. She pulled the trigger of her submachine gun, firing a series of rapid, three-round bursts. The MP5SD chattered, bucking hard against her grip as it punched 9mm rounds toward the gunman.

Near misses tore sections of the railing behind him to pieces, sending jagged, flame-bright sparks flying as bullets ripped through brass and shattered marble. Other bullets struck the dangling remains of the ruined chandelier. More fragments of glass and crystal broke away to smash onto the tile floor far below.

Hit repeatedly by several rounds that splattered across his Kevlar vest with bone-crushing force, the dark-haired gunman stumbled back, hunched over in agony. He crashed into the weakened section of railing and then screamed in sudden terror as it bent and gave way under his weight.

Randi kept shooting, grimly holding the submachine gun on target as it kicked higher with each burst.

With his arms flailing wildly in a vain effort to regain his balance, the wounded man toppled through the gap, hammered backward by more hits on his armor. Still screaming shrilly, he vanished into the darkness. His eerie, horrified wail ended abruptly in a dull, meaty thud.

Breathing out, Randi eased off on the trigger. Her submachine gun fell silent.

"Scheisse!" a voice growled behind her.

Oh, hell.

She twisted in place, urgently trying to bring the MP5SD around far enough to bear on the slender, thin-lipped man she saw framed in the open door to Kessler's study. Like the others, he wore black clothing and Kevlar armor. His submachine gun, though, was slung across his back, freeing his hands to carry a large, rectangular metal gasoline can. They were less than ten meters apart.

Snarling, the man dropped the can. Gasoline splashed out across his legs and dripped onto the hall carpet as it crashed down. He yanked a Walther semiautomatic pistol out of the holster at his side.

At such close range, the pistol looked enormous. White flame spurted out of its muzzle as the gunman fired.

Randi felt the bullet rip past her head, so close that the hot gases trailing behind it slapped her hard in the face. Her ears rang. The salty-sweet taste of fresh blood filled her mouth. Desperate now, she shot back without aiming, just trying to spray enough rounds in the right direction to drive this new enemy into cover.

One slug hit the gasoline can.

The container rocked under the powerful impact and toppled over. More fuel sprayed high through the air. A spark leaped from the torn metal.

With a soft *whoosh*, the gasoline ignited.

Rivulets of fire raced outward in every direction, feeding on every drop of spilled fuel, setting everything in their wake ablaze.

The thin-lipped man looked down in horror as his gasoline-soaked pants burst into flame. His face twisted in panic as he dropped the Walther to swat wildly at the roaring blaze. But then a mad, inhuman shriek ripped from his throat as the flames seared his fuel-stained hands and flashed up his arms, reaching for his face. In less than a second, he turned into a human torch, wreathed from head-to-foot in fire. Shrieking and screaming in torment, the dying man blindly staggered forward toward her. The flames were consuming him alive.

Sickened, Randi took careful aim and shot him through the head. The burning man tumbled to the floor and lay still. The flames roared higher, spreading up the walls and across the carpet. Thick, choking smoke boiled upward.

Through the open door, she could see Kessler's study was already fully engulfed in fire. Through the swirling smoke and flame, she could see another blazing corpse — this one lying twisted near the big antique desk. No doubt that was Kessler himself, she thought darkly, fighting down the urge to be sick. And with him went the faint, flickering clues she had hoped might lead her to Professor Wulf Renke's new lair.

Abruptly, Randi tossed the submachine gun aside and scrambled to her feet. She needed a closer look at the man she had just killed. She turned and sprinted back down the hall. Without slowing down, she skidded into one of the villa's guestrooms, snatched a heavy wool blanket off the bed, and dashed back the way she had come.

The flames and smoke were even thicker now.

Still running, Randi draped the blanket over her head, shut her eyes tight, and leaped straight through the curtain of fire. For just a split-second, she felt a wave of intense, scorching heat. Then she landed heavily on the floor and crouched down beside the dead man. Staying low to keep below the dense pall of lung-searing smoke rolling through the hallway, she whipped the heavy blanket off her head and swiftly smothered the flames that were charring his clothing and flesh.

Wincing in pain, she ran her hands over the still-smoldering corpse, ransacking pockets and pouches in a desperate hurry. She found what looked like a cell phone, strangely twisted and blackened by the fire, and shoved it into one of her jacket pockets. Then she did the same with a set of scorched papers, a passport, and a wallet.

The flames roared louder. Large flakes of burning paint broke loose from the ceiling and drifted down around her, tumbling end over end in the boiling currents of superheated air. The carpet, walls, and ceiling were a solid sheet of fire.

It was time to leave.

Hurriedly, Randi wrapped the charred wool blanket around her head and shoulders and hands. Coughing now as the raw, acrid smoke bit deep into her lungs, she staggered upright and plunged back into the flames, sprinting fast toward the main staircase.

Again, she felt a wave of intense scorching heat. This time she smelled burning wool. But then, suddenly, she was out of the wall of fire. Frantically, Randi tossed the smoldering blanket aside and threw herself onto the floor, rolling over and over down the hallway while slapping at the smaller flames that were burning through her jeans and jacket.

Once they were snuffed out, she scrambled back to her feet and ran on, racing down the stairs at full speed, leaping down them two and three at a time. Behind her, the fire spread rapidly, growing ever stronger and hotter as it fed on Ulrich Kessler's expensive antique furniture, his precious books, and all of his priceless works of art.

Coughing harder now, Randi reached the ground floor, found the front door, and staggered outside, into the infinitely welcome cold, fresh air. Wearily, she turned and looked back. The whole second floor of the villa was on fire. Orange, red, and white tongues of flames leaped and danced madly, exploding out through shattered windows and erupting toward the heavens through holes torn in the steep slate roof.

Feeling strangely numb, Randi stared at the inferno for a few moments more. She was trembling in reaction, shaking hard as the shock of her narrow escape set in. She had come way too close to dying in there, she realized suddenly. Her right hand closed slowly on the cell phone and papers she had retrieved. It scarcely seemed possible that these bits and pieces of scorched debris contained any information that was worth the risks she had just run. Or the lives of three good men and women, the members of her slaughtered surveillance team.

She sighed. If nothing else, she owed it to them to find out.

Slowly and painfully, Randi turned away from the burning villa and limped off into the darkness.

CHAPTER THIRTY-NINE

Outside Moscow

Vladik Fadayev followed the road all the way up to the top of the little hill and pulled over to the shoulder. He killed the headlights and shut off the engine of his small, Russian-made Lada, listening carefully as it coughed and sputtered to a stop. He had earned enough money in his years with the Brandt Group to afford a better car, but the lean, hollow-cheeked sniper preferred his rusting, often-dented Lada, for all its many faults. Newer vehicles stood out, especially the expensive Western makes, and Fadayev liked to be able to blend anonymously with his surroundings.

He pulled a long, heavy flashlight out of the glove box, pushed the door open, and then stepped lightly out onto the hard-packed, frozen dirt. For a minute, he stayed where he was, shining the beam around the road and into the woods on either side. To his trained eye, it was easy enough to see what had happened here. Tire marks showed where Brandt's big vehicles had stopped suddenly. Spent shell casings glittered in the bright light, half-buried in the trampled snow under the trees where the Group's gunmen had opened fire from ambush.

Fadayev snorted in disgust. Leaving those casings behind for anyone to find was sloppy. Real professionals prided themselves on making a hit and then moving on without leaving any telltales behind that could link them to their work. But he supposed Brandt and the others had been in too much of a hurry to police the area properly.

The sniper shook his head slowly. He did not much care for this new contract Brandt had accepted. Urged on by their mysterious employer, the big, gray-eyed German was always pushing for speed, taking risks with the lives of his men to produce quick results. Fadayev frowned. This constant haste was not safe. It was not sound. He preferred the old days, back when the Brandt Group did most of its well-paid work discreetly and without so much fuss, eliminating a political dissident here, and kidnapping and murdering a business rival there.

He turned in the other direction, noting the deep gouges in the snow and dirt leading straight down the slope. That was where the GAZ jeep he had spotted earlier had plunged to its doom. Broken branches and pieces of torn metal and shattered glass strewn across the slope painted a trail of destruction that ended at the lip of a steep-sided gully.

Fadayev reached into his car and grabbed his pistol off the seat, a heavy old 7.62mm Tokarev. Though he preferred killing at a distance, the pistol was a better choice of weapon to take down that slope. It was handier at close range than his SVD rifle, and more suited to finishing off a wounded man — which was the most he expected to do in the circumstances. He shoved the Tokarev into the pocket of his winter camouflage smock.

Slowly at first, and then with increasing confidence, Fadayev made his way down the slope, picking his way through the trees until he drew near to the edge of the ravine. He paused briefly, pulled the pistol out of his pocket, and went forward with the flashlight in one hand and the Tokarev ready in the other.

Cautiously, he peered down into the gully.

The wreckage of the GAZ jeep lay tilted on its side about ten meters below, sitting at an odd angle in the middle of a pile of large boulders. Splintered saplings and crushed underbrush showed where it had rolled over and over down the side of the ravine before smashing into those rough-edged rocks. The beam from Fadayev's flashlight picked out more than a dozen bullet holes along the vehicle's torn and dented chassis. A few shards of glass stood in its windows, but otherwise they were only dark openings into the ravaged interior.

The sniper sighed.

Climbing down into that ravine in the dark was not a job he relished. It would make more sense to wait for daylight. After all, the dead man inside that jeep was not going anywhere, nor were any of the identity documents or other papers he might be carrying. But orders were orders, and Brandt was not a patient or forgiving man these days. No, it was better to get this job over quickly, Fadayev thought. Then, at least, he could turn around and drive back to the comfort of his apartment in Moscow.

It took him several minutes to reach the bottom.

Probing the rough ground ahead with his flashlight, the sniper moved confidently toward the wrecked jeep. He climbed over a pair of boulders and dropped easily into a little hollow, and then leaned carefully against the side of the vehicle, craning his neck to peer inside.

His eyes widened.

There was no one there. A shoulder

safety belt dangled empty in the driver's seat. Which meant . . .

Fadayev froze suddenly as he felt the ice-cold muzzle of a pistol press firmly against the back of his neck.

"Drop your weapon," a stern voice commanded.

Numbly, the sniper obeyed. The Tokarev clattered against the rocks.

"Very good," the voice said coolly. "And now, get rid of the flashlight."

Again, Fadayev did as he was told, still completely bewildered by his failure. No enemy had ever managed to take him by surprise before. He was always the hunter, never the hunted. The flashlight fell to the ground at his feet and rolled away. It ended up shining off into the tangle of boulders and underbrush in front of him. He swallowed hard. His mouth had gone completely dry.

"Excellent," the voice said, with a hint of bleak humor. "You may live through this night after all."

"What do you want with me?" Fadayev croaked.

"A great many things," the man behind him said flatly. "We will start with a few basic, easy-to-answer, questions. Remember, though, that this is a game with two simple rules. Rule Number One: If you tell me the truth, I will not kill you.

Rule Number Two: If you lie to me, I will blow your spine right out through the front of your throat. Is that clear?"

Fadayev nodded nervously. "Yes, that is very clear," he stammered.

"Good," the other man told him. The muzzle of the pistol pressed even harder against the back of his neck. "Then let us begin —"

Air Defense Force Headquarters, Kiev

Deep in a command bunker beneath the Defense Ministry building, the senior officers responsible for defending Ukraine against air and missile attack sat around a horseshoe-shaped table, listening closely while a middle-aged colonel briefed them on recent developments. Together, they commanded an array of MiG-29 and Su-27 fighter regiments, long-range surface-to-air missile batteries, and early warning radar sites.

"We have evidence of increasing activity at fighter and bomber bases within easy striking range of our country," the briefer said seriously. "We have intercepted air-to-ground transmissions and ground controller replies that may show new aviation regiments deploying to airfields around Bryansk, Kursk, Rostov, and others."

One of the officers sat forward. "But

these transmissions are not conclusive?" he asked sharply.

"No, sir. They are not," the briefer admitted. "But in several cases, we have overheard pilots identifying themselves from new air units and requesting landing instructions at these bases. In each case, the controllers have sharply reminded them to maintain strict radio silence and to follow the visual cues they were given earlier, before leaving their original bases."

"That is certainly suggestive," another Air Defense Force major general said grimly. He commanded one of the MiG-29 regiments stationed near Kiev. "No rational commander asks his pilots to fly into a new base on radio silence for training purposes. Not in the winter! Not unless he is willing to lose aircraft and pilots in otherwise avoidable accidents. Why should the Russians do that unless they are trying to hide their movements from us?"

The colonel conducting the briefing nodded. "Yes, sir. And in fact, all Russian military transmissions have fallen off dramatically over the past twenty-four hours, those involving air, ground, and missile forces . . . the lot of them."

Faces around the table frowned. Transitioning to radio silence was a security measure sometimes employed to conceal forces massing for combat. In peacetime, it was faster, easier, and safer for aviation, tanks, artillery, and infantry units to communicate with each other and with their headquarters using radio signals.

"Are there any other signs of possible imminent action?" one of the missile complex commanders asked quietly.

"The Russians are flying significantly more sorties very near and along our common frontier," the colonel told him. "In several cases, they have 'accidentally' penetrated our airspace — sometimes by as much as twenty or thirty kilometers."

"They're testing us," another of the generals said bluntly. Thick-necked and in his early fifties, he commanded a key radar site near the eastern Ukrainian town of Konotop. "They're probing our defenses to evaluate our detection capabilities and to find out how fast we can react to hostile aircraft crossing into our territory. In all probability, they have electronic intelligence aircraft flying close by during these 'accidents,' monitoring our radar frequencies, communications, and intercept patterns."

He turned toward the head of the table, where the gray-haired commander-in-chief of the Air Defense Force, Lieutenant General Rustern Lissenko, sat with his head down, apparently listening to their discussion while intently examining the notes prepared by his staff. "What is your impression, General?"

Lissenko said nothing.

"General?"

One of the officers sitting next to him reached over and gently touched Lissenko on the shoulder. The gray-haired man fell forward onto his notes. Tufts of his hair fell out, revealing a virulent rash across his scalp. He began shaking, clearly wracked by a skyrocketing fever.

There were astonished gasps around the room.

The colonel who had touched Lissenko stared down at his hand in horror. Then he grabbed for the nearest command phone. "Connect me to the medical center! This is an emergency!"

An hour later, a short, nondescript Air Defense Force captain stood at the window of his small office. He looked down into the Ministry's inner courtyard, watching the panicked activity below in undisguised satisfaction. Doctors and medical technicians wearing biohazard suits were busy shepherding a long line of worried-looking generals into waiting ambulances. So many high-ranking soldiers and political leaders had fallen ill over the past week that no one still in authority in Kiev was taking any more chances. Everyone present at the command conference had been ordered into strict quarantine.

He smiled. Three days ago, he had added the contents of a vial to General Lissenko's customary breakfast, a bowl of *kasha,* or seasoned porridge. Now, the results of this one, simple act far exceeded his expectations. In effect, the Ukrainian Air Defense Force had just been decapitated, stripped of its most senior and experienced officers at the worst possible moment.

The captain, Ukrainian by law but a Russian by ethnicity and loyalty, turned away from the window and picked up a phone. He dialed the secret number he had been given weeks before.

"Yes?" a quiet voice asked.

"This is Rybakov," the captain said calmly. "I have good news to report."

The Kremlin

Russian President Viktor Dudarev looked across his desk at the stocky, gray-haired man standing before him. He frowned. "Castilla is organizing a meeting of his allies to discuss ways to confront us? A secret meeting? You are sure about this?"

Alexei Ivanov nodded coolly. "The report from our special asset in the White House is quite detailed. And reliable

sources inside the other invited governments confirm this report."

"When?"

"In less than two days," the head of the
Thirteenth Directorate answered.

Dudarev rose from behind his desk and
stalked over to one of the windows of his
private office. For a moment, he stood
peering down into the floodlit courtyard
below. Then he glanced back at Ivanov.
"How much do the Americans know?"

"Not enough," Ivanov assured him. "At
most, they have rumors and speculation."
He shrugged. "But we know that they are
probing ever more desperately, seeking the
answers they lack."

The Russian president nodded curtly. He
glowered. "Your courier with the HYDRA
variant has arrived in the United States?"

"Yes," Ivanov confirmed. "He is in New
York now, en route to Washington, D.C."

"Good." Dudarev turned back to look
out the window. His own distorted reflec-
tion stared back at him from the glass. His
scowl deepened. "Signal our mole. I want
Castilla out of the way at the earliest possible moment. I want him dead or dying
before he can conduct this secret conference of America's allies." He swung back
to Ivanov. "Is that clearly understood?"

"It is," the other man assured him quietly. "It will be done."

CHAPTER FORTY

February 21
U.S. Embassy, Berlin

Randi Russell stiffened suddenly, feeling a wave of pain race through her body. For a few terrible seconds, the pain was so intense that the third-floor conference room around her seemed to turn red. Her forehead felt both boiling hot and freezing cold, all at the same time. Slowly, she breathed out through her clenched teeth, forcing herself to relax. The pain ebbed slightly.

"Stings a bit, doesn't it?" the embassy doctor said cheerfully, taking a close look at the cut he had just finished stitching up.

"If by 'a bit,' you mean 'a hell of a lot,' well then, yes," Randi said drily. "It does sting."

The doctor shrugged, already turning away to pack up his medical gear. "If I had my say-so, we would be having this conversation in a hospital emergency room, Ms. Russell," he told her calmly. "You have enough cuts, scrapes, and minor burns for any three people, let alone one young woman."

Randi eyed him. "Are any of my injuries disabling?" she asked pointedly.

"In and of themselves? No," the doctor admitted reluctantly. He shrugged again. "But if you ever slow down long enough for your body to figure out how badly it's been hurt, you're going to wish you were lying quietly in a nice, soft hospital bed, hooked up to an IV loaded with the best painkillers on the market."

"So I guess the trick is to keep moving," Randi said, grinning crookedly. "Well, Doctor, I should be able to manage that. I've never been really comfortable just sitting still."

The doctor snorted. Then he shook his head, accepting defeat. He set a small, capped medicine bottle down on the table in front of her. "Look, Ms. Russell, if the pain you're suffering ever does spill over that rather high threshold of yours, at least promise me that you'll take two of these pills. They'll help you cope with it."

She looked at the bottle and then back up at him. "What are the side effects?"

"Minimal," he said with a slight smile. "Nothing beyond a slight drowsiness." As a parting shot, he added, "But you should probably be careful when operating heavy machinery — which includes firing automatic weapons, chasing down bad guys, and burning down expensive villas."

"I'll keep that in mind," Randi told him coolly.

Once the doctor was gone, she tossed the bottle of painkillers into the closest wastepaper basket. Then she pushed herself up out of her chair and limped over to where Curt Bennett, the head of the special technical team sent out from Langley, was busy trying to pry his way deeper into Wulf Renke's secure communications network. The short, fidgety man was using a combination of the first telephone number her surveillance team had unearthed — the one registered in Switzerland — and other numbers, these taken from the memory of the scorched and blackened cell phone she had captured at Kessler's house a few hours before.

Randi leaned over his shoulder. The computer screen in front of Bennett was filled with what looked, to her untutored eye, like a mishmash of strings of random numbers and symbols. Solid lines connected some of them. Others were linked by dotted lines. Still others sat alone in splendid isolation. "How's it going?" she asked quietly.

The CIA analyst looked up at her. His eyes were bloodshot, but they still gleamed brightly behind the thick lenses of his wire-rimmed glasses. "I'm making progress," he promised. "But whoever created this network was really very good. It's a remarkably complicated web of different phone numbers, with a great many loops and blind alleys built into it. Still, I'm beginning to be able to trace some of the patterns."

"And?"

"So far I've identified numbers belonging to accounts that are registered in several different countries," Bennett told her. "Switzerland, Russia, Germany, and Italy — for a start."

Randi frowned. "Can you tie any of them to Renke?"

"Not yet," the CIA expert said. "Most of those accounts look like fakes to me. Basically, I suspect they're the electronic equivalents of a post office box rented by someone using a fake name and fake ID."

"Damn."

"All is not lost," Bennett reassured her. He raised an eyebrow. "Let's say you found that real-life post office box. What would you do next?"

"I'd put a tail on anyone who came to collect mail from it," Randi said. "And I'd trace any mail forwarded from it."

"Exactly." The CIA specialist grinned toothily. "Well, we can do the same thing electronically. As calls pass through those different numbers, we can track them, following them up the ladder to the next set of accounts and so on."

"How long will it take you to zero in on the core numbers?" Randi asked quietly. "The ones connected to honest-to-God phones?"

"That's difficult to estimate," Bennett said. He shrugged. "Maybe a few more hours. Maybe a couple of days. To a large extent, it depends on the traffic through this secure network. Now that we're inside the outer layer, the more calls the bad guys make using their system, the more information we acquire."

Randi nodded. "Then keep on it, Curt," she said grimly. "I need to know where Renke is hiding out. As soon as possible."

She turned away, seeing another CIA staffer hurrying into the conference room. "Yes?"

"Langley thinks it may have a name for that last man you shot inside Kessler's house," the other woman told her quickly. "That scorched passport you grabbed was definitely a fake, but they were able to match what was left of the photograph with one already in the archives."

"Show me," Randi snapped. She took the TOP-SECRET message sent from CIA headquarters. At the top, there was a scan of an old, black-and-white photo, one that showed a thin-faced man with dark hair. He was wearing a military uniform, an East German officer's service jacket with the four diamonds of a captain on his shoulder straps. She compared this picture with her mental image of the black-clad gunman who had tried so hard to kill her just a few short hours ago. She nodded tightly. It was the same man.

Her eyes moved down to the text of the message. "Gerhard Lange," she read aloud. "A former captain in the East German Ministry of State Security. After the fall of the DDR, initially taken into custody by the Bonn government in connection with several political murders in Leipzig, Dresden, and East Berlin. Released for lack of evidence shortly thereafter. Believed to have emigrated to Serbia one month later. Rumored to have worked as an internal security consultant for the Milosevic regime from 1990 to 1994 before emigrating again, this time to Russia. No further information on file."

"Well, well, well," Randi murmured. "It appears that the good doctor Renke prefers working with his fellow countrymen. I wonder how many other former Stasi goons he has at his beck and call."

Cologne

Bernhard Heichler sat numbly at his

desk inside the headquarters of the Bundesamtes für Verfassunsschutz, the BfV. He stared down at the urgent reports from Berlin, reports that could easily lead to absolute disaster for him. He groaned aloud and then stopped abruptly, appalled by how far the sound seemed to carry in this strangely silent building.

At three o'clock in the morning, the offices of the BfV were almost completely deserted, inhabited only by a skeletal night shift of counterintelligence officers and clerical staff. His continued presence would undoubtedly draw raised eyebrows and lead to sardonic comments, especially from his own subordinates in Section V. Heichler was widely known as a man who craved routine and who ordinarily despised grandstanding. Seen in that light, his decision to stay so late at the office to monitor new developments in yesterday afternoon's massacre of three American intelligence officers in Berlin would strike many of his colleagues as evidence that he was angling for yet another promotion.

No one would guess Heichler's real reason for wanting to read those classified Berlin police reports first, before anyone else in German counterintelligence.

He read through them again, still in disbelief. Police forensics teams had managed to connect the weapons used in the murder of the CIA agents with those found — along with six more bodies — in or around the burned-out home of a high-ranking official in the Bundeskriminalamt. Heichler swallowed hard, fighting down the acid taste of bile. What kind of hellish conspiracy was he now caught up in?

His phone chirped suddenly, frighteningly loud in the unnatural quiet of his office. Startled, Heichler snatched the receiver off its cradle. "Yes? What is it?"

"An incoming call from America, Herr Heichler," the operator said. "From Herr Andrew Coates, a senior aide to the director of the Central Intelligence Agency. He wants to speak to the ranking officer in Section V."

"Put him through," Heichler said harshly. His hands trembled. "Hello?"

"Bernhard?" a familiar voice said into his ear. Coates was the liaison between the CIA and Germany's confusing array of foreign and domestic intelligence organizations. He and Heichler met fairly frequently to exchange information. "Boy, am I glad that you're still there! Listen, I wanted to bring you up-to-date on our investigation, and to let you know that we've had some good news. One of our people survived that goddamned ambush. Not only that, but we're pretty sure that she's managed to get her hands on some crucial evidence that will lead us to the bastards who ordered the attack —"

Heichler listened in growing terror while his counterpart in the CIA shattered any hopes he had harbored of easily escaping the noose of treason and betrayal drawn so tightly around his neck. Somehow he managed to make it through the ensuing conversation without screaming. When the American at last hung up, he sat staring into space for several minutes.

Then, slowly and reluctantly, with hands that shook harder than ever, Heichler picked up his phone one more time. If the Americans captured those responsible for butchering their field officers in Berlin, they were sure to uncover evidence that would lead them right back to the BfV — right back to him. Once again, he thought despairingly, he had no real choice. None at all.

CHAPTER FORTY-ONE

Moscow

Konstantin Malkovic sat calmly at the breakfast table in his luxury apartment, which occupied the top floor of a building overlooking the Kitay Gorod financial district. He sipped the last of his morning tea while reading through summaries of the overnight trades made by his commodities brokers in the United States and Asia. For the first time in the past several days, the billionaire felt able to concentrate on the routine operations of his far-flung business empire. Brandt had the two Americans — Smith and Devin — safely in his grip, and last night's late news reports from Berlin were also extremely satisfying.

HYDRA was once again completely secure.

Quietly, one of his servants appeared, holding a phone. "Mr. Titov is on the line, sir."

Malkovic looked up in some annoyance. Titov was responsible for managing the Moscow offices in his absence. What was so important that it couldn't wait until he arrived at Pashkov House a bit later in the morning? He took the phone. "Well, Kirill?" he demanded. "What's the problem?"

"We have received an e-mail addressed to you personally," Titov told him. "It is marked urgent. I thought you should know about it."

With an effort, Malkovic suppressed his irritation. Like many Russians who had grown up under the old Soviet system, Titov had difficulty acting on his own initiative, without explicit orders from his superior. "Very well," he sighed. "Read this e-mail back to me."

"Unfortunately, I cannot," Titov said carefully. "It appears to be coded using the SOVEREIGN encryption program."

Malkovic frowned. The SOVEREIGN cipher system was one reserved for the most sensitive communications, those involving his most secret and illegal enterprises. Only Malkovic and a few of his most trusted subordinates possessed the ability to decode these messages. "I see," he said, after a pause. "You were quite right to bring this to my attention. I will handle the matter myself."

After breaking the connection with Titov, he rose from the breakfast table and went back into his study. With a few quick keystrokes on his computer, he brought up the e-mail and ran it through his decryption program. It was a frantic report sent by one of his top operatives in Germany, a man who controlled the various puppets and spies Malkovic had planted in several of that country's most important government ministries.

Malkovic read through the message in increasing alarm. The hunter-killer team sent by Brandt to Berlin had been wiped out. Worse, this man Lange and his men had failed in their primary mission. The Americans were still hot on Renke's trail. The HYDRA secret was in greater jeopardy than ever.

Coldly, the billionaire contemplated the likely reaction to this news by the Russian president. He grimaced. Dudarev's threats had been explicit. Could the details be kept from him? The Russian leader had his own sources of information, and one way or another, he would soon learn of this disaster. When he did, it would be unwise in the extreme for Malkovic to rely on his forbearance. With his armies already on the march toward their unsuspecting enemies, too much was at stake for Dudarev to easily forgive failure.

Still scowling, Malkovic deleted the damning message and shut down the computer. For a short time longer, he sat moodily staring at the blank screen, mulling over possible courses of action. HYDRA could still be salvaged, he knew, but the work would be best done personally — and from well beyond Dudarev's reach.

Abruptly, with his decision made, he pushed away from his desk and stalked over to a wall safe concealed behind a centuries-old icon of St. Michael the Archangel. Keyed by his fingerprints, the heavy metal door swung open, revealing an assortment of CD-ROMs, folders of photographs, and a small box full of audiotapes of surreptitiously recorded conversations. Together, this material documented his secret transactions with the Kremlin. It also included a detailed summary of everything he had learned about Russia's military plans.

Quickly, the billionaire began transferring the contents of the safe to one of his briefcases. Once he was safely outside Russia, he would be able to use this information to renegotiate his agreements with Dudarev, securing ironclad guarantees of his personal safety in return for bringing HYDRA to completion. Malkovic smiled thinly, imagining the Russian president's outrage at being blackmailed by his confederate. Then he shrugged. Fortunately, like him, Dudarev was fundamentally a cold-eyed realist. Their alliance had never rested entirely on the basis of mutual trust.

Outside Moscow

Jon Smith was drowning, sinking down and down through the waters of a bottomless black pool. His lungs were on fire, straining against the increasing pressure as he tumbled deeper and deeper into the crushing depths. He writhed in a desperate attempt to claw his way back up to the surface. Then, to his horror, he realized that his hands and his feet were frozen, completely immobile. He was pinioned and helpless, falling ever faster headfirst into nothingness. There was no escape.

"Wake up, Colonel!" a harsh voice demanded suddenly.

Smith shuddered and gasped, retching as another bucketful of ice-cold water hit him right in the face. He coughed violently and then doubled up in pain. Every nerve ending felt raw. Warily, he forced his eyes open.

He was lying on his side in a puddle of freezing water. His hands, bound behind his back, were numb. So were his feet, tied together tightly at the ankles. A rough, worn stone floor stretched away into darkness. For a long moment, nothing he could see made any sense. Where was he? What the hell had happened to him? He could hear what sounded like a woman moaning softly nearby. Slowly, wincing involuntarily at the agony it cost him to make even the slightest movement, Jon turned his head to look upward.

A tall, blond-haired man stood there, staring down at him with an appraising look in his winter-gray eyes. The tall man studied him for a bit longer in silence. Then he nodded in cruel satisfaction. "Now that you are conscious, Colonel, we can begin — all over again."

Unwelcome memories rushed back, flooding into Smith's pain-clouded mind like a rising river bursting through a weakened dam. The gray-eyed man was Erich Brandt. And he and Fiona Devin were Brandt's prisoners. They had been dragged into this dank cellar not long after the ambush that had killed Oleg Kirov.

The cellar itself lay below the ruins of a church, part of a Russian Orthodox monastery that had been closed by the Bolsheviks after the 1917 Revolution. Jon remembered seeing hundreds of bullet holes pockmarking the walls and hearing the tall German explain, with grim amusement, that this chamber had been used by Stalin's secret police, the NKVD, as a place of execution for political prisoners during one of the dictator's brutal purges. Now the monastery's grounds and its buildings, what was left of them, were wholly abandoned, slowly being swallowed up by the surrounding forest.

The terrible hours since they were brought here had passed in an endless procession of torment as Brandt and two of his grim-faced henchmen took turns interrogating them. Every question they asked was punctuated by pain, either by a short, sharp punch to the ribs or the head, or an open-handed slap to the face, or by the application of electric shocks. In the brief intervals between these sessions, Jon and Fiona had been drenched with freezing water, and bombarded by a dizzying succession of shrill, earsplitting sounds and blinding strobe lights — all as part of an effort to disorient them and weaken their resistance.

Brandt had been watching him closely. The blond man smiled coldly. He nodded to the other men standing unseen behind Jon. "Our American friend here is ready. Help him back into his seat."

Two pairs of rough, callused hands grabbed Smith under the arms as Brandt's underlings hauled him bodily upright out of the icy puddle of water. They shoved him back into a chair and then again looped a leather strap around his chest, binding him to the sharp-edged wood frame. The strap tightened unmercifully.

Jon gritted his teeth. He glanced to his left.

Fiona Devin was strapped into a chair

next to him. Her hands and feet were also bound. Her head lolled. Blood trickled out of the corner of her mouth.

"Like you, Ms. Devin has been . . . uncooperative," Brandt said easily. A humorless smile appeared on his face and then vanished swiftly without leaving a trace on his lips or in his eyes. "But I am a forgiving man, so I will grant you both another chance to save yourselves more of this unnecessary pain."

He snapped an order over his shoulder to one of his men. "She looks thirsty, Yuri. Give her another drink!"

His subordinate, a brawny, shaven-headed man, obeyed, tossing a bucket full of cold water into Fiona's face. She choked and spluttered, leaning back against the chair in a vain effort to avoid the deluge of freezing water. After a few seconds, she slowly opened her eyes. Noticing Smith looking at her with evident concern, she forced a wry, painful grin. "The service here is really rather awful. Next time, I'll choose different accommodations."

Brandt snorted. "Very amusing, Ms. Devin." He turned back to Smith. "Now, Colonel, let me try being reasonable one last time." His voice hardened. "Who do you work for? The CIA? The Defense Intelligence Agency? Some other organization?"

Jon braced himself for the blow he knew was coming. He raised his head, staring the former Stasi officer straight in the eyes. "I've told you before," he said tiredly, surprised at how slurred his voice sounded. "My name is Lieutenant Colonel Jon Smith, M.D. I work for the U.S. Army Medical Research Institute —"

But instead of hitting him, Brandt spun around and slapped Fiona hard across the face. Her head rocked back. Blood from a new cut inside her mouth spattered off into the darkness. The sound of the blow echoed like a gunshot in the damp silence of the cellar.

"You're a dead man," Smith growled through his clenched teeth, shocked by what he had just seen. He strained uselessly against the wide leather strap holding him in place.

Brandt swung back with a sly, satisfied grin on his face. "Oh, didn't I tell you, Colonel? The rules have changed. From this moment on, Ms. Devin will suffer for each of your lies, not you." He shrugged. "The pain she endures in the process will be on your conscience, not on mine."

Christ, Smith thought bleakly, feeling light-headed. The big, gray-eyed bastard had read him perfectly. He had been tortured before, and he knew the limits of his own endurance. But how long could he sit helpless and watch another person being brutalized to satisfy his own stubborn pride?

"Pay me no mind, Jon," Fiona Devin said quietly, spitting out a mouthful of blood. "This murdering bastard will kill us both no matter what we tell him, or don't tell him —"

Yet another open-handed blow from Brandt's hard hand rocked her head to the side.

"*You* will be silent, Ms. Devin!" he said coldly. "My conversation is with the colonel here, not with you. You had your chance to tell me what I wished to know. Now it is his turn."

Smith raged inwardly, maddened by his inability to stop this devilish game. If he could just get free, even for a second, he thought desperately . . . but realistically he knew there was no chance of that. He also knew that Fiona was right. They were both going to die here in this dark, dank cellar, this place already haunted by the ghosts of hundreds of others murdered by men like Brandt and his thugs. The only real question remaining was whether or not they could win at least one small last victory by denying the Stasi officer the information he demanded.

He closed his eyes briefly, steeling himself to endure the long, pain-filled, and bloody hours to come. Then he opened them and looked up again at Brandt in front of him. "My name is Lieutenant Colonel Jon Smith, M.D.," he repeated steadily, in a stronger voice than he would have thought possible. "And I work for the United States Army Medical Research Institute of Infectious Diseases . . ."

Brandt stared down at the lean, dark-haired American in frustration. He had been sure that Smith was on the edge of breaking. He had sensed it. But now he could see the man's resolve stiffening. Meanwhile, time was moving on. Sooner or later, a militia patrol would discover the carnage inside the Zakarov dacha. And sooner or later, they would find the wreckage of that bullet-torn GAZ jeep lying in a ravine by the side of the road. Once either of those things happened, Alexei Ivanov would start asking some very awkward questions.

He rubbed his jaw. At least Fadayev had finally called into the Group's headquarters, reporting that the driver was definitely dead and that he had retrieved the dead man's identity papers. If nothing else, Brandt thought, that would make it slightly more difficult for Ivanov to connect the two incidents. But only slightly.

His phone rang suddenly.

Scowling, Brandt yanked the device out of his pocket. "Yes?" he snapped irritably, walking back toward the stairs out of the cellar, moving out of earshot of the two prisoners. "What is it?"

"Your man Lange has bungled his assignment," Malkovic told him bitterly. "And by now the CIA must have penetrated very deeply into our communications network."

Brandt listened in stunned disbelief while his employer ran through what he had learned about the disaster in Berlin. Lange dead? Along with all of his hand-picked team? It scarcely seemed possible.

"We have no choice now," Malkovic said flatly. "We must transfer the key elements of the HYDRA lab to a new location — without further delay. I intend to oversee the work myself, and I want you there, too. Both for security purposes and to make sure that Professor Renke appreciates the need for immediate action."

Brandt nodded, understanding what the other man really wanted. He wanted personal protection against any danger. The billionaire was frightened to death of what the Russians might do once they learned that all of his fine promises to them about HYDRA's operational security were worthless.

His jaw tightened. Malkovic was right to

be afraid. "When do we leave?" he asked harshly.

"My personal jet is scheduled to take off in just under three hours," Malkovic said. "But first I want you to shut down all of your operations in Moscow. Make arrangements for your key people to rendezvous somewhere outside Russia. Dump the communications system. And wipe your files, all of them. Understand?"

"Yes." Brandt considered the work necessary to implement those orders. He nodded again. "It can be done."

"Make sure of it," the other man told him coolly. "I will not tolerate any more mistakes." The phone went dead.

Brandt spun on his heel. "Yuri!" he growled. "Over here!"

Openly curious, the brawny, shaven-headed man ambled over. "Yes?"

"We've got new orders," Brandt told him brusquely. "I'm heading back to Moscow straight away. Close up shop here, sanitize the area, and follow me when you can."

"What about the Americans?"

Brandt shrugged. "They're useless to us now. Finish them."

CHAPTER FORTY-TWO

With their hands still tied behind them, Jon Smith and Fiona Devin were hustled up the stairs and out of the cellar at gunpoint. They came up into the ruins of the church, a square stone building topped by the broken remains of a central onion-shaped dome. Gray light from an overcast sky streamed in through empty windows and gaps in the dome. Small patches of weathered, fading paint on the moss-covered walls were all that was left of the bright frescoes of saints and scenes from the Old and New Testaments that had once decorated the church interior. Everything else of value — the marble altar, the golden tabernacle, chandeliers and candelabras — had long since been carted away.

Brandt wheeled at the main door to the church and sketched an ironic salute. "And here I will say farewell to you, Colonel. And to you, too, Ms. Devin." His teeth flashed white in the gloom. "I will not see either of you again."

Jon said nothing, staring back at him

with an impassive face. Show no fear, he told himself. Don't give the bastard any satisfaction. He noticed that Fiona had the same faintly bored look on her bruised face. She glanced at Brandt with no more interest than she might have shown if he were a common housefly buzzing against a window.

Visibly irked by their lack of reaction, the gray-eyed man turned on his heel and left. Not long afterward, they heard the engine of his Ford Explorer roar into life and listened to its thick tires go crunching away across the snow and ice.

"Go on!" one of the two gunmen still guarding them growled. He gestured with his pistol, a 9mm Makarov, pointing toward a smaller, arched doorway at the side of the church. "Out through there!"

Smith glanced at him, not bothering to hide the contempt he felt. "And if we refuse?"

The gunman, the shaven-headed man Brandt had called Yuri, shrugged carelessly. "Then I will shoot you here. It makes no real difference to me."

"Do as the man asks," Fiona murmured. "If nothing else, we buy a little more time. And at least we get the chance to breathe a bit of clean air."

Jon nodded slowly. In the end, resisting here would make no real difference to their fate, and perhaps it would be better to die outside — under the open sky — than here in this musty pile of stone.

Of course, not dying would be even better, he thought wryly. Cautiously, he tried again to loosen his bonds, straining his wrists hard against the length of heavy-duty plastic cable binding him and then relaxing, trying to stretch them out slightly. Over time, the constant expansion and contraction might create a point of weakness that would let him break free. He sighed. It was a technique that might succeed, but only if he were given an uninterrupted ten or twelve hours to spend working away at the cable. Unfortunately, his remaining life span was probably measured in minutes at best.

"Come!" the gunman snapped again. His comrade, shorter and with a mop of coarse brown hair, prodded them forward from behind with the muzzle of his submachine gun.

Smith and Fiona stumbled out through the little door, down a few cracked stone steps and out across a snow-covered patch of waste ground. It was largely overgrown with weeds and brambles and little clumps of saplings. A few paths wandered off through the old and gnarled trees, heading for darker heaps of broken stone — all that was left of a small hospital, a school, a refectory, cells for the monks, and other buildings. The remnants of a stout stone wall could be seen rising beyond those ruins.

They were pushed and shoved down a path running off to the left, one that led through an open gate in the monastery wall and out into a small, equally neglected, and overgrown graveyard. Many of these markers had fallen over and lay half-buried in the snow. Others were pockmarked with old bullet scars, probably made decades ago by NKVD execution squads amusing themselves while off-duty. All were surrounded by clumps of tall dead grass and weeds.

Looming up on the far side of the graveyard, Jon could see a shallow open pit, probably once used to burn rubbish. Cans of gasoline and a collection of dirty, oil-soaked rags were stacked at the rim of the pit. He stopped abruptly, digging in his heels. Their planned fate was clear. He and Fiona were going to be herded down into that pit, shot to death, and then their bodies would be doused in gasoline and burned.

From somewhere behind him, he could hear the two gunmen murmuring to each other. By the sound of it they had dropped back several meters behind their two captives.

Smith grimaced. They were out of time and out of options. And if they were going to die anyway, it was better to go down fighting. In that same moment, he heard a muffled gasp from Fiona and knew that she, too, had seen the waiting pit and the gasoline. Jon glanced across at her. "Are you with me?" he said quietly, jerking his head slightly to indicate Brandt's thugs coming up behind them.

Now there were tears in her eyes. But she lifted her chin and nodded bravely. "To the bitter end, Colonel." Then she actually managed a very slight smile.

Smith grinned back appreciatively. "That's the spirit. Let's see if we can lure them in within reach. I'll take the guy on the left. You take the one on the right," he murmured under his breath. "Trip yours if you can. Otherwise just kick the hell out of him and then keep kicking. Okay?"

She nodded again.

"No talking!" the shaven-headed man snapped. "And keep moving!"

Smith refused to move. He stood still with his back to the two gunmen, waiting. His skin crawled, anticipating the sudden smashing impact of a bullet. Just come a little closer, he thought grimly. Just a bit closer.

He heard footsteps crunching across the snow, drawing nearer. He tensed, preparing himself to spring. A shadow fell across his shoulder.

Now!

Jon whirled around, lashing out with his right foot in a lightning-fast kick. Out the corner of his eye, he saw Fiona making the same move.

It was no good.

Brandt's men must have been waiting and watching for one last desperate escape attempt. With contemptuous ease, they evaded the kicks wildly aimed in their direction. Both quickly stepped back well out of range, grinning cruelly.

Thrown off balance by his sudden movement, Smith stumbled. With his hands still tied behind his back, he could not recover and wound up falling forward onto his knees. Panting, Fiona dropped to the snow at his side.

The shaven-headed man slowly wagged a mocking finger at them. "That was very stupid." Then he shrugged. "But it doesn't really matter, I suppose. Nothing does — in the end." He signaled to his colleague. "Kill them here, Kostya."

Nodding coolly, the brown-haired man moved forward, raising his submachine gun.

Surprised at his own calmness, Smith forced himself to stare straight into the other man's narrowed eyes. He had fought the good fight. What else could he do but take what was coming as bravely as he could? He could hear Fiona murmuring words softly under her breath, possibly a prayer of some kind.

The gunman's finger tightened slowly on the trigger. A breath of wind ruffled through his mop of coarse brown hair.

Crack.

And the gunman's chest blew apart in a spray of blood and bone, blown open from front to back. The submachine gun fell out of his nerveless hands. His body swayed and then crumpled sideways, collapsing in a clump of brush between two grave markers.

For a split second, no one moved.

The other man stared in absolute astonishment at the mangled corpse of his comrade. Recovering suddenly, he threw himself down.

Crack.

A second high-velocity round smashed the snow-covered cross right behind where Brandt's bald henchman had been standing. Snow and shattered pieces of marble flew away from the point of impact.

Smith rolled to the left, into the shelter offered by a headstone that appeared on the verge of toppling over but that was somehow still standing. A sculptor had carved the likeness of a sleeping mother and child deep into its surface. Fiona followed him. Together, they crouched low on their knees, being very careful to keep their heads well below the top of the monument.

"What the devil is going on?" Fiona whispered. Her eyes were wide and her face had gone very pale. The red handprints, welts, and cuts left by Brandt's cruelty were plain on her smooth clear skin.

"Damned if I know," Smith said softly, putting his mouth close to her ear.

An eerie silence descended across the weed-choked cemetery. Cautiously, Smith turned his head, studying the terrain more closely. The graveyard lay at the bottom of a little bowl, with gentle slopes rising all around. The ruins of the monastery crowned one of those shallow hills. Groves of birch and pine trees covered the other elevations.

He heard the sudden crackle of dry brush not far off, the sound of someone slithering closer through the dead weeds and grass. Brandt's surviving gunman was stalking them, Jon realized coldly, inching carefully from cover to cover to avoid drawing fire from the marksman lurking somewhere among the trees. From the noise, Brandt's man was swinging wide to their left, crawling through the crowded tangle of crosses and grave markers that still separated them from him.

Smith leaned closer to Fiona. "You go off that way," he muttered, jerking his chin to the right, away from the ominous, crackling sounds coming steadily and stealthily closer. "Go a few meters. Once you're behind another big marker, make some noise. As much noise as you can. Understand?"

Wordlessly, Fiona nodded back. Without waiting any longer, she rolled rapidly away across the hard-packed earth and snow.

And Jon moved himself, rolling to the left as quietly as he could. He crossed a small gap and reached the next pair of headstones over, one leaning drunkenly against the other. He stopped behind the largest, a solid slab of dark-colored stone, and listened intently. More weeds rustled. The shaven-headed gunman was coming closer, creeping slowly through the snow and tall grass.

Quickly, Smith twisted around onto his back, lying with his legs drawn up to his chest, coiled and ready to strike. With luck, he might get one chance, he knew. But only one. If he muffed it, he was a dead man.

Off to his right, he heard a sharp thud, then another, and another, and finally what sounded like someone weeping in sheer terror and frustration. Fiona was playing her part well, he realized, mimicking the noises that might be made by a frightened woman desperately crawling away through the cemetery in a panic.

Jon held his breath, waiting.

Flat on his belly, Brandt's man wriggled out from around the weathered edge of the tall stone slab, moving faster now that he thought he had pinpointed the position of the two Americans, with the 9mm Makarov pistol held ready in his right hand. His head swung sharply toward where Smith lay watching him.

Jon saw the other man's eyes widen in utter dismay. In that instant, he kicked out with both feet, smashing them as hard as he could straight into the gunman's face. He felt a sickening crunch and saw the man's head snap backward under the force of the blow. Droplets of blood spattered across his boots.

Smith kicked out again.

The shaven-headed man writhed backward, away from the American's second attack. Below his glaring eyes, his face was a gruesome mask of fractured bone and shattered teeth. Enraged and in agony, he rolled up onto his feet, taking careful aim at Smith's head.

And a third rifle shot rang out, echoing sharply across the little hollow.

Hit in the back, the man screamed once,

clawed desperately at the huge hole torn through his stomach, and then folded over, hanging limp across the tall stone slab. His head and hands trailed in the weeds. More blood slid down the marker and pooled on the ground, staining the white, ice-crusted snow a sickly pink.

Slowly, painfully, Jon sat up. He inched away from the dead man and leaned his head back gratefully against the ice-cold stone of another grave marker, waiting for his nerves to stop twitching.

"Colonel?" a soft voice called out. It was Fiona Devin. "Are you still in one piece?"

"I seem to be," he called back, not bothering to conceal the relief in his own voice. He caught a flicker of movement among the trees on the slope rising above them and sat up straighter. The movement resolved itself into the figure of a tall, silver-haired man, striding down the little hill toward them with a Dragunov SVD rifle cradled casually in his arms and a wide grin wreathed across his broad, large-nosed face.

Jon stared in total disbelief. He was looking at a man who should be dead. He was looking at Oleg Kirov.

"How in hell . . . ?" he asked, when the other man drew nearer.

For an answer, the Russian pulled open the torn winter coat he was wearing. Underneath, he wore a bulky black vest. It was pockmarked and stained with what appeared to be smears of once-molten copper. He patted it affectionately. "British-made body armor, Jon," Kirov said with satisfaction. "Some of the best in the world."

"Which you just happened to decide to wear last night?"

Kirov shrugged. "Before I became a spy, I was a soldier. And what soldier in his right mind would go out on sentry duty without the proper equipment?" He grinned again. "Old habits die hard, my friend, and old soldiers die even harder."

CHAPTER FORTY-THREE

Rural Maryland

Ten minutes after turning off the Beltway that ringed Washington, D.C., Nikolai Nimerovsky glanced down at the odometer of his rental car, a plain white Ford Taurus, checking how far he had come. Five miles. He was getting close to his destination. He looked back up at the little country road stretching ahead of him. On either side, thick stands of trees choked by underbrush were lit by the car's headlights and then disappeared in the predawn darkness. A small signpost loomed up out of the blackness on the right, marking a turn-off that his map indicated meandered deeper into this state park until it came out a few miles away in a new housing subdivision.

He pulled off onto the shoulder and got out, holding the briefcase he had been given in Zurich. Following the instructions given to him in Moscow, he found the dead drop easily enough. It was a hollow tree just a few yards from the signpost. Acting quickly, he slid the briefcase into the tree trunk, made sure it was not visible from the road, and then walked unhurriedly back to his car.

Along the way, he punched in a local phone number on his cell phone. It rang three times before someone answered.

"Yes?" a voice snapped, sounding irritated at being woken up so early in the morning.

"Is this the Miller residence at 555-8705?" Nimerovsky asked carefully.

"No," the person on the other end said tartly. "You've dialed the wrong number."

"I'm very sorry," Nimerovsky said. "My apologies."

There was a sudden click as the person he had called hung up.

Smiling now, the Thirteenth Directorate agent climbed back into his rental car and drove away. His mission was complete. The HYDRA variant had been delivered.

Berlin

Curt Bennett swore suddenly and violently. He bent forward, peering even more closely at the computer screen in front of him, while his fingers raced across the keyboard sitting in his lap.

Randi looked up from her end of the long conference table. Her eyebrows rose in surprise. The CIA technical analyst was not ordinarily a profane man. "Trouble?" she asked.

"Big trouble," Bennett confirmed tightly. "The network we've been probing is going dead."

Randi hurried to his side. "Dead in what way?"

"In every way," Bennett told her. He nodded at the screen. Most of the cell phone numbers whose ownership he had been tracing were now showing up in red, indicating they no longer belonged to active accounts. While she watched, the others shifted to red, too.

"Professor Renke and his friends are pulling the plug," Randi realized.

"Not only that," Bennett said. He tapped a key, switching to a new screen. This one showed long columns of information — date and time stamps and locations — all broken down by separate telephone numbers. One by one they were disappearing, vanishing into the ether. "They're also purging the database records of every call made or received by those numbers."

Randi whistled softly. "I thought that was supposed to be basically impossible."

The CIA analyst nodded. "Yeah, it is." He pushed his glasses back up his nose and frowned. "Unless, of course, you happen to have access to the proprietary software and top-level security codes used by all of the different telecom companies involved in completing those calls."

"So who would have that kind of high-level access?"

Bennett shook his head. "Before now, I would have said nobody." He watched the rest of the screen fade to black and then turned away in disgust. "Most of those companies are fierce competitors. They don't share that kind of data."

"A third party, then," Randi suggested. "Someone from the outside who can hack in past their safeguards."

"Maybe," the analyst admitted. He looked troubled. "But anyone able to break into those phone company computer systems so quickly and easily could do just about anything else he wanted to them."

"Such as?"

"Loot their corporate bank accounts. Steal the private account information for tens of millions of customers. Crash whole switching subroutines so badly that it might take weeks before anyone in the affected areas could make a phone call." The analyst shrugged. "You name it."

Randi nodded slowly, thinking very fast. "And yet," she pointed out, "even with all of that incredible power at their fingertips, the only thing that these guys seem to have done with it is piggyback their own secure communications network onto those systems."

"No kidding," Bennett said. He looked frustrated. "None of it makes any sense. Why go to so much trouble to protect just one man, even if he is a top-notch weapons scientist?"

"I'm beginning to think we're looking at something bigger than that," Randi told him grimly. "Much bigger." She nodded toward the analyst's computer. "How far did you get before Renke's friends pulled their disappearing act?"

"Not far enough," Bennett admitted. "I thought I was seeing some significant patterns in the data, but I can't be sure of how close I was to the core."

"Show me," Randi ordered.

Quickly, the CIA specialist called up the results of his work, displaying them graphically on his screen as a series of separate circles — groups of apparently related phone numbers — with thicker or thinner lines showing the frequency of calls made between them. Each circle also carried a tag identifying the approximate geographic location assigned to each set of numbers.

Randi studied the layout carefully, seeing the patterns Bennett had uncovered. Most of the calls made using this secret network seemed to originate in either one of two places. Moscow was the first. She nodded to herself. No real surprise there, considering Wulf Renke's past affiliations. But the second concentration seemed to make far less sense. It showed a flurry of phone calls made from and to Italy, especially to a group of numbers registered in a section of Umbria, north of Rome.

Umbria, she thought, bewildered. That was a region of ancient hill towns, olive groves, and vineyards. What could be so important to Renke or his backers in Umbria?

"Ms. Russell?"

Randi looked away from the screen. One of the junior-grade CIA officers attached to the Berlin Station stood there. Like her murdered lookout, he was another of the many highly intelligent, but woefully inexperienced rookies who had been rushed through training at Camp Peary after 9/11 as the Agency rushed to rebuild its human intelligence capabilities. She searched her tired mind for his name and found it. Flores. Jeff Flores. "What is it, Jeff?"

"You asked me to work on that scrap of paper you found on Lange," the young man said quietly.

She nodded. Besides Lange's passport, wallet, and phone, that torn and badly blackened bit of paper had been the only piece of hard evidence that she had rescued from the chaos inside Kessler's villa. Unfortunately, that piece of paper had seemed completely worthless as a source of information. At first glance, it was much too scorched to be legible. "Were you able to make out anything?"

He looked worried. "It would be simpler to show you what I found." The younger man glanced cautiously at Bennett. "In my office, I mean."

Curbing her impatience, Randi followed him down the embassy's third-floor corridor to a small windowless cubicle. Flores's desk and a locked filing cabinet for classified disks and documents took up most of the floor space. She looked around with a dry smile. "Nice digs, Jeff. It's always a delight to see patriotism and self-sacrifice rewarded."

He grinned back, but his eyes were still troubled. "My instructors out at the Farm always told me that you got a choice after putting in your first twenty years in clandestine work: either the Medal of Freedom or a desk with a view."

"Hate to break it to you the hard way," Randi told him, "but they were pulling your leg. It takes at least thirty years of service to get a window." She turned serious. "Now fill me in on this document that has you so spooked."

"Yes, ma'am," Flores said. "I scanned that paper, or what was left of it, into our system here. Once it was in digital form, I was able to do a pretty decent job of washing off the burn marks electronically and then enhancing what was left. I've recovered about forty percent of the original text."

"And?"

Flores entered his combination for his filing cabinet and pulled out a single sheet. "This is a printout of what I could read."

Randi studied it in silence. It seemed to be part of a long list of license plates and various car and truck makes and models. Her eyes narrowed. Several of those plate numbers and descriptions sounded familiar. Then her eye dropped down the list to SILVER AUDI A4 SEDAN, BERLIN LICENSE: B AM 2506. She had walked by that car yesterday evening, sitting with a bullet hole in the rear window and the body of poor Carla Voss splayed across the steering wheel. She looked up suddenly in shock.

"They're all ours," Flores confirmed. "Every single one of those vehicles is either leased to or owned by the Agency and assigned to the Berlin Station."

"Christ," Randi murmured. "No wonder Renke's hit team spotted us so easily." Her jaw tightened as she tried to control her growing anger. "Who could put together a list like this?"

Flores swallowed hard. He looked as

though he had a bad taste in his mouth. "It would have to be somebody here, someone in the Station itself, I mean. Or back at Langley. Or else with the BfV."

"The BfV?"

"Germany is an allied host country," the young man pointed out. "It's policy to keep their counterintelligence folks posted on most of our activities."

"Just peachy," Randi said acidly. "Now, who else knows about this?"

"No one."

Randi nodded. "Good. Let's keep it that way." She picked up the printout. "I'll take this copy, Jeff. And I want the original, too. Make sure you wipe everything else you've done off your hard drive. If anyone else asks, you play dumb. Tell them you didn't make any progress and then I pulled you off the assignment. Is that clear?"

"Yes, ma'am," Flores said somberly.

Randi stared down at the damning list in her hands. Another pattern, a very ugly pattern of betrayal and treachery, was becoming disturbingly clear. Someone with access to the results of her hunt for Wulf Renke was working for the enemy.

The White House

President Sam Castilla listened with increasing concern to Admiral Stevens Brose, the chairman of the Joint Chiefs of Staff. In preparation for tomorrow's secret conference with America's allies, he had asked the admiral to brief him on the latest warning signs that the U.S. military was beginning to detect in and around the Russian Federation. The president needed to be able to make the strongest possible case and nothing he heard was particularly helpful in that. But neither was it reassuring. Although no one inside the Pentagon was very happy with the overall quality of intelligence available to them, it was clear now that growing numbers of Russia's best-equipped and trained army and aviation units had completely dropped off the Defense Department's situation maps.

"Meaning what, exactly?" Castilla asked.

"Put bluntly, Mr. President, we don't have the faintest idea of where these divisions and other combat units are right now, where they're headed, or what they might be planning."

"How many soldiers are we talking about here?"

"At least one hundred and fifty thousand troops, thousands of armored vehicles and self-propelled guns, and hundreds of front-line fighters and bombers," Brose told him grimly.

"Enough to start one hell of a war," the president said slowly.

"Maybe several wars," Brose admitted. "At least given the relative combat power of the other countries around Russia. Of all the former Soviet republics, only the Ukrainians have a reasonably strong and well-equipped army and air force."

"Or they would, if it weren't for the fact that their best leaders have been hit by this damned disease," Castilla realized.

Brose nodded his large head ponderously. "Yes, sir, that's true. Right now, from what I've seen of the confusion they're in, the Ukrainians would have a devil of a time putting up much of a fight. As for the rest?" He shrugged. "Even at the best of times, the Kazakhs, the Georgians, the Azerbaijanis, and the others can't field anything more than lightly armed militias. If the Russians are planning to hit them, those militias won't stand a chance against modern armor and crack assault troops."

"The Russians thought that in Grozny, too," Castilla pointed out, referring to the first major battle of the ongoing Chechen war. Overconfident Russian troops storming the city had been slaughtered by coordinated ambushes by Chechen guerrillas. Taking the city had finally required a massive campaign, one that had left tens of thousands of civilians dead and Grozny in ruins.

"Grozny was more than ten years ago," the chairman of the Joint Chiefs said quietly. "The Russian Army and Air Force have learned a lot since then — both from their own experiences, and from watching our forces in action in Iraq. If they really are going to war to reclaim their old territories, they won't make the same mistakes this time."

"Damn." Castilla looked straight across his big pine desk at Brose. "All right, Admiral," he asked, "what's your best estimate for when the balloon might go up — assuming that our worst fears are right?"

"All I have is a guess, Mr. President," the other man warned him.

"In the absence of facts, I'll settle for anything I can get," Castilla said drily.

Brose nodded. "Yes, sir. I understand that." His eyebrows knitted together as he concentrated. After a moment, he looked up somberly. "In my view, Mr. President, the Russians could be ready to strike any time within the next twenty-four to ninety-six hours."

Castilla felt cold. Time was evidently running out faster than he had imagined.

One of the secure phones on his desk beeped. He snatched it up. "Yes?"

It was Fred Klein. "Colonel Smith and Ms. Devin are alive — and they're in contact," the head of Covert-One reported, quietly exultant. "What's more, I believe they have uncovered a major piece of the puzzle."

"But do they have the hard evidence we need?" the president asked carefully, aware of Admiral Brose sitting within earshot.

"Not yet, Sam," Klein admitted. "But Jon and Ms. Devin are confident they know where to go to acquire that evidence. First, though, we've got to get them safely out of Russia."

Castilla raised an eyebrow. The last he had heard, Klein's agents were on the Kremlin's Most-Wanted list. Security officers at every Russian airport, train station, harbor, and border crossing were already on the highest possible alert. "Good grief. That's not going to be easy, is it?"

"No, sir," Klein told him firmly. "It won't."

Near the Russo-Ukrainian Border

Snow was falling across the empty fields and wooded hills, swirling in drifts as gusts of wind blew harder from the east. There was no sight of the noon sun beneath the heavy mass of clouds covering the sky. Safe from any possible observation by American photo-reconnaissance satellites, long lines of T-90 and T-72 tanks, BMP-3 fighting vehicles, and heavy self-propelled guns crowded the narrow roads and logging tracks that wove south through the forests toward the frontier.

Hundreds of vehicles sat motionless, already thickly blanketed by the fast-falling snow. Thousands of men stood at attention in formation beside them, waiting for the signal to move.

Suddenly a white flare soared up from the south and burst beneath the overcast sky. Whistles blew shrilly up and down the waiting columns of men. Instantly, the rigid formations dissolved, with tank crews, infantry squads, and gun crews all swarming onto their vehicles.

Captain Andrei Yudenich pulled himself up onto the low, rounded turret of his T-90 tank and then dropped lightly into the open commander's cupola. With an ease born of constant practice, he donned his headset and plugged it into the tank's radio gear. Glancing down, he checked the settings, making sure his microphone was set on intercom. Like the other units assembled here, the 4th Guards Tank Division was still under strict orders to maintain radio silence.

For Yudenich and his men, the last twenty-four hours had passed in a blur, consumed by the frantic work — fueling up, stowing ammunition and food, and running last-minute maintenance on every major system — necessary to prepare their tanks and other vehicles for possible combat. No one yet knew quite why they were really here, but rumors of imminent war had swept through the huge camouflaged cantonments with increasing frequency and conviction. And the claims by some senior officers that this was all just an elaborate readiness exercise sounded increasingly hollow.

The captain looked up, seeing another flare arc through the sky. This one was red. He keyed his mike. "Stand by. Driver, engine start!"

Immediately, the T-90's powerful diesel engine roared to life, echoed by all the others in the column. Clouds of thick black smoke drifted away across the white fields and dark woods.

And a third flare soared high, this one green.

Yudenich watched closely, waiting for the tanks ahead of his to start moving before ordering his own driver to advance. One by one, starting from the front, the massive armored vehicles clanked into motion, treads squealing and clattering as they headed south, rumbling toward new assembly areas that lay within closer striking range of the Ukrainian border.

The clock was running on a countdown toward war.

CHAPTER FORTY-FOUR

Rome

Ciampino Airport lay on the outskirts of Rome, only fifteen kilometers from the center of the city. Plowed fields, parkland, suburban homes, low-rise apartment buildings, and light-industrial areas surrounded the small, single-runway airport. Eclipsed by its larger rival, Fiumicino, Ciampino was now used primarily by low-cost international charter flights and smaller private, government, and corporate aircraft.

Shortly after three in the afternoon, local time, a twin-engine corporate jet broke through the thin layer of overcast, flew parallel to the Via Appia Nuova in a gradual descent toward the airport, and then dropped lower. It touched down only meters after clearing the boundary marker, braked hard, and slowly taxied past the small terminal used by arriving and departing charter flights.

At the end of the runway, the jet swung left and pulled up on the section of concrete apron ordinarily used by cargo aircraft. Two Mercedes sedans were parked there, waiting.

Eight men, all dressed in winter clothing, emerged from the aircraft. Six of them formed a tight ring around the seventh, an older, white-haired man who was already striding purposefully toward the parked cars. The eighth man, much taller and with pale blond hair, moved forward to intercept the lone Italian customs official coming to greet them.

"Your papers, *Signor?*" the customs officer asked politely.

The blond-haired man reached inside his coat and took out his passport and other documents.

Smiling politely, the Italian scanned through them quickly. He raised an eyebrow. "Ah, I see that you are assigned to the ECPR. We see many of its staff here at Ciampino. Tell me, what is your work for the Center?"

Erich Brandt smiled mirthlessly. "Auditing and quality control."

"And what of those other gentlemen?" the customs officer asked, nodding toward Konstantin Malkovic and his bodyguards as they climbed into the waiting sedans. "Do they also work for the Center?"

Brandt nodded. "They do." He reached inside his heavy coat again, this time for a white letter-sized envelope. "Here are their required papers. I think you will find that everything is in order."

The Italian pulled open the envelope just far enough to see the thick sheaf of high-denomination euro notes it contained. He smiled greedily. "Quite correct, as always." Then he stuffed the envelope away inside his own coat. "Once again, it is a pleasure doing business with you, *Signor* Brandt. I look forward to your next visit."

Within minutes, Brandt, Malkovic, and their six heavily armed bodyguards were speeding away along the Via Appia Nuova, beginning the next leg of their journey to Orvieto.

Sheremetevo-2 International Airport, Outside Moscow

Night had already descended on the birch and pine forests surrounding Sheremetevo-2. Lit by harsh white lights, the airport's approach roads sliced through the darkness with rigid precision. Long lines of cars, trucks, and buses were backed up along those roads, waiting to pass through the special militia checkpoints set up outside the single passenger terminal, an ugly block of steel and concrete. Away from the terminal, armored scout cars manned by elite Ministry of the Interior commandos patrolled Sheremetevo's perimeter fence.

The Kremlin's orders were explicit. Under no circumstances were the two American fugitives to be allowed to escape from Russia. As part of the manhunt for them, security around the airport had been tightened to levels not seen since the height of the Cold War.

A TransAtlantic Express 747-400 cargo plane sat on the tarmac at the other end of the airport. Packages, boxes, cartons of overnight mail, and other pieces of heavy air freight were being taken off a number of different trucks, strapped onto standard-sized pallets, and then loaded into the 747's main deck cargo holds.

Squads of gray-coated militiamen prowled through the loading area, keeping a wary eye on the activity going on around them. Their officers had firm instructions to arrest anyone attempting to stow away aboard any of the cargo aircraft that flew out of Sheremetevo-2.

Senior Lieutenant Anatoliy Sergunin stood with his hands clasped behind his back, watching the heavy pallets as large scissor-lift loaders picked them up off the concrete and slid them into the enormous TranEx aircraft. Waiting cargo handlers guided the pallets in through the 747's hatches, rolled them into position, and then locked them down to the deck. For the first several hours of his shift, Sergunin had found the whole process fascinating. Now he was merely bored and cold and tired.

"Gate Security reports that another vehicle is on its way over, sir," his sergeant reported, listening to the detachment's radio.

Surprised, Sergunin checked his watch. This aircraft was scheduled to depart in less than an hour. By now, all of the freight assigned to the 747 should already have arrived. Sorting and securing the various sizes of packages onto pallets was a complicated and time-consuming process, one governed by the absolute need to safely balance the aircraft's load. He turned around and looked away across the vast stretch of darkened tarmac. Sure enough, he could see a pair of bright headlights coming toward them at high speed.

He glanced at his sergeant. "What kind of cargo is this new vehicle carrying?"

"Two coffins, sir."

"Coffins?" Sergunin repeated in amazement.

"Yes, sir," the sergeant said patiently. "It's a hearse."

A few minutes later, Sergunin stood off to the side of the hearse, which had come from a Moscow mortuary, observing the proceedings closely. The driver, wearing a white smock, wrestled each of the heavy metal caskets out of the back of his vehicle and onto a folding gurney. The coffins were sealed by tape as proof that they had already been x-rayed and cleared by Customs.

Sergunin's eyes narrowed in suspicion. Customs officials could be bribed. And what better way to smuggle two fugitive spies out of Russia than in a pair of coffins? Especially aboard an aircraft that was bound first for Frankfurt, then Canada, and finally on to the United States? He laid his hand on the butt of the pistol holstered at his side. Huge rewards were promised to anyone who captured the two wanted Americans, and equally serious punishments were ordained for anyone who let them escape. Under the circumstances, even excessive caution was warranted.

The militia officer waited until the mortuary worker finished his awkward task. Then he approached the tall, silver-haired man. "You are in sole charge of this material?"

The big man, who stood mopping the sweat off his forehead with a red handkerchief, nodded. "That's right, Lieutenant," he said pleasantly. "Twenty years in the business, and never a single complaint from any of my passengers."

"Spare me the jokes and show me the

shipping warrants for these . . . corpses," Sergunin snapped.

"Always happy to oblige the authorities," the man said, shrugging. He handed over a clipboard. "As you see, everything is in order."

Sergunin read through the documents with a skeptical eye. According to the paperwork, the caskets contained the bodies of a husband and wife — both quite old when they were killed in a car accident. Although the dead man and woman were Russian citizens, their children, émigrés now living in Toronto, were paying to have the bodies shipped to Canada for burial there.

The militia officer frowned. The story was feeble. He looked up at the silver-haired hearse driver and tossed the clipboard back. "I want those coffins opened for inspection," he demanded.

"Opened?" the big man asked. He sounded surprised.

"You heard me," Sergunin told him coldly. He drew his pistol and thumbed off the safety. With his free hand, he signaled his sergeant and a waiting squad to close in around the hearse. "Open them up," he said. "And do it now."

"Easy there, Lieutenant," the man said quickly. "If you want to see inside, that's fine with me." He shrugged again. "But I should warn you, neither stiff is exactly a wholesome sight. They're both a real mess, in fact. A bus hit the car they were driving head-on. There wasn't much our cosmetics girls in the back room could do to pretty them up."

Sergunin ignored him. He stepped forward and rapped one of the caskets with the muzzle of his service pistol. "This one first. And be quick!"

With a sigh, the hearse driver obeyed. First he cut through the customs tape with a pocketknife. Then, one by one, he flipped open the latches holding the lid shut. Before going any further, he looked over his shoulder at the militia officer. "You really sure you want to see this?"

Sergunin snorted, holding his pistol ready. "Get on with it."

With one last expressive shrug, the other man lifted the casket lid.

For a moment, Sergunin stared down into the coffin. His face turned deathly pale. He was looking at a corpse so terribly mutilated and burned that it was impossible to tell whether or not it was that of a man or a woman. Empty eye sockets and teeth grinned back at him out of a skull only partly covered by scraps of blackened flesh. Withered hands, twisted into claws by intense heat, were raised above the shattered body in what appeared to be a last, grotesque appeal for help.

Retching, the militia officer swung away and was violently sick all over his boots and the tarmac. His sergeant and the others backed away in disgust.

The big man closed the lid of the coffin. "There was a fuel tank fire after the crash," he murmured apologetically. "Maybe I should have mentioned that first." He moved to the second coffin and took out his penknife.

"Stop," Sergunin gasped, still mopping at his mouth with the back of his hand. Desperately, he waved the driver back from the unopened casket. "Hurry up and get those damned horrors aboard that plane. And then clear off!"

With an effort, the lieutenant straightened up and staggered away, looking for somewhere private to clean the humiliating mess off his boots. Equally repulsed, his sergeant and the other gray-coated militia busied themselves with inspecting the other pieces of air freight left in the area. So when the hearse drove away into the darkness ten minutes later, neither Sergunin nor his subordinates noticed that the man who was now behind the wheel was much shorter and had light brown hair.

One hour later, with the 747-400 flying west at more than thirty-five thousand feet above the ink-black Russian countryside, Oleg Kirov tugged off the cargo netting surrounding the two coffins. He wore a TranEx flight crew uniform. With the netting out of the way, he knelt down beside one of the caskets and began quickly unfastening a series of screws set into the bottom. Once the last screw dropped out into his hand, he pried open the edge of a panel running the length of the coffin. It clattered onto the cargo pallet, revealing a hidden compartment roughly six feet long, two feet wide, and barely a foot high.

Slowly and painfully, Fiona Devin wriggled out through the narrow opening and slid to the deck of the aircraft. She wore an oxygen mask coupled to a small metal cylinder.

Gently, Kirov helped her sit up and take off the oxygen mask. "Are you all right?"

She nodded weakly. "I'll live, Oleg." She smiled faintly. "But if I wasn't claustrophobic before, I certainly will be in the future."

"You are a brave woman, Fiona," Kirov said seriously. "You humble me." He kissed her lightly on the forehead and then turned away to open the hidden compartment in the second coffin.

Jon Smith crawled out through the opening and fell onto the deck. His muscles, already bruised and battered by

Brandt and his thugs, felt as though they were on fire. Wincing, he stripped off his oxygen mask and took a deep, shuddering breath. He saw Kirov and Fiona looking down at him with concern and forced a twisted grin onto his face. "Never again," he said with heartfelt passion. "Never, ever again. The savings just aren't worth it."

They both looked blank. "Pardon, Colonel?" Fiona said, puzzled.

Smith pushed himself up into a sitting position. He motioned toward the cramped compartments concealed inside the coffins. "No more super-economy class for me. Next time I'll pay full fare," he explained.

Kirov chuckled. "I will be sure to pass your complaints on to the management, Jon." He turned more serious. "Or you can do that yourself, as soon as you are ready."

"Do we have secure contact with Covert-One?" Smith asked.

"We do," Kirov replied. He nodded back up the darkened cargo deck toward the cockpit. "I've patched through the TranEx system, using one of our own scramblers. Mr. Klein is standing by."

Ignoring his aches and pains, Smith levered himself upright. Fiona did the same. With Kirov coming behind to help steady them, the two Americans hobbled forward, feeling their knotted muscles gradually starting to loosen up. By the time they reached the cockpit, Jon was walking on his own.

The 747's pilot and copilot sat in their seats, apparently intent on monitoring the aircraft's controls. Neither seemed to take any notice of their unexpected "guests."

"As far as they are concerned, we do not exist," Kirov explained quietly. "It is safer for them that way."

Smith nodded his understanding. Once again, Fred Klein had demonstrated a remarkable ability to pull strings from his position in the shadows. He took the headset offered by Kirov. "Smith here."

"It's very good to hear from you, Colonel," Klein's familiar voice said. Even at a distance of several thousand miles, his relief was audible. "I was beginning to get rather worried."

"Me, too," Jon admitted. "The thought of you having to handle all that extra, death-related paperwork brought tears to my eyes."

"I'm touched," Klein said drily. "Now, what can you tell me about this disease?"

"First, that it's not a disease — not in the classic sense, anyway," Smith said seriously. "My best guess is that we're facing a very sophisticated biological weapon, a weapon set up to attack individual genetic sequences. Based on the symptoms, I'll bet that Renke is engineering each variant to interfere with cell reproduction in some fashion." He sighed. "I don't know how the victims are infected, but it could be as simple as introducing it into their food or anything they drink. And once this weapon is inside the person who's been targeted, I doubt that there's any way to stop the process or to reverse it. Of course, in anyone but the intended victim, this material would be completely harmless."

"Which is why those who get sick don't seem to be infectious to anyone else around them," Klein realized.

"Bingo," Smith said. He frowned. "Basically, Renke has invented the perfect precision weapon."

"Assuming you can gain access to your target's DNA," Klein commented.

"Yeah. And that's where this Slavic Genesis study comes in," Smith told him. "The researchers at the ECPR have been sampling DNA in Ukraine, Georgia, Armenia, and the other former Soviet republics for years. If we dig hard enough, I'm pretty sure that we'll learn that most of those who've been killed were also participants in one or more ECPR projects."

"What about those who weren't part of these research studies?" Klein wondered. "How is this illness being tailored for use against so many of our intelligence analysts and military people? Or the Brits, the

French, and the Germans, and others?"

Jon shrugged. "If it came down to that, Fred, I could isolate your DNA from your fingerprints on a dirty glass — or from hair clippings given to me by your barber. It's not as easy or as cost-effective, but it can be done."

"You're not seriously suggesting that Renke or the Russians or Malkovic have been bribing every barber and bartender in Washington, London, Paris, and Berlin to collect samples for them, are you?" Klein asked wryly.

Smith shook his head. "No, sir. Not *en masse.*"

"Then how?"

Jon stiffened suddenly as a horrible possibility occurred to him. "Take a good hard look at anyone with unrestricted access to the OMEGA medical database," he advised grimly.

There was a long silence on the other end as Klein considered his suggestion. OMEGA was a top-secret program designed to ensure the ability of the U.S. government to continue functioning in the event of a catastrophic terrorist attack on Washington and its suburbs. The OMEGA medical database was just one small part of that much larger program. To assist in identifying the dead from any large-scale attack, it contained tissue samples taken from tens of thousands of American government and military personnel.

"Good God," the head of Covert-One said at last. "If you're right, this country is in even graver danger than I had first supposed." He sighed. "And it also seems that we're running out of time faster than I had anticipated."

"Meaning?" Smith asked.

"Meaning this is not just a biological weapons threat, Jon," Klein said quietly. "Those rumors Kirov passed on from his FSB contact were solid. It now appears almost certain that Dudarev and his allies in the Kremlin are ready to launch a major military campaign, one designed to take advantage of the confusion caused by this new weapon."

Smith listened closely while the other man brought him up-to-date on the most recent military and political developments along Russia's frontiers. If anything, the Pentagon's time estimate struck him as optimistic. Russian tanks and aircraft could begin rolling to the attack at any moment. His blood ran cold, thinking about the carnage that would be caused by a war of the scope Klein feared. "What countermeasures are we taking?"

"The president is scheduled to meet with representatives of our key allies in less than twenty-four hours," Klein told him. "His goal is to persuade them that we must act to deter Russia before it is too late, before the first bombs fall."

"Will they listen to him?"

The head of Covert-One sighed again. "I doubt it."

"Why not?"

"We need evidence, Colonel," Klein said flatly. "The problem is still the same as it was when I ordered you to Moscow. No matter how persuasive they may be, we need more than theories. Without better proof that the Russians are behind this disease, we cannot persuade our allies to act — or force the Kremlin to stand down by ourselves."

"Listen, Fred, get us to Italy with the right equipment, and we'll do our damnedest to find that evidence," Smith promised.

"I know you will, Jon," Klein told him somberly. "The president and I are counting on the three of you."

CHAPTER FORTY-FIVE

Washington, D.C.

Nathaniel Frederick Klein looked up from his desk to the large monitor on the wall of his office. It was set to display a computer-driven map of Europe. A small icon blinked on the map, showing the position of the aircraft carrying his three agents. He followed its progress for a moment, watching as it slowly slanted southwest through Hungarian airspace, en route to the U.S. Air Force base at Aviano, in the northeast corner of Italy. Another aircraft icon indicated the heightened alert status of the U.S. fighter wing based there.

He touched a key on his computer and saw more aircraft icons appear on the map, some in Germany, others in the United Kingdom. Like the icon at Aviano, they depicted the tactical fighter, bomber, and refueling wings alerted by Sam Castilla for possible emergency deployment to Ukraine, Georgia, and the other threatened republics around Russia.

Klein took off his glasses and rubbed

601

wearily at the bridge of his long nose. Right now, no American combat aircraft were going anywhere. The F-16s, F-15s, and refueling tankers were just sitting near runways or in their hardened shelters, waiting. Approached quietly through back channels, the NATO allies were expressing grave doubts about allowing the use of their airspace for any U.S. military deployment to the east. Ironically, the conference the president had summoned for tomorrow morning was now working against him because it gave the French and Germans and others an excuse to delay any decisions until after their representatives reported back. Perhaps even more important, none of the countries that were threatened by Russia were willing to invite U.S. forces into their territories.

Renke's DNA-based weapons had done their work well, Klein decided sourly. Too many of the best and bravest political and military leaders in Ukraine and the other smaller states were dead. Those who were left alive were too frightened of angering Moscow. They were paralyzed, fearing the blow that might be about to fall — but unwilling or unable to take actions that might deter a Russian attack. If the United States could prove that what it said about Dudarev's actions was true, they might find the courage to decide. Otherwise, they would not, preferring the uncertainty of inaction to the perils of action.

He put his glasses back on. Almost unwillingly, Klein found himself staring again at the small dot representing the plane carrying Jon Smith, Fiona Devin, and Kirov, as though he could somehow urge the 747 to even greater speed by sheer willpower.

"Nathaniel?"

Klein looked up. His long-time assistant, Maggie Templeton, stood in the doorway that separated their two offices. "Yes, Maggie?"

"I've finished running that search you asked for," she told him quietly, walking all the way into the room. "I cross-checked every file we had on OMEGA with the FBI, CIA, and other databases."

"And?"

"I found one serious correlation," Maggie told him. "Take a look at your in-box."

Klein obeyed, using his keyboard to call up the documents she had downloaded and sent to his computer. The first was a local news story from the archives of *The Washington Post*, dated roughly six months ago. The second was a copy of an updated police investigative report covering the same incident. The last was a personnel file from the Bethesda Naval Medical Center. He compared them quickly. One eyebrow rose.

He looked up. "Very good work, Maggie," he said. "As always."

Before she left his office, he had already hit the button that would connect him to President Castilla's private line.

The president answered it on the second ring. "Yes?"

"Unfortunately, Colonel Smith was right," Klein told him flatly. "I'm convinced that OMEGA has been compromised."

"How?"

"Six months ago, the metropolitan police found a body floating in one of the canals near Georgetown," Klein said, reading the relevant facts from the *Post* story. "Eventually, they identified the dead man as a Dr. Conrad Horne. According to the police, Dr. Horne appeared to be the victim of a routine mugging that went very badly wrong. But no one was ever arrested for his murder and there are no pending leads."

"Go on," Castilla said.

"It turns out that Horne was a senior researcher at the Bethesda Naval Medical Center," the head of Covert-One told him.

"With clearances for the OMEGA medical database," Castilla guessed bleakly.

"Exactly," Klein said. He went through the police report, noting key details. "Horne was divorced, with huge, court-mandated alimony and child-support payments. His bank balances were always near zero. And his colleagues often heard him complaining about the lousy pay given to government-employed scientists. But the detectives searching his apartment after the murder found several thousand dollars in cash and thousands more in brand-new furniture and consumer electronics. There were also indications that he had been shopping around for a brand-new car, probably a Jaguar."

"And you think he was selling access to the tissue samples in the database?" Castilla interjected.

Klein nodded solemnly. "Yes, I do. What's more, I think he got greedy — or that he was simply too indiscreet — and that he was murdered to keep his mouth shut."

Castilla sighed. "So what you're telling me is that Professor Renke and his patrons could already have the DNA for every key player in our government?"

"Yes, sir," Klein replied grimly. "Including yours."

Aviano Air Base

The U.S. Air Force base at Aviano lay in the Friuli-Venezia Giulia region, roughly fifty kilometers north of Venice, right at the foot of the Italian Alps. From the flight line at Area F, Mount Cavallo dominated the northern horizon, towering nearly twenty-three hundred meters above the surrounding highlands. The pale rays of the rising moon glittered off vast expanses of snow and ice covering the mountain's rugged slopes.

With its engines howling as the TranEx pilot reversed thrust, the 747 rolled down the long, main runway at Aviano, braking hard as it passed rows of hardened aircraft shelters. Each had its blast doors open, revealing brightly lit interiors where hangar crews were busy prepping the F-16s of the 31st Tactical Fighter Wing for a long flight east into possible combat.

At the end of the runway, the massive cargo aircraft swung off onto a wide stretch of concrete apron and came to a full stop. A truck equipped with a set of mobile stairs appeared and maneuvered into position at the 747's forward door. As soon as they were in place, Smith hurried down them, with Fiona Devin and Kirov following close behind.

A young Air Force captain in a green flight jacket stood waiting for them at the bottom. He carried a helmet with night-vision goggles clipped to the visor. "Lieutenant Colonel Smith?" he asked, rather dubiously eyeing the three apparent civilians, all of whom looked very much the worse for wear.

Jon nodded. "That's right." He grinned at the worried expression on the younger officer's face. "Don't worry, Captain. We'll try not to bleed all over your nice shiny aircraft."

The Air Force officer looked abashed. "Sorry, sir."

"No problem," Smith told him. "Are you ready for us?"

"Yes, sir. We're right over that way," the captain said, nodding toward a large black helicopter sitting off by itself across the concrete. Smith recognized it as an MH-53J Pave Low, one of the world's most advanced special missions aircraft. Heavily armored, bristling with weapons, and crammed full of sophisticated navigation systems and electronic countermeasures, Pave Lows were built to carry commandos deep into enemy-held territory, flying as low as thirty to forty meters off the ground while dodging enemy radar detection and surface-to-air missiles.

"What about our gear?" Smith asked the captain.

"Your clothing, weapons, and other equipment are already stashed aboard the bird, Colonel," the younger man assured him. "Our orders are to get you and your party airborne as soon as possible."

Five minutes later, Smith, Fiona, and Kirov were strapping themselves into seats in the twenty-one-ton Pave Low's gray-painted rear compartment. One of the helicopter's six crewmen handed around helmets and earplugs. "You'll need them when we crank this baby up," he said cheerfully, hooking them into the intercom system. "Otherwise, the noise will pretty much pound your brains into mush."

Overhead the huge rotor blades began turning, spinning faster and faster as the two turbo-shaft engines revved up. By the time the engines were at full power, the whine and roar were deafening. The aircraft rattled and shook, vibrating and rocking from side to side.

Through the intercom, Smith heard the flight engineer, a sergeant with a thick Texas drawl, running through the checklist with the MH-53J's pilot and copilot. "Ready to taxi," the sergeant said at last.

The helicopter crept down the taxiway.

The three Air Force crewmen in back with Smith and the others leaned out through the open hatches and rear ramp, watching carefully through their night-vision goggles. In flight, their job was to help warn the pilots of any obstacles that could endanger the helicopter — mostly trees and power lines.

Slowly, the Pave Low lifted off the

runway. Wind whipped up by the pounding rotors screamed through the crew compartment. Smith tightened his seat belt. He noticed Kirov helping Fiona with hers and hid a grin.

For a few minutes more, the huge black helicopter hovered in place while the crew finished its last-minute navigation and systems checks. Then, with its engines howling, the MH-53J spun right and flew south at nearly one hundred and twenty knots, racing low over the Italian countryside with all of its running lights off.

Near Orvieto

Erich Brandt struggled to control his mounting impatience. The main HYDRA lab was a hive of activity as Renke shepherded his assistants through the time-consuming task of crating up their DNA databases and specialized equipment. The work was necessarily complex, but once it was complete, the scientist and his team would be able to vanish, and then restart their lethal production line in a new and even more secure location. Almost as important, any American agents investigating the European Center for Population Research would find only an ordinary lab dedicated to routine genetic analysis.

He turned to Renke. "How much longer?"

The scientist shrugged. "Several more hours. We could cut that time significantly, but only at the cost of leaving precious equipment behind."

Standing at Brandt's side, Konstantin Malkovic frowned. "How much delay would that cause in reopening your lab?"

"Perhaps as much as several weeks," Renke told him.

The billionaire shook his head firmly. "I have promised Moscow that HYDRA will be back in operation by the time their armies go into action. Even with Castilla already marked for death, our Russian allies want the ability to act directly against others in Washington if the new president is also stubborn and refuses to accept their *fait accompli*."

"Dudarev will still deal with you?" Renke asked curiously.

Now it was Malkovic's turn to shrug. "What choice does he have? The secrets of the HYDRA weapon are mine, not his. Besides, I've promised him that our security problems are being resolved. Once your equipment and scientists are safely out of Italy, what proof can Washington possibly find in time — especially with its agents in Moscow already dead? Anyway, once the shooting starts, it will be far too late for the Americans to intervene."

The financier's secure cell phone beeped

suddenly. He flipped it open. "Malkovic here. Go ahead." He glanced at Brandt. "It's Titov, reporting from Moscow."

Brandt nodded. Malkovic had left the manager behind to monitor developments in the Russian capital.

Malkovic listened intently to his subordinate's report. Slowly, his face tightened to a rigid, expressionless mask. "Very well," he said at last. "Keep me informed."

He flipped the phone closed and turned back to Brandt. "It seems that the Moscow militia have found two bodies outside that old, ruined monastery you use for your dirty work."

"Alas for poor Colonel Smith and Ms. Devin," the former Stasi officer quipped, with grim amusement.

"Save your sympathy for them," Malkovic snapped icily. "Smith and Devin are still alive. The dead men were yours."

Brandt stared back at his employer in shock. Smith and Devin had escaped? How could that possibly be true? For a moment, he felt a shiver of superstitious dread course down his spine. Who were these two Americans?

CHAPTER FORTY-SIX

Near Orvieto

With its rotors churning, the Pave Low helicopter swept low over a steep, wooded ridge and dove into the broader valley beyond. Treetops flashed by only meters below. Bathed in moonlight, a narrow river, the Paglia, snaked south, roughly paralleling the wide *autostrada* and the railway. Vineyards, groves of gnarled olive trees, and rows of tall, shapely cypresses spread across the gently rolling landscape. Patches of square black shadow marked the location of old stone farmhouses. Lights that seemed to float in the sky ahead outlined the towers and spires of Orvieto, set high on its volcanic plateau. More lights gleamed on a shallow ridge west of the city.

"ECPR in sight," one of the pilots commented. "Two minutes out from infiltration point."

Gradually, the MH-53J began decelerating, slowing as it began its approach to the designated landing zone. Occasionally, the nose of the helicopter flared higher as the pilots climbed sharply to avoid colliding with taller trees or the telephone and power lines crisscrossing the Paglia valley.

Jon Smith hung on tight to a strap dangling from the ceiling. His stomach lurched.

"Hell of a ride, isn't it, Colonel?" one of the crewmen commented, flashing a quick grin over his shoulder. "Beats the best roller coaster in the whole wide world!"

Smith forced himself to smile back. "I was always more partial to the bumper cars myself."

"That's a sure sign you were meant to be a ground-pounder, Army-type, sir," the same crewman said with a laugh, again craning his head out through the open hatch to keep a careful eye on their flight path. "Begging your pardon, of course."

"Guilty as charged, Sergeant," Smith said, smiling more genuinely now. He hung his head in mock surrender.

Fiona Devin, sitting across from Jon, offered a sympathetic shrug. Beside her, Oleg Kirov appeared to be deeply asleep, leaning back against the bulkhead with his eyes closed.

The Pave Low slowed further, turning more to the west as it crossed the ridge well to the north of the ECPR compound. It slid lower, flying over a spur of forest spilling down across the slope. Tree branches swayed and rocked behind the large helicopter, pummeled by its powerful rotor wash.

"LZ dead ahead. One hundred feet, fifty knots," the flight engineer drawled out.

Smith let go of the strap and sat up straighter. His right foot nudged the bag wedged under his seat, making sure that it was still in easy reach. It contained an assortment of clothing, weapons, and other equipment drawn from U.S. Special Operations Command caches stored at Aviano. He glanced up and saw Kirov and Fiona making their own preparations for landing. The silver-haired Russian gave him a quick thumbs-up.

Guided by constant chatter from his crew, the Pave Low pilot edged slowly forward and brought his big helicopter safely into their landing zone, a wide clearing in the woods. The ridge running south toward the ECPR compound rose off on the left, a dark mass against the paler, moonlit sky. The wheels thumped down. Immediately, the engine noise began fading, descending rapidly from a shrill, howling roar, to a deepening whine, and then to absolute dead silence. The rotors slowed and stopped turning.

The helicopter crew had orders to wait here until Smith or one of the others called for a pickup. But the six Air Force officers

614

and enlisted men aboard the big MH-53J were also under strict orders to sit tight and do nothing else. Once their feet touched the ground, the improvised Covert-One team would be completely on its own. If they met with disaster while breaking into the ECPR labs, this mission had to be completely deniable by the U.S. government.

Smith unbuckled his seat belt with a feeling of intense relief. It wasn't that he minded hazardous, nap-of-the-earth flying so much, he told himself, it was just that he preferred having his fate in his own hands. He bent down and tugged the heavy duffel bag out onto the metal deck. Fiona Devin and Kirov followed suit. Together, they slung the bags over their shoulders, trotted down the ramp, and moved off to the east, heading straight across the clearing and into the deeper darkness among the trees.

Jon led the way, pushing up the gentle slope at a fast walk until they were well away from the helicopter. Near the top of the ridge, they entered another clearing, this one much smaller. A little heap of roughly hewn stones, mostly covered by moss and bracken, lay in the center of the clearing. Were those tumbled stones all that remained of an ancient shrine? he wondered. This was an old, old land,

615

fought over for thousands of years by the Umbrians, Etruscans, Romans, Goths, Lombards, and other peoples. Their ruins and tombs dotted the landscape, buried in some places by new towns and cities, swallowed up by forests and ivy in others. Seen by moonlight, the small open space glowed eerily.

"This will do," Smith whispered to the others. "We'll change into our gear here, before moving closer to the Center." He lowered his duffel bag to the ground and knelt to unzip it. Swiftly, he started tugging out articles of clothing and equipment and handing them out to his companions.

Shivering in the cold night air, the three shifted out of the ordinary street clothes and shoes they had been wearing, rapidly donning dark-colored sweaters and jeans. Camouflage sticks blackened their faces and foreheads. Comfortable hiking boots and thick leather gloves gave better protection and traction for their feet and hands. Night-vision goggles offered them the ability to see in the dark once the moon went down. Padded cases stuffed inside the duffel bags contained a collection of high-tech digital cameras, lightweight tactical radios, laser-surveillance equipment, bolt-cutters, and other tools.

"No body armor?" Kirov asked, pulling an assault vest studded with equipment pouches out of his duffel. He slipped both arms through the vest and zipped it up, checking the fit.

Smith shook his head. "Nope. Armor's too heavy and too bulky for what we're supposed to do. If possible, we want to get inside the Center, find out what the hell's going on in there, and then get out without being spotted. But if we have to run, we're going to want to run fast."

"And if someone starts shooting at us?" Kirov asked drily. "What then?"

"Try very hard not to get hit," Jon advised, with a quick grin. He handed the Russian a 9mm Makarov pistol and three spare magazines, then took a SIG-Sauer sidearm for himself, along with extra ammunition. Both men slung Heckler & Koch MP5 submachine guns across their backs. Spare thirty-round clips went into pouches on their vests.

Fiona Devin slid a lightweight Glock 19 pistol into the holster belted around her waist and then stood back, watching the two men finish checking their weapons. "That's quite an arsenal you requested from Fred Klein, Colonel," she said with a slight, impish smile. "Didn't you just tell Oleg we were here to walk softly?"

Smith nodded. "Yep." He patted the pistol at his side. "But frankly, I'm getting tired of being outgunned. This time, if someone starts shooting at us, I want enough firepower along to hit back hard and fast."

Groves of age-bent olive trees and ancient vineyards surrounded the European Center for Population Research, running right up to the edge of the fifty-meter-wide clear space maintained all the way around its chain-link perimeter fence. Most of the compound's modern steel-and-glass buildings were totally dark this late at night. The sole exception was a large laboratory set apart from the rest. Lights glowed behind the blinds on every window. And bright white arc lights and television cameras mounted on its flat roof covered every square centimeter of the approaches to the lab. Between the cameras and the complete absence of any cover, no one could hope to get across the fence and up close without being spotted first.

About one hundred meters from the lab, a slender woman wearing black from head-to-foot lay prone in a shallow drainage ditch bordering one of the old vineyards. Camouflage netting studded with leaves and twigs broke up her silhouette and concealed the pair of image-intensifer binoculars she focused on the building. Even in the silver moonlight, she was effectively invisible from more than a few meters away.

Once the moon slid behind the horizon, the only way anyone else would ever spot her was by walking right through her camouflaged hide.

Suddenly the black-clad woman stiffened, alerted by soft, dry, rustling sounds coming from somewhere behind her. Moving with extreme caution to avoid making any noise herself, she swung around and propped up her binoculars on the edge of the ditch, intently surveying the shadow-filled vineyard for any signs of movement. She held her breath, waiting.

There. One of the shadows changed shape, gradually becoming a man crouching near a row of bare and gray vines that had been pruned back to lie dormant for the winter. Seconds later, another man flitted across the vineyard and joined the first. Then a third figure appeared. This one was a woman.

She focused the binoculars, first on one man's face and then on the other. One of her eyebrows rose in utter disbelief. "Well, well, well . . . look who the cat dragged in," Randi Russell murmured coolly to herself.

Sighing, she put down the binoculars and then slowly and carefully stood up, abandoning her concealed position. She kept her hands away from her sides, palms out. Startled by her sudden appearance, the three people crouching among the vines swiveled in her direction. The two men drew their pistols with lightning-speed.

"Please try not to kill me, Jon," she said quietly. "It's not like you have a surplus of friends as it is."

Stunned, Smith eased off the trigger. "Randi?" he said in amazement. "What the hell are you doing here?"

The slender CIA officer came closer, emerging from the darkness. She crouched down beside them with a grimly amused expression on her smooth, good-looking face. "Since I was here first, it seems to me that should be my question . . . not yours."

Almost against his will, Jon grinned back at her. She had a point. He shrugged. "Fair enough."

He thought fast, trying to come up with a plausible story, one that Randi could choose to believe. She was the sister of his dead fiancée, and an old friend to whom he owed his life several times over, but she also worked for the CIA — which meant she was not privy to the closely held Covert-One secret. Until that changed, he was forced to find ever more inventive ways to dodge her awkward questions.

"Some people high up in the Pentagon have asked me to track down the origin of this mysterious disease," Jon said at last. "The one that's been killing our intelligence analysts and key leaders in the former Soviet republics. We're sure now that the illness is man-made, a sort of genetically targeted assassination weapon."

"But why you exactly?" Randi demanded.

"Because I was the one first approached by a Russian scientist, a colleague of mine, at a medical conference in Prague," Smith told her. Quickly, he briefed her on Valentin Petrenko's claims and the murderous attack used to silence him. "When I passed the word back to Washington, they sent me to Moscow to check out his story, figuring that I had the contacts and the expertise to nail down the facts."

Randi nodded reluctantly. "That almost makes sense, Jon," she admitted. She looked skeptically at Kirov, whom she had gotten to know years before while working as a field officer in Moscow. "I assume this is where Major General Kirov of the Russian Federal Security Service comes in?"

The big, silver-haired man shook his head with a smile. "It's just plain Oleg Kirov these days, Ms. Russell. I'm retired."

Randi snorted. "Yeah, I just bet you are." She waved a hand at the submachine gun slung across his back. "Most pensioners don't go wandering around the

Italian countryside at night while armed to the teeth."

"Oleg has been working with me," Smith explained. "As a sort of private consultant."

"So who is this?" Randi asked pointedly, nodding toward Fiona Devin. "Your secretary?"

Jon winced, seeing Fiona stiffen angrily. "Ms. Devin is a freelance journalist based in Moscow," he said quickly. "She was already investigating the first disease outbreak when I arrived."

"A journalist?" Randi said in disbelief. She shook her head. "Let me get this straight, Jon — you actually brought a reporter along on a covert mission? Don't you think that's carrying this whole Pentagon media-embedding program a bit too far?"

"I am not exactly here as a journalist," Fiona said coldly, speaking for the first time. The trace of her Irish accent was stronger now. "Not anymore."

"Meaning what?" Randi demanded.

Smith filled her in on the various attempts made by Erich Brandt, acting for Konstantin Malkovic, to kill them. He ended by telling her about the orders issued by the Kremlin for their immediate arrest. "In the circumstances, Oleg and I thought she should stick with us," he finished lamely, realizing how improbable that all sounded.

There was a moment's silence.

At last Randi threw up her hands. She stared hard at Jon. "Am I really supposed to believe this cockamamie story of yours?"

"As wild as it sounds, it is the truth," he said stoutly, glad that the darkness hid his red face. Well, at least part of the truth, he told his abraded conscience silently.

"So I guess the three of you just waltzed out of Moscow, right under the noses of half the militia and the FSB?" Randi asked sardonically.

"I have friends in shipping," Kirov said calmly.

"Right," the CIA officer said drily. She looked all three of them up and down, clearly noting all of their weapons and other equipment. "And these friends of yours . . . in shipping . . . just happened to be able to provide you with all this nifty hardware?"

Smith grinned at her. "Not quite. That was my part. Remember, I have friends in the Air Force."

"Naturally." Randi sighed, apparently accepting defeat, at least temporarily. "Okay, Jon. I give up. You three are just the pure, accidental heroes you claim to be."

"Then perhaps it's your turn to tell us what you're doing out here in the dark,

Ms. Russell," Fiona Devin suggested coolly.

For a second, Randi bristled. Then, surprisingly, she smiled. "My what big teeth you have, Ms. Devin." She shrugged. "It's pretty simple, actually. You're hunting for the source of this genetically aimed biological weapon. Well, I'm hunting the man who undoubtedly created it."

"Wulf Renke," Smith said quietly.

"That's the guy," Randi agreed flatly. She ran through the long and bloody trail that had led her all the way from Baghdad to Berlin, and then, finally, here to Orvieto. "I had to guess at the end," she admitted. "The phone network we were tracing went dead before my technical experts could nail down any specific locations. But when I did some research on my own, this place popped out as the best fit for Renke in Umbria. There are other medical research facilities around, but the ECPR seemed a natural — plenty of money, plenty of scientists from all parts of Europe working together, and all the top-of-the-line equipment his black little heart could desire."

"So you hopped a flight down here?"

"To Rome, and then up here by car," the CIA officer confirmed. "I've been in position since early this afternoon."

Smith heard a strained note in her voice,

one that he had been noticing for a while. "You keep saying 'I,' Randi," he commented. "Where's the rest of your team?"

"There is no team," she said grimly. "Just me. And nobody at Langley or anywhere else knows where I am right now. At least I hope not."

Now it was Smith's turn to be surprised. "You're working without a net? Without any Agency support? Why?"

Randi grimaced. "Because Renke, or maybe this Malkovic bastard you mentioned, has a mole somewhere high up, someone who's been feeding him everything I've learned." Her mouth tightened to a thin, angry line. "Playing by the rules has cost the lives of three good people already. So now I'm not taking any more chances."

Smith, Fiona, and Kirov nodded slowly, understanding both her reasoning and her fury. Betrayal by someone in your own ranks was the ultimate nightmare for every intelligence agent.

"We should join forces, Ms. Russell," Kirov told her quietly. "It is unorthodox, I admit, but when we are faced by such dangerous enemies, working together is only common sense. And time is very short. We cannot waste any more of it arguing among ourselves."

Jon and Fiona nodded in agreement.

Randi stared at them for a long, painful moment. Then she nodded slowly. "All right, you people have a deal." Her mouth twisted into a wry smile. "After all, this isn't exactly the first time Jon and I have stumbled across each other in the field."

"No, it isn't," Smith said quietly.

"Perhaps you're fated to be together," Fiona Devin suggested, with just a hint of mischief in her voice.

Randi snorted softly. "Oh, sure. Jon and I are a regular dynamic duo — the Mutt and Jeff of the espionage business."

Smith wisely decided to keep his mouth shut. This was one of those wonderful moments when anything he said was bound to land him in hot water. Or maybe even boiling water, he thought warily, eyeing the tight-lipped expression on Randi's face.

But then she shook herself back to the present. "You'd better come and see what we're up against. Because, believe me, whatever you heroes have in mind is not going to be easy."

CHAPTER FORTY-SEVEN

General Staff Command Bunker, Outside Moscow

A large display map of Russia and its neighbors occupied one concrete wall of the elaborate command center buried far below the surface of the earth. Symbols scattered across the map showed the current position and readiness of the major military units slated for ZHUKOV. The room itself was filled with rows of consoles, each equipped with the latest secure communications to allow staff officers to maintain constant contact with the troop commanders in the field.

Russian President Viktor Dudarev stood at the back of the room watching as the array of generals, colonels, and majors moved unhurriedly through the intricate work of bringing his long-held plans ever closer to reality. One of the last yellow symbols — depicting the two divisions assembled secretly in the snow-bound Caucasus Mountains — turned green.

"Colonel-General Sevalkin reports that his command is in position," Major Piotr

Kirichenko, his military aide, murmured. "All ZHUKOV ground forces are now deployed to their final pre-war bivouacs. The senior commanders will begin briefing their regimental and battalion leaders in twelve hours."

Dudarev nodded in satisfaction. The decision to hold back those operational briefings until practically the last possible moment had been his, one intended to prevent leaks that could jeopardize ZHUKOV's success. He glanced at Kirichenko. "Are there any signs of a reaction among our targets?"

The younger man shook his head. "No, sir. Intelligence confirms that the Ukrainian and other armies are still in their peacetime quarters, with absolutely no sign of any higher alert status."

"What about the Americans or NATO?"

Kirichenko frowned slightly. "We are picking up fragmentary signs that American aircraft squadrons at bases in Germany, Italy, and the United Kingdom may have been ordered to higher readiness, but there is no indication of any significant movement of those planes toward our frontiers."

Dudarev turned to the stocky, gray-haired man standing behind him. He raised an eyebrow. "Well, Alexei?"

"So far the Americans have been denied any permission to move aircraft eastward,"

Ivanov confirmed. "The European governments have their heads well down in the sand. Each is waiting to see what, if anything, Castilla can prove about our intentions."

"And he will find it very difficult to prove anything from an intensive care ward," the Russian president said with a cold smile. "In the meantime, let us hope that the Europeans continue to choose wisely over the next twenty-four hours. By the time they wake up to the new balance of power on this continent, it will be far too late."

Near Orvieto

"See the problem, Jon?" Randi murmured. They were lying next to each other in her camouflaged hiding place overlooking the brightly lit ECPR building she had picked out as Wulf Renke's lab facility.

Smith slowly lowered the powerful binoculars she had lent him. He handed them back to her with a tight, worried nod. "Yeah, I do. The damned place is practically a fortress."

"A fortress is right," Randi agreed, ticking off on her fingers the defenses she had observed. "We're talking about lights, remotely controlled security cameras, motion sensors, bullet-proof windows, a solid steel main door, bank-vault quality locks — plus maybe a dozen highly alert armed guards inside."

He nodded again, grimly this time. "I think it's time we held a council of war."

Jon and Randi slid cautiously out of the shallow drainage ditch and faded back into the vineyard. Kirov and Fiona had set up some of their gear in a spot where a small fold in the ground offered concealment from the cameras and lights mounted on the lab building. They had their heads close together, studying the dozens of digital surveillance photos the CIA officer had shot during her long afternoon and evening vigil.

Kirov glanced up when Smith and Randi returned. "We've definitely come to the right place," he said somberly. "See for yourself."

While Jon watched, the Russian clicked through several color images taken with a telephoto lens. The first showed two black sedans arriving at the lab building. The next set showed a large group of men climbing out of the cars and moving toward the lab. Kirov zoomed in on two of those men.

Smith whistled softly, staring at the familiar faces of Erich Brandt and Konstantin Malkovic. The sight of the ex–Stasi officer's cold gray eyes raised the hairs on the back of his neck. Jon's jaw tightened. While he and Fiona Devin were being tortured, Jon had promised to kill that arrogant bastard. That was a promise he meant to keep. He looked away, fighting to regain a measure of control over his anger. This was a time for coolly rational thought, not avenging blood lust. "Are Brandt and Malkovic still inside?" he asked.

"They are," Fiona said. She sounded surprisingly calm. "Ms. Russell's admirably complete set of pictures shows no one else entering or leaving."

"That's one piece of good news anyway." Smith squatted down on his haunches. The others grouped themselves around him. "The bad news is that our first plan — to run a quick sneak-and-peek into that compound, looking for evidence — isn't going to fly. Their security is too tight. We'd be spotted the second we started toward the perimeter fence."

Kirov shrugged. "Since we know where Renke's lab is, I suggest we strike now, without worrying about stealth. Our enemies have done us the favor of putting themselves in one place," he said coldly. "We should take advantage of their error."

"I'd like to kick in the door," Smith agreed. He grinned tightly. "But only if we had a full company of infantry, with a couple of M1A1 Abrams tanks for fire support. And even then we'd be sticking our hands into a meat-grinder."

"The building is that closely guarded?" the Russian asked.

Jon nodded. "It is."

"There are F-16s based at Aviano," Randi said coolly. "They could be here in an hour. Maybe less."

"You want to call in an air strike?" Smith asked.

"Why not?" The CIA officer's eyes were hard. "One laser-guided bomb would solve a great many problems."

Jon understood her feelings. The vicious genetic weapon set in motion by the men inside that lab, Renke, Brandt, and Malkovic, was already responsible for dozens of cruelly painful deaths around the world. It was incredibly tempting to contemplate watching a single massive explosion engulf them in flame. But there were too many arguments against an air strike, both practical and political.

Sighing, he shook his head in regret. "The president would never approve an F-16 strike, Randi, and that's how high up the decision would have to go. Most of the Center's work is legitimate scientific research, and there's too much chance of collateral damage. Can you imagine how the EU would react if we dropped bombs on friendly territory, especially without permission or even consultation?" He frowned. "Our alliances are already too fragile as it is."

"Destroying that lab would also destroy the evidence we need — the evidence that the Russians have been involved in creating and using this new weapon," Fiona pointed out quietly. "So would killing these men, or at least all of them. We may need their testimony to make our accusations against the Kremlin stick."

Kirov nodded heavily. "Ms. Devin is right. Whatever we do, we must try to take at least one of these men, Renke or Malkovic especially, alive."

"Spiffy," Randi said, shaking her head. "This gets better and better." She turned back to Smith. "Okay, Jon, you claim that you're tied in with the Pentagon. Why don't you whistle up a commando unit? Like the Delta Force or the SEALs?" She jerked a thumb over her shoulder toward the ECPR compound. "Kicking in doors is what they train for, isn't it?"

"Believe me, I'd like nothing better," Jon told her softly. "But there aren't any Delta Force or SEAL teams in striking range. They're either in the States refitting and training, or tied up in combat operations in Iraq and Afghanistan." One side of his mouth curved up in an ironic grin. "I'm afraid you're looking at the only special-ops team available . . . and it's the four of us."

"What about the Italians?" Fiona broke in. She nodded at the darkened landscape around them. "This is their country. Don't they have special police or Army units capable of raiding that lab?"

Smith thought about that. The Italians had two very highly regarded counter-terrorist units, the GIS (Groupe Interventional Speciale) and NOCS (Nucleo Operativo Centrale de Sicurezza). And this was their jurisdiction. Why not ask Fred Klein and the president to kick the responsibility over to the government in Rome? But how far would the Italian government be willing to go without seeing anything more than vague and circumstantial evidence?

Then another, even more unpleasant thought, occurred to him. He looked around at the others. "We know, from Randi here, that Malkovic is already being tipped off by someone in Germany, or maybe even inside Langley. But what if Malkovic has another mole — this one in the Italian security services?"

"It seems likely," Kirov growled. "This financier has shown himself to be a man with a near-infinite capacity for corrupting others, in Russia, Germany, and many other countries. I doubt very much that he would leave himself blind and deaf here in Italy."

Fiona frowned. "That's pure speculation, Oleg."

"Yes, it is," Smith agreed. "But even if Malkovic doesn't have a secret source in Rome, bringing the Italians into this operation would take some pretty fancy diplomatic maneuvering —"

"For which there is no time," Kirov said suddenly and forcefully.

The others looked at him in surprise.

"Our enemies must know that their cover here is tattered and perhaps even on the verge of falling apart completely," Kirov explained. He showed his teeth. "Think, my friends. Why else do you think a man like Malkovic would come all this way, especially now, with events in my country moving so fast toward war?"

"Renke and his pals are getting ready to pull another disappearing act," Smith realized.

"Could they really pull that off?" Randi asked curiously.

"Sure," Smith said. He rubbed at his jaw, thinking it through out loud. "All Renke really needs to set up shop again somewhere else are his DNA samples, any special equipment he's using, and a few of his trained technicians. Most of the equipment and other material would probably fit in one small truck or a couple of vans."

"Then it's simple," Randi said coldly. "We wait until they drive out of here, and then we jump them."

"Look more carefully at your photographs, Ms. Russell," Kirov advised. "Do you see any trucks or vans outside that lab?"

She shook her head reluctantly. "No."

"But there is a large stretch of bare concrete, is there not?"

Jon saw what the Russian was getting at. "Hell," he muttered. "Malkovic and Renke are going to fly the stuff out."

Kirov nodded. "Probably by helicopter to a jet waiting at Rome or Florence or any one of several other nearby airfields." He shrugged his big shoulders gloomily. "Malkovic's native Serbia is not far from Italy, not much more than an hour's flying time across the Adriatic Sea. Libya and Syria are also within easy reach. As are any number of other unsavory regimes that might offer so rich a man refuge."

Frowning, Smith summed the situation up. "Which means if we wait too long, Renke will vanish again — with everything he needs to restart Malkovic's genetic weapons business."

"So we can't go in. We can't bomb them. And we can't wait for them to come out. Mind telling me what other options we do have, Jon?" Randi said sharply, reining in her temper with difficulty.

Smith gritted his teeth, feeling equally frustrated. "I don't know." He shook his head grimly. "But we've got to find a way to push these guys off their game, to make them react to *our* moves for a change."

Unable to bear inaction any longer, he stood up and began pacing around their small campsite. There had to be something they could do, some angle they could play, to get at Malkovic and his subordinates, to pry them out of that fortified lab before it was too late.

Abruptly, Jon stopped and stood still, waiting while the faint glimmering of a wild idea took on real form and substance. Maybe Randi had already given them the hook they would need. A fierce gleam appeared in his eyes. He swung round to Kirov. "I need your phone, Oleg!" he snapped. "Now!"

Nodding, the Russian tossed him the last of their Covert-One secure cell phones. "Use it wisely," he suggested drily.

Smith grinned back at him. "Acting wisely is the last thing on my mind right now."

He moved off out of earshot and punched in the code for Covert-One headquarters.

Fred Klein listened intently while he summarized the situation they faced. "An ugly dilemma, Colonel," he said quietly when Smith had finished. "Do you have a plan?"

"Yes, I do. But we need action from Washington to make it work. And we need it as soon as humanly possible."

"What do you want me to do?" Klein asked.

Smith told him.

There was a long silence on the other end of the line. At last, Klein spoke again, sounding troubled. "You're asking me to skate very close to the line on this one, Jon."

"I know I am."

Klein sighed. "The president and I can probably conceal Covert-One's existence from those involved here in Washington, but I'm worried about Ms. Russell. She already knows far more about our activities and access than is prudent. What you suggest may very well give her enough information to break through this organization's cover."

"She's already suspicious as hell, Fred."

"There is a wide gulf between suspicion and certainty, Colonel," Klein said tartly. "And I would prefer to keep Randi Russell on the proper side of that gulf."

Smith shrugged his shoulders. "What choice do we really have?"

"None," the head of Covert-One admitted at length. "All right, Jon. Stand by where you are. I'll let you know when we're ready to kick things off back here."

"Standing by," Smith acknowledged.

The line went dead.

February 22
Joint U.S.-German Intelligence Secure Videoconference

Large television monitors in Washington, D.C., Langley, Virginia, Berlin, Bonn, and Cologne flickered simultaneously to life, linking groups of men and women seated around conference tables separated by thousands of miles and hours of relative time. Those in Germany looked tired and nervous. It was already past midnight when they had been hurriedly summoned back to their various offices for what was being billed as an extraordinary emergency briefing by the new U.S. Director of National Intelligence, William Wexler.

Wexler himself appeared cool and collected. His body language radiated absolute confidence and conviction in what he was about to say. As he spoke, he looked straight into the camera, maintaining the illusion that he was making eye contact with everyone else on the secure circuit.

What none of those joining in this satellite-linked videoconference knew was that a feed was also going straight to the White House. And Fred Klein, watching the transmission with President Castilla from the Oval Office, cynically suspected one reason for Wexler's apparent ease was because the former senator was used to delivering televised speeches that he either did not understand or did not believe.

After a few preliminary formalities, Wexler jumped straight to the core of the matter. He spoke clearly and concisely. "Intelligence agencies of the United States have now definitively identified the production site of the biological weapons being used against us, against our NATO allies, and against countries around the border of the Russian Federation."

Those listening and watching sat up straighter.

The screen split, with half showing a satellite photo taken months before. It depicted a large fenced-in complex spread across what appeared to be a low ridge. One of the several buildings was circled. "These weapons are being secretly manufactured at a laboratory near Orvieto, in Italy," Wexford said firmly. "A lab that is part of the European Center for Population Research, the ECPR."

Shocked murmurs spread through the background audio feed.

Wexler overrode them. "The intelligence confirming this target is clear and irrefutable. Accordingly, the President of the United States has authorized an immediate all-out military assault on this clandestine weapons facility."

The German and American intelligence officials fell silent, plainly stunned by what they were hearing.

The satellite photo disappeared, replaced by a map showing Italy and the seas around it. Another circle appeared on this map, enclosing a graphic of ships positioned in the Mediterranean Sea, off Italy's western coast. "A U.S. Marine Corps quick-reaction force is now prepping aboard the ships of the Sixth Fleet," Wexler continued. "This force will be in position to conduct the raid within two hours. Several teams from our Special Operations Command are already in place several kilometers to the north and south of Orvieto — preparing to set up roadblocks on the main highway."

One of the Germans spoke up. A crawl beneath the screen identified him as Bernhard Heichler, a high-ranking officer in the Bundesamtes für Verfassunsschutz. "What do the Italians think of this risky plan of yours?" he asked stiffly.

"To ensure complete surprise, this assault is being made without the knowledge or consent of the Italian government," Wexler replied coolly.

Heichler's mouth fell open, a reaction shared by many of his colleagues, of both nationalities. "Then why are you giving us this information?"

With a slight smile, Wexler dropped his next bombshell. "Because the man responsible for creating this biological weapon is Professor Wulf Renke," he told them. "One of your own countrymen, and a dangerous criminal you have long hunted." Speaking firmly and forcefully, he outlined what U.S. intelligence now knew about Renke, including his escape from German justice with Ulrich Kessler's assistance.

"We would like you to form a task force of experts to assist us in exploiting every scrap of intelligence our Marines lay their hands on," Wexler said carefully. "Their mission will be to ferret out any critical information contained in the lab's phone logs, computer files, and shipping records, and to interrogate the prisoners we intend to capture." He smiled winningly. "Now? Are there any questions?"

Immediately, a confused babble of voices broke out, with everyone trying to speak at once.

Castilla hit the mute button on his remote. The agitated voices fell silent. He turned toward Klein, with a thin smile on his broad, blunt face. "Looks like that little stunt of ours just tossed a coyote right into the middle of some real nervous cattle."

"Yes, sir," Klein agreed.

"You think this will actually work the way Colonel Smith hopes?" Castilla asked quietly.

"I hope so," Klein said, equally quietly. "If not, Jon and the others are not likely to survive the next several hours." He checked his watch. The furrows on his high forehead grew deeper. "One way or the other, we should know very soon."

CHAPTER FORTY-EIGHT

Estelle Pike sat primly at her desk in the antechamber outside the Oval Office, typing up one of President Castilla's handwritten action memos to the National Security Council. Her eyes flicked rapidly from the screen in front of her to the scrawled notes on her desk, and then around the rest of the room. The other desks and workstations were empty. She smiled slightly. One by one, she had found errands for her assistants to run in widely scattered parts of the White House office complex.

A white-gloved steward entered the room, carrying a covered tray.

She stopped typing and looked up with a frown. "Yes? What is that?"

"The president's meal, ma'am," the steward told her politely.

Estelle Pike nodded to the empty corner of her desk. "You can leave it there. I'll take it in to him in a moment."

One of the steward's eyebrows went up in astonishment. The president's secretary was well known and widely disliked among the White House household staff for her strict insistence on protocol and rank. She only rarely, if ever, volunteered for duties she considered beneath her station.

"The president is extremely busy, Anson," she explained coolly. "He does not wish to be disturbed at the moment."

The steward looked at the closed door behind her and then shrugged. "Yes, ma'am. Please don't wait too long, though. Otherwise the salad will start to wilt."

Estelle Pike waited until the door closed behind him and then bent down to open her purse. Inside, wrapped in tissue paper, she found the small sealed glass vial she had retrieved earlier from the Maryland countryside. Then, moving calmly and precisely, she opened the vial, lifted the silver cover off Castilla's salad and sprinkled the liquid contents liberally over the tossed greens, salsa, sour cream, cheese, and pieces of grilled chicken. She dropped the vial back into her purse and stood up, reaching for the tray.

"That won't be necessary, Ms. Pike," a quiet voice said from behind her.

Startled, she froze and then slowly turned around toward the door into the Oval Office. Nathaniel Frederick Klein stood there, framed in the open doorway. His narrow, long-nosed face was impassive. Two uniformed Secret Service agents stood ready on either side of him, both with drawn weapons.

"What is the meaning of this, Mr. Klein?" Estelle Pike demanded icily, trying to brazen it out.

"The meaning, Ms. Pike," Klein said bluntly, "is that you are under arrest."

"On what grounds?"

"The attempted assassination of President Samuel Adams Castilla will do for a start," he replied. His eyes were cold. "No doubt other charges will arise as we dig deeper into your conduct and background."

Later, sitting across from a visibly shocked Castilla, Klein slid the glass vial across the president's big pine table desk. "We'll have what remains of the contents analyzed, but if Jon Smith's suspicions are accurate, I doubt that we'll find much of use inside."

Grimly, Castilla nodded. His mouth turned downward. He shook his head in disbelief. "Estelle Pike! She's been with me for years, ever since I came to the White House." He looked up at the head of Covert-One. "What made you suspect her?"

Klein shrugged his narrow shoulders. "Suspicion is too strong a word, Sam. Once we learned how easily this targeted biological weapon might be administered to its victims, I had a quiet chat with the head of your Secret Service detail. They've been monitoring every aspect of White House food preparation ever since. Ms. Pike's domain was the only potential gap in our security, so it was one I've had closely observed. When she started finding reasons to send her people away after you called down to the kitchens for that salad, I thought it would be a good idea to see what she might be planning."

Castilla tapped the vial gently. His eyes were still troubled. "But why? Why would she do this?"

"I rather think we will find that your Ms. Pike has a great many hidden depths," Klein said flatly. "I've sometimes wondered about her. Her position here at the White House gave her access to an enormous range of secret information. And her background — widowed at an early age, no family, no real friends — well, it just seems too convenient, too perfect. If I wanted to create a legend, a cover, for a deep-penetration mole, that's exactly the sort of thing I would work toward."

"You think she's a Russian spy?" the president asked.

Klein nodded again. "Almost certainly." He stood up. "But we'll find out for sure. You can count on that."

"I do, Fred," Castilla said with a grateful

smile. "I always do." Then his smile slowly faded. "Just as I am counting on Colonel Smith and the others."

Near Orvieto

Konstantin Malkovic stared down at the decoded message on his laptop in dismay. "Impossible!" he muttered. He turned to Brandt, who was standing at his shoulder. "How could this be?"

"The Americans are closer to us than we realized," Brandt snapped, reading through the urgent warning sent by the financier's agent in Germany. "That's all."

"But what can we do?" the other man asked. His voice, usually a deep baritone, now sounded shrill.

Brandt stared at his employer in disgust. Malkovic was crumbling in front of him. All of the rich man's bluster, all of his famous self-confidence, was largely a charade, the gray-eyed man realized coldly. Oh, the Serbian-born financier was brave enough when he was winning, or when he speculated in abstractions — like currencies, or oil and natural gas, or other men's lives — but he was a physical coward, a man who flinched when his own life was in peril. Like many greedy men, always hungry for more power or for more money, he was fundamentally hollow inside.

"We must evacuate at once," Brandt said carefully. "Professor Renke's DNA databases and his design files are ready to go. We'll take them, and Renke, and leave now."

Malkovic stared back at him in confusion. "But his equipment —"

"Can be replaced," Brandt said brutally.

"What about Renke's assistants? His lab team?" the financier stammered. "The helicopters won't arrive until it is too late, and we don't have room for them in the cars."

"No," Brandt agreed coolly, looking out into the main lab where the scientists and technicians were still working hard, preparing their expensive machines for a move that would now never be made. He shrugged his powerful shoulders. "We'll have to leave them behind. Along with the Italian security guards."

Malkovic paled. "What? Are you mad? When the Marines storm this building, they will be captured and then they will talk."

"No," Brandt said bluntly. "They won't." He drew the Walther pistol from his shoulder holster and inspected the weapon quickly. As a last measure, he checked that he had a full fifteen-round magazine, and then slid the clip back in.

The financier looked sick under the lab's bright fluorescent lights. He sat down heavily, staring at the sterile tile floor between his feet.

Turning slightly, Brandt waved one of the bodyguards over.

"Yes, Herr Brandt?" the man said, sounding bored. "What is it?'

"Order the staff to assemble in the lounge, Sepp. Everyone, without exception." The former Stasi officer lowered his voice slightly. "Then tell Karl and the others that we have some necessary killing ahead of us. And ask Fyodor to bring his cases from the car trunk. We will need his explosives after all."

For the first time, the bodyguard's dull eyes flickered to life. "It will be a pleasure."

Brandt nodded coolly. "I know. That is why I find you and your comrades so useful." For a few seconds, he watched the man move away and begin herding the fatigued scientists and technicians out of the main lab.

Renke came over. A slight tightening around his mouth betrayed his supreme irritation at seeing his assistants ushered away, leaving their work unfinished. "What are you playing at, Erich?" he demanded.

"Read that," Brandt told him flatly, nodding toward the message still displayed on Malkovic's laptop.

The scientist skimmed through the

warning of an imminent American assault. One thin, white eyebrow slid up in mild, annoyed surprise. "Unfortunate," he murmured. Then he looked back over his shoulder at Brandt. "We're leaving?"

"Correct."

"When?"

"Within minutes," the gray-eyed man said. "Retrieve what you need from your office as quickly as you can." He nodded coolly toward Malkovic, still sitting slumped over in his chair. "Take him with you. And keep an eye on him, Herr Professor. His resources and connections are still of use to us."

With that, Brandt swung away, stalking toward the lounge with his pistol out and ready.

Renke watched him go for a moment and then looked down at the shaken billionaire. "Come, Mr. Malkovic," he snapped. "This way."

Numbly, the taller man got to his feet, grabbed his briefcase and laptop, and followed the weapons scientist down the central corridor.

Inside his windowless office, Renke crossed quickly to the bookcases concealing his combination wall safe and freezer. After entering his code, he pressed his thumb to the built-in fingerprint scanner. Cold vapor puffed out as the door swung open.

Gunfire erupted inside the building, muffled by thick, soundproofed walls. There were high-pitched wails and shrieks. When the quick fusillade ended, only a few agonized moans broke in the sudden, eerie silence, along with the sound of a man weeping in sheer terror. A pistol barked three times. The silence became absolute.

"My God!" Malkovic groaned. "The Marines are here already!" He shrank back against the nearest wall, clutching the briefcase containing information on Dudarev's military plans and the Russian leader's involvement in HYDRA to his chest as though it would protect him from American bullets.

Renke snorted. "Calm yourself. That was only Brandt eliminating my unfortunate assistants." He donned a heavy glove and pulled out the rack of vials inside the freezer. Carefully, he lowered them into an insulated cooler.

He smiled down at the rows of his specially crafted HYDRA variants in satisfaction. Labels on each clear glass tube bore different names, many of them Russian. In less than forty-eight hours, the material inside Malkovic's briefcase would be useless as a means of pressuring Viktor Dudarev. Once Russian troops and tanks crossed the border, the Kremlin leader would no longer fear the exposure of his plans. He would be free to act against the trembling financier as he saw fit.

Still smiling to himself, the scientist shut and sealed the container. Malkovic was doomed, whether or not he realized it yet. But the undetectable and incurable weapons in those vials would give Wulf Renke a firm grip on Dudarev and his cronies for the rest of their lives.

Lieutenant Colonel Jon Smith crouched low behind the front end of the car rented by Randi Russel, a dark green Volvo four-door. It sat sideways across the two-lane road, blocking the main route running around the base of Orvieto's rugged volcanic plateau. The road, the Strada Stratale No. 71, split here, with one fork heading toward the train station, the lower town, and then on eastward toward the foothills of the distant Apennines. The other climbed gradually up the side of the massive rocky outcropping and entered the cliff-top city of Orvieto itself.

Smith looked to his left. The plateau loomed there, a huge black shadow against the starlit sky. Just beyond the intersection, the ground rose steeply in a grassy slope dotted with stands of small trees and withered bushes. It ended abruptly in a sheer wall of cracked and crumbling tufa, a type of limestone, and basalt.

He glanced to his right. Kirov was a couple of meters away, kneeling behind the Volvo with a Heckler & Koch MP5 submachine gun gripped in both hands. The Russian saw him looking and gave him a cool nod to show that he was ready. Beyond the road there, the ground descended in a gentle slope covered in barren fruit trees and vines. Small lights from distant farmhouses glowed here and there across the valley.

"Here they come," Randi Russell whispered over the radio. The CIA officer was stationed in cover a little bit farther down the road, on a low rise that offered a view of the well-lit ECPR compound, roughly a kilometer away. She was their forward observer. "I count two cars. Both black Mercedes, moving fast." She hesitated and then went on. "Looks like you were right, Jon. Maybe you're getting better at this soldier stuff."

"Understood," Smith said softly.

Despite the knowledge that he was facing imminent action, part of him relaxed slightly. Randi had argued vehemently for setting up their ambush much closer to the Center. She had wanted to make sure that Malkovic, Renke, and their subordinates couldn't slip past them by taking one of the other, smaller country lanes that crisscrossed the valley. But Jon had vetoed her idea, pointing out that hitting the enemy too close to that fortified lab building only offered them the chance of retreating back into its impenetrable protection. And then, once Malkovic and the others realized the U.S. Marine assault they had been warned about was only a gigantic bluff, they would be free to follow their original scheme and fly out to safety.

Instead, Smith had gambled that Brandt would lead his employers this way, since this road offered the fastest means of putting distance between them and the ECPR. And once they crossed the north-south *autostrada* near the Orvieto train station, the fugitives would be able to cross the Apennines on little-used secondary roads and make for Italy's Adriatic coast.

He tensed, hearing the noise of powerful car engines drawing nearer. He yanked back on the cocking handle of his MP5, forcing a 9mm round into the chamber. One hand made sure that the weapon's firing selector was set for three-round bursts. He crouched lower, staying out of sight behind the heavy Volvo.

The approaching engines grew louder.

Headlights suddenly washed over the Volvo, throwing its strangely distorted shadow farther up the slope. Tires squealed sharply as the lead Mercedes braked hard to avoid crashing into their improvised roadblock. A second later, more brakes squealed as the second black sedan swerved abruptly and stopped in the middle of the road to avoid slamming into the first.

Immediately, both Smith and Kirov stood up from behind the Volvo, leveling their submachine guns at the lead car, just fifteen meters away. There was more movement higher up the slope. Fiona Devin jumped up from her own hiding place, a half-buried limestone boulder that must have tumbled from the cliff face centuries before. Peering intently through her Glock semiautomatic's front and rear sights, she took careful aim at the second car.

"Come out of the car!" Smith shouted, with his eyes narrowed against the glare of the headlights. "Now! With your hands up!"

His pulse roared in his ears. This was the critical moment. Their need to take prisoners if possible outweighed every other consideration, even their own safety.

The two Mercedes sedans just sat there, angled awkwardly across the road. He could not see any movement through their darkly tinted windows.

"This is your last warning!" Jon snapped loudly. "Get out of the damned cars! Now!" His finger tightened on the trigger.

One of the lead car's back doors popped open. Slowly, a man, one of Malkovic's bodyguards, climbed out and stood facing them. He kept his empty hands spread carefully apart at shoulder height. "I am unarmed," he said, speaking in heavily accented English. "What is it that you want? Are you with the police?"

"No questions," Kirov growled. "Tell Malkovic and the others to get out! They have ten seconds before we open fire!"

"I understand," the other man said quickly. "I will tell them."

The bodyguard half-turned, just as though he was going to lean back in through the open door and talk to those inside. But then, moving with incredible speed, he whirled back around. One hand darted inside his heavy wool coat and came out gripping a pistol-sized Uzi submachine gun.

Smith and Kirov fired at the same time.

Hit by several rounds that tore right through him, the bodyguard toppled backward. He was dead before he hit the ground.

But in that same instant, the driver of the lead Mercedes stamped down hard on the accelerator. The black sedan roared ahead, aiming straight for the front end of the Volvo. The second Mercedes swung back behind the first and accelerated, too.

Too late, Smith realized his mistake. Those bastards had sacrificed a man to decoy him out of position. He swung the barrel of the MP5 through a short arc and fired again, this time aiming straight into the first oncoming car's engine compartment. His bullets punched huge holes through the hood. Sparks and pieces of shredded metal danced up under the series of impacts.

Beside him, Kirov started shooting, aiming for the tires. Further uphill, Jon could see flame jetting from the muzzle of Fiona Devin's Glock as she fired at the second sedan, pulling the trigger as fast as she could. Like the Russian, she was aiming for its wheels, trying to immobilize their enemies before they could break past the roadblock and race off into the night.

Jon stood his ground behind the Volvo for a split second longer, seeing the speeding Mercedes loom up out of the darkness in front of him like a maddened elephant. He fired one more three-round burst. More torn metal flew away from the black sedan's engine compartment.

But then it was time to go.

Smith dove away from behind the parked car, landed on the hard surface of the road with a teeth-rattling jolt, and then rolled frantically off into the grass. Behind him, the Mercedes slammed into the Volvo's front end with an earsplitting crash. Locked together for a brief moment by the impact, the two cars slid up the road in a grinding spray of broken glass, shattered fiberglass, and crumpled metal. Slowly, the Volvo spun away from the crash, opening up the right-hand fork of the Y-intersection.

With a scream of rending steel, the first Mercedes scraped past and rattled away, heading uphill toward Orvieto. Chunks of torn tread from three blown tires scattered behind it, bouncing and tumbling across the road in what looked like slow motion. Sheets of glowing sparks whirled across the gravel and asphalt surface. And then the second black sedan, also running on its metal wheel rims roared past the mangled Volvo, grinding slowly after the lead car.

Smith rose to one knee. He opened fire again, walking bursts up the road toward the fleeing vehicles. Kirov stood close by, shooting calmly, still aiming low. Fiona came sliding down the slope toward them, snapping a new magazine into her pistol. Her face was a mask of frustration.

"They're getting away," she yelled.

Kirov fired another burst, holding the submachine gun on target as it sprayed copper-jacketed rounds uphill. Then he shook his head. "No," he told her. "Look."

With a final, coughing roar from its

dying engine, the first Mercedes sputtered to a stop about two hundred meters up the road. Four men scrambled out and sprinted uphill, still fleeing toward Orvieto. One of them had a shock of thick white hair and ran awkwardly, clutching a briefcase in both hands. Another, taller, had hair that glowed pale blond in the moonlight. "Malkovic and Brandt," Smith realized. He jumped up. "Let's go!"

Ahead of them the second sedan careened off the road, trying to pass the stalled first car. Instead, it bottomed out in the soft soil, lurched forward a few more meters, and then ground to a halt. Four more men jumped out of this one. Two fanned out across the road, weapons in hand, evidently intending to act as a rearguard for their retreating comrades. The last two, one of them a slender man with a white beard carrying another case, hesitated for a moment while looking up the long, open stretch of road leading to Orvieto. Then they turned instead and faded uphill off the road, moving in among the trees and bushes growing at the base of the cliffs.

Jon heard footsteps pounding up the road behind him and whirled around, raising his MP5.

Randi Russell came loping out of the darkness, pistol in hand. "That was

Renke!" she growled, pointing to where the two men had disappeared among the shadowed trees. "You and Kirov and Devin take the rest of them. I'll go after Renke!"

Smith nodded quickly. "Good luck."

Randi clapped his shoulder as she ran past him. "You, too!" Then she turned and began climbing the slope.

Jon stripped the spent magazine out of his submachine gun and slapped in a fresh clip. He turned to Kirov and Fiona. "You ready?"

They nodded, eyes alight — gripped, like him, by the strange exultation, verging on madness, of combat.

"Right, then," Smith snapped, already starting to move up the road. "Let's finish this!"

CHAPTER FORTY-NINE

Smith ran up the left side of the road while Kirov and Fiona moved up on the right. Far ahead of them now, still illuminated by the moonlight, he could see Malkovic and Brandt and their two bodyguards hurrying away, straining to reach the top of the plateau before their pursuers came within range. Renke and one of the other gunmen had vanished up the slope to the right, disappearing among what looked like small orchards of peach and apple trees and rows of grapevines that were planted right up to the base of the cliffs. Small yellow signs by the side of the road pointed in that direction, identifying the area as Tombe del Crocifisso del Tufo, the site of an ancient Etruscan necropolis, a city of the dead.

It was the men lurking up ahead who most concerned Jon now. Two of Brandt's gunmen had stayed behind while the others fled, probably under orders to kill or at least delay the Americans chasing after them. One had dropped into cover among the bushes and trees on the downhill slope.

The other was hiding somewhere to the right, in the rocks and brush higher up.

Smith frowned. Charging straight up the open road toward those guys was a really good way to get killed. Courage under fire was one thing. Suicidal madness was quite another.

He slowed down and then dropped to one knee, carefully scanning the tangled vegetation along both sides of the road over the barrel of his submachine gun. Kirov and Fiona went prone off to his right, peering ahead with their own weapons ready.

"See anything?" Jon hissed.

Kirov shook his head. "No." He glanced over at the American. "But we have to keep moving, my friend, despite the risks. All this shooting will soon draw the police."

Smith grinned back at him. "You don't think the *Carabinieri* will buy our story about being tourists out for a midnight stroll?"

Kirov snorted. He hefted his MP5 and ran a quick finger over the dark camouflage paint smeared across his cheeks and forehead. "For some reason, Jon, I doubt it," he said drily.

"Then we'd best cut the chitchat and get going," Fiona said, sounding both amused and irritated at the same time. She scrambled to her feet and started up the road again, staying close to the verge. "I'll draw their fire. Then you two shoot them."

Startled, Kirov turned, putting out a hand to stop her. "No, Fiona. Let Jon and me handle this. We were trained as soldiers. You were not. The risk is too great."

"Oleg is right," Smith agreed.

She shook her head impatiently. "No, he's not, Colonel. And neither are you." Fiona showed them the pistol in her hand. "I can't count on hitting anything with this at more than twenty or thirty meters. Those submachine guns you're both carrying give you an edge at longer range. So let's make use of that."

Jon grimaced. Reluctantly, he shrugged at Kirov. "She's right."

The Russian, scowling himself, nodded heavily. "Yes. As she is so often." He dropped his hand, though not without a gruff plea. "But please do not get yourself killed, Fiona. If you do, I —"

His voice thickened and then fell silent.

Smiling now, Fiona patted Kirov gently on the head. "Yes, I know. I'll be as careful as I can." Then she walked on ahead, crouching slightly.

The two men waited a few seconds and then followed her, staying low, moving cautiously through the grass on the edge of the road and keeping to the shadows wherever possible.

★ ★ ★

One of Brandt's gunmen, Sepp Nedel, lay hidden behind a little pile of weathered, brush-covered rocks. He peered down toward the road, watching for any signs of movement over the sights of his Micro-Uzi. He settled the weapon's folding stock firmly against his shoulder, waiting calmly. Shooting Renke's unarmed scientists had been a pleasant enough diversion, but this duel against armed opponents was more to his taste.

There was a faint stir among the bushes across the road. Nedel sneered. That was typical of Fyodor Bazhenov, nervous and twitchy as always when holding a gun. The onetime KGB man was competent enough with explosives. But he was a menace to himself and others in the field.

Something flickered at the edge of his vision. Someone was coming up the road. The German tightened his grip on the Uzi and shifted his aim. Now he could see a black-clad figure drifting closer, crouching briefly from time to time to watch and listen. A scout, Nedel thought. The correct move was obvious. Let this one pass unharmed and then kill the others who would come later.

The scout drew nearer.

He held his fire. Something about the moving figure's shape intrigued him. Then he realized what it was. The American scout was a woman! Nedel bared his teeth in the darkness, anticipating even more pleasure once he had eliminated her companions.

Suddenly another Uzi stuttered harshly, spitting bullets down the road. Pieces of asphalt and shredded grass and dirt exploded all around the black-clad woman. She fell forward and lay still.

Nedel swore silently. Bazhenov had panicked.

Suddenly he saw the Russian poke his head out above the bushes, trying to get a clearer shot. The demolitions expert brought his submachine gun up, aiming intently at the motionless figure curled up beside the road.

And then another weapon fired, this one from farther down the hill.

Hit in the face, Bazhenov screamed shrilly once and then fell sideways, sprawling out from the bushes to lie in a heap. A second burst tore him apart.

Instantly, the black-clad gunman who had killed him leaped to his feet and raced toward the fallen woman. He dropped to her side, apparently fumbling for a medical kit in one of the many pouches on his assault vest.

Nedel nodded slightly to himself. That was a worthwhile target. Slowly, with great care, he rose up from behind his little pile of rocks. He stared down the short barrel of his Uzi, breathing shallowly, waiting until the sights settled on the kneeling man and hung there. His finger tightened on the trigger . . .

Lying prone about one hundred meters away, Smith fired. The MP5 chattered loudly, punching back against his shoulder. Three spent cartridges flew away into the grass. Hit twice, once in the neck and once in the shoulder, Brandt's gunman slumped forward. Black in the pale light, blood pulsed across the rocks briefly and then stopped flowing.

Grim-faced, Jon sprang up and sprinted forward to where Kirov knelt beside Fiona Devin.

She was already sitting up when he got there. "I'm okay," she insisted, pale and plainly a bit shaken, but smiling with relief nonetheless. "They missed me."

"You say they missed?" Kirov growled. He reached out and touched a long tear through the dark cloth covering her upper left arm. A thin trickle of blood welled up from a bullet graze there. "So what is this?"

"That?" Fiona said, grinning back at him. "That's nothing but a scratch."

"You were lucky," Smith told her

bluntly. His heart was still pounding. Like Kirov, he had been sure that she was dead or badly wounded.

She nodded calmly. "Indeed I was, Colonel." She looked down ruefully at the radio clipped to her equipment vest. It had been smashed, either by a bullet or by a rock when she dove for cover. She stripped off the now-useless headset. "But it looks as though I'll have to rely on you two to make any calls for me."

Abruptly, bright white light flared through the night behind them, throwing their shadows ahead up the slope. They whirled around, in time to see a huge fireball rising in the west. Shards of twisted steel and shattered concrete spun away from the center of the explosion, soaring hundreds of meters into the night sky before tumbling back to earth. The sound of the blast reached them in that same moment, a rumbling, thunderous freight-train roar that died slowly, leaving only a stunned silence in its wake.

"There went Renke's lab," Smith said bitterly, staring at the pillar of flame still rising from the ECPR compound. "Along with most of the evidence we needed."

Kirov nodded somberly. "All the more reason to capture Malkovic and Brandt, then." He shrugged. "But at least we no longer have to worry so much about being stopped by the police."

"No kidding," Jon agreed absently, still looking at the fires consuming the shattered ruins of Renke's weapons lab. "Every municipal police and *Carabinieri* squad in Orvieto will be swarming over that compound in ten minutes or less." He leaned down and helped Fiona back to her feet. "We'd better not waste the opportunity."

Together, the three Covert-One agents turned and sprinted east along the road, running flat-out now toward the top of the plateau.

Pushing carefully through a tangle of vines, Randi Russell saw the sudden glare light up the slope around her, casting its stark illumination across a landscape of tall grass, leafless fruit trees, waist-high rail fences, and eroded terraces covered in brush. She dropped flat, waiting until the flash faded and the hillside returned to darkness.

In the sudden silence following the explosion, she heard a quick murmur of startled voices from ahead and off to her left. Cautiously, she rose and moved forward again, heading in that direction. The voices fell silent abruptly.

Randi came to a rail fence and crouched lower. In the faint moonlight, the terrain ahead looked far more open. It was difficult, however, to make out details. There was a succession of what appeared to be grassy mounds with gray stones set in the top, but the areas between these mounds were bathed in impenetrable shadow. It was time to get a better look at what lay ahead of her, she decided. She raised her image-intensifier binoculars. Set to amplify even the smallest amount of ambient light, whether from the stars or the moon, they turned night into effective day.

Immediately, the landscape leaped into clearer focus.

She was looking at what appeared to be a rectangular grid of streets. Small houses built of large blocks of quarried tufa, a form of pitted gray limestone, lined these narrow, stepped roads cut into the hillside. Some of their roofs were conical, others were flat, but almost all of them were covered in grass and hard-packed earth. Low, dark, trapezoidal openings gaped in the center of each building. Letters in some archaic script were carved on the large stones set above the empty doorways. Beyond the buildings she could see a path with railings leading up shallow steps to an empty parking lot.

This was the old Etruscan city of the dead, Randi realized, remembering the quick research she had done on her flight down from Germany the day before. Some of the tombs here were nearly three thousand years old. Excavated beginning in the mid-nineteenth century, the vases, drinking cups, weapons, and armor found inside were now on display in a museum next to Orvieto's cathedral.

She frowned. Renke and his bodyguard must be hiding somewhere in the necropolis, probably with the intention of slipping away back down the hill when all the shooting died down. Not a bad plan, Randi thought coldly. Anyone trying to hunt for them up and down those narrow streets would be exposed, a sitting duck for anyone shooting from cover inside one of the tombs.

She stuffed the binoculars back into one of her equipment pouches and slid under the bottom rail of the fence, moving slowly to make sure she did not snag any of her gear. Then she wriggled toward the tombs through the long grass, gliding quietly from one patch of shadow to another.

Periodically, Randi stopped moving to listen, trying to ferret out the slightest sound that could tell her where her enemies were lurking. But she heard nothing, only the sound of police and fire and ambulance sirens speeding toward the explosion-ravaged ECPR compound.

At last she made it to the position she had been aiming for, a small stand of scrub trees growing out of the slope above the necropolis. From here, she could look down into most of the streets, especially the lanes that ran back toward the Orvieto road.

Again, Randi dug out her binoculars. Methodically, she swept them across the ancient cemetery, focusing first on the entrances of tombs that she thought offered the best vantage points. Unless she missed her guess, Renke and his bodyguard would have picked a hiding place that would let them spot anyone entering the tomb complex from the road or the parking lot.

Her binoculars slid slowly past a tomb opening about halfway up the central street, paused, and then came back. Was that paler shape inside the darkness just a chunk of fallen stone or a trick of the moonlight?

Randi held her breath, waiting patiently. The shape moved slightly, taking on form and definition. She was looking at the head and shoulders of a man, a clean-shaven man who was crouched just inside the low opening, peering down the street toward the entrance to the necropolis. He shifted position again and now she saw the weapon in his hands.

She held still. Was Renke inside the tomb with this man? Or had the weapons scientist chosen another lair?

The bodyguard looked back behind him for a moment, apparently listening to something being whispered to him, nodded, and then turned back to his post.

Randi smiled thinly. Wulf Renke was there, crouching patiently in the darkness, waiting for his chance to slip away and disappear again, as he had so many times before. That was the answer she had been hoping for. She put her binoculars away and crawled down the slope, staying low and angling away from the street where Renke and the other man were concealed.

She dropped quietly into the little lane that marked the northern boundary of the necropolis and crossed it quickly, slipping into the shelter of one of the small square mounded tombs. Then she slid her Beretta back into the holster on her hip, snapped the flap shut, and used both hands to haul herself up onto the grass-covered roof of the burial chamber.

From there, Randi made her way from rooftop to rooftop, jumping lightly across the narrow gaps between buildings until she reached the flat-roofed tomb just north of Renke's hiding place. She drew the 9mm pistol, crawled to the corner, and looked down over the edge.

There, just a few meters away, lay the low open door where she had seen the scientist's lookout. She took aim with the

Beretta, waiting while her eyes adjusted. Gradually, the blackness took on different shapes and shades, again revealing the head and shoulders of the sentry crouching there with his submachine gun. Her finger tightened on the trigger and then eased off slightly. She decided to give this guy the chance to be smart.

"Drop the weapon!" Randi called softly.

Taken completely by surprise, the guard reacted instinctively. His head jerked up and he spun desperately, bringing his Uzi up to fire.

She shot him in the head.

Before the Beretta's sharp, ringing report stopped echoing back from the stone walls around her, she was in motion. She rolled off the roof, landed in a crouch on the street, and brought her pistol back up, aiming straight at the opening to the crypt.

There was no noise. No sign of movement from inside.

"Wulf Renke!" Randi said quietly in perfect German, pitching her voice just loud enough to be heard inside the tomb. "It's over. You've got nowhere left to run. Come out now, with your hands up, and you'll live. Otherwise, I will kill you."

For a moment, she thought he would stay silent, refusing to talk. But then the scientist replied. "So those are my two choices?" he said calmly. "I either meekly surrender to you and face prison? Or else I die at your hands?"

"Correct."

Renke snorted. "You are wrong," he said bleakly. "You forget, there is always a third option. And that is the path I choose."

Suddenly Randi heard a faint *crunch* from inside the tomb, followed by a startled gasp and then a long, drawn-out sigh that ended in absolute silence. "Oh, hell," she murmured, already moving toward the entrance.

She was too late.

Wulf Renke sat slumped over on one of the stone benches used by the Etruscans for their dead. His eyes stared back at her, rigid and unblinking. Foam had dripped out of his slack mouth and into his neat, white beard. The fragments of a broken glass ampule lay on the ground at his feet, next to an insulated carrying case. The air inside the burial chamber smelled faintly of almonds.

The fugitive biological weapons scientist had committed suicide, probably with cyanide, Randi thought grimly. She bent down and entered the tomb. When a quick search of Renke's pockets produced nothing of value, she took the case and backed out again, into the narrow moonlit street.

Inside the container, she found a row of

glass vials packed in dry ice. And when she read the labels on each vial, her eyes widened in absolute astonishment and horror. At a guess, Randi decided that she was looking at lethal disease variants keyed to the precise genetic makeup of Viktor Dudarev, his senior ministers, and many of Russia's highest-ranking military commanders. Quickly, she slammed the lid back down, grabbed the case, and then raced away through the cramped streets of the city of the dead.

CHAPTER FIFTY

Smith slid quietly through the shadows thrown by a row of tall pine trees. He came out on the edge of a small public park dominated by the foundations of an Etruscan temple — not much more than a few stone steps, a raised, grass-covered platform, and the circular bases of what must have once been towering columns. The main road up had turned sharply as it climbed and entered Orvieto and now he was facing south.

He dropped to one knee, signaling Kirov and Fiona to come ahead. They ghosted through the trees and joined him.

The bulk of the medieval city loomed on their right, a maze of little, twisting streets and low, irregularly shaped stone houses that were mostly between eight and nine hundred years old. Arches crossed the streets in many places, linking the ancient houses, and turning the narrow lanes into alternating pools of wan silver moonlight and Stygian darkness.

The eastern end of the plateau fell away on their left, plunging steeply toward the lights of Orvieto Scalo, the lower town. A wide terrace ran along this edge, all the way to the tall, round, open-topped bastions and massive outer stone walls of the Fortezza dell'Albornoz, a papal fortress built in the fourteenth and fifteenth centuries.

"Which way would Brandt and Malkovic go?" Jon murmured. "West into the old city?"

"Not into the old city," Fiona said flatly. "That's a dead end for them. The only real way out from there leads straight back toward the Center compound, and that road will be swarming with Italian police and emergency crews."

"Ahead," Kirov said firmly. He pointed to a small sign with an arrow, pointing the way south along a tree-lined avenue to the Piazza Cahen and the Stazione Funicalore — the station for the funicular railway connecting Orvieto with the lower town. "Their only realistic hope of escape is to beg, buy, or steal another car, and the only place to do that safely is down below, near the main train station. That funicular railway is probably closed for the night, but there must be other roads or tracks down from this side of the city."

Smith nodded tightly. "Sounds reasonable." He stood up. "Okay, I'll take the left flank. Oleg, you take the right."

"And I'll tag along like a good little girl, safe in the middle," Fiona said, smiling slightly to take the sting out of her words.

Spread apart in a skirmish line, the three of them crossed the little park, skirting the raised platform of the ruined temple, and kept moving south, sticking close to the left edge of the wide road leading into the open square called the Piazza Cahen.

"But where is Professor Renke?" Konstantin Malkovic forced out between panting gasps, still clutching his briefcase to his heaving chest. He was sitting propped up with his back against the locked doors of the funicular station. Sweat matted his thick mane of white hair and ran in rivulets down his terrified face.

"Either dead or a prisoner," Brandt snapped. "He should have kept up with us."

Coldly furious with himself and with his panic-stricken employer, Brandt contemplated his options. They were increasingly limited. With Renke gone and the HYDRA lab destroyed, his usefulness to the Russians would last only so long as the Americans were kept in the dark about the invasion plans for Ukraine and the other former Soviet republics. The gray-eyed man glanced sidelong at Malkovic's briefcase. It contained information that must not be allowed to fall into American hands. And the financier himself was rapidly becoming a liability.

At this point, Brandt suspected, the only way he could win back his own life from the hard men in the Kremlin would be to eliminate Malkovic for them and then hand over the briefcase and all of its contents. He raised his Walther pistol, then stopped himself. Not here, he decided. The square was too open and the sound of a shot would echo across the city. No, he would kill the older man later, Brandt thought grimly, when they were safely away from this damned medieval maze. Once they were high up in the Apennines, it would be a simple matter to hide a bullet-riddled body where it might never be found.

Bending down, he roughly yanked Malkovic back to his feet. "Come on!" he snarled. "There's another road down, just around the corner of that fortress."

Trembling both with fear and fatigue, the older man obeyed.

In that instant, one of his two remaining men crouched lower, hissing, "Herr Brandt! The Americans! They're here!" He raised his submachine gun, using the Uzi's short black barrel to point toward the entrance to the Piazza.

Startled, Brandt spun round with his pistol ready. In the dim light, he could just

680

make out three black-clad figures entering the square. They were less than a hundred meters away. "Kill them!" he snapped.

Smith saw a sudden flurry of movement near the funicular railway station, a small, modern building, on the eastern edge of the square. There were four men there. Two were in cover behind a row of terracotta planters, with their weapons out. Brandt, taller and blond-haired, crouched behind them. The fourth man, Konstantin Malkovic, was turning to flee, scuttling wildly away from the station. He disappeared into the darkness, heading for the tall arched gateway leading into the papal fortress.

"Down!" Jon roared, trying to warn Kirov and Fiona. He dove for the pavement. "Get down!"

And then Brandt's gunmen started shooting, firing on full automatic.

Bullets ripped through the air all around Smith, cracking past low over his head. Others ricocheted off the paving, spinning wildly away in every direction. Chunks of concrete and torn strips of asphalt spattered across the square.

He rolled away, frantically trying to throw off their aim.

A few meters away, Fiona Devin cried out suddenly and went down. She lay curled up, with her teeth tightly clenched, clutching at her right thigh. Blood welled up between her locked fingers. Grim-faced with worry, Kirov hurled himself toward her, ignoring the 9mm rounds screaming around him.

The two Uzis fell silent. Both gunmen had expended their full twenty-round magazines in just a couple of seconds. Each man crouched low, desperately slapping in a fresh clip.

Smith stopped rolling. Either they started fighting back or they were dead. His eyes narrowed and he took rapid aim at the row of planter boxes. He pulled the trigger, firing as quickly as he could while swinging the barrel from one end of the little train station to the other. The MP5 stuttered loudly, punching rounds toward Brandt and his men. Hit by one of his bursts, a terracotta planter exploded, sending pieces of shattered pottery, dirt, and bits of shredded bark and leaves swirling through the air.

The gunman crouching behind that planter toppled backward and lay still. His Uzi clattered to the pavement.

One down, Smith thought grimly. He shifted his aim again, swiveling toward Brandt's second gunman. Brandt himself was next to his subordinate, down on one knee with his semiautomatic pistol out.

The three men opened fire at the same time.

Again, bullets hammered the paving and the air around Jon. One round tore a line of fire across the top of his right shoulder. Another near miss ripped through his assault vest, sending a torn equipment pouch tumbling away across the Piazza. Bits of broken plastic and glass littered the ground in its wake, all that was left of a handheld laser surveillance kit. A ricochet punched off the pavement and slammed into his left side, hitting with enough force to crack one of his ribs.

Deliberately, Smith fought down his fear-laced instincts to duck or to dive away from the incoming fire. Instead, his finger tightened again and again on the trigger. The MP5's barrel jumped and bucked against his grip. Jon clenched his jaw against the searing pain from his cracked rib, and kept shooting, forcing the submachine gun back onto his targets.

Multiple 9mm rounds smacked into the funicular station, shattering glass, punching through the locked doors, and gouging huge craters in the brown basalt walls. The rest of the planter boxes blew apart. Brandt and his gunman crumpled and fell, one heaped on top of the other.

The cocking handle slammed forward as Smith fired the last of the thirty rounds in his magazine. Reacting swiftly, he snatched out the old clip, tugged a new magazine out of his ammunition pouch, and slid it into the MP5. Then he yanked back on the handle, chambering a new bullet.

He scanned the front of the station, finger on the trigger, looking closely for any sign of movement from the three bodies littering the torn pavement. Nothing stirred. There was only a sudden strange silence — the total absence of noise after the staccato, clattering roar of so much gunfire.

"Jon!" Kirov called to him. The Russian was crouching over Fiona Devin, working frantically to staunch the bleeding from the wound in her thigh. "I need your help," he said bleakly.

Smith rolled back to his feet, staggering slightly as a new wave of pain from his cracked rib ripped through him, and then hurried over to the wounded woman. Fiona was still conscious. But she was pale and shivering, starting to go into shock.

He glanced across at Kirov. The Russian was just as pale. "Go after Malkovic, Oleg. He ran into the fortress over there," Jon said softly. "I'll take care of her."

Kirov shook his head angrily. "No, I —"

"I'm a doctor, remember?" Smith said urgently. "Let me do my job. Now you go and do yours. If Malkovic escapes, everything we've done has been in vain. Now move!"

Kirov stared back at him for a second longer. He scowled darkly, but then he nodded. Without saying anything more, he bent down and touched Fiona's forehead gently. Then he grabbed his submachine gun, jumped to his feet, and loped away, heading for the fortress gate.

Smith went down on his knees beside Fiona and began examining the injury, pulling the torn cloth of her jeans away carefully to get a good look at both the entry and exit wound. He felt around her leg with his fingers, pressing hard in places to check for any pieces of broken bone. She hissed sharply through gritted teeth.

"Sorry," Jon told her quietly. He tore open a field dressing kit and shook out a pressure bandage. Then he began wrapping it tightly around her wounded leg. She winced again. Next, he stripped off his assault vest, balled it up, and used it to elevate her wounded leg.

"How bad is it?" Fiona asked softly.

"You were lucky," Smith replied flatly.

She forced a smile. "That's the second time tonight you've told me that, Colonel. Somehow I don't feel quite as fortunate this time around."

Jon smiled back at her. "All luck is relative, Ms. Devin." He turned serious.

"Somehow the bullet that hit you missed every major blood vessel and the bone itself. Your thigh muscle is torn to hell, but it should heal nicely — once we've got you in a decent hospital."

Once he had finished stabilizing Fiona, he shook open another field dressing, pulled up his sweater, and then used pieces of adhesive tape to strap his cracked rib, holding it in place. With that taped down, Smith used another length of bandage to form a sling for his left arm and looped it around his neck.

Randi Russell's excited voice suddenly came through his headset. "Jon," she said quickly. "Renke's dead, but I've got some of his materials. I'm heading up the hill now. What's your situation?"

Smith keyed his mike. "Brandt is dead, too. But Malkovic slipped away and Ms. Devin is wounded." Speaking quickly, he briefed her on the rest of the situation, including their location in the Piazza Cahen. "How soon can you get here?"

"Give me five minutes," she promised.

"Understood," Smith said. "Come as fast as you can. And whistle up the Pave Low helicopter using the codes I gave you. Tell them to stand by to extract us."

"Where will you be?" Randi asked.

"I'm going after Malkovic myself. I'll keep you posted. Out." He picked up his weapon, stood up, and looked down at Fiona. "Randi will be here soon. Will you be all right until then?"

Still pale, she nodded. "I will. Now go help Oleg run that bastard down."

"And you sit tight. No trying to walk on that wounded leg of yours," Smith said firmly. "That's an order."

Then he turned and sprinted away across the Piazza.

Erich Brandt swam up through the darkness, fighting against the pain that threatened to drown his senses. His eyes blinked open as he came back to full consciousness. He was lying on the pavement with a dead weight pressing down across his legs. The hot, coppery smell of fresh blood filled his nostrils. He turned his head slightly, wincing at the agony that caused him. More blood dripped onto the Piazza.

One of his men lay heaped on top of him, plainly dead — shot multiple times.

Brandt carefully raised his own hand, gingerly touching his forehead. A crease torn there stung like fire. He felt broken bone grate beneath the loose flap of skin. His vision darkened and he jerked his bloodstained fingers away hastily. It would not do to think too closely about what this head wound might mean.

He heard footsteps racing toward him

and closed his eyes until they were only narrow slits. Breathing shallowly, he watched a lean, dark-haired man go running past, with one arm in an improvised sling and the other holding a submachine gun.

It was Smith, Brandt saw in amazement. Somehow the American had escaped from Russia, and now here he was in Orvieto, hot on Malkovic's heels. The realization jolted him into action. Slowly, he inched his way out from under the corpse. He found his pistol and then crawled away, staying low to the pavement until he reached the shelter of some trees and shrubs planted near the high arched gate that opened into the Fortezza dell'Albornoz. Once in cover, the gray-eyed man stood up and then staggered on, following in Smith's wake.

Using both hands, Fiona levered herself up into a sitting position, being careful to keep her bandaged leg stretched out in front of her. The effort left her feeling dizzy. She waited a few moments for her head to stop whirling and then looked up, staring out across the moonlit square. Frightened voices were calling out to each other in the city behind her, as Orvieto's citizens tried to make some sense of all the explosions and gunfire ringing through their ancient town.

Fiona frowned. She looked down at her watch, wondering where Agent Russell was. If the local police got there before the CIA officer arrived to help her, she was in real trouble. Neither Klein nor President Castilla could break the Covert-One secret to explain her actions, and she suspected the Italian authorities would look severely on a supposed freelance journalist caught wandering around their country armed to the teeth.

She studied the bullet-riddled funicular railway station, noting the two corpses sprawled across the Piazza in front of its shattered windows. Her eyes narrowed sharply. Two corpses? There should be three.

For an instant, Fiona sat rigid, feeling ice-cold. One of Brandt's men, maybe Brandt himself was on the loose . . . and without her radio, she had no way to warn the others. Painfully, she pushed herself to her feet and hobbled slowly toward the fortress.

Smith found Kirov and Konstantin Malkovic standing together on the upper ramparts of the fortress. The cliff face fell away sharply below the walls, plunging almost vertically through a tangle of scrub trees and bushes to the lights of Orvieto Scalo and the *autostrada* below. The finan-

689

cier had his hands high up in the air. An opened briefcase lay at his feet.

The Russian held his submachine gun pointed casually at the older, white-haired man. He glanced over his shoulder at Jon. "Mr. Malkovic has agreed to cooperate with us," he said drily. "It appears that he bitterly regrets his unwise decision to assist President Dudarev in his various conspiracies."

"I'm sure he does," said Smith, equally drily. "What's in the briefcase?"

"Important information for our government," Malkovic said eagerly. "Everything that I've been able to learn about Russia's military plans."

For the first time in days, Jon felt some of the weight lift off his shoulders. With Malkovic alive and talking, and with evidence of Dudarev's plans to invade his smaller neighbors, it was just possible that the United States might be able to fend off open hostilities with Russia.

"Drop your weapons," a harsh, pain-filled voice said suddenly from behind them. "Do it now. Or I will shoot."

Smith stiffened. He knew that voice. But Brandt was dead. He'd shot the bastard himself.

"You have three seconds," Brandt said coldly. "One. Two —"

Drained by the sudden reversal of fortune, Smith let go of his submachine gun. It clattered against the parapet. Beside him, Kirov did the same, carefully setting down his own MP5.

"Excellent," the German told them. "Now turn around . . . slowly. And keep your hands up where I can see them."

They obeyed.

Brandt stood there, just a few meters away along the battlement. His face was a horrible mask of dried blood. Bone gleamed white from a jagged cut across his forehead. He held his pistol in a one-handed grip, constantly shifting his aim slightly to cover them each in turn.

"Erich!" Malkovic said gladly, starting forward. "Thank God!" He smiled broadly. "I knew that you would save me from these men."

"Get back," Brandt growled, jabbing his pistol at the financier.

The smile faded from Malkovic's face. "But Erich, I —"

"You thought you would live through this night?" The former Stasi officer sneered. "Well, I'm afraid that your speculations were in error this time. One might even call it a fatal miscalculation." He shrugged, still holding his weapon on the three men. "Dudarev may not reward me for killing you. But your death should at least protect me from the worst of his anger."

"You intend to kill us all?" Kirov asked bluntly.

Brandt nodded. "Naturally." He stepped back a few paces, widening the gap between them, making it impossible for any sudden rush to reach him before he shot them all down. "The only question is which one of you dies first."

Again the Walther's muzzle swung from one man to the other. Then it settled on Jon and stayed there. "You, Colonel," Brandt said coldly. "You are the first."

And then Smith saw a lithe, pale-faced shape loom up out of the darkness behind Brandt. He shook his head. "I don't think so," he said quietly. "Remember that I once promised that you were a dead man?"

Brandt smiled icily. "Yes, you did, Colonel." He took careful aim at Jon's head. "But you were wrong about that, as about so much else."

A gunshot rang out, deafening at point-blank range.

Brandt's smile froze. Slowly, very slowly, he twisted and then fell sideways, toppling over the edge of the parapet. There was a short silence, and then a dull, crunching thud.

Smith scooped up his submachine gun, walked toward the parapet, and looked over. There, about twenty meters below, he saw Brandt's broken corpse splayed out across the gravel path running along the foot of the fortress walls. He shrugged. "I never said I would be the one who would kill you," he murmured to the dead man.

He looked back over his shoulder.

Fiona Devin stood there, slowly lowering her Glock. The bandage wrapped around her right thigh was dark, stained with fresh blood.

"I thought I ordered you to stay put," Smith said mildly.

She smiled at him, with a gleeful light dancing in her eyes. "So you did, Colonel. But I'm a civilian, and I never was much good at following orders."

"Fortunately for us," Kirov said gruffly, coming forward to take her gently in his arms. "Thank you, my dear, dear Fiona," he said simply. He bent down to kiss her.

Grinning, Smith looked away to keep an eye on the trembling financier. In the distance, he heard the muffled clatter of rotor blades growing louder. Their ride home was on the way.

EPILOGUE

February 23
Air Force One
Navigation lights blinking steadily, the 747-200B that served as Air Force One, the president's official aircraft, flew steadily east through the night sky over Europe. The cloud cover below the aircraft was unbroken, but at this altitude the night sky was ablaze with stars. Relays of U.S. F-15 and F-16 fighters flew close by, providing continuous protection. More lights blinked in the sky some distance behind Air Force One. Two mammoth KC-10 tankers were on station there, making sure the escorting fighters were always fueled up and ready for immediate action.

"Our ETA is one hour, Mr. President," the steward said, standing at the open door to the fully equipped cabin that served as his airborne office.

President Sam Castilla looked up from his desk. "Thank you, James." When the door closed behind the steward, he turned to Fred Klein, who was sitting patiently on a small couch. "Ready for the big show?"

The head of Covert-One nodded. "Yes, sir." He smiled. "Let's hope your performance is appreciated."

Castilla grinned. "Oh, I think it will be — though probably not in a friendly way." He picked up the intercom phone on his desk. "General Wallace? This is the president. You may initiate that hot-line call to Moscow we talked about earlier."

Both Klein and the president waited for several minutes while the communications staff aboard Air Force One made contact with the Kremlin. At length, an American voice spoke up, coming over the speakers hooked up inside Castilla's office. "President Dudarev is standing by, sir."

"Good morning, Mr. President," Castilla said cheerfully. "I apologize for disturbing you so early, but the matter I'd like to discuss is fairly urgent."

Dudarev's smooth, calm voice came clearly over the secure circuit. "The hour is not a problem for me, Mr. President," the Russian leader said politely. "I often work very late these days . . . an unfortunate fate which I am sure we both share."

Castilla snorted quietly. Slick, very slick, he thought. But now it was time to drop the hammer. "Yes, I'm sure you're extremely busy just now, Viktor," he said coolly, deliberately deciding to use

Dudarev's first name. Bluntness could be just as much a weapon of statecraft as could subtlety and indirection. "Plotting unprovoked wars of aggression against your smaller and weaker neighbors is just so darned time-consuming, isn't it?"

There was a moment's frozen silence before the Russian replied. "I really don't understand what you are driving at, Mr. President."

"Let's cut the crap, shall we?" Castilla said forcefully. He winked at Klein. "Hell, I've seen your mobilization schedules, operational plans, and target lists. I've even heard audiotapes with your voice on it discussing those same plans. And Ukrainian police units and bomb disposal squads have already found the explosives your agents rigged in Poltava, for your little piece of phony 'anti-Russian terrorism.' "

"I do not know who could have provided you with these monstrous fabrications," Dudarev said stiffly.

Castilla leaned forward in his chair. "Your good friend, Mr. Konstantin Malkovic, Viktor. That's who."

"Malkovic is a capitalist and a speculator who does business in my country," Dudarev snarled. "Beyond that, I know nothing about him."

Castilla shrugged. "That's not a lie that's going to stick, Viktor. I'd advise you to come up with some other story, real quick." He glanced out the window, catching a brief glimpse of the blinking red and green navigation lights of his fighter escort. "Let's talk instead about the fact that you're going to turn around those three hundred thousand or so troops you've massed near Ukraine, Georgia, Kazahkstan, Armenia, and Azerbaijan and send them marching back to their peacetime barracks . . . and pronto."

"Can I speak candidly, Mr. President?" Dudarev asked grimly.

"By all means," Castilla told him, grinning across the small cabin at Klein. "I always enjoy candor. Especially since I hear it so rarely from you."

"If I really did have so many tanks, soldiers, and aircraft ready for war, why would I abandon my plans so easily? Do you think your voice is so frightening?"

"Not in the least, Viktor," the president said easily. "I just don't think you're ready for an all-out conflict with the United States — and with NATO. You've been thinking in terms of a lightning campaign against weak and disorganized local forces, not a slugging match with the most powerful alliance in history."

"But you have no defense agreements with Ukraine or Georgia or the rest," Dudarev pointed out sharply. "Nor any forces stationed on their territory. And somehow I do not believe that your country — or your allies — will oppose us so seriously. No one in London or Berlin or Paris or New York will support a war against Russia for the sake of a few bare-assed Azerbaijanis and the like!"

"Maybe not," Castilla agreed. He straightened up. "But they will if your attacks put Americans at risk, especially political leaders who are pretty well known and respected." He paused modestly. "Like me, for example."

"What?" the Russian leader demanded. "What are you talking about?"

Castilla checked his watch. Outside, the noise of the 747's four big engines was changing as the jet began its gradual descent. "I think you should know that I'll be on the ground in Kiev in a little less than forty-five minutes. And that I don't expect to be leaving Ukraine for a few days. Their new leaders and I have a lot of business to transact, especially negotiating a mutual defense treaty."

"Impossible."

"Not in the least," Castilla said carefully. His voice hardened. "Ukraine is an independent country now. I guess you forgot that one little fact, Viktor."

Dudarev said nothing.

"And so are the other former Soviet republics," Castilla continued. "Which is why a host of U.S., NATO, and Japanese senior officials, including my secretaries of State and Defense, are going to be visiting those countries over the next several days. And if a single Russian bomber, tank, or foot soldier crosses those borders, I can guarantee that you're going to wind up dragging your country into a war it cannot afford — a war that it will most certainly lose."

"You are insulting," the Russian leader snapped.

"On the contrary," Castilla said coldly. "I'm being remarkably patient. But let me assure you that neither my country nor I will ever forget or forgive your decision to unleash the HYDRA weapon on us."

"HYDRA?" Dudarev asked, but for the first time there was a discernible note of uncertainty, perhaps even of fear. "I do not know what you are talking about."

The president ignored him. "There's an old, old saying that when you lie down with a dog, you get up with fleas, Viktor. Well, Professor Wulf Renke was one damned, dirty dog, and now you have one hell of a case of fleas. When we caught up with Renke, we found something very interesting in a little case he was carrying — a whole set of glass vials filled with some kind of liquid."

Dudarev said nothing.

"Now, the interesting thing about these vials is that many had Russian names on them — and one of them was yours, Viktor."

Even across the thousand miles separating them, Castilla could hear the other man suddenly swallow hard.

"But I'm a civilized man, unlike you," the president went on, not bothering to hide his utter contempt for the Russian leader. "So I've decided not to see how you like the taste of your own weapon when it's thrown back at you. Instead, well, we'll just hang on to these so-called HYDRA variants for the time being. As a form of insurance against any future bad behavior by you or by your pals in the Kremlin."

"That is blackmail," Dudarev growled.

"Blackmail is such an ugly word, Viktor," Castilla said calmly. He shrugged his broad shoulders. "I'll let you know when I think of a better one. *Da svidaniya*."

He pushed a button on his phone, cutting the hot-line connection. Then the president looked across at his old friend. "Well?"

"I think you enjoyed that, Sam," Klein said, grinning crookedly. "But then, for a politician, you've never been the most diplomatic fellow around."

"Nope, I'm not," Castilla agreed contentedly. "But what I'm really going to enjoy is watching Czar Viktor's pedestal start wobbling. Hell, I may even decide to give it a few, well-timed kicks myself. With a bit of luck, the Russians will get a chance to make a new start for themselves one of these days in the not too distant future."

"You think Dudarev's regime is going to be in serious trouble?" Klein asked, raising an eyebrow.

"I do." The president nodded seriously. "Once the word of what Viktor and his chums were up to leaks out, there'll be hell to pay inside Russia. Some very influential folks will be mad at him for almost dragging them into a war, and others will think he's a weakling for backing down at the last minute. This fiasco will be the first real chink in his armor." He shrugged. "Once that sense of invulnerability wears off a would-be dictator, it's pretty much the beginning of the end. It'll take a while, and my guess is that he'll cause us some more trouble before he goes down, but I'd say that Dudarev just gave his political enemies a big piece of the rope they'll use to hang him."

**March 15
U.S. Naval Station,
Guantanamo Bay, Cuba**

Camp Five, one of the several maximum-security facilities at Guantanamo Bay, was reserved for high-level terrorist detainees, most often senior members of al-Qaeda or other dangerous terrorist groups. It was also used, on rare occasions, to house "ghost detainees" — those men and women whose names were kept out of any official records for security and intelligence purposes.

U.S. Army Staff Sergeant Henry Farmer knocked politely on the wire-mesh door of the cell occupied by Prisoner Number Six. "Time for your lunch, sir," he said, sliding a tray through the slot at the bottom of the door.

Number Six, a tall, white-haired man with high cheekbones and pale blue eyes, sat up wearily from his bunk and padded over to collect the tray. "Thank you, Sergeant," he said. He tried to smile. "I'll hope that the chef has taken a refresher course since yesterday's disaster."

"Maybe so," Farmer said with a disinterested shrug. "Just to let you know, your next session with those fellas from Langley is scheduled for a little later this afternoon."

The prisoner nodded moodily. His discussions with the CIA debriefers were never very pleasant. He carried the tray back over to his bunk and then began eating.

Farmer watched him in silence for a moment, then turned, and went on with the rest of his duties.

Later that afternoon, the sergeant found the time to go for a stroll along the beach. He found a stocky, gray-haired man waiting for him, a man whose passport and sober business attire proclaimed him to be Klaus Wittmer, a visiting representative of the International Red Cross.

"Was there any trouble?" the gray-haired man asked.

Farmer shook his head. "Not a peep." He tossed something to Wittmer, who caught it one-handed and held it closed in his palm. "And the rest of my payment?"

"Will be made on schedule," the gray-haired man assured him placidly.

Once the American noncom was trudging away down the beach, Alexei Ivanov, the head of Russia's Thirteenth Directorate, opened his palm. An empty glass vial glinted there, reflecting the warm Caribbean sun. Frowning, Ivanov stared down at it for a few seconds more. *A futile gesture,* he thought grimly, *but then what other options are open to us now?*

Abruptly, the Russian spy chief turned and tossed the vial out into the bay, well beyond the waves lapping gently at the shore. Then he, too, turned and walked away.

The last HYDRA variant had been delivered.

March 22
Alexandria, Virginia

The small Vietnamese restaurant on King Street, across the Potomac from Washington, D.C., was a favorite among those who appreciated good food, reasonable prices, and quiet, unpretentious service. In other words, Jon Smith thought wryly, studying the menu, it was not fashionable — just popular.

"Is this seat taken?" he heard a familiar voice ask.

Smith looked up with a welcoming smile. A slender, pretty woman with short, golden hair stood there. She smiled back, but he thought her eyes looked wary. "Hello, Randi," he said, getting up to greet her. "I was afraid the boys at Langley had decided to lock you up after all."

Randi Russell shrugged. "The seventh-floor quill-pushers can't seem to make up their minds," she said calmly. "Half of them, including the DCI, think I'm a lone-wolf menace to the Agency who ought to be slung out on my rear end before I cause a major scandal. The other half of them, including my boss in Operations, think nailing Renke was worth cutting a few corners."

He waited until she sat gracefully, and then took his own chair. "So which half do you think will win?"

"Oh, the Agency will keep me on," she said confidently. A slight smile creased her lips. "The top-echelon guys will compromise, just like they always do. So I'll probably wind up with another few pages of scathing comments in my personnel file — and maybe an extra week's leave that I'll never find the time to take."

Smith laughed. "You're getting cynical."

"I was born cynical, Jon," she told him. "That's why I fit in so well at the CIA." She picked up the menu in front of her and then put it back down. "You heard the Germans have finally confirmed the identity of their mole?"

"Heichler, right?" he guessed. "The guy who shot himself the day after we grabbed Malkovic?"

She nodded. "It took a lot of digging, but they managed to trace a whole slew of cash payments to him from one of Malkovic's front companies."

"I heard about Malkovic, too," he told her quietly. "I guess Guantanamo Bay isn't quite as secure as everyone thinks it is."

Randi raised an eyebrow. "Word gets around fast in those rarefied circles you travel in — whatever circles those are. With so much egg on people's faces for letting the Russians get to him before we were through wringing him dry, I thought the details of his death were strictly top-secret."

"I may have a few friends who tell me things they shouldn't," Smith admitted.

She snorted. "Spare me." Randi picked up her menu again. "I understand that Ms. Devin is out of the hospital and up and around," she said casually.

"So I hear," he said carefully.

"I don't imagine she'll be very welcome back in Moscow."

Jon grinned. "Not exactly." He looked across the table at her. "But it seems that Fiona is the type who always manages to land on her feet. Apparently, she's already wangled a job at some prestigious think tank headquartered in New York."

Actually, he knew that it was Fred Klein who had arranged the assignment for Fiona, since it would give her useful cover for other Covert-One missions.

"New York's not very far from here," Randi commented coolly.

"Nope, I suppose not," Smith agreed. Then he took pity on her. "But it's an awfully long way from Moscow and air tickets aren't cheap. So I have a funny feeling that Oleg Kirov's clients are going to find their consulting bills going up."

She looked narrowly at him. "Kirov?"

He nodded. Once Klein was convinced that the Kremlin had no knowledge of the part played by Kirov in recent events, he had allowed the Russian to go back to his own country. So the former FSB officer was still in play as a deep-cover Covert-One asset.

"Oleg Kirov?" she asked again, still skeptical. "And Ms. Devin?"

Smith crossed his heart. "Honestly. No lie."

"Gee, that's nice," Randi said innocently. Then, smiling to herself, she sat back in her chair, studying the menu with real interest now. "So, what do you recommend?"

The employees of Thorndike Press hope you have enjoyed this Large Print book. All our Thorndike and Wheeler Large Print titles are designed for easy reading, and all our books are made to last. Other Thorndike Press Large Print books are available at your library, through selected bookstores, or directly from us.

For information about titles, please call:

(800) 223-1244

or visit our Web site at:

www.gale.com/thorndike
www.gale.com/wheeler

To share your comments, please write:

Publisher
Thorndike Press
295 Kennedy Memorial Drive
Waterville, ME   04901